C000153420

The Path of the Gods

Joseph Geraci

Strand Fiction

Copyright © 2009 Strand Publishing UK.

The right of Joseph Geraci to be identified as the author of this work has been asserted in accordance with the Copyright, Designs and Patents Act 1988.

All rights reserved. No reproduction, copy or transmission of this publication may be made without written permission. No paragraph of this publication may be reproduced, copied or transmitted save with the written permission or in accordance with the provisions of the Copyright Act 1956 (as amended.) Any person who does any unauthorised act in relation to this publication may be liable to criminal prosecution and civil claims for damage.

First published 2009 by Strand Publishing UK Ltd. Golden Cross House, 8 Duncannon Street, Strand, London WC2N 4JF

E-mail address: info@strandpublishing.co.uk
Internet address: www.strandpublishing.co.uk

Paperback ISBN 978-1-907340-05-5

I. Prologue: Lord of All.

1. 368 BC. In Paraitoniom.

I, Amyntas, son of Alcetas of Methone in Macedon, the goldsmith, not the illustrious King after whom my father named me, am now about to set down for the record all that I know of the character and murder of my beloved friend and mentor Socrates. Some call it justice, and some tragedy, but murder it surely was, although it was his own hand hat held the cup. Why did the people do this? Under the influence of a trio of infamous men, they sentenced him to drink the hemlock for crimes against religion and the corruption of youth. His three accusers blinded themselves to his truth and the ways of the God within him, and so would blind others. Meletus was their spokesperson. He was a second rate poet who wished to further his ambitions. The populist orator Lycon was hired to proclaim their case in the Agora, and sway the people through the force of his rhetoric. He knew the ways of crowds and the ability of populist notions to mask themselves as reason and have broad appeal, if little truth. But Anytus was the real instigator of the charges. He deemed himself paragon and savior of the democracy, but he was motivated by jealousy of his son's love for Socrates and Socrates return of the friendship. If Athenians were tired of decades of war, and angry with those of Socrates' friends who had attempted to overthrow the democracy two or three years before, the roots of Socrates' arrest went far deeper. Decades before, Aristophanes had reflected the readiness to scorn Socrates in *Clouds*. I attended that performance in my youth. The

3

poet did as much as any to foster doubts about Socrates, and he called himself his friend. We who loved him wanted to refute the accusations, or rescue him with a daring plan, but the inner divine voice that had guided him since childhood told him neither to deny his fate nor to flee. Blinded by love we could not understand this and wanted him to go into exile; he would not. Did his death fulfill a divine purpose? If it did, we were too overcome with grief to see the intervention of the God.

It was through a dream, some weeks before his trial, imprisonment, and death, that I first received news of his troubles. I was in the Oasis of Zeus Ammon, down in the Great Desert, paying honor to Zeus and pursuing banal business and personal interests when Socrates visited me in a dream. Filled with dread I consulted the Oracle who confirmed that I should hasten back home and thence to Athens. It was but the last in a series of dreams that had been leading me. Was not our great hero Agamemnon speaking the truth when he said, "God will always have His way"?

How peaceful it is now, sitting here in Paraitonion so many years after the events, writing by the open window, looking out over my beloved Great Sea. How remote it seems from the turmoil and sorrow of that year, or the glories and passions of my youth in Athens. Zeus, Lord of Olympus, Leader of the Fates, and Apollo, your son and famed archer, healer, God of Truth, guide my hand until the last word is written.

***

Why I was chosen to play a role in this story I cannot say; we do not know the minds of the gods. No matter how hard we try to see their pattern in events it remains a mystery. As a youth I was beloved by Socrates who saw in me a potential I do not claim to have fulfilled. Among those surrounding Socrates were many illustrious men. I was only a craftsman unworthy of his affection, but which I strived to return. I had no special gift for rhetoric or logic; I was not a poet of any skill, nor could I tell the ancient stories with much fluidity. I sometimes tried my hand at lyre and song and had a pleasing but common voice. My love of the comedies and tragedies was as spectator. I was shy around eminent men and either spoke too much out of nervousness or kept too silent; I hid my virtues out of false modesty. My classmates in the Lyceum often called me a dunce because I was so often at a loss for words. Yet in the exercise of my goldsmith craft I was filled with confidence, shaping pure gold into intricate, innovative designs. I swiftly earned a reputation. Socrates set great store on the crafts. His father was a talented sculptor who had worked on the Parthenon friezes, and had taught Socrates that craft. When he spoke of his father, his face glowed with affection.

At his trial it was insinuated that the beauty of youth counted more with Socrates than their welfare, and that he corrupted youth through false religious beliefs. Athenians were more religious than most - more than we Macedonians, I think - and these charges counted among the most serious. His inner voice, they said, could not be divine because it had no name and would not allow others to worship it, make sacrifices to it, or hold festivals in its honor. From boyhood it had told Socrates what not to do, and through him what others should not do. But it had not prevented Alcibiades or Critias from doing great harm to Athens. As a boy I often asked Socrates for advice, and his *daimon* through him. He never led me astray. Athens was rife with gossip, and it was said that I was only one more *kalos kagathos* in Socrates' stable of many. I could never take the rumors seriously because I did not think I was beautiful. My face seemed misshapen, my nose too large; my ears jutted out too far; my chin was too sharp, and my eyes too often filled with befuddlement. Nothing about me seemed to fit together into a whole; everything was in contradiction. I knew only that Socrates prized the crafts and thought that this was why he befriended me. He said he "saw my worth."

It was also said that Socrates could see things in the souls of men to which most men were blind, and if he saw such things in me, they have remained a mystery to me. Others said that Socrates had a knack for gathering influential and wealthy people around him. As the years past I did become a master of my craft, and did acquire a considerable fortune by trading gold in Scythia, and by designing extravagant objects for arrogant kings to satisfy their vainglory. But as a boy I only showed promise. They further had the temerity to compare our friendship to his friendship with Alcibiades son of Cleinias. For sure we were both of royal line. Alcibiades, through his mother's side, was the most prominent member of the Alcmaedonidae, direct descendants of Nestor son of Neleus, an Argonaut. Through my father, I was cousin to our king, Perdiccas II of Macedon, Perdiccas the Mad, as we called him privately, because of his uncontrollable fits of rage. Our family was descended from Temenus of Argos, so there was some validity to the comparison with Alcibiades. When my older brother died in battle I became my father's eldest son and prince in line for title of leader of our house, and I suppose the throne of Macedon, if distantly. Perdiccas was always fearful of plots, and he was the ostensible reason why I was sent to Athens, for "safekeeping" as my father called it, although there were many other reasons as well, about which I will tell later in this history. If I had good looks and royal Argonaut blood in common with Alcibiades, in all other ways I would like to think that we were dissimilar. I never divided my loyalties between Athens and Macedon, as Alcibiades did between Athens and Sparta, and I never seduced other men's wives.

Everyone knew that wealth and worldly things mattered little to Socrates. His wife Xanthippe frequently complained about this, but his sons, Lamprocles, Sophroniscus, and Menexenus never went wanting, if there was never excess. After his death I helped to provide for her and his sons' welfare, through our friend, Crito. When he was a young man Socrates had assisted his father long enough to accumulate sufficient wealth to invest. It earned him a small income that would provide for the necessities without much left over. He refused to take money for his teaching, distinguishing himself from the sophists who always taught for money. He believed that teaching "should be imparted for free to be freely learned", and was more than half serious. His house in the Alopeke district, inherited from his father, was simple, certainly not opulent. His own room was nearly bare, and he slept on a low pallet away from his wife. Crude jokes were made in Athens about how he had sired his sons. He had one pair of sandals, but nearly always went barefoot, in winter too, as did many Athenians. He had no expensive cloaks, and his clothing was made from homespun wool and flax. Rumors persist until today that he never washed and smelled badly, but this was not only false but it also violated his own principal of taking care of the body as well as the soul. As I was just a boy when he took me under his wing, I found his eccentricities rebellious and inspiring. I was always ready to defend him to all and sundry, not to mention imitate him too. His eccentricities strike me still as virtues.

Early on Socrates began to call me his friend, and more. How can I explain this? His affection puzzled me, and others too. They thought he must have lost his head or heart to me, a sure path to clouded judgment. One day, during those youthful years in Athens, as I lingered by a window waiting for Socrates, I overheard his physician friend, the pompous Eryximachus the Physician, asking him, perhaps in exasperation, "What do you see in this boy? He may be beautiful, as Alcibiades and others of your boys were beautiful, but otherwise it seems to me that he has little distinction. And as for the poet Simonides, why the boy treats him disgracefully. Really, Socrates, sometimes I think all your thoroughbreds are mules."

This remark was by no means the first or last to challenge Socrates' judgments about the young friends he made, or the first or last about me for that matter. I was still a boy hardly fifteen and Eryximachus had in mind my troubled friendship with Simonides son of Bacchylides who was not well liked in Socrates' circle. Simonides, his father, and his grandfather were poets, but the father's gifts were greater than the son's and the grandfather's gifts were the greatest of the three. Simonides made himself disliked by flaunting his bad verse in the Agora and otherwise proclaiming himself the new great poetic talent of the day.

Hiding from view, I heard Eryximachus say too, "The boy may be a prince in Macedon, but his father has sent him away here to learn a lowly trade. He must think his own son a dunce."

Lowly trade indeed! It was an insult to my master, Athenades, and to Socrates, son of a stonemason, to my father's reasons for sending me to Athens, and to myself. I nearly dashed out at him in anger. Had not the crafts forged Socrates' body into a solid block, fierce and tireless in battle? Were not songs sung of his exploits? I wanted to cry out, "What kind of a friend are you to Socrates!" But I did not.

Socrates was a patient man, and chided Eryximachus gently. "Did I hear wrongly yesterday when you said that true beauty reflects the virtues within?"

"I cannot deny that I did."

Socrates said, "And just yesterday did you also not say that you found Amyntas *truly beautiful*? Were these not your exact words?""

"Well, yes, I suppose they were, although I was only speaking figuratively."

"Figuratively?"

9

"Yes, you know, rhetorically, with a little hyperbole."

"Do you think Amyntas is truly beautiful or not?"

Eryximachus laughed, "I see what you are driving at, but I won't fall into your trap, old friend."

"It is a simple question. You said he was truly beautiful, and seemed to say it with conviction, as if some moment had revealed his beauty to you."

"Well, yes, all right, all of that is true."

"So then you do?"

"I suppose I do."

Socrates said, "What are his virtues then?"

Eryximachus said, "I can name one that everyone calls a virtue but that I would question. They say that he resists Simonides advances and when Simonides asks him why he says that he would not lead Simonides feelings astray because he could not return them. Of course he continues to see Simonides and be shown off all over Athens by him. Not a few are calling this opportunism. You might suppose that it is a virtue to resist someone out of honesty, so long as it is not false idealism. But as a physician I have to condemn it because it makes Simonides love sick."

Socrates said, "Do you think Amyntas is being an opportunist?"

"To tell you the truth I put the very same question to Simonides and he defended the boy, saying that he had never met anyone so honest and true to his feelings. Of course the poor poet is so besotted that he would say most anything wouldn't he?"

"Then do you agree or disagree?"

Eryximachus said pompously, "I would rather reserve judgment. Simonides may not be as great a poet as his grandfather, but I rather like him. And the boy seems to be inspiring some of his better lyrics, although they are about unrequited love, and I am sure he would rather write about fulfillment."

"Then Amyntas' *resistance*, as you call it, is doing good? The good of inspiration?"

"I suppose you could say that. Simonides is bursting with creative energy and writing more than ever."

For reasons that escaped me Eryximachus found his own statement funny, and Socrates joined in the laughter. I mention this because it has been said that Socrates never laughed.

Did Socrates know that I was listening that day? I do not think that he did. He had great simplicity. If he had known of my presence he would have called out to me to join them. This was more his way than to talk about me knowing that I was there but pretending not to know. That was not his way.

I had just turned fifteen at the time and my desire to experience everything in Athens sometimes overpowered me. I knew full well how to manipulate another's affections for the sake of personal gain, and see myself as a crafty boy who thought too highly of himself. Perhaps the conversation I overheard did me good. It made me feel vain and unworthy. As I sneaked away, lest I be caught eavesdropping and earn Socrates' displeasure, I resolved to rise to the ideals that Socrates saw in me. If we have mirrors to reflect ourselves back to ourselves, we seldom have a mirror to affirm our inner virtues, except through friends like Socrates who act as mirrors to the soul. If I did not have virtue on the day I skulked eavesdropping in the shadows, then being the object of Socrates friendship instilled it in me, as if my virtue were there in a fitful sleep, and he would startle and shake it awake.

2. 407-400 BC. The Cretan Oracle.

By the time of Socrates' trial, I had been living away from Athens for many years. By the age of sixteen, when some were just beginning to think of their apprenticeship, I had already completed two years in Athenades workshop, as his ward. A faction within the ruling Macedonian house had plotted an assault against me in order to show the reach of their power down to Athens and the vulnerability of my family's claim to accession. Violence was committed against me by factions of the ruling Macedonian house, and it was hastily arranged that I go to Egypt. Athenades had powerful friends in Thebes, and it proved a safer haven than Athens. I was to stay there for several years, although I periodically returned to Attica to visit Socrates, Aspasia, and other friends. These visits became less and less frequent as war and political turmoil disrupted the sea-lanes and made travel increasingly hazardous, or as life took over and my responsibilities grew.

I did well in Thebes, so well that the Master of the Workshop and Athenades conceived an ambitious plan to send me to organize branches of their businesses in Lydia and Scythia, where gold lust thrived and the gold supply was ample, and later to manage an outlet on Crete, because of its geographical position mid-way along the trading routes between Athens and Egypt, central to a myriad of cities around the Great Sea. The island was, moreover, a hub of information, as valuable a commodity in the gold trade as it was in politics or war. I formed a great affection for Crete, especially the mountainous western region, not solely for its supreme beauty like some elaborate piece of natural jewelry set in lapis lazuli – crystalline mountains snow-capped for most of the year, emerald valleys undulating with grain and grazed by goats and sheep, the blue sea surrounding—but also because those inaccessible peaks harbored the birth and boyhood caves of beloved Zeus.

In boyhood I was devoted to Apollo, but as I matured I heard the call of Zeus, Lord of Oracles, Lord of All. On Crete there was great devotion to Zeus-Ammon and the Egyptian rites. The poet Pindar had introduced the devotion to Hellas. Pindar died around the year of my birth and he was much quoted to me as a child. My tutor had made me memorize Pindar's great hymn "To Zeus Ammon". It came to resonate deeply, as those things do that are learned in childhood. "Who if I cry out will hear me among the heavenly powers . . . Zeus alone hears and answers me." On Crete I felt at home again, if not intensely, as I felt in Athens, more securely. I began to draw designs for a grand villa, and chose a young Egyptian wife, Eshe, her name meaning life; within a year our daughter Azeneth was born, "pride of her father", a birth delighting. Eshe was seventeen when we married, and I was thirty-two. This was six or seven years before Socrates' death. Eshe's family had settled on Crete for two generations and become prosperous in the cotton cloth trade. With her dowry and my accumulated wealth we could live well.

My plan was to build my house near Knossos, down by the sea for my health, but the gods were soon to ask other things of me. It is said, "In all things set the gods first." What should be said is, "The gods set all things first for us."

A year or so after my marriage I was struck down by illness. I mark this as fate, of being led by the gods. My health had been failing in fits and starts for several years. I would be seized with sweats and fevers, fainting spells, and chronic stomach disorders. For days I would feel weak; my nerves on edge; I would be moody and stumble when I walked. One of the banes of the goldsmith trade is poisoning from the compounds used in processing the gold. Baser metals are added to the gold to help mold it more easily. It had also been my practice, no matter how successful the workshops, to work the gold myself. I could not bear to stand by the benches of my apprentices and see them making something crude that I knew could be delicate and refined; I often interfered when I felt too ill to stand, without realizing that the thing that obsessed me was afflicting me. The effects accumulate incrementally. Long exposure brings first mild aches and pains to elbows, hands, knees, ankles and feet; but these gradually become more and more acute over the years. I began to suffer from severe headaches, nausea and vomiting, and these all grew steadily worse. Finally, on Crete, I was so stricken that I had to set all else aside in order to find the cause and cure.

While sitting at my table one day in my workshop in Knossos filling an order for a piece of jewelry for some Scythian Lord, they who loved gold more than women, I lost consciousness and the assistants could not revive me.

14

A physician-priest was summoned and they carried me to the healing temple nearby where the Egyptian healing arts were practiced based on divine causes, not the new natural healing methods of Hippocrates of Kos based on physical causes and the balance of the four elements already popular in other parts of Hellas. There was much Egyptian and Cretan resistance to these new healers. They were considered too rational and profane. The priest sects had much power and political influence on Crete because of their ties with the priest castes in the upper Nile cities of Memphis and Thebes, and the wealth of the healing temples both there and on Crete. They perpetuated the old medical ways and were linked to a network of physicians with considerable influence in the Egyptian court that wished to spread its imperial power through religious and cultural means as much as military. Egyptian healing was considered the finest of its time. It was said that if you had to be sick it was best to be so in Egypt. But it would fail me, and I would worsen, until a meeting with the Hippocratic physician Philiscus of Kos in the great oasis of Ammon set me on the right path. With external symptoms, such as a cut or wound, Egyptian treatments were almost always successful, through use of herbs and poultices and the like. When the ailment was internal and hidden, as it was in my case, they were too often unsuccessful.

I was a well-known figure on Crete and gave generously to the temples, and Eshe's great uncle had also been a High Priest. When they brought me to the Asclepiad the chief priest, Annen, was called to attend to me. He was an imposing man with large, warm, dry hands.

When laid upon my forehead and head I felt instantly comforted.

There were three possible causes of my affliction, he said. Either an evil spell had been cast over me, or an evil spirit or spirits had taken up residence, or I had committed some offense to one of the gods for which I was being punished. The first step of the examination was to interrogate me about my friends, enemies, devotional practices, actions, and dreams. The agitation and distortions of my dreams, Annen said, fit the pattern of certain malign spirits, and so the soothsayers were consulted in order to discover which chthonian visitors afflicted me and how they might be counteracted. The remedy included wearing certain amulets, and imbibing bitter herbal remedies. Foul smelling creams were applied to every orifice but one in order to seal them off from further intrusions, while a sweet smelling cream was applied to the only open orifice. In this way the malignant spirit would be repelled by the foul smells and attracted out of the body by the sweet. Complete rest and abstention from work for three months, a diet of whole grains and purgatives, daily sacrifices at the temple in my name, and hourly prayers before our household altars were also required.

At the end of this period I did indeed feel better, if only because I was away from the offending substances. But no sooner did I go back to work than I collapsed again. This time, in a dream vision, I saw an eagle circling a snow-capped peak from right to left three times. The High Priest said that my dream was a summons to prayer and sacrifice by Zeus himself. I must also visit His temple in the west of the island. As soon as I was well enough, I was to set out for the Cretan mountains in order to consult the oracle at the mountaintop temple. I had been about to build a house, and settle at Knossos. The dream visit would change this.

***

The mountain temple is unusual, not being built by laborers out of marble or stone, but by hewing out rooms in a natural cave. It is remote, and arduously accessible. Indeed, the great traveler Hellenicus does not mention it in his chronicles of a journey in that region, a rare copy of which I have here in my library at Paraitonion. It is a simple shrine with one oracle, unlike some shrines with three, and is devoted to the boyhood and childhood of Zeus-Ammon. The priests who serve there serve first in Thebes at the small Temple of Khensu, son of Ammon by Mut. The Theban rituals are said to be the origin for those on Crete to Boy-Zeus, but the two gods are dissimilar in many ways. Khensu is a moon god and god of good advice. He is the son of a greater god but not himself Lord of All. They say also that the Egyptian practice of circumcision had its origins in the cult of Khensu, a ritual sacrifice devoted to male fertility. The Cretan sect of Zeus does not practice circumcision, but male rites revolving around sunrises and sunsets and changes of the seasons similar to those at the Temple of Khensu are practiced at the Temple Cave.

I made my way from Knossos to a village on a plateau half way up the mountain. A priest-guide was to meet me there and conduct me further. With my slaves and a priest

17

that Annen had sent, I waited in a small, peaceful village square noisy with flies and bees buzzing around the food laid out for us by the innkeeper. He had the enlarged throat so common among mountain people, so common that I did not consider it an ailment until I met my friend Philiscus. He told me that Hippocrates had diagnosed the swelling as a deficiency that could be corrected with diet. Philiscus had great success healing this disfigurement.

The small square commanded a view for miles of the mountains and sea. I felt my normal energy returning, excited by the prospect of seeing one of the sacred sites of Zeus and receiving insight from the Oracle concerning my dream and illness. The current oracle had a good reputation. Our priest friends in Knossos told me that I could trust his word. Yet I was anxious too. A large tree shaded me as I sat drinking an infusion made with mountain herbs that an attending physician in Knossos had recommended. A stirring among my slaves distracted me. They had seen the priest-guide coming down the slope and were making ready to depart. At that precise moment two ravens, birds of Apollo, glided into a nearby tree, cried out, rose suddenly, and flew off in the direction of the caves. I felt a chill go through me. If it had been one raven the journey would have been marked by ill fate, but two ravens was a harbinger of good fortune.

Our priest-guide was portly and garrulous, with the dark complexion, hooked nose, and black hair of an Egyptian. It was customary when consulting the Oracle to give gifts. I had made a gold ritual platter from a design I had seen on the temple walls at Thebes and, to my amusement, the priest-guide put it in a large sack that he threw over his shoulder as if it were vegetables. The day was warm and bright, but our ascent brought us into mist. He was barefoot. My sandals clicked on the stones disturbing the peace and I wished I had learned Socrates' discalced ways better as a boy.

I asked, "Do you have many visitors at this season?"

"No, not many," he said. It was early spring. "The weather is unstable on the peaks. Most come in summer."

"Have you lived at this temple long?"

"Two years and some."

"Were you at Thebes before that? "

"Yes. You are well informed."

"I have worked at Thebes. You must know the gold workshop?"

"Of course I do! You were there long?"

"Yes, many years. We made many objects for the temple.

"And for our sister shrine in the Great Oasis?"

"No. Never."

The path was becoming increasingly treacherous, strewn with loose, wet pebbles, and sometimes so narrow as to force us to the edge of a precipice. I was feeling a little dizzy and breathless from the thinning air. Despite my first enthusiasm I could see how far I was from health, and the good priest sometimes took my arm to steady me. For a time we could still hear shouts and cries from the villages below, or the sound of braying or a goat bell, the shriek of a hawk. Soon only the slapping of my sandals, the sighing of wind and clicking of the mules' hooves marred the eerie, solemn silence. We came out onto a circular rock ledge from which the path forked upwards in three directions. The priest said that he was required to attach us each to the other with a rope and to blindfold us, which he did this with strips of black cloth he took from his sack. A rope was placed in my hands, and I was cautioned to hold it tightly.

We continued for perhaps half an hour or more before he removed the blindfold. The path had narrowed between high rocks and afforded no views. I could have never found my way back there on my own. It was an hour or more before we emerged suddenly into a large flat open area at the far end of which was the mouth of the cave. Two pillars, in an Egyptian rather than Hellenic style, flanked the entrance. The carved lintel was decorated with scenes from the childhood of Zeus, such as I had never seen before or since, and resembling phallic representations of Hermes.

I glanced around greatly amused. We were on a high peak, on a large, wide plateau, and had come there with great difficulty. But at the far end there were stone visitor huts, some makeshift shelters for slaves, and two or three small shops selling amulets and open for business. I went into one before going back down to Knossos, to find gifts for my wife and child. They sold statues of body parts such as legs, hands, feet, and male and female parts. Some objects were made in great detail, to suggest certain illnesses such as deformed feet, or eyes with drooping lids, swollen male organs, and hands with gnarled fingers. One shop sold objects relating only to babies and children. On Crete many babies were stillborn, died soon after birth, or within the first year or two. I was an anxious father and feared for Azeneth's health, perhaps compounded by worries about my own. If she had a sniffle I would tremble and so I bought charms to hang above her bed. During Eshe's term we had made special prayers and sacrifices, especially at the onset of labor. I found an interesting amulet, which I bought for Eshe. It was a gold coin depicting Asclepius and a snake. There was a hole at the top so it could be hung around the neck; from a gold chain I also gave her. Most of the objects for sale were disease or health related in keeping with the dedication of this Oracle and temple. I could not locate where I stood in relation to other peaks or the sea as it was too overcast both the day of arrival and departure.

I wanted to stop in order to study the frieze but the priest ushered me into an antechamber where I was left to wait alone. Visitors could stay one night inside the caves but there was no dream chamber as there was at the Great Oasis or at Epidaurus. Within the caves all outside sound was blocked. A white robed priest came to fetch me, and I was led down a vaulted, stone corridor into a small room with a wooden door. I would have to spend the night there in prayer and fasting. There was only a small oil lamp for light, but I was given fresh water that tasted sweet. I slept restlessly, troubled by violent dreams.

The following morning, at least I think it was morning because time became confusing there, having been ritually bathed and cleansed, I was given a simple white robe to wear and led into an enormous inner room lit with torches set in niches in the wall. There were stone benches along one side and to my surprise five other supplicants whom I had not seen until then. The room was perhaps ten times my height, and as long and wide as the deck of the largest

Athenian trireme. At one end was an enormous gold plated statue of bearded Zeus seated on a pedestal, with a scepter in his left hand and his right hand on the head of a boy, also plated in gold. At his feet there was an altar covered with a white cloth, and in the walls to either side of the altar were arched doorways into antechambers. Over one exit there was a golden ram's mask, and over another a golden eagle with wings spread. These must have led to the priests' and oracle's chambers. There were pungent oil lamps on the altar and set on tripods to either side of it, adding to the room's brightness and filling the air with the smell of burnt unguents. Three priests entered silently, dressed in simple white robes and wearing ram's masks. Two took up positions to either side of the altar and the third went to the altar to acknowledge our gifts already heaped there. The other offerings were simple, an oil lamp, a basket of food; mine alone was lavish, but it was treated as equal to the others.

Chanting began in one of the back chambers, the signal that the questions for the Oracle were to be presented. Unlike Delphi, where the oracle prophesied the future, here the custom was to ask straightforward questions for which a yes or no were given. And unlike Delphi the Oracle was never a woman. The petitioners had to write their questions on pottery shards, one to each fragment, and lay them face down in a vertical row on the altar. We were each allowed five questions, and the others chose the maximum but I had decided on only three. Mine were placed last on the altar, to the far right side.

From the left side came more chanting, gradually growing louder until a procession emerged led by a boy carrying a torch, followed by the Oracle and three priests supporting a large planchette one to a side on which there was a gold and ivory eagle. A boy followed at the end carrying another torch. The procession moved three times around the room and then paused before the altar and the questions. Each time the Oracle came forward to read and answer a question the chanting would grow louder, and subside as he withdrew.

The questions were not read aloud, nor did the Oracle answer in words. One of the priests would first read the shard silently and hand it to the Oracle while prayers were being chanted. If the Oracle moved forward towards the altar the answer was affirmative, if backwards the answer was negative. The questions needed to be short, so my first was simply, "Should I build a house and settle on Crete?"

I thought surely that I would receive a positive answer and that would be that. Crete had everything I needed and wanted: competent physicians, temples and rituals to further my knowledge and devotion to Zeus, business connections, my wife's family and their connections, and so much more. The Oracle swayed back and forth, and then backwards. The dismaying answer was no.

My second question was about health. For decades the Temple of Asclepius at Epidaurus was known as the greatest healing temple anywhere. While I was a boy in Athens I heard many praise it, and this praise stayed with me. Asclepius is the son of Apollo son of Zeus, and my devotion to Zeus was forged out of illness. And so my second shard read, "Should I build a house and settle at Epidaurus?" But the answer to this question was also no.

I had prepared a third question, but as it was not one I

thought I would ask, having given diligent thought to the first two, it reflected more a whim than a considered thought. Once, as a young man, I had been to Paraitonion on the coast of Africa almost directly south of Crete, and had found it a peaceful and beautiful place. There was a natural harbor, and a small town with not much in it. What there was catered to those making their way down into the desert to visit the Oracle of Zeus-Ammon in the Great Oasis, then and now one of the greatest of the oracles, the oasis the center of much devotion, and mystery cults, and as well an important trading crossroads. I had been on my way to the Oasis to deliver gold artifacts that the King there had ordered, but I never reached it. At the port I was taken ill and I sent emissaries instead. When I felt better I thought it best to return home to Crete instead of making the difficult desert crossing. I had found the Great Sea there restorative. Perhaps it was only my mood, or the prevailing northwestern winds carrying soft scents, but the port had become fondly fixed in my mind. I promised Zeus that I would return there and make the pilgrimage across the desert to his shrine.

Perhaps because I thought I would not have to ask it, my third shard read simply, "Should I settle in Paraitonion?"

I was sure that the answer would be no and that I had been a fool not to ask the full five questions allowed. The Oracle bowed deeply and moved forward to the altar placing my shard in the middle of the cloth. The answer was yes.

In this way the god began my journey. Would it end in Athens?

3. A Home in Paraitonion.

With a fair wind, I set sail due south on a Cretan ship for Paraitonion, intending to bring my wife and daughter there if the signs were indeed propitious, and I could find a suitable dwelling. I did not doubt the Cretan oracle's positive answer. But I knew that an oracle's answer was often obscure, including a simple yes. They could not warn of obstacles, nor could they predict sudden changes in the God's plan. An answer on one day might change on another. I had long ago started to bring my own soothsayers on my travels, for daily readings, a practice I learned from Aspasia.

The ancient Cretans invented navigation by the winds, those most temperamental of the gods. We made record time reaching the isolated stretch of the North African coast, as if the gods, having willed me there, would now facilitate my journey. The port owes its renown to the Oracle of Zeus Ammon in the Oasis of Ammon some eight to ten days journey south through the most forbidding of deserts. In that year Ammon was purportedly the greatest oracle after Delphi, but this reputation also reflected Egyptian political and religious ambitions. Long dominated by Persia, the Egyptians longed for a return of the old glory. Indeed, a year or two after my move to Paraitonion, Amenidiris threw off the Persian yoke and declared himself Pharaoh of all Egypt and the founder of a new dynasty. He spread his influence rapidly westward into the desert, increasing the importance of the Great Oasis as a crossroads of Persian, Egyptian, and Hellenic intrigue.

As I sailed into that most beautiful of bays that summer morning, standing at the prow of the ship watching the kingfishers hover, no other place seemed so imbued with peace, hope, and the possibility of building a new life. To the east and west of the harbor are deep lagoons separated by jetties, and in both directions as far as the eye can see undulating beaches of perfect sand. A natural cove shelters the town from sea gales, and cliff walls shelter it from the sharp, sand-laden desert storms. In summer a fresh wind off the sea dispels the heat. But the sea is what truly astounds. Many seas are of great beauty, the Scythian Sea, dark and restless, or the sea around Crete, but the sea at Paraitonion is of another order; alive with colors unlike any others I have seen. Azure there is to be sure, and green from a variety of sea plants; shades of emerald, surprising ambers, lush purples, deep blacks, and vivid yellows, each merging and mixing into hues hitherto unknown. Nor are these ever still. Stirred by the slightest breeze or strong wind they shift and blend, and shift again with sunrises and sunsets. On calm days the white sails of new ships arriving or departing add contrast, as do white caps stirred by the breath of playful gods. Each day from minute to minute the elements renew themselves with deep brilliance.

I was there three or four months before I was given a sign. A sharp knoll rose above the western edge of the town. It offered a commanding view of the surrounding area and coastline and I would go there often to sit and escape from the close quarters of the densely packed streets, or simply to enjoy the view. At sunset I imagined that the gods were riding sun trails to earth. Sounds from the town drifted up, of braying mules, crying children, and hawkers selling bread or fresh fruit. Since my arrival I had prayed and made sacrifices for divine guidance. How small and limited the town seemed, hardly more than the smallest of Spartan villages, but with less intensity. How could this be a place for me I wondered, a place for a woman as sophisticated as Eshe, a place to raise Azeneth?

I was on this knoll one morning watching the sponge fishers at work. Below me eastward was the main harbor, and to the west high jagged rocks forming a quiet, crescent-shaped cove where the sponge boats could anchor at the fringe of the open sea. A path led from the knoll along a ridge to a rocky bluff overlooking the cove. I had been going there every day to sit and watch the sea, and the divers at work. Because of my illness, I was always thinking of other ways to supplement my income. The main economy of Paraitonion depended upon the supplicants en route to the Oasis: filling the inns and restaurants, flocking to the shops for offerings, or to the Agora for supplies to make the long desert trek; seeking guides, camels and desert horses, or guards to protect them from brigands. If Paraitonion became wealthy, as the gateway to the Oracle, it did not have the religious establishment to direct its greed to religious practices, as did Delphi. Some in the city abhorred the dependence on the Oracle and encouraged other trades to flourish. Its theater was becoming famous in that part of Africa and attracted people seasonally to the dramatic festivals. But the trade with the most hope for competing with the oracle was sponges. They commanded a premium price; indeed, in Athens they had the reputation of being better than

27

those from Kalymnos. "Sponges fit for Hephaistos", the Athenians called the sponges of Paraitonion, because that god was the first to use a sponge, and the best.

Seeing the sponge boats set out from the harbor day after day, returning at nightfall with such plentiful catches, made me wonder if there might not be some opportunity here, and so I took it into my mind to watch from the bluff to see if I could be inspired with some plan. The boats worked close enough to the shore to make notes on the numbers fished from the sea, and which sites produced the most. Sponge fishing is a risky craft. The diver holds in one hand a large rock tied around with a long rope, and in the other a bag for the sponges, also attached to a long rope. A three- pronged Poseidon spear is strapped across the shoulder and easily swung into use. The diver launches himself from a small platform in the boat's mid-section, or directly from the rail. Once at the proper depth, he releases the rock and tugs on the rope to have it hauled back up again. After much training, they are able to work underwater for many minutes, but it takes a terrible toll on the body over the course of just a few years, and often the sponge divers die young, what with the perils of the sea and the rigors of the dive.

One boat I had come that day especially to see. I had studied it before, had heard rumors in the harbor, and made discreet inquiries about the owner. They said that its divers were the most successful, and I wondered what they were doing that could be better.

I sat on a dock in the harbor one fine morning talking to an old diver as the sponge boats made ready to sail. I said to him, "That captain is very successful."

28

He turned to reply. His cheeks were sunken and he was so thin that his ribs showed through his thin tunic. His breaths were long wheezes. As I looked closer I wondered if he were only as old as I and not twice, as I had at first supposed, but I did not dare ask for fear of insulting him.

He said, "Yes he is. They fight to serve under him, but he will only take the best."

"Is that his secret? That he only takes the best?"

The old man thought a while and said, "He has a unique way of paying."

"And what is that?"

"He pays his men a percentage of the profit and so they work harder to find more because they know they will have a share."

"Then they are not slaves?"

"He treats all the same."

"That is an interesting practice." I decided that I should meet this captain with his unusual ways. "So you think that is his secret?"

"Yes, and that he makes generous sacrifices to all the sea gods and does not favor one over the other. He does this every day that he sets out."

Was dividing devotion equally among the gods the wisest practice? I had noted that he had named his boat Triton, so perhaps he was protecting himself too. I said, "Favoring the son of Poseidon can do him no harm."

A crude carving of Triton adorned the prow of the ship: he who had the tail of a fish and roamed freely the deep sea. It was believed that if you caught sight of him it would bring good fortune, so long as you were not entrapped by his spell.

The old diver said, "He is a good captain who goes to great lengths to protect his men and so they are loyal to him."

This conversation made me all the more interested in the activities of his boat. The following morning I went out to the bluff at daybreak to watch them. My vantage point was also close enough to wave to the men and recognize them individually. The divers dove naked, not only because those depending on the sea should bare themselves to it to be truly in the hands of god, but also because their bodies could be oiled to withstand the cold of the greater depths in a sea warm at the surface, thus preventing shock. The last remnants of summer still lingered and the sea was calm. From the height on which I stood I could at the same time see to my right side the activity in the harbor, ships setting or furling sail, and to the other side the spongers working quietly in isolation and in peace with great diligence as if in their own paradise.

A boy caught my eye that morning. I first saw him standing with the other men winding a rope into loops, gathering up his spear and bag, and removing his chiton to dive with the others. I noticed too that the captain of the boat treated him with more deference than the others, paternally hugging his shoulder and touching his hair. The boy took up his rock and hung the sponge bag from his shoulder, following the other men to the side of the ship. A ladder led down into the water, but he stepped onto the narrow platform to dive feet first, the early sun turning him golden. The challenge of the dive had excited him. He paused to pray. At that moment the shrill cry of a bird overhead made us both look up. Soaring in a great circle that embraced both the boy and me, so that we were centered within it, was an eagle. I felt that chill again; such as I only feel from sacred things, as I had felt when the ravens called on the Cretan mountain. The boy had noticed the eagle too because he raised his hand to shield his eyes against the glare, looking first up and then towards me to see who was standing within the circle. He put a hand to his heart in greeting, and I did the same.

This was my first glimpse of Alexis, son of Thessalos of Kalymnos. And I heeded Socrates' warning too, for I had learned he was right through painful experience. To think that your beloved is beautiful is common to all lovers, but to know that he is *kalokagathia*, good and beautiful, must stand the test of time.

He plunged into the sea and I waited tensely for him to rise to the surface again; twelve times my life span it seemed before his head broke the surface. He prided himself on staying down as long as the best. I would like to think that day he did this for me. When he pulled up his sack he triumphantly spilled out a large catch and the others gathered around to look. As I watched I knew that the sign I had sought in Paraitonion had been given, that Alexis was an omen of love and good fortune. I knew also that it was here on this knoll, within the circle described by Zeus, that I should build my house. This is what the eagle told me and this I have done. I write there now.

I went down to the harbor at the end of the day in order to wait for his boat to pull into harbor with the day's catch, having the plan to pretend that I was already a sponge merchant. Alexis was standing at the prow ready to jump ashore with a rope; he wore a simple, homespun chiton come lose from the shoulder. As the boat slid up onto the sand he jumped ashore nearly at my feet, laughing. His eyes were a grey-blue, and his brown hair had blond streaks that caught the sun; his nose was aquiline and his chin pointed, his skin a rich olive. Such features are called Median beauty, and are rare among the Greeks, although sometimes I saw them in Macedon among the King's retinue. Alexis saw that he caught my eye. He smiled shyly. How fast my heart beat. Had he accepted the will of the circling bird? I knew I should give a calm impression and raised my hand again as I had done on the knoll. He blushed, but he raised his hand too. Some philosophers say that we should flee from the glimpse of beauty because it instills madness in all the senses, but I did not.

Alexis's father was not just captain but the owner of the Triton, and several others there in that same lagoon, having staked that place for himself in his rivalry with the other sponge fishers. Alexis was not his oldest son, but was his favorite. That evening I invited the two of them to a feast ostensibly to talk about the sponge trade and a possible investment, but really to get a closer look at Alexis. Tired and worn as he was that evening, I could not imagine anyone finer: small of frame, shorter than I am, and I am not tall, shy, and modest. His clean chiton was of finely woven homespun. Hellenic clothing lends itself to coquetry but he kept his modesty when seated. I had known many boys who did not, and that was a mark against them, as modesty is to their credit. It can proceed from honesty or be feigned for effect, but his was genuine. His chiton he treated as a child that should obey him and not be unruly, but when he wished to seduce he could be charming and direct, as I later discovered.

At dinner that night I learned they were, in fact, from Kalymnos itself. They had come here because they now dominated the trade there, and were ambitious to dominate all the best sponges everywhere. Alexis was fifteen; he had not been that far and wide, had never seen Athens for example, nor even Crete that was not too distant a sail from his home. He knew nothing of fine food or wine, or of the wider world. I will be his mentor if he permits, I thought, remembering what Socrates had said, that mentoring must proceed from virtue in order to instill virtue. As he sat next to me that evening, I prayed to Zeus who bestows such things that we should be together as long as the god willed, and we still are, thanks to His great blessing. His house is near mine. His children are as my children.

Entering Alexis' life as I did created great conflict. Alexis' loyalty to his father was fierce, but I did not want him to continue to dive because of all of the accidents that occurred almost on a daily basis. The face of the old diver on the dock that day flashed before my eyes. Life held such wonders. I could not believe that Zeus wanted us to shorten it. His father saw it differently. Not that he wanted him to dive. This Alexis insisted on. His father's wish was for him to captain a ship himself or manage the business on Kalymnos. His father was harsh and driven, and Alexis and I argued about his influence more than about anything else. For two years he did continue to work with his father before coming to live near me. The intermittent stays were painful but I continued to pray and bide my time patiently.

I did not want to win Alexis through trickery or force.

In the days that followed this first meeting with Alexis I should have felt secure in the sign the God had sent me and made preparations immediately to secure the knoll and surrounding land in order to build my house there. Did the Cretan Oracle not direct me here? I was seeing Alexis every day, but the more I saw of him the more doubts I had. What could this remote stretch of coastline, this remote village offer us? Paraitonion was no Athens, no Delphi, or Sardis, or Memphis. I worried about Eshe and Azeneth's happiness, and now about Alexis too. Would I limit his possibilities at the same time that I wished to expand them? What would he do, I wondered? He was too young to command his own boat, and I finally admitted that I knew nothing about the trade. There were other fears: that the well water on the knoll would be too brackish for my child; that the summer climate and desert winds would not agree with Eshe; that the doctors and physician-priests were not skilled enough to treat me; that I could not raise falcons as I wished or find my favorite foods. In other words, some of my fears were real, and some childish.

The soothsayers I had brought from Crete were skilled but I had also discovered a very clever dream reader in the village. This dream had visited me one night, I think after the third or fourth meeting with Alexis. A snake entered my bedchamber, slithered across the floor and licked my toe. The next day I went to find the dream interpreter in his shop. It was down a small alleyway that I would come to know well as it was on this same byway that Philiscus opened his practice. There was a small outer room where you were offered a calming desert herbal tea. When I was ushered into the diviner's room I was struck by his piety. Innumerable niches were carved into every wall, some illumined with small oil lamps, some not. Apollo dominated, not as muse or musician but as the archer god of healing, perhaps because a plague had afflicted Paraitonion many years before, as it had Athens, and was still remembered and feared. Before these statues were small offerings: a piece of fruit, a clump of bread, a pile of dates. I gave a gold medallion, reclined, and told my dream.

The seer was thin and middle-aged. His teeth were blackened as I had often seen in the town perhaps because of a desert plant that was chewed.

He said, "The god who rid Delphi of the giant python has touched your soul."

"What does it mean?"

"That seeking god and seeking healing for you are the same. Praise to Him from whom all healing flows. He has blessed you."

Suddenly he bent and touched my foot, as if to honor the spot Apollo had touched with his divine tongue.

I told him too of my dream on Crete of the eagle, of the purpose for my coming to the town, and of the eagle circling.

He answered, "Zeus draws the two of you into a fate known only to him. That is the circle."

"But should I build my house on that knoll? Is this what He commands?"

For a time he silently consulted a chart and he also called for a liver, so that he could read all the omens

35

before pronouncing.

He said, "This knoll is owned by the God."

"Then should I build on it?"

"If you build you must consecrate."

I said, "Our lives belong to God. I have always known that. So I shall build."

He was looking at his charts again and said, "There is something more. When precisely did the eagle cry out the third time?"

"Precisely? I think it was just as it finished the third circle, just as it turned south. Yes, I am sure."

"He bids you follow. At Zeus-Ammon more will be told."

I longed to ask what would be told but was foolhardy enough to ask only, "Do the signs say when?"

"His time is His time."

The knoll belonged to a herder's family, seven sons who could not agree on the terms of a sale, some wanting it sold and some not, some wanting one sum and some holding out for a sum threefold greater. There were several builders in the town but each had his own set of enemies so that there was always someone ready to talk against one or the other of them making a choice confusing. Materials were scarce and the cost of importing them exorbitant. The local stone was of poor quality. There was no apparent water supply on the property and finding a water-diviner would prove time consuming and costly. There was only one who worked that entire coast and he would not return for many weeks. To purchase without knowing there was good water would have been foolhardy. The local tiles were of such poor quality that I could snap them easily. I wanted painted murals in the central hall, special tiles for the floors, sculpted friezes over every door interior and exterior; an internal fountain, fig trees, plants, a special cage for my wife's birds. Without water I could not plan a fountain or garden and the town craftsmen were too amateurish. I would have to find those in Memphis or Sardis willing to come for many months, and would also have to send emissaries to these and other cities where I knew experts worked. Putting all of this together was to take many months, during which I dared not send for Azeneth and Eshe.

Alexis was also soon beset by conflict. As our bond strengthened his father grew jealous. He rested the future of his sponge trade on Alexis and would not see him deflected from that course. I had also proposed to Alexis that he become involved in the planning of my villa, paying him for his tasks; he had shown natural talents for design, and for overseeing the men. Despite his youth he was freeborn and would have been respected, but he earned respect by showing sympathy for the workers from being on board his father's ships from an early age. When I asked him to supervise the installation of the tiles or the design of the bedrooms so that they would have a cross breeze in summer, he handled it as I wished. I often pretended ignorance of something I knew quite well and would have him find out the answer.

The villa would take two years to finish, but after one year there was a small central structure where I could at last live with Eshe and Azeneth. At the base of the knoll was a small fisherman's cottage sitting by itself on a sheltered ledge; I repaired it for Alexis, so that by the age of seventeen he had his own home. The sea was always tempting him, and I knew that he often longed for that life. At first I thought I needed to distract him so that he would forget sponge diving, its dangers and adventures. No sooner was the water situation solved than I decided that I wanted a garden filled with rare specimens, not content alone with the amaryllis that through the open window filled our view with rich flame, or the red bougainvillea that draped along a portico. Profuse gardens were a luxury in Paraitonion because fresh water was so scarce; rare plant specimens might cost more than my gold jewelry. I used the search for rare plants to introduce Alexis to a wider world. It took us far afield, to Melissa were I heard a rare orchid grew, and to Persepolis where there was a market for rare plants.

Building my house brought bittersweet days. My happiness with Alexis often seemed complete, but my health was worsening, and my daughter fell ill.

4. 399 BC. The Oasis of Zeus-Ammon.

In those first years in Paraitonion I did not go much to the Oasis of Zeus-Ammon, despite the bidding of Zeus in my dream. The high cost of building the villa had made me turn to gold work again, through ignorance stumbling back into illness, like a blind man into snakebite. The mere thought of venturing far from home, no less undertaking the arduous desert crossing, made me feel insecure. The few visits I did make to Ammon were in search of new healers who might offer me more hope than those I had around me on the coast. These visits proved devoid of dreams or prophecy. Nor did I meet any healers who could offer me more help than I was already receiving back on the coast, and this was not much. Another concern had emerged at home to keep me there, yet finally drive me to seek answers. Soon after Eshe and Azeneth joined me, my daughter had the first of her seizures, gradually growing in frequency and intensity. The physicians we consulted called it "the sacred disease", a form of possession by a god or demon, but which they would not say. One prescribed an old Hellenic remedy, of having Azeneth breath in the fumes of burning ram's horn, the goat being prone to this illness, but it was not successful; nor the exorcisms they submitted her to. King Meneclush, I knew, was ever bringing new healers to Ammon, again drawing me there.

Frequent caravans were setting out from the coast for the oasis, in low season, fortnightly, but in high season, weekly; I could join any one of them. But the truth is that the desert terrified me, admittedly an ignorant response, as are all governed by fear. I hated the eight to ten day's journey across, to me, utterly desolate terrain, despite the rewards promised at the end by the green paradise set in the middle of the arid waste. Except for a short spell in spring, there were no fresh water wells along the way, and what water we carried with us from Paraitonion needed to be boiled with medicinal herbs to make it less brackish and more palatable. The fine desert camels are Bactrian and are bred in northern Persia. There were times when I envied their plodding endurance, as I did those extraordinary desert horses their fortitude and ability to go so long without drinking. Strong winds would sweep across the waste table of loose pebbles, hurtling tiny fragments against exposed skin and chafing it raw. Wild fevers could rage through a camp and far fewer arrive than had set out. Above all it was the vipers that inspired my deepest fears. They darted across the desert floor forward and sideways and would strike without warning, most often fatally, after terrible agony. They were small and impossible to detect until they were upon you; they were vicious and loathed us, invaders of their land. The vipers were said to manifest the awesome might of Zeus, He who might dart into your life unawares and cause havoc. Fear of the gods is a form of wisdom, or of expediency. Zeus had always seemed to me benevolent, and my belief was that the vipers were lower demons exiled to the waste for their malevolence, and filled with rage. The carrion birds were also dreadful. The least taint of death and they would hover above a caravan. We knew that they needed sacrifices and would not depart until someone satisfied their black hunger. There was a lesson to be learned from them; we must bear harsh realities with courage and caution. The evening encampments were eased with song, stories, and camaraderie, but the days were tense with threat, and stifling heat. Add to this my poor health, the building of the villa, my daughter's illness, Alexis's familial troubles, and a thousand other things that filled daily life, and there seemed to me excuses enough not to go to Ammon. If it had not been for Azeneth, my own illness, and the call of Zeus, I might have stayed away altogether and practiced my devotions at home bent before His household altar. The divine winds were blowing and would again urge me towards Ammon, as swift winds unfurl resistant sails.

But illness continued to force me to look for new ventures for quick profit, if I had given up on sponge fishing. One night over dinner in Paraitonion by accident or fate I hit on one of my wilder schemes, yet one that would play a role in Socrates' last days. We had guests who had come from the oasis and they had brought us a handful of the most delicious but scarcest of all dates, grown only in Ammon. These small red or white dates made all others seem crass and dull. They were simply the finest in the world. But few had ever tasted them. King Meneclush of Ammon reserved the entire harvest for himself and used them to reward the desert chieftains for their support. The small grove where the dates grew was part of his royal grounds, and guarded night and day. The number of trees was kept at about forty so that the harvest in any given year would be small enough to keep the dates few, and the price as high as possible. Meneclush jealously guarded his right to sell them and went so far as to make sure to remove the pits before they were sold so that no one else could propagate them. He was known to go into frenzies of pillaging and burning when he heard that someone was trying to grow the trees elsewhere. He need not have. They could only grow in the soil, weather, and water conditions of Ammon. Certain select traders were allowed to handle their sale, those with rich clients who could pay the exorbitant prices. I knew that I could sell the whole harvest back in Athens for a staggering sum, but decided to test the market first. At one of the banquets I attended in Ammon I managed to bribe a slave to smuggle out a few in the folds of his robe. These were carefully wrapped in special cloths and sealed boxes that would keep them fresh until they reached my emissary, Oloros, in Piraeus. Indeed, they were all the rage, as I thought they might be.

I had one advantage over other traders who might also have schemed after the fruit. I was acquainted with Meneclush, and knew that his lust for gold objects might overwhelm his hoarding of the precious dates. He was as cruel and untrustworthy as his avarice was immense. It was said that he had poisoned his father Lysis in order to have the throne, and many rivals as well. I heard it from Daryush the Persian that he had a certain woman's husband murdered because he desired her for himself but then soon tired of her and traded her into slavery. If such vices would let nothing stand in their way, how could my plan to trade mean dates for gold fail? He had purchased many gold objects from me, and had commissioned me to build the four gold statues of Egyptian gods that he housed in a temple room within his palace. These are the statues they said spoke to him. My scheme was simple. I would supply the King with a truly magnificent ceremonial wine cup such as he had never before beheld, and in return request a "few small boxes of the white and red date harvest for my table", as if it were nothing more than the request of a child for sweets. Two large saddle baskets full per camel and four camels would suffice to earn me a small fortune back in Athens.

The date harvest in general was between November and January, but I thought it wiser to go in March after the curing process was over and the dates were ready for transport. It was in the middle of March, the year of Socrates' death that I set out there, having learned all I

42

could about the harvesting and packing of the cargo. A small white worm nests within them, but if properly cured they will crawl out leaving the fruit perfect within and ready for export without spoiling.

Besides my health, and my daughter's, there was another reason for going to Ammon. It was because of Alexis. Weaning him from the sponge trade had added purpose and intensity to our relationship. His father never did give up his wish to have him take it over. But now that he was fresh returned from his military service he began to take an interest in the new medicine from Kos, as impatient as I with those trying to cure me and my daughter. I was encouraging him in his desire to be a doctor, but I had also lost faith in the old methods. The traditionalists, following Egyptian practices, had failed to cure me. They had referred me to new practitioners from Cnidus. I was mistakenly told that they were following the rational regimen of Hippocrates of Kos and I had put great store in them. Kos and Cnidus are very close to each other, and I wrongly concluded that Cnidus must be a branch of Kos, but they were worlds apart. The Cnidian pathology of diseases was pure Egyptian, and part of the greater Egyptian plot I have mentioned to establish the New Kingdom.

Alexis had also received encouragement to study the Hippocratic methods by our friend Dareios the Persian. I did not know his father's name and always referred to him thus. Besides being a trader, he claimed expertise with aphrodisiacs, and love charms. I was skeptical. Aspasia was the only one I ever knew who genuinely practiced the love arts; she had taught Socrates these too, although some secrets she would never reveal. Others were, if not outright fakes or swindlers, then hit and miss amateurs. I sometimes followed Dareios' advice in matters of the bed, especially in the early days of my relationship with Alexis, but never took his herbal potions. He traveled widely in search of new stimulants and remedies, and because he traveled so widely, he was one of my best sources of news. I also used him from time to time as my business agent. Shortly before visiting us, he had been to Kos, hearing that Hippocrates was successfully treating male performance dysfunctions through diet. He had made friends with Hippocrates' pupil, Philiscus, and was becoming a convert himself to the new medicine.

Dareios and I shared another connection, Meneclush, who had long ago befriended Dareios and brought him regularly to Ammon. The King was obsessed with his virility, and brought to the oasis anyone claiming success with a new aphrodisiac or remedy, true or false. He became dependent on Dareios' potions; it gave Dareios access to the court and court secrets, which he would pass on to me, as gossip, or for profit. One such had an influence on my decision to brave the desert once again that March. He claimed a mystery rite was being performed at the Temple of Zeus in Ammon in which men and youths were married. The ritual also pledged them to honor Zeus-Ammon above other gods. It had its origins in the Mysteries of Ammon-Khensu and was a closely guarded secret, but I recalled having heard a passing remark about this from Aspasia when I was young. I wanted to know more before speaking to Alexis, having learned not to trust Dareios. Driven by the wildness of love, the possibility made me resolve to set out as soon as matters at home permitted my absence. The thought of being so closely bound, at the same time yet separately, to both Eshe and Alexis was incentive enough to brave the desert.

***

In the popular imagination, and most of the time in reality, an oasis is a few palms or a bit of scrub encircling a muddy well, a watering hole for desperate animals and travelers. There are countless of these in the Great Desert. The Oasis of Ammon was something other, a paradise rewarding suffering.

I never adjusted to the camel's rhythm and pace, two left and two right legs moving in unison swaying the rider side to side for the entire march, and preferred to go on horseback. Countless supplicants over many decades had forged grooves in the impacted rock and mud, a makeshift road between Paraitonion and Ammon. Setting out at dawn from home, and every morning of the trek, there would be song, the cry of falcons far overhead, and the clatter of pebbles driven by wind. The main concern was water. For a few days in spring it could be dangerous to get caught in low areas in heavy downpours because of the flash floods. A torrent would rush through a declivity that should have been hard-packed mud, careening around bends with a roar. At all times the wells were unreliable, often dry or fouled by carrion. But the winter downpours rushing off into the greedy sand brought forth bright desert flowers in yellows and reds, and wisps of promising green among the barren rock crevices. In March there was still bountiful wildlife to feed us. If we sighted an occasional gazelle we would hunt it and feast, shared thinly among so many. If a hare ran across our path as we were ready to encamp, it was a sign to move on to another place; hares fled before harm they said. This happened but once. Knowing how long the trek should take, I would nevertheless lose count of the days. Each morning the desert again stretched arduously before us.

Dulled by seemingly endless days of trekking, the arrival at Ammon was always a surprise. On my first journey it seemed so sudden that I was left breathless. We had ascended for a day into rough terrain. The path had narrowed, forcing us to walk single file. I was often near the front. The guide had stopped and bid me come forward. I spurred my desert horse. We were on a flat plateau. Stretching before us southwards, as far as the eye could see, was an immense sea of waving green. The sun glittered off the surface of two olive brown lakes, and four hills rose to the sides, above the undulating palms. On the eastern bluff, several hundred feet long were the gleaming palace and the oracle Temple of Zeus Ammon. Built from Libyan limestone, the wind driven sand had cleansed and kept them as new since the time of their construction by Pharaoh Amasis of Thebes some two hundred years before. What joy I felt each time I stopped on the plateau to give thanks to God for bringing me safely to worship at his Temple of the Sea of Palms so proudly commanding the white town spilling up the hillocks and bluff face to be nearer the gods. After the silence of the desert, there was again the hum of life: bells from the grazing goats, the bellow of camels and livestock, the crowing of roosters, the cry of birds, the shouting, singing and drone of the thousands who lived there, and the temple's plaintive chant echoing over all. The streets and marketplace would be teeming when we entered. So weary, if not desperate, was I from such a long and arduous trek, that I had to hide my face in weeping as we picked our way carefully from the plateau down the steep cliff face among huge boulders and into the oasis valley. Black flies and gnats would be our first reminder that we were near reed beds and water.

It was the much beloved Herodotus who coined the word "oasis", meaning "a fertile place to dwell". He was referring to Ammon, and so it might be called the first oasis. But it was my friend, the traveler Hellenicus, who wrote the first account of Ammon in his book *Account of a Journey from the coastal city of Paraitonion to the Sanctuary of Zeus Ammon*. If beauty depends on opposites, as it is said it must, it was the most beautiful of all oases because nowhere could the contrast have been greater, an explosion of wet, fertile green in the most arid landscape imaginable. To the north, days away, was Paraitonion, and two weeks to the east was Thebes. To the south for weeks there was nothing. Westward too there was bleak terrain before high mountains blocked passage. How then was it that this wondrous emerald island so watered and fruitful, came to be there in such a desolate place? Seashells abounded and so it was said that Poseidon drove the Great Sea beneath the desert to resurface clean and pure of salt as testimony to his power, and the might and reach of his domain into unexpected places. But Zeus, God of Surprises, could have commanded it into being as well.

Hellenicus says that to some the desert is a place of desolation, but to those who lived in it and knew its ways, it was a haven of silence and great purity valued for the freedom it gave from enemies too timid or foolhardy to try to conquer independent men. Whole armies were lost there. A Persian force, some fifty thousand strong under General Cambesis, had simply disappeared into the sands not far from Ammon, perhaps in one of those blinding storms. That had been some hundred and fifty years before but still struck terror. For the Libyan nomadic tribes, Ammon was a reminder of how dependent we are on the beneficence of a God that can bring such fertility from nothing. With my first glimpse of Ammon came a revelation, that Ammon surely was the work and will of Zeus. It was sensible of God to make somewhere so unexpected a place, to remind us of his command of time and place and his ability suddenly to break into our lives. The Great Oasis came to signify for me, so reluctant at first to visit, that place that was made by the God himself, much as the Parthenon was made, or all the Acropolis. The thousands of waving palms, the refreshing breezes, and the dark mysterious pools were the God's handiwork.

Descending into the town was like entering a giant, intricate, active beehive of some ten thousand drones. The houses are open to the street day or night, doorways draped with various curtains; there is little theft. The inhabitants live simply, with few furnishings. Locally woven carpets are laid on the floors but they are shaken each day and the floors swept. The lightest wind can blow fine sand and dust in from any direction, infiltrating everything. Rolled mats are used for sleeping. Some grander houses on the hilltops were more sumptuously fitted, as was the palace, and the temple quarters of the priests.

There was much intrigue in Ammon. Meneclush wanted control of the desert tribes, to use them to extend his rule to the edges of the vast desert and beyond. Emissaries and spies, slave traders, and brigands came to sell information, as much as devotees seeking answers. Meneclush made much of secrets. He knew they attracted like honey, filling the town with adventurers and speculators, and others seeking pleasures. Indeed, secrets in Ammon were more rife than the dates from the thousands of date palms, though not always as nourishing. Some of these secrets had nearly become customs. For example, men could come there to exchange wives with each other, as did the inhabitants. Outsiders made much of this, mostly pious condemnation masking envy. There were a number of rules around the practice, as there were among the Spartans who also slept with another man's wife so long as the husband did not disagree, one reason why Alcibiades was so attracted to Sparta. Perhaps the Ammonites took this from the Spartans, or perhaps it was the other way around, but I was told that, if there were no objections, a man might ask another's wife to spend a night together. She had to agree. Abduction, or force was punishable by death. Another rule was that whoever sired a child was responsible for the child's upkeep. Meneclush encouraged these practices, and indulged in them himself. Exchange of wives was also a thriving business needing negotiators, intermediaries, and lavish gifts. It would happen too that a man might want his son initiated and that his friend's wife being kind and pretty might be asked to introduce the boy into the passions. An exchange of presents was customary. My friend Dareios had a theory that Meneclush encouraged these practices in order to preoccupy the town's people who might otherwise descend into rebellion or crime. Their pleasures earned him their gratitude, and kept him in power.

If the air hummed with talk of illicit affairs, the talk of war, and plots to further empires, was greater. The high priests were also tribal chiefs of immense power and influence in conflict or competition with each other; the temple plots and strife added to the general atmosphere of intrigue in Ammon. In the gathering around the five date marketplaces there was more buying and selling of secrets and rumors than of the fruit itself, and higher prices paid. The abrupt cliff, at the top of which the temple stood, formed one natural wall of the marketplace. Against it the most interesting vendors sold their goods, and information. I would walk the long length of the market beside that imposing wall every morning at daybreak, buying the daily news, and selling some too. I foolishly thought that I had come to Ammon for trade or secrets, but the gods were working their design.

5. Dareios at Ammon.

I had used Daryush, as his friends called him, for several years as representative for my gold trade in Salamis. The arrangement had gone smoothly enough, that is with only a small percentage of the profits unaccounted for, a sort of purse tax he exacted and I let pass. He was amusing, if challenging, company. Only Aspasia was better informed about secret practices. Knowing them could be useful in getting himself out of predicaments with married women, and for increasing his yearly income. This expertise had secured him the friendship of the High Priest at Ammon, who liked to be treated roughly by slave girls, whom Daryush supplied. He always stayed at the High Priest's villa, and that in turn gave him access to the oasis's secrets, and the king.

Daryush was tall, handsome, with black eyes. His black beard he had curled with hot irons. His voice and mannerisms were that of an actor rather than a trader, stentorian, self-conscious. Athenians were fond of saying that the Persians valued three things above all: riding, archery, and telling the truth, the latter being one of their religious duties. Daryush told the truth, but not always with discretion. He appeared to be vulnerable and self-doubting, but he was ruthless. You had to have your wits about you when dealing with him, friend or foe. As with men who are known to have secret proclivities, rumors about him were rife. One will suffice. I first heard it soon after arriving in Paraitonion so it must have been some four or five years before the death of Socrates. When I discovered that it was true, I suspected that Daryush had spread it himself.

The Spartan General Lysander, no hero of mine, was receiving money from the young Persian Prince Cyrus to aid and abet his plotting against Athens. The Prince, but a boy of fifteen, had been made governor of the entire western Persian territories. Rumors were that Lysander was infatuated with Cyrus and that they were lovers. It

51

was not the practice of Spartan men over thirty to take boys. But Lysander was an ambitious man and in his twenties had been the lover of the Spartan prince and heir apparent, and so was practiced in the art of using the skills of the bed for political advancement.

Now Daryush had been a tutor in the royal court at the ceremonial capital of Persepolis and had gone west with Cyrus. He bragged to me that he had introduced Cyrus and Lysander, fire and tinder. He knew about Lysander's early affairs in Sparta, and encouraged the Prince to consort with Lysander in order to secure a Spartan alliance; it took no more coaxing than some strong potions. Daryush achieved a number of things through this affair. The Persians needed Sparta. They had decades-long grievances against Athens, and Egyptian power was in the ascendancy, threatening their western front. An affair with Lysander would also have implications in Persia. Cyrus's older brother was the pretender to the throne; he looked for every opportunity to undermine his younger brother's influence by questioning his youth and judgment. Daryush hated the heir presumptive, or so he said, but some suggested that he played both sides against each other by spying for him in the tent of Cyrus and Lysander. He vowed to me that he had witnessed Lysander and Cyrus' love making through a secret spy hole, which was enough like him to be true. He must have had Lysander's trust. Lysander allowed him to live, knowing Dareios knew of the affair. There may be some truth in this. When Lysander conquered Athens and destroyed its walls - this was some three or four years before Socrates' death - one of Daryush's Athenian allies was appointed a Spartan intermediary and it was through Daryush and his intermediary, Oloros, that I planned to hire mercenaries to secure Socrates' escape from Athens. Lysander would not have trusted a confidant of Dareios unless there was some bond between them.

Daryush was temperamental, given to deep brooding and fits of temper over small things, while underneath calm and calculating. He always treated me straightforwardly, perhaps because I was Macedonian. Macedon was allied to the Persians in the invasion that resulted in the sacking of Athens. Since then the Courts at Susa and Persepolis had harbored ambitions to resurrect the alliance with us. If I never had political ambitions, I had friends in high places, and was well informed about Macedonian intrigues and events. I had proved a good listener. In fact, I liked the tales of his bedroom exploits. He was incapable of desiring a woman unless she was married and the husband disapproved. Otherwise, he might have lived permanently in Ammon where you could have your way if the husband approved. He had never married himself. Perhaps this was out of fear of others like himself, a rare breed so he need not have worried. I have heard of only one other like Daryush, that is Alcibiades, who practiced this craft on a grander scale than Daryush, if less systematically and more irrationally. Daryush never kept a mistress or went with courtesans, nor did he like virgins, widows, or boys. But set him among married women and he was like a rooster among hens, often creating as much noise and flying of feathers. If a marriage is an officially sanctioned and publicly recognized rite, as was my marriage to dear Eshe, then

Daryush wanted the opposite, secrecy, intrigue, and conflict. Great danger excited his desire. Escaping through a window as a husband entered through a door was one of his specialties. Because of all the wars, husbands were away more often than at home, and there was ample opportunity to practice his art. In fact, because he reveled in married women, lavished attention on them, and treated them like goddesses, married women sought him out and fought over him, whether it was out of revenge against some husband's philandering or absence, because of the attention he paid them, or his attributes, I cannot say. I do not know how he managed such a life, filled as it was with the risk of being murdered or chased by enraged men and whole families, or balancing several women at once, but we all perfect our skills through practice as I had with gold, or Olympic champions their sport. He said he was only imitating the gods, for they were always in and out of beds, and called his libidinous pursuits pious, only half in jest.

And so, the evening of our arrival in Ammon, I made my way through the town to meet him. The Agora was teeming with those beautiful, blue-eyed, light skinned desert men with their impervious, independent air. The streets were overrun with the half-wild, white and yellow dogs that the inhabitants kept as guard dogs. They scavenged freely, boldly snatching food from merchants' stands no sooner did they turn their back to make a sale, or from your hands if you walked along with a cake. Children feared them. If pursued they might turn on their pursuer. Goats, cats, chickens tangled the legs of the throng; small sturdy horses were being led to auction;

small boys darted among the crowd like shoals of small fish amid coral. My favorite stalls were the falcon breeders'. The birds perched proudly on poles, their heads hooded. They were magnificent birds, much prized for their hunting skills and speed, worthy cousins to the eagles of Zeus. Purse-snatchers and thieves were as plentiful as oranges. I had learned to walk cautiously and keep my wits about me.

"There you are, Amyntas!" Daryush said greeting me, already having arrived at the place by the wall near where we would dine. "I surely expected you to be blue," he joked, "Still not painting yourself?"

In this he referred to the myth that Macedonians painted themselves blue, which was a custom among some of my warrior countrymen if not my tribe.

I said, "That is no more true than saying that all Macedonians hate the sea."

"You are proof! Nevertheless, building a villa overlooking the sea is a radical act for a Macedonian. How is it going with the search for good water and digging wells? Any luck since I was there?"

"We dug where the diviner told us, but it was brackish, and we were forced to dig a second and third hole, each of them costing a ransom fit for King Midas himself. But we did find good water at last, and on the plateau too. So the diviner was right, if not precisely enough to suit me."

"Is it not the same with divining as with the divine, obscurity muddling revelation?"

Daryush was not really a believer, but I did not want to argue and said, "Indeed!"

"And Alexis? Did that little aphrodisiac I told you

about have the desired effect? Where is he anyway? Seeking pleasure I hope."

"He is out buying horses. He is particularly fond of the desert stallions and wants to breed them. He will join us soon. And as to the other matter, lentils mashed with artichoke hearts, I simply added it to our meals and in a day or two his passions were more than adequate for his wife and me."

"I thought it would work. I must tell Philiscus of your success. It was he who prescribed it, you know and he has a scientific interest in knowing the results of his remedies."

I said, "I was just going to ask whether Philiscus was here with you? I am very eager to meet him, as is Alexis."

"He is here indeed. He went off to talk to some of the local healers, but will join us later. I outlined Azeneth's symptoms to him, and he said he thought he could help."

"But Daryush, that is splendid news! Splendid!"

Daryush liked to link arms, or drape one over my shoulder as we walked, an easy matter as he was a head taller. He leaned close to my ear to whisper conspiratorially, "And speaking of Alexis, on that other little matter, you know, I did speak to the High Priest and he is willing to discuss the Khensu rites privately between the two of you."

"Did you explain that no decisions have been made? I have still not mentioned it to Alexis and thought I should know all there was to know before discussing it."

"Yes, I did just as you asked. He did tell me that both parties had to express willingness. There is a contract of some sort, and it is not cheap. In any case, he will tell you

56

everything. There is only one small problem."

"What is that?"

"The earliest he can see you is a week from now, because of the festival and other obligations."

I spoke too soon, not accounting for the play of the gods, "We meant to stay that long. Will you send word today and confirm the appointment?"

"Of course."

"Then, once again I am in your debt."

I usually said some such to make it clear that I understood the monetary aspect of our dealings. We had nearly reached the market when I realized we were no longer headed in the direction of the restaurant.

I said, "But where are you taking me? I thought we were going to Salim's to eat and I am famished?"

"I have a surprise for you. And don't worry. It will include food, in fact food such as you have never tasted!"

"A surprise? With food?"

"It is a new private bath house, quite sumptuous. The king recently opened it, but only for himself and a chosen few. It has only been going a few weeks but it is already the heart of court life, and the town. If you want to conduct any business or obtain any information that is where you have to go. Not to mention the nomad girls and boys! You mean you have not heard of it yet?"

"No. I can't say I have."

"You are too isolated there in Paraitonion. Why word spread to me in Sardis weeks before it opened."

We were nearing a stairwell carved in the rock that led up the bluff to the palace.

"Where on earth is it then?"

57

"Attached to the back of the palace of course, so it is easier to regulate and guard. Do you think the King would admit just anyone to such a place? You need introductions, passes, a fee. I had to call in many a favor to get us in. And wait until you see the Persian tiles I supplied for Meneclush!"

"But Alexis then? He thinks we are dining at our customary spot, and will meet us there."

"That is easily managed. One of my slaves can wait by the restaurant and bring him to the bath house."

He pointed to a handsome Scythian slave following us some feet behind and went for a moment to speak to him. Alexis, with his brown hair streaked with gold, his blue eyes, his light dusting of fair beard, would be easily recognizable. "He is wearing a chiton decorated with a silk band," I called to Daryush.

A sumptuous bathhouse in the middle of the desert sounded just like the sort of grandiosity Meneclush would think up, but if it were in the high Persian style it might not be pompous or pretentious. The marketplace was just beginning to empty at the end of the day. The streets were still crowded with merchants and beggars, jugglers and musicians, storytellers, children crying and running. Horse or mule driven carts were being reloaded with unsold bolts of Egyptian cotton, jars of olives, woven baskets now half full of their myriad of spices casting exotic spells. Heaps of bruised and rotting lemons, oranges, a variety of fruits and vegetables were being discarded, the poor descending on the rubbish in droves.

The palace loomed high above us on our right as we made our way along the rock face. Daryush turned a sharp

58

corner and when I sped to overtake him we nearly collided. Two guards stood beside the narrow entrance to a stairwell. He stopped to pay them, gesturing back to me, and disappeared up the smooth stairs. In the rains a torrent would flood down them; morning mists made them treacherous to sandaled feet, but in the dry evening I made a safe ascent. At the top was a small square between the temple and palace hardly large enough to call a square but with a wonderful view over the town. We stopped there to catch our breaths from the steep ascent. A light breeze that never made it to the town below refreshed us. Meneclush was not in residence, nor expected for a day or two. Few people milled about and it was too late in the day for the slaves to be working still on the construction of the new wing, the walls only half raised. Daryush pointed out a carved wooden door in the side of the palace and rapped sharply. A slave immediately opened for us. There was a narrow dark corridor lit only by a single lamp and then another door of less grand design leading into an antechamber tiled with geometric designs imitating sunbursts in deference to Ammon, who was both a sun and a fertility god. In the baths themselves the tile theme was dolphins, tridents and shells, tribute to the stories of Poseidon's role in creating the oasis, not as superbly executed as those in Aspasia's old house in Athens.

As we went in to disrobe Daryush said, "I have a special treat for you. I ordered it before hand. A wonderful wine you may not know, and some of your favorite dishes."

"I look forward to it all."

"And the greatest luxury is that there are two bathing

pools, one cool and the other hot. You are meant to take the hot one first and then the cool. Philiscus has said that it is very good for your health."

"But wait. We arranged for Alexis but what about Philiscus?"

"Oh, he is to meet us here. We arranged it previously. He should be along soon too. Come now, the wine will refresh us."

It was brought to us in silver goblets on a silver platter. When I tasted it I found it chilled and quite delicious.

Daryush asked, "Can you guess where it is from?"

"I take it that is the surprise?"

"Yes."

I sipped it again, indeed better on the second taste. It was light and fragrant with the scent of familiar mountain flowers.

I said, "It is not vulgar like Pisidian medicinal wine, nor as full as those from Hios, or as delicate as those of Thassos. Yet it is fruity, perhaps with figs, almost herbal."

I was baffled and finally had to admit defeat.

Triumphantly, he said, "It is from Chalkidike in your very own Macedon!"

"Macedonian wine! Of this excellence!"

Somehow the mention of my birthplace as a small gesture towards me moved me greatly, perhaps because by contrast the oasis was the antithesis of the snow capped mountains I knew as a boy, or perhaps because there were difficult health concerns in my life then, and still more difficult ones to come. I was overcome with nostalgia, or the power of the wine.

I said, "As a boy we had home grown wines but

nothing of this excellence. And father made and loved wines." I took another draught and asked, "How is it that there are warm and cool pools. And chilled wine?"

In the oasis there was a pool that was as large as a lake, he explained. The King had let down test ropes to measure its bottom, and divers had gone to dangerous depths, without discovering the bottom. They had, however, found the entrance to an underwater cavern with an exit above ground in one of the cliff faces. Jars were filled with the finest wines and brought to the cavern; some were also lowered into the lake to cold depths.

As we settled into the hot bath, we were handed our wine, and served with plates of extravagant delicacies. Lightly salted Sicilian tuna and *horaion* from Byzantium no less, seemed more savory than ever down there in the desert so far from the sea. The surroundings loosened my restraint and I asked him, "Now Daryush, you told me the King's new and favorite wife is most beautiful, and you also told me that Meneclush just happens to be away right now while you are here. It does not seem coincidental. So tell me, have you taken advantage of the circumstance?"

Daryush moved closer to me so as not to be overheard by the slaves. Meneclush had his household spies and we had to speak cautiously. He whispered, "She is an exquisite Assyrian girl, not sixteen. Such a one!" Slaves were coming and going and musicians had entered to play for us. We waited for the music to grow louder to cover further talk. Daryush continued, "I am told that she married Meneclush against her will and had a lover at home. Meneclush knew that if her father heard about her lover he would have them both killed and blackmailed her into marriage."

"She must be very angry with Meneclush. Did he ever tell her father?"

"No, he holds it over her head. You are right. She is very angry and seeks revenge."

"And you are, well, sympathetic?"

"Most. But don't get the wrong impression. I must be growing older, because I am trying to reunite her with her lover and not have her for myself, perhaps find safe haven for them in a northern outpost."

"You really intend to help both of them reunite? You *are* mellowing."

"Well, not entirely. You see, the King's second favorite wife would then become his favorite again. Let us just say she would be most grateful to me if this strip of a girl were to disappear. We are concocting a way of getting them out of Ammon that makes it seem as if they have been killed so no one will search for them."

"This is really one of your wilder schemes! If Meneclush finds out, well, I don't want to think of the consequences. You know how jealous he is of his possessions, wives included. And this second wife, is she worth all the risk?"

"Oh yes. Her father is a chamberlain at the court in Memphis, a most valuable ally for us Persians right now. You lead too staid a life, Amyntas. You should take more risks; create more of a fuss around you. It helps keep things interesting you know."

I said, "I have enough worries. But I did hear rumors that Egypt and Persia were negotiating an alliance."

But he was not selling me the information, he would

not say much, and I did not ask. Yet, his capacity for intrigue, and his contacts in the Piraeus underworld would be useful in the days and weeks ahead.

6. I dream of Socrates.

Half way through the evening, the servant Daryush had sent to intercept Alexis arrived without him. He had waited for hours, but there was no sign of Alexis, and I began to worry. Ammon was the sort of place where anything could happen, and did. Despite Daryush's reassurances, I decided to make my way back early to the villa we had rented, not far away at the other end of the plateau on which the temple stood, in the hopes of finding him, or word from him. I was tired from the long desert trek and a recurrence of my symptoms, and took my leave.

Alexis was there when I arrived, with a perfectly good explanation. Seeing that he would be delayed in his negotiations for the horses, he had sent one of our servants to the restaurant to warn me. Of course, our slave did not see me, and the slave that Daryush had sent did not recognize him, so there was a mix-up worthy of the bawdy Megarian comedies that I reveled in as a child. Alexis was doubly fortunate that day. He heard in the marketplace that the King's chamberlain monopolized the best horses and went immediately to see him. The rumors were true. The corral was filled with those splendid desert horses so favored of the nomads, and bred in the southern most regions of the Persian Kingdom. Alexis had settled on three: with magnificent refined heads and the bright look of superior intelligence. Their strong, sleek flanks were shaped for speed, and their high tails flaunted spirit. The negotiations had been conducted over strong wine. The show of enough money to buy a dozen of his best loosened the Chamberlain's tongue and greed, and Alexis saw his opportunity to ask about the dates. "But I have heard that you are also able to supply special buyers with the finest dates in the world and my Master happens to have a fetish for these and will pay *any* price for a years supply." The Chamberlain had exclaimed, "A years! I do not know if I can convince the King of so many." By his reply Alexis knew that the man already intended to mediate the sale of some, a "generous complement," it was decided. The weather had been favorable that year with just the right combination of hot dry days and cool evenings, and so that year's harvest was bountiful. The king had also tried a clever, successful experiment. He daily watered a select group of prize trees from the sacred lake nearby. This water was sweet and blessed. The first tasting of the new crop had evoked enthusiastic praise, for the perfection of the fruit, and the inventiveness of the king. Alexis had also mentioned gold to the Chamberlain, gold such as he had never seen before, and the Chamberlain immediately suspected that I was the would-be buyer. We were confident that the platter I had made, with date tree and leaf pattern to honor this special aspect of Ammon, and commemorate the King's innovative groves, would secure us our supply.

I was more excited by the forthcoming meeting with the physician Philiscus than the fantasy of profits. It was near dawn when we went to bed, impassioned by fine wine and the possibilities raised in Ammon. Before falling asleep, sated with embrace, I wished that Alexis would step over into my dream and so extend the bliss of a hopeful day. I fell into that deep sleep where gods roam and hold court with us about their mysteries. This dream visited me.

Our bedroom had no windows. Socrates entered through the keyhole of the closed door and hovered in the air at the foot of my bed. He commanded, "Amyntas, awaken and see!"

I sat up in bed. An enormous black snake slithered across the floor to the foot of the bed, reared, ready to strike or devour me, but coiled instead and swallowed its own tail.

Socrates pointed and said, "Look."

I now saw that his feet did not touch the floor. He hovered in the air and glided towards me, which also terrified me. I said "Socrates, why are you here? You never travel. Is something wrong that it brings you here to the desert so far from Athens?"

"Look closer!"

He held out his arms to me and I saw that they were shackled.

I cried out. "Socrates! What have they done to you?" A soft light grew within the room. A cage descended and enclosed him. He seized the bars. I cried out again, "Socrates!"

"Watch!" he commanded. As I watched he ascended, still encaged. His voice faded but I heard clearly, "Come."

I must have shouted out in my sleep. Alexis was shaking me. "Amyntas, wake up. You've had a bad dream. Wake up."

I was trembling and sweating as if in a high fever. He

65

put his arms around me. "Amyntas, what is it? What is it? Tell me."

But it took many minutes to calm down enough to relate the dream. And what was so familiar about it? I could not guess.

Dawn was breaking. I arose now, unsteady, and said, "Alexis, go down and awaken our diviners in their tents and bring them here immediately. I must ask the gods the meaning of the dream. And send a slave to the temple to see how soon I can consult the oracle. There on the table is a bag of coins. Take some for the priest. And bring our best rider. I might have to send messages home today."

Alexis was distraught. He could not love Socrates as I, but he loved him nonetheless. "Whatever happens, we shall face it together," he said.

7. New hope for better health.

I went early that same morning to the small public fountain by the temple wall in order to perform my ablutions. Priests guarded it day and night, to prevent villagers or travelers from profaning the sacred water for household or personal uses. Just after dawn, I found the guard asleep, and could pray privately and devoutly, my spirit lifted by peaceful bird song. Dionysus, lost in the desert and dieing of thirst, was led, by Ammon the Sun God in the guise of a ram, to the spring that fed this Fountain of the Sun. Blind, black fish swam in its depths. The penalty was death for catching them. I was eager to see the oracle, she whom they called Phemonoe, daughter of Apollo, second in reputation only to Delphi. As I cupped the cool water to my face, I hoped that Zeus would

66

guide me, not knowing that He already had.

The priest awakened. He was surprised to find someone there so early, glad to break the silence of the night and his long watch with chatter. He gave bad news; I could not possibly consult the oracle for many days. Had I arranged it with the High Priest to have my name added to her waiting list? I had not. Did I realize that she was awaiting Meneclush's return and that the King would have first consultation rights? I did not. He threw up his hands and looked at me as if I were an ignoramus.

If I were to see the oracle at all I would need the help of Daryush, and his connections with the High Priest. We had made plans already to meet again, and the day of our appointment, I went mid-morning to our spot along the wall, before the heat of the day made moving about insufferable. He knew nothing of my dream. When I arrived he was already standing there with a young man. He might have greeted me the more enthusiastically had he known that I had decided to turn over the dates' transaction to him because of my dream, uncertain how long Alexis and I would remain in Ammon.

He saw me staring at the stranger and introduced us, "Amyntas his is the physician Philiscus, son of Demetrios of Kos. I have told you about him. Philiscus, may I present Prince Amyntas of the House of Temenidai, son of Alcetas of Methone. I have told you about the library he is amassing in Paraitonion."

Indeed I had already collected a large number of traveler's tales, histories, and Egyptian medical treatises; I hoped to add some on the new medicine. Hippocrates wrote prolifically, one of the reasons his methods are now prevailing.

Philiscus was tall and thin, in his early thirties. His warm, firm hand earned my confidence. His face was ruddy with health, his hair and beard had a lustrous sheen; his eyes were bright with curiosity. It is said that eyes that dart inquisitively indicate intelligence and imagination. His hands too were restless, as if driven by his eyes, yet he was serene. I caught him staring at me, but not impolitely. When our gazes met he did not turn his eyes away; he smiled.

He said, "Daryush said you were building a most extraordinary library and that you already had some rare volumes on diseases and healing?"

"Not many, only a handful, mostly Egyptian Asclepian. My wife is Egyptian. There are priests in her family at Memphis and Thebes and, knowing of my interest, they had copies made of a few texts they found in their temple archives. I am a follower of their methods. Have you come here from Kos? You were studying there? Like most, I have heard a great deal about the new healing, true or false."

"I have come from there. I was born on the island and also did my apprenticeship there in Hippocrates' school, but now I practice on some of the nearby islands where we have spread our methods. I brought a book you might like to see. It is on epidemics. At least it is the first part of a work in progress. Hippocrates is still writing it."

"I would very much like to see it! Is it based on his theory of bodily humors? I know that much. Of course, those I have been following believe that illness is of divine origin."

68

Daryush said, "And those methods prescribed for you have not produced much success. Tell him about it, Amyntas."

I replied, "I am afraid that is true." I asked Philiscus, "Did you apprentice with Hippocrates then?"

"Yes, for several years. It is a long training. He is looking for a synthesis of the two different healing approaches, you know, the sacred and the physical. He wishes to bring them together before he dies." We were nearing our favorite café, where private conversation was still possible among the throng. They also served the best almond cakes, those laced with honey. Philiscus said, "He is sixty now. Dareios -- if he will not mind my mentioning it-- tells me that your daughter is ill with seizures? How old is she and when did they start?"

"She is six now and they started about a year ago but are getting worse."

"Can you describe her symptoms?"

"She trembles all over; her teeth rattle, and she falls to the ground shaking. It is terrible to see. I feel helpless to ease her suffering."

"Is there white froth at her mouth? Does she bite her tongue? Is it hard to revive her?"

"Yes, all of these. We have been told that it is the sacred disease. This much we know already. But the treatments so far have been useless."

"Yes, I thought it might be the sacred disease from what you and Dareios have told me, but Hippocrates does not think it is sacred. He has been gathering notes about it for several years, and intends to make this into a book as well."

"Really! But what does he say? The priests and healers we consulted were convinced it was sacred in origin and is either a demonic curse, or the harbinger of prophetic powers. We thought perhaps the gods wanted our daughter Azeneth to be an oracle."

"Hippocrates believes it is a disorder of the brain entirely natural in origin. He is experimenting with various herbal and diet remedies. I am glad to hear that the fits started not too long ago. Her treatment must begin at once. Once the disease becomes chronic it is nearly impossible to cure, but if caught early there is every reason to hope for success."

I was overcome with relief and joy. "Then it is not too late?"

"No. I think not."

"Praise God! But it means you must come back north to the coast at once, or as soon as possible. I would also show you my library, of course, and you will both be our guest."

Daryush said, "He has a beautiful villa overlooking the sea. I am treated better than kings there."

Philiscus replied, "My needs are simple. But I am treating Meneclush. I might be able to leave for a while and return. What do you think Dareios?"

Daryush said, "I see no reason why you cannot travel back with Amyntas so long as you leave enough remedies with the King to ease his manhood anxieties, and he knows you will be back on a certain date."

Philiscus said, "I shall have to seek permission from his Chamberlain. But Dareios tells me that you also are ill?"

We stood now before the café. Some tables were laid out in the shade under palms and we looked for one free. I said, "Perhaps if you have time today we can talk privately. Dareios here has heard the stories of my illnesses so many times I do not think he would want to sit through their recitation once more time. Perhaps tell me about Meneclush instead? He is a great collector of physicians. Are his complaints real?"

"I am not at liberty to say."

"How so?"

"We are taught to keep the confidences of our patients. What I might say is that some complaints become real if the person is convinced they are real, real or not. "

"Yes. That seems correct.

We found a table now and Philiscus whispered something to Dareios and turned to me. "It is all right with our friend here, and if it is all right with you as well, of course, I can examine you a little right here."

Physicians often advertised their skills publicly but I had never been examined in a café. I agreed and he looked at the whites of my eyes, my tongue, squeezed my skin, and smelled my breath.

He said, a little sheepishly, "In fact, Daryush has told me enough about your symptoms to guess what might be causing your illness. I would have to do a full examination, of course and hear your history and that of your family too. There is a family connection with diseases, more often than you might suppose. But from everything Dareios has told me about your work and lifestyle I think the cause is not divine, but something physical and simple."

"But I would like to hear what you think now. If you change your mind later I will not hold it against you."

"Oh I do not think I will change my mind. I think you are suffering from metal poisoning. You have all the symptoms."

"Metal poisoning!" I exclaimed. "And you can cure it?"

"Yes, I think I can. It will take time though. We have to discover first which specific metal has pervaded which humor, and then we have to find which remedy can attract a specific metal within each of the humors and also whether another remedy is not also necessary to eliminate the offending substance from each. It is all trial and error and time consuming I am afraid. It will require testing and patience before we hit on just the right regimen."

"But you think it feasible?"

"Yes. Very much so! The fact that you work with gold further complicates the matter because so many other metals are used in the process and we do not know if one, many, or all are responsible for your troubles. Several metals might have polluted you, and they have probably caused imbalances in all four humors. It will take time to sort it all out."

"I assure you I have patience." After years of suffering I was overwhelmed by the possibility of health, and I added, "Do you really think there is hope of restoring my health?"

"Oh yes. It is really a matter of establishing the right routine and watching your reaction and progress. There are herbal teas I can recommend right away, a change of diet, foods that will cause the metals to bind to them so that they can be eliminated. The first step is to stay completely away from the offending substances. Of course, you will not be able to touch or be in contact with gold or any

72

metals used in your processes."

"For how long?"

"Well, the truth is that if you have become so ill from these things then you are susceptible and that means complete abstinence."

"You mean never!"

"I am afraid so."

"Just like Alexis and his sponge diving," I burst out.

"How is that?"

I said, embarrassed, "Oh that is another story. But no contact with gold! It has been a good craft to follow, one that I took to naturally as a boy and led to many good things. But, if the God wills it and it is time to find something else, well, it will be difficult, but not impossible. Praise the God of wholeness." I fell silent for a minute or two, and then said, "How much longer do you need to treat the King? I have not told you yet Daryush, but something has occurred. Alexis is out now seeing about a caravan back to the coast and we might want to leave soon."

Dareios said, "Amyntas! What has happened? You should have said something immediately. Not bad news from home?"

"Well, in a way. A dream. In fact I wanted to speak you today about helping to secure a consultation with the oracle as soon as possible. I will tell you both if you do not mind? It is about my dear friend Socrates." When I had related the dream both were silent and I added for their benefit, or mine, "Socrates is dearer to me that my own life and nothing could stop me from going to his side if that is what the dream means."

Daryush said, "Socrates in a cage, it is very odd. And the snake! Do you know Philiscus?"

Philiscus said, "I am not an oracle, or diviner. Of course, Socrates is famous on Kos. He is the wisest man alive. The oracle of Delphi said so herself many years ago."

I said, "Please, I would value your opinion."

"Well, certainly Socrates beckons you. And the snake eating its tail implies a divine, eternal purpose. I am afraid I cannot say more."

I said, "And you Daryush? I was hoping you had heard some rumors from Athens, but you have not?"

He looked disconcerted and said, "No, I am afraid that I have not, but I have been away from Sardis for many weeks. We must send word at once to our informant Oloros in Piraeus. He will know the whole story."

"It is a good idea and I shall word to my overseer at once. Let us hope there are ships at Paraitonion willing to ail. There were sea storms before I left."

Daryush said, "Five or six days across the desert to Paraitonion with fast horses, and then a ship to Athens. Perhaps I had better send my own messenger home to Sardis, and have copies of the news brought to you in Paraitonion? Or accompany you back as well? What do you say Philiscus? Shall we both accompany Amyntas back to the coast?"

"There certainly seems reason enough, with your health, and your daughter's to attend to. I am very curious to see how this matter with Socrates plays itself out."

Daryush said, "Settled then!"

8. The oracle of Zeus Ammon.

As on Crete, the Oracle of Zeus-Ammon gave simple yes and no answers for things favored by God. Consultations were grouped together on one day each fortnight and were accompanied by pageantry. Zeus' effigy, of a bearded man sporting a ram's horn, or of a ram encrusted in emeralds, was carried in procession on a long gold boat with as many as forty priests in attendance. A chorus of young girls followed, chanting sacred hymns to Ammon and Zeus, some Egyptian in origin and some from Hesiod and Hellenic sources. Questions were also scratched on shards, which has led me to think that the practice originated in Memphis or Thebes, the source for Crete. At Ammon, the questioner was allowed to mark the shards with his own symbols so that they could be identified later. The priests or oracle did not read the shards. They were held up and the answer given without the priest knowing what was being asked, preserving the divine origins of the answers.

The answers were given in an ingenious way that I have not seen practiced at any of the other oracle temples. Along with your shards, pebbles were put in the jar, one white and one black, yes and no, for each shard. When the oracle, or priest serving her, reached in to take a question one or the other of the pebbles was also taken in hand and laid upon the altar, one shard and one pebble, question and answer.

The oracle chamber was at the center of a series of enclosures within enclosures, the outer leading to the divine world; the sanctuary also protected from marauding desert tribes. Outermost was the palace structure, living quarters, a colonnaded garden, and within this the temple itself, which in turn had enclosures within enclosures, rooms where the priests could robe and prepare for the ceremony, or others where the sacred objects were stored for the oracle rites. There was also a large room where supplicants assembled and the inner most, central oracle chamber containing a large altar, with several small altar niches carved into the walls, and an archway leading back into a further temple space where secret rituals were performed such as the male marriages; this secret room, I discovered, was decorated with elaborate murals showing Ammon in various erotic pursuits.

I had come for the consultation with Alexis and as we approached the temple gateway Alexis pointed out an old woman crouched in the shadows beside the door. She was gesturing to us. As we approached she shuffled out and took hold of my sleeve. She smelled badly. I tried to pull away but she had a firm grip.

She said, "Why are you here?" Her voice was firm and made me try to look closer, but her face was hidden. I had heard that eastern soothsayers haunted the temple precincts but I had seldom encountered one. Beggar women were also common, and I did not know which she was.

"To consult the Oracle, of course," I said, pulling my sleeve away.

"You are devotees of Zeus-Ammon?"

"I would call us such." Alexis said.

She held out her hand to offer me something hidden in her palm. "Go no further. Here is your answer."

I said, "Go away. We don't want to buy anything. We're

76

here to consult the oracle."

I took Alexis's arm and tried to step around her, but with great alacrity she blocked our way again.

She said quite firmly, "Hold out your hand, fool. The God has told me to give this to you."

I did not believe her and said, "The God? Which God?"

She said in a firm voice, that of a young woman, not of an old, "Your God, of course."

I scoffed at this, "My God? That is strange. Whoever you refer to would not prevent us from entering. Now stand aside. We do not want what you have to sell, and we shall be late for our reading."

But she persisted, "I sell nothing but give something. It is the God's work I do."

She pushed her closed fist closer to my face so that I pulled back.

"What is it then? Tell me first."

"Beware! Are you prepared?" She added sharply, "Now take it!"

Alexis had become pale and afraid. I hesitantly opened my palm and into she dropped a tiny black snake eating its tail. I cried out, nearly dropping it, but Alexis's hand shot out to steady me.

"It's all right, Amyntas," he said, "it is obsidian."

He had misunderstood. I was startled by its association with my dream and knew it to be an omen.

I mumbled, "Yes, of course, obsidian."

I turned to ask the old woman why the God had sent it and which, but I saw only a black, fleeting form disappearing into shadows.

II. My Life in Athens: Simonides and the Odeion.

1. 399 B.C. Spring.

Dareios remained in Ammon to complete the purchase of the dates, but Philiscus accompanied us on the journey back through the desert to Paraitonion, a return to Hestia filled with hope and dread, bringing as I did a physician who might hold the cure for my beloved daughter, no less for me, yet burdened by my dream of Socrates. Never before had the goddess of hearth and home seemed so real, so mysterious. I was also heartened during the journey to see Philiscus and Alexis becoming friends. In the evenings when our party stopped to pitch tent, eat, and sleep, they would stay up late, talking by the fire about their lives and the new medicine. I would join them sometimes, but most often I would crawl exhausted into our tent and be asleep by the time Alexis came to my side. That the new healing excited him was an understatement. By the time we reached home he was a true disciple of Hippocrates. To be a healer was revealed to him in a flash; as if Asclepius had handed him the healing snake.

By the campfires, surrounded by the deep desert stillness, spontaneous plans burst from us like sparks from dry kindling. Flashes streaked across the starlit sky, the gods spreading insights and fates. One night I suddenly said, "But, Philiscus, we must open a practice for you in town. I know an empty space that would be perfect, on the side street of the soothsayers. You could also give classes, and perhaps take an apprentice or two."

Of course, I meant Alexis, as was instantly understood, if laughter at my transparency be the judge.

78

Alexis said, "You are not very subtle, Amyntas. Give our friend here a chance to see the town first. He might find it awful, and run away the first chance he gets."

But Philiscus did not think this would be the case.

Another night, our plans well advancing, Alexis said, "If we are to make Paraitonion a Hippocratic center then, perhaps, you could use your library to preserve the new teachings?"

I exclaimed, "Yes, a study center filled with books. When we were first together we went everywhere looking for plants for our garden. Why not medical texts now?"

Philiscus said, "If it's a library you want to build all you need do is go to Kos. I'm sure I can convince Hippocrates to supply you with copies of his own writings. He is eager to disseminate them. He also has rare Egyptian works in his personal collection. We could go to Kos together. I would like to visit my family in any case."

We did not know that with such plans we were also laying the groundwork for our plot to rescue Socrates. He was much on my mind. I slept restlessly; half hoping he would visit me again in dream, this time released from his cage. Fond memories of him would catch me unaware, when I dressed in the morning to begin that day's march, bend to pick up a robe, or fix a clasp. At the *palaistra* he had sometimes adjusted my clothing after exercises so that I could go home presentably through the Agora. I tried to tell myself that my anxieties were imaginary, but I knew that the gods had told me the truth; Socrates was in grave danger. Through that vast waste, as we trudged along so slowly, what could I do but pray? Had I not already sent home slaves on fast horses with instructions to return to find me in the desert with messages from Athens, or to set out immediately for Athens to find out what was happening? The steady pace at which we were forced to travel drove me mad with impatience. If Socrates' were under threat, should I not make haste? A threat to him seemed like a threat to my own soul. What might have happened that was so severe it could threaten his freedom? I never imagined the truth was worse. Socrates was seventy that year, the year of his death. Neither in his youth nor in his old age was he known for his caution or conformity, or as someone who would avoid conflict by holding his tongue. His opinions and friendships had always been a source of controversy: the notorious and extraordinary Alcibiades; those who betrayed the republic such as Critias, but nothing more than his inner voice, and the fear and envy instilled in others by an unknown god. Why then had he beckoned me to come?

In the desert, one terrible night, I was awakened by dread. How peacefully Alexis slept; my comfort! The desert night was cold. Wind whistled down from some hidden cave of the wind gods, they who brought pestilence and disease. Stones hurled against the side of our tent. His deep breathing and warmth sustained me. I arose, thinking to write, agitated by the image of a cage. A memory was just out of reach and I wanted to retrieve it, the image of Socrates long ago descending in a cage, as in my dream he had ascended. What was it then? Would it shed light on his summons? I could not remember.

Alexis stirred, disturbed by my restlessness. "What time is it? Is it time to break camp?"

"No. Go back to sleep. I am restless. I'm sorry I

80

awakened you."

"Is it Socrates?"

"Yes. It is Socrates"

"Come back to bed. I know you are worried."

"I want to write something."

"At this hour? What could it be?"

"You remember my dream of Socrates descending in a cage?"

"Yes."

"I've seen this before somewhere."

"Socrates in a cage?"

"Yes, well, no, Socrates descending from the heavens though. I cannot quite put it together."

He was fully awake now, and said, "Come back to bed and tell me about it. There is no use my trying to get back to sleep. In an hour or two it will be dawn and we will be on our way again."

"But I want to write it down before I forget."

"If you tell it to me then between us we shall not forget."

"No, I suppose we shall not."

"Come beneath the blanket. It is cold tonight here in the desert. Tell me his story."

"Like the old times," I said.

"Yes, like the old times."

In those first months when he was fifteen I often told him the old stories to lull him to sleep; of the gods' conflicts and heroes' deeds, of wars, and Odysseus' travails. He liked the bond of those nights curled together. I laughed now. "You're still a boy. A boy who loves stories." But I went to lie beside him.

And so began my story, "In the days of my youth, when my father Alcetas sent me to Athens to save me from the clutches of the mad King Perdiccas, the poet Simonides, besotted with love, took me one day to the Odeion to see the preview of *Clouds*, knowing that I loved the theater, and ready to indulge my every whim. It was there that I first saw Socrates all those years ago. Blame it on Simonides. Blame it on Aristophanes, whose play it was. But, really, this history begins before that…"

2. 423 B.C. Leaving Macedon.

When I was fourteen, father sent me to Athens for safekeeping. The timing was not accidental. The Athenians had suffered a major defeat in their war with Sparta, at the battle of Delium the year before. Capitalizing on war fatigue, the Athenian peace faction had gained influence again. Father had friends among them, including Athenades the famous goldsmith, and Aspasia, the mistress of Pericles. I would be entrusted to their patronage.

During the long Peloponnesian war, Macedon shifted its allegiances like the sea winds, one year favoring Athens, another Sparta, and after Delium Athens again. Father knew from his court sources that King Perdiccas had sent a delegation to Hellas seeking new trade privileges from the depleted city. The renewal of ties was propitious. I could be sent there without father seeming disloyal to royal interests, be protected from the endless court intrigues back home, and become self sufficient in a trade, one of father's education principles.

Father headed the house of Temenidai, one of the three principal houses of Macedon; his father and the King's father were half-brothers. After the death of my older brother in battle I was my father's firstborn son and therefore also an heir to the throne, if no more than tenth or twelfth in line. If I had been twentieth it would not have mattered to the king should he choose to consider me a threat. Perdiccas had fits of madness in which he imagined that everyone around him was plotting his assassination, or the assassination of his favorite son and designated heir of the moment in order to prevent him from inheriting the throne in favor of some other favorite son from some former wife. He thrived on real or invented plots; the court intrigues, which he encouraged and sometimes contrived, rationalized his brutality. Because of the assassinations and father's dire warnings about the threat of poisoning, I feared going to the court at Aigai for the ceremonial occasions that I was required to attend. The legend had it that wild goats led the founders to the spot where they built the capital. I trembled at the thought that I might be slaughtered, as were the sacrificial goats each year on commemoration day.

My father was a vintner and our villa a short day's ride east of Aigai, down near the coast. Methone was the market town for the fertile hill regions around. My grandfather had amassed our lands and slaves, but father managed them with more skill. I sometimes thought he was too worried about money, but if it were not for him I would not have acquired whatever acumen I have in business. He taught me by example, by keeping me by his side while he conducted the vineyard's affairs. He had been lamed in the same battle in which my older brother was killed, at Potidaea when I was five. Macedon fought alongside Sparta against Athens at Potidaea, so that my father and my brother might have fought against Socrates who served there as a hoplite. I hid my family's role in battle from my classmates at the Lyceum when I arrived in Athens, although Potidaea had occurred a decade before. Memories of war live long, and harbor division.

I loved my brother dearly. There had only been sisters between him and me; he had taken me under his wing and taught me how to shoot a bow and ride. He had comforted me when I fell, or had bad dreams. Potidaea was a battle that Macedon should never have fought, father felt; but to criticize the king openly would have risked execution. He considered Potidaea an act of royal arrogance that cost him his wholeness and his son's life, and from that battle sprang his revulsion for Macedon's role in abetting it, and for war itself. From father's revulsion, and the loss of my beloved brother, came mine. When father was fit enough to travel again, in a special carriage he commissioned in which he could recline, he began to frequent Athens again, ostensibly for business. He was cementing his political ties, however. Here is an irony: if the two battles of Potidaea and Delium, some ten years apart, had not occurred I might never have lost a brother, or been sent to Athens. And, Socrates fought at both, and I came to love him. Battlefields are fertile ground for fate.

A special bond grew between father and me after the death of my brother. He often told me that he caught glimpses of the gods in me more than in my younger half-brothers or my cousins. Many days, when I wandered out to play, I would find him seated on some hillock at the far end of our vineyards brooding over the loss of his eldest son, his hampered mobility, and the fate meted out to Macedon by war and politics. He decided sometime in those dark, disturbing days, to set his life and mine on a different course.

When I was a few weeks short of fourteen he told me one day to ride with him to inspect the vines on some of our more remote hill-slopes. The vine-strewn hills were glorious to see and I always liked these special times together. We stopped to rest at the hottest part of the day.

He said, as we took a simple meal of figs, olives, wine, and bread, "I want to tell you something. But it must be between you and me."

He seemed so serious that I felt something must be terribly wrong, and replied, "What is it father?"

"When your brother died, when I was first recovered enough, you will remember that I made the long journey to Dodona out of reverence for Apollo."

I only vaguely remembered this but said I did.

Father said, "I made a vow to Apollo to find a different life for you than one filled with blood, loss, and strife. And so I consulted the oracle and through her it was confirmed that the God would bless you. But there was more."

I saw his sadness and said, "What is it then?"

"It was predicted that Apollo would call you away from me, to somewhere He would designate. The time would come and it would be announced in dream or heard on the wind. It has come."

It was a harsh thing to hear, that I might some day be sent away from home.

I said, "Oh father! Sent away! Should I be punished then? What have I done? What wicked things? Do not punish me! Please! I could not bear to go from you. Have I not always tried to be a good son? Tell me what I have done and I will make amends."

"No, no, Amyntas, neither I nor the gods think that you are wicked; quite the contrary. You are blessed and loved of the gods."

The Spartans were prepared at birth for such separation and did not see it as abandonment, as I saw it then. I said, "But I do not understand! Macedon is not Sparta where boys are sent to live with other boys when they are six. And I am fourteen, if a day."

"You are not to blame. If anyone is to blame then it is your great uncle, Perdiccas. And even then it is not really the king. I have consulted our soothsayers and they too have told that the gods wish special things for you. The stars write it."

"And you have dreamt that I must go away?"

"Yes. A raven visited me in dream, perching on my bedside. It spoke and said you were to follow. I did not understand the words, nor did our soothsayers. A long time passed and there was no further word until some weeks ago. The hand of the God startled me awake. I went to the window to see if there were intruders and there was a large raven perched on the branch of the old larch, the same I had seen in dream. It cried out, and flew off southwestward towards Athens, crying out until I could hear no more. The soothsayers confirmed it was the sign I awaited. Soon after that, with a heavy heart I went to Athens to prepare the way for you."

"To Athens? So far from you and Macedon? Surely, I am being punished by the gods, but for what I do not know! Is it a punishment, father? Have I wronged you?"

"It is my love that would send you, and if it is love, as I know it is, then it will bring great good."

I could hardly control myself but I managed to ask, "Am I to go soon from you?"

"In a few weeks. The arrangements are nearly complete."

I was grief-stricken and could only say, "I do not think I can bear it."

I loved Macedon, our farm at Methone and its nearness to Mount Olympus a day or so to the south, and my friends. My stepmother was not cruel as are those of legend. I was heartbroken to leave. But Athens! How excited I was too.

Father said, "Perdiccas is busy rebuilding his army after Delium and not thinking much of court intrigue. But that will not last long. So it is a good opportunity for you to go now. With all his mistresses, wives, and sons, and all the confusions of the court, perhaps he will forget you and you can build another sort of life for yourself."

I do not think I asked him that day to whose house I would be sent. Too many feelings confused me. A few weeks later, just as I turned fourteen and thought that father had forgotten the plan to send me away, word came to us in Methone that another assassination had occurred at court and retribution was imminent. The day that word came, I was working up in the vineyard alongside the men tying vines. Father rode up to find me. I saw the sadness in his face, and knew it was time.

"Has the moment come?" I asked him quietly.

"Yes," he said, hardly able to speak for the tears.

"The King again?" He bent his head, and I tried to protest, "But Bouselos of Oion has been teaching me the sword. If the king sends men against us we can fight them off. Please do not send me away."

"We have spoken about this before. You must go to Athens. The arrangements are made now. I shall come to see you and I shall write to you every day. I have purchased fit slaves only to carry messages between us. The way is ready."

"When am I to go then?"

"At dawn. Things are being prepared already. Athenades the goldsmith will take you into his household. He is a freeborn citizen. His petition was successful. We were waiting for that. He is adopting you into his household. You will be given his rights and the rights of his district under the law. You will go to school and you will learn his trade to make your way in the world. You are a Temenidai and will not disgrace our honor."

"No, father, I never would. And I do not mean to sound disrespectful either. It's just being without you."

"You are upset. I know. We shall pray and make sacrifice when we go home. Come, let us ride back now. There is much to do."

So it was that I first heard of my new life. Long roads led from our farm in all directions, all the way to Athens it seemed, to Athenades' workshop, and to Socrates.

3. Autumn-Winter. 423 B.C. The house of Athenades.

How fickle and selfish a boy's moods! When I awakened before dawn the next day from a restless sleep, my first thought was not that I was leaving home, perhaps for good, but that I might fulfill my dream of attending a play at the Theater of Dionysius. I was passionate about the theater, and had written pitiful dramas for my friends about Odysseus' homecoming, Herakles' labors, and murder and mayhem among the gods. Father had taken me the summer before to Thebes for the Herakleia festival and when I returned I poured out worthless verse onto valuable parchment. The stages of Macedon could never match the lavish productions of Athens, the quality of the acting, the excellence of its masks. Athens set the standards. Was it grief or gratitude that made me kiss father a thousand times before departing?

Upon my arrival, Athenades son of Euphronios came out into the street to greet me. He held up his right hand, an Athenian greeting also marking an end. He was not at all what I had imagined. The Macedonian and Scythian goldsmiths were portly and shifty. He was tall, stately, fifty, with large brown eyes and a keen, steadfast gaze. He belonged to the Athenian cultural aristocracy, his father having been a potter much esteemed by Pericles. He was naturally conservative, but he also cultivated conservative mannerisms and attitudes, modesty and piety in the main; although aristocratic he was no oligarch. His thick white hair and beard were neatly trimmed. Weekly attendance at the barber, I would quickly learn, he considered a moral duty; it encouraged dignity of person. His tunic was plain white, but of the finest wool. I never saw him wearing a necklace, bracelet, or ring. He had strict views on women. His wife never went shopping in the Agora, and kept to her part of the house. In the two years I lived there I only glimpsed her a handful of times, and exchanged not more than a dozen words. She was also the main organizer of the yearly, married woman's feast, the Thesmophoria, perhaps because Athenades was so religious. Every day there were household sacrifices and I often heard him muttering some prayer or other, about the weather, the success of a sale, the Athenian grain crop, or for his two wastrel sons. Father thought that Athenades' piety was the reason for his stance on peace with Sparta. The city was diverting too much wealth to war that should be spent on ritual and religious festivals. He resented his civic obligation to provide money for building the fleet. His politics was more complex than that, but father was also right.

Athenades' house and shop, both were combined, was in the craft district, at the base and spilling up the slopes of the Kolonos hill, not among the luxury shops under the colonnades along the Panathenaic Way, but "under the eyes of Hephaistos", as the district dwellers called it, an area devoted to Athena patron of workers, and Hephaistos god of craftsmen. The Temple of Hephaistos could be seen from most every street in the quarter; it was resplendent, if gaudy. Painted in blue, pink, orange, and green, the gilding on the friezes and columns caught the Athenian sun at all times of day, every day of the year; it rarely rained a full day in Athens.

Athenades greeted me politely, "Praise Hestia you are here safely. Come say a prayer before we go in."

90

Flanking the entrance of the shop were statues of Hestia, and Athena Ergené, goddess of workers. Potted flowering plants were placed before the gods, and kept fresh by a female slave said to have the touch for growing things. We entered through a curtain. The room was small and crowded. Beside and behind a long counter were rows of locked wooden boxes containing samples of jewelry designs, or ready-made objects you could take away with you, and behind these four high stools and workbenches. In the left wall there was an open archway to another workroom; in the back wall there was a curtained doorway leading into a square hallway. The workbench closest to the door was empty. I hoped it would be mine, as it had more natural light and air, and it turned out to be so, not as a favor, but so that Athenades could oversee me better, a disadvantage in every advantage, as they say.

A slave in my party had run ahead to announce our arrival, and refreshments had been prepared. Three of the workers, resident alien apprentices, had been given permission to interrupt their work to greet me. Athenades preferred to employ metic apprentices rather than train slaves. They were more motivated, and once they had finished their training could teach the craft back home or become managers. All three were from the eastern regions where Athenades had workshops or partnerships, that is, two were from Scythia and the third from Lydia. The Scythians had disabilities, and had used them to avoid military service, or bribe their way free, I never found out which. One had a clubfoot. The other squinted and saw distant objects in a blur. He could also see finer details than anyone I have known, the wispy sub-veins of a plane tree leaf, for example. This was useful in fashioning intricate jewelry designs, and the reason Athenades employed him. He had a perpetual squint and wrinkled his nose when looking at you.

Athenades introduced me to the Lydian, Assur. He was short, seventeen, with hardly a beard, not hirsute like his countrymen, warm, and with a good sense of humor. He seemed to have a trick for everything, whether it was adding a twist to a molten strand of gold with a flick of his wrist, or playing knucklebones so cunningly it took me months of practice to win a game. He also collected grasshoppers, and had built little wooden cages "to give them good homes," he said. On the rare free day we went a few times to the countryside to add to his collection. He made me feel instantly at home, with his enthusiasm and instant approval of me. I think he was feeling a bit alone and sad before I came. The Scythians excluded him. My arrival made both our lives better, and we became friends.

Assur said, "You must be tired after the long trip from Macedon. Did you have any adventures? Were their robbers? Why did your father send you overland? Of course, we have heard the Macedonians hate the sea, but wouldn't it have been the quicker way to come? Are you afraid of the sea? But you are not painted blue! We were expecting you to be painted blue. And you're not wearing pants. Don't you all wear pants? You have the room next to me, if you want to call it a room. It is very small I am afraid. I cleaned it for you and didn't find any spiders. Not a one. A few centipedes though, and they can bite, you know. Did you know they bite?"

I laughed, "One question at a time! I can't answer them

all at once! Well, if I remember them all. Thank you for cleaning my room. But I do not mind spiders. As for coming overland, father had friends along the way who could see us safely through the mountains, but he was not sure about keeping us safe at sea. Some of us do paint ourselves blue for the festivals, and some of the army legions paint their faces blue for battle, to make them fiercer, but most of us don't. And I never wore pants. Have I missed any questions?"

Assur said, "Oh it doesn't matter. You must tell us everything about your trip. Surely there was at least one attack from brigands? Maybe, this evening, when we are off work and are eating? What about it lads? Shouldn't he tell us everything? You know, your Attic Greek is really excellent, far better than mine. How did you learn it? Perhaps you can give me some tips? I hardly hear one guttural of an accent. And tell me, do I have to call you Lord something or other?"

I said, "Oh please you must not make anything of my title. They are nothing in Macedon. Every house is related to the king through brothers, or brothers of brothers and half-brothers, so every house has heaps of lords and princes. It is all just a formality that means nothing, really it doesn't. Just consider it one of our strange Macedonian ways."

Athenades had been settling the slaves and guards who had accompanied me but now interrupted. "What have I told you boys? Amyntas will have no special privileges in this house. In fact, if anything, he will have more to do than the rest of you." He turned to me, "Besides your duties learning the trade, as your father wished, you will

93

also have to attend classes at the gymnasium, and a palaistra. There is a fine grammar and rhetoric Master who holds classes at the Lyceum. I am trying to arrange for you to study with him. Your father expects you to do well in everything and has asked me to send him regular reports. Indeed, one of the messenger slaves accompanying you will take a letter back first thing tomorrow morning, reporting on your safe arrival. You may include a letter, if you like."

My heart fell. Would I have any free time for the theater? But I saw that Athenades meant to impress upon me his authority at the very beginning, and said, "Yes, Master. I would like to send a letter. Father had me pack writing equipment."

"Very well, then lay your scroll here on my counter before retiring. Now Assur, help Amyntas with his box and show him where he will stay."

As Assur was accompanying me to the back of the house where the metic apprentices lived, I asked him what free time we had and whether he liked the theater. He laughed and said, "Don't talk about free time too loudly. It will get you into trouble with the house steward, Plator. He's not to be meddled with, that one, and if he hears you talking about enjoying yourself he'll immediately accuse you of shirking. There's a lot to tell you, but we better be somewhere where we can't be overheard." He leaned closer and whispered, "He has his spies among us. Be careful what you say."

We took a circuitous route to our quarters, so that he could familiarize me with the floor plan. I had heard that Athenian homes were very small, usually only a room or two, with mud walls. But Athenades' house was a maze. I said, "Where on earth are we going? There are enough twists and turns to make a Minotaur dizzy."

As Athenades wealth grew over the years, he had cleverly acquired not just the house at the front that was our workshop but also the house adjoining at the back and gradually the houses, to each side both back and front. These he connected by piercing walls and by creating interlocking courtyards giving free access to any one part of the growing establishment. He had also replaced the ringing outer mud walls with stone, and some of the interior walls as well, to make secure storerooms for his precious stock. Pious men like Athenades frowned upon too much decoration. His concession was to use expensive wood everywhere he could; cedar, fir, and oak, all of which were imported.

At the end of a quiet passageway was our small, plain courtyard, filled with potted plants and flowers, and also acting as our dining and common room. There was a small kiln, used to make small objects such as rings, fired only in winter. Most of the smelting was done at Athenades' country villa. My room, if you could call it that, was so small there was only room for the straw, sleeping pallet and one of my wooden cases, so that the second had to be stacked on the first, encouraging me in the art of organization. I had to squeeze past the cases to get to bed. More difficult an adjustment than the size of the room was the lack of a window. At home I had the same room from birth, with a window overlooking the countryside. Athenian homes did not as a rule have windows; Aspasia's being an exception.

Life did not go smoothly in those first weeks. I was homesick for father and the countryside, and found the city air sickening. The autumn weather was warmer than I was used to in rural Macedon where the sea and mountain breezes refreshed us. On the closest nights, Athenades permitted us to take our mats to the roof, or to one of the interior courtyards cooled by a fountain, but he considered too few nights intolerable. On still days human and animal stenches choked the air. The dust rose from the dirt streets and Athenades was forced to hang a thick curtain over the door so as not to pollute our work. Coarse wool headbands trapped our sweat. I welcomed the cold weather. The north wind seemed to bear messages from home.

Work piled up on my table before I knew what to do. Athenades hovered over me trying to teach me the rudiments as quickly a possible, impatient with my slow progress. We were the only goldsmith and jewelry maker in Athens using the best Scythian gold. All the others used inferior ore from the Pangeon in western Thrace. With Scythian gold came commissions from their King and aristocracy. They were beset by gold fever, as life-threatening as the plague, lusting after gold objects as much as Meneclush of Ammon. I had little time to dream, but my workplace at the front of the shop did give me a vantage point onto the lively street, by no means the Panathenaic bustle, but still a colorful parade of men and boys. It made me nostalgic for the freedom to roam, as I had the hills by Methone.

The worst adjustment was not the work or weather, but the arrogant metic Plator, about whom Assur had warned me. He had charge of the entire household, including overseeing our work. I had known tyrants at court but never at home and did not like the new experience. He monitored our work and gave us claps on the side of the head if he thought we were not working hard enough or had made a foolish mistake. He did all the mean things to us that Athenades, not being mean tempered, would never do, but seemed to tolerate in another so long as they were done behind his back. Plator was Illyrian. His hair and beard were red; he drank too much. Some men are silly and amusing when drunk, others cruel and barbaric. Plator was of the latter humor. Rumors were rife in the house that he was beating and abusing the slaves and I stayed clear of him; you did not want to cross or be in debt to someone cruel. As a youth I was very idealistic, emotional, and intolerant. Plator increasingly upset me, but I was unsure just what to do. In the evenings, after work, he became the favorite topic of conversation between Assur and me. We were allowed to take walks at the end of the day, so long as slaves chaperoned us. No sooner were we ten steps from the shop than Plator's latest horror would spill out of one or the other of us.

One evening Assur told me that he had found a young slave boy crying in one of the cupboards when he went to fetch a supply of lamp oil. He had howled when he felt an arm trying to pull him out, but was reassured when he saw it was Assur, whom he trusted. Plator was beating and using him for pleasure and the boy was frightened for his life. He had that morning dropped a wine cup and spilled a few drops, but had not broken it, a minor household infraction hardly worth a slap. His back, buttocks, and thighs were covered with stripes, Assur said. I was furious.

97

Right then and there we resolved to stop Plator.

Assur said, wisely enough, if I did not want to hear it, "You must be careful. If you tell Athenades and he does nothing except reprimand Plator, then Plator will leave no stone unturned until he finds out who informed on him. He will make your life miserable after that, but very secretively, so Athenades will not find out, by planting stinging ants in your bed, for example, or putting bitter herbs in your food to make you vomit."

Later in the week, Assur also found out from the slave boy that Plator was visiting a witch down the street from us, one of those women, filled with hatred, who practice the dark arts. She cast spells over anyone he wanted, and in return he brought her some of Athenades' slaves to satisfy her. Assur and I decided to follow him one day, thinking that he was going to see the witch. This was very dangerous because we did not know who his spies were and it might have been one of the slaves accompanying us. But we had had enough. Plator wended his way through the city to a very poor district, and entered into a small shop on a disreputable street near the Ceramica. We stood hidden to either side of the doorway and heard that he was selling gold. He had been taking the sweepings and scraps from our tables and the floor around, hoarding them in a string bag, and was selling them. It was enough to get him flogged to death.

We rushed straight home. I was jubilant, but Assur cautioned me, "It is still just our word against his, so we will need proof."

I brooded over this, and feel terrible. I hated injustices and knowing about such great ones and being able to do

98

nothing about them was intolerable. Father had often enough impressed upon me the need for self-protection; our court politics was too unstable to depend solely on him. To risk myself, or help another? That was the dilemma upon which I reflected. I was sitting in a courtyard one day, in a corner where I could hide and not be seen, when suddenly Athenades father-in-law Leagros stumbled upon me; a fateful encounter. He also lived in our household.

"Amyntas! What on earth are you doing here at the back of the house? Are you ill?"

I began to cry, more out of frustration than sorrow, and he thought I was merely homesick. He knelt beside me to comfort me, and out spilled the whole Plator story, the beaten slave, the stealing of gold.

He said, "There, there, it will be all right. It will be all right. But you must put it out of your head."

I tried to protest but he insisted.

The very next morning Assur shook me awake. The whole house was in an uproar. Plator had run away. They said he had taken refuge in the Temple of Hephaistos or the Altar of the Twelve Gods, where those hunted could find sanctuary. In fact, it was later said that he had fled the city, but he was never found and no one knew for sure. The Anatolian slave boy also told me that he had not had the courage to complain, but I was sure that it was Leagros' doing. I might stop and praise Leagros here, but days later, when I mentioned the conversation with Leagros to Assur he scoffed at the notion that Leagros might do something noble. Assur said, "You see, Leagros and Plator were drinking buddies and he found women for

99

Leagros and settled some gambling debts for him. So, Plator had too much over his head for Leagros to have ratted on him. Besides there is no love lost between father-in-law and son-in-law."

But I was sure that Leagros had rid us of Plator.

When the stories of Plator's misdeeds spilled out, and threatened to blacken the reputation of our household, Athenades blamed himself and was very remorseful. He was also more solicitous towards me. My father had entrusted me to his care and he had failed my father by exposing me to a brute. Praise Apollo I was never beaten! Athenades did not quite apologize but he did start to allow me to go out and about more. Father was paying him a good fee to house and teach me, but I do not think Athenades was craven. His remorse seemed genuine.

He took me aside one day and said, "Your father wishes you to have all the advantages of Athens. I have arranged for classes for you with a fine teacher I know at a private school out on the grounds of the Lyceum, which means you will be out and about more in the city. Of course, you will need a permanent chaperone. I have asked my father-in-law Leagros to do it rather than a slave and he has agreed. You must be sensitive to his age, but none know the city better than he and you can learn much from him."

In fact, Leagros had suggested this to Athenades and not the other way around, as I might have guessed but did not. Somehow it was all linked to Plator, but I was new to Athenian intrigues, and it did not matter to me. Thanks to Leagros, I would be able to have some freedom in Athens, because he chaperoned me, not despite.

To be out and about in Athens, what bliss! Athens! How

excited I was to be in Athens! The name had conjured magic, having been nowhere larger than backwater Boas, or the dangerous court of Aigai, whereas Athens was twenty, no thirty times the size of these not just in space but in spirit and intensity. And the theater! When would spring come? No more rural festivals and bad performances! If I did not worship Dionysus himself, the Lord of the Theater, Apollo being still much in my favor, I worshipped Dionysus' theater. Most wondrous of all, my boyhood passion for the theater would soon bring Simonides and Socrates into my life.

4. Spring. My first glimpse of Simonides.

No sooner did Athenades loosen control than I began to drag Leagros, Assur, and my new school friends to any performance I could find anywhere in the city. Drifters would stage Homeric scenes in the Agora for money. My favorites were the mimes. I would stand enraptured until Leagros pulled me away out of boredom. I haunted the poet's corner. Aspiring actors strove to catch a playwright's attention by mimicking scenes from last year's comedies or the old stories, hoping against hope to secure a part in the next play at the next festival. They would place a woven basket down on the ground into which you threw a few small coins to help them eat and survive until they were discovered. Some of them were very talented and for these the people would clap and shout, but for the bad there were whistles and hisses of derision.

Two of my classmates shared my enthusiasm, if not my obsession. We knew the names of every actor and their careers, of every first, second, and third place winner of the Dionysia, the Lenaia, and the lesser competitions as far back as there were awards. We could recite whole scenes together from Sophocles' tragedies. Aristophanes liked to insult famous men in his comedies. Indeed he had been sued because of this, litigation being one of the favorite Athenian pastimes. As we walked about the city we often held contests to see who knew the most insults by Aristophanes and I won as often as not. Aristophanes lived near the Agora and we occasionally saw him there alone or with the actors, scene painters, and mask artists working on his plays. We learned their names and accomplishments, the prizes they had won, their place of birth, whether they were married and had children, were of drunken or sober temperament, had lovers, and the gods to whom they were beholden. Boys are collectors of gossip and facts, the two often in contradiction. If you see a group of boys gathered in any Agora near an accident they are the ones to ask for details. In Athens there seemed a thousand times more gossip to collect than facts.

It was because of my love of the theater that Simonides took notice of me. I had been at Athenades workshop for several months when he came in one day with the actor Lygis to order some costume decorations. This was, I am certain, in the ninth year of the Great War, several months after the battle of Delium, and a month or two before the City Dionysia, so I can date our meeting with some accuracy. My head was bent over my work drawing intricate filigree designs for a pair of earrings. It needed close attention and a steady hand because I had to keep the drawing to scale. It was a windy day. When they lifted the covering to enter a gust whirled around my feet raising dust and threatening to ruin my drawing. I looked up with annoyance, recognizing them both.

They were there to discuss the objects they needed for the forthcoming Greater Dionysia, I heard them say, and "had the latest gossip about Socrates," Lygis announced.

Athenades said, "Why I was wondering when I would see the two of you. They told me that you both were back in Athens but when you did not come in I thought I had aggrieved you in some way."

Lygis said, "Aggrieved? Not at all! We were later getting back from our tour than we thought. After the lesser festival in Myrrhinus we went to Acharnai with some comedies. I took sick there and had to rest before traveling again. Lost my voice, of all the curses of some offended god the worst. They are a barbaric audience out there, you know. We had to shout to be heard over their insolent hubbub. Praise to be back in civilization."

"If I had known you were ill I would have sent my own doctors to treat you."

"As you can hear I am fine now."

Athenades might well have been glad to see them. Simonides spent lavishly on his festival productions, so lavishly that it meant the difference between an exceptionally good year for Athenades, and a mediocre one.

He said, "And you Simonides? You are looking well. I hear that you might be sponsoring the new Aristophanes?"

"You are well informed as always, Athenades. I shall indeed. We have high hopes too."

Athenades said, "Aristophanes won't tell anyone the

103

title. Not even Aspasia. Surely you can tell an old friend. Especially one giving as generously to the rituals for the festival as I."

At the name of Aristophanes, one of my heroes, I rested my hand a moment while I listened, but pretended to survey my work lest I be reprimanded in front of strangers. The title of his new play interested me; I would then know something my friends did not and could rush to them excitedly with the news.

Simonides said, "Lygis and I had quite an argument with Aristophanes over the title, did we not Lygis?"

"We did indeed. He had come up with a terrible title and we had all we could do to talk him out of it. "

Athenades said, "What was it then?"

Simonides replied, "He wanted to call it *Cloud Cuckoo Land*. Can you imagine anything so absurd? It would have been to mock his own handiwork and we simply would not have it."

"I can see what you mean. It is quite awful and would be a disaster. Did you convince him to change it?"

"Yes, praised Apollo. But you do give your solemn word not to tell anyone the new title?"

I trembled with anticipation, all the more keeping my gaze averted for fear they would pledge me to the self same secrecy.

Athenades said, "You have my word."

"Your word is enough. It is called simply *Clouds*. Short and sweet."

"*Clouds*? It does sound better, of course depending on what it means."

Simonides said, "I get the hint. You are very greedy,

wanting not just the title that almost no one else knows, but the content as well! Now you wouldn't want all the suspense taken out of your waiting would you?"

"No. Of course not."

At that moment I could not resist and finally, for the first time, dared glance up, and found Simonides staring directly at me, his stare drawing my gaze. He looked startled, like someone who sees a chimera. I could not help smiling, but shyly looked down. Had he recognized me from the Agora, I wondered? Some friends of mine and I had stopped to hear him read at the poet's corner a few days before. I had called his verse "pleasant but not Pindar", which was very unkind. I was sure then that he had not overheard me, but was not so sure now. I glanced up quickly again and he was still staring at me. I was sure this time that his expression was one of disapproval, but of course it was not. In those days, I thought that everyone had some critical assessment or other of me, that I was ugly, or had a stupid grin, that my ears protruded, or my neck was too long, that I looked dull or stupid or that my vices and not virtues were glaringly obvious. I dared a third glance but he was politely looking away. I need not have worried. Only Socrates had the ability to read my face, as I feared others did. And with Socrates it did not matter because he wished the best for me, or rather it mattered for that reason.

Simonides had turned back to his conversation with Athenades and so I had a chance to study him as he had studied me. He was very handsome I decided, his clothing tastefully expensive but not ostentatious. His beard was carefully trimmed; he must recently have been to the same barber I frequented, known for his meticulous trims. His eyes were hazel, which I had not often seen, and I liked their absent-minded expression as if poetry was ever distracting him. I noticed his trait of raising an eyebrow in scrutinizing me, which I thought a bit affected. His hands were long and refined, but I was critical of the number of rings he wore. I was not sure he looked like a poet; at least he did not look like my image of a poet, someone unkempt and ragged. His father had conceived him in old age and had died some thirty years before. I calculated that he must be in his early thirties, therefore, but there was no trace of grey in his beard, or his moustache, which turns first. I disapproved of his mouth. It was too sensual. Everyone knew that the best poets lived otherworldly lives, dedicated to Apollo and godly things. At least he was slender and fit, not pudgy like some other poets making the rounds in the marketplace. I found it hard not to laugh at him, however. Simonides, of course, means snub-nosed, and his nose was just that. His enemies cruelly used his name to impugn his intelligence, but he was no fool, if he was a little mad. In other words, upon first glimpse, my opinion of him was mixed.

I quickly found out these things about him. Simonides, son of Bacchylides, was from a line of Attic poets. You could say that like Athenades he belonged to the Athenian cultural aristocracy. His father, the poet Bacchylides of Kos, was the nephew of the esteemed poet Simonides of Kos, the teacher of Pindar. Perhaps this is why Pindar called Kos the Supplier of Poets? Simonides the Elder had amassed a fortune from poetry by praising the heroics of soldiers, mostly generals who could pay the high price for

106

his encomium. His odes to Olympian champions were prized. These champions were sometimes princes, or from the wealthy class, and it is easy to see how, with war and the games recurring events in Attic life, Simonides the Elder was quickly able to become rich. There is no greater vanity than among those victorious at war or games. Before he died he began to transfer his clients to his nephew Bacchylides. And by the time Bacchylides died his son, Simonides the Younger, had inherited one of the largest poetry clientele in Hellas.

Simonides the Younger, "my Simonides" I might call him as he was my first real suitor, is now most famous for his erotic verse. Some he penned on commission for Aspasia and her lover Polydamus, and some privately for me, or I should say for my eyes, for he seemed to see in them all the depths of his misery and desire. He also tried his hand at comedies in the manner of Ameipsias, and had them staged out in the provinces. They were never very good or popular and none won a competition, as did Ameipsias' *Connus*, in the same festival where *Clouds* was staged, in fact. "Better to fail away from Athens," I heard Simonides once say. "Failure in Athens is worse than ostracism." He gave up his theatrical ambitions after two or three failures. He told me that the life of the theater was too demanding and took too much away from the commissions that paid for his extravagant lifestyle. He was content being a producer and not dramatist. He was a bit vain and did not want to own up to a lack of talent, not understanding that humility is to know yourself as you are.

He liked to claim that his family was descended from the original Dorians who settled Kos, but that seemed to me more wishful thinking than fact. He had two virtues that impressed everyone, and that I can attest to also, and these were his honesty and generosity. Honesty is one of the strangest of all virtues, because if it is not tempered with common sense and discretion it can be vicious and hurtful and no virtue at all. I was never sure that honesty could ever be called a virtue in the first place. Simonides had honesty in abundance, although I often wished he would keep his honest remarks to himself. It might have been due to his upbringing on Kos. The story was told to children there that Cadmus was entrusted by Gelo of Syracuse, who ruled Kos at the time, to take a huge sum of money to Delphi during the war against the Persians. If the Persians were victorious the money would have to be paid Darius in tribute, but if they were defeated Cadmus was to bring it all back to Gelo. The Persians were defeated and Cadmus returned with all the money, not pretending any had been lost, or keeping one coin for his trouble. This was all the more remarkable and worthy of legend because Cadmus was not particularly trustworthy.

Simonides was also very free with his wealth, I would say squandering it on too many pleasures as happens sometimes when a fortune passes to you through generations and is not earned. But he gave generously to actors and the theater. Were it not for him many a production by Sophocles or Aristophanes would never have been staged. To the festivals, rituals, and sacrifices to the gods he also gave lavishly. No festival season was successful without his largesse. As a boy I had a long list of pruderies, and his generosity to me became a source of conflict between us.

I now took up my work again for fear of reprimand, but did not stop listening avidly. Athenades was saying, "Yes, the more I think of it the more I like this new title. *Clouds*. Have you started rehearsals already?"

Simonides said, "Not quite. We're taking over the Odeion for a day before the festival you know. You might come by."

Renting the Odeion would have been possible only for the wealthiest with the right connections. Its mention also greatly interested me, as I had not been there yet. I was like a dry sponge, soaking up essence of theater.

Athenades said, "I will if I am not too swamped with work."

"Not so swamped for a little more work? We thought of a handful of things we will need for the opening besides the order we sent in with slaves a few weeks ago. Unless it is too late to fill it?"

"Of course not, of course not. For you we can work double shifts and put lesser things aside. You know I always give you and Aspasia preference. But your tour must have been a success, if you have such money to spend!"

Simonides said, "It was a success, but not the plays so much as the odes."

Lygis did not seem to like this comment and said, "We used old décor for the tour and no one likes to come long distances just to see old things."

Simonides quickly replied, "Yes. The next time we will announce new sets and the like and of course the old things will never do for Athens. They could use refreshing for sure. In fact, I've heard from Aspasia that you have a new designer?"

My hand froze but I did not dare to look up. Athenades lowered his voice but I heard my name mentioned and blushed. They knew better than to address me. You did not interrupt work in Athenades' workshop.

Lygis said, "We wandered all the way up to the furthest corner of Scythia you know. Those Scythians. They are a most receptive audience. They cry like babies or laugh until they collapse. Just like children. Some say they lack sophistication but I like their emotional exuberance. Better play to them than to the intellectuals of Corinth."

Athenades had a thin skin when it came to Athens, and asked, "Are you not happy to be back then?"

Lygis said, "Of course we are happy to be back. As they say, east west Athens best."

Simonides added, "There is nothing like the intensity or intrigues of Athens, thicker than the thickest sea fog and just as blinding, but exhilarating beyond belief. I am most certainly glad to be back. There are so many possibilities here."

I glanced up again and again found him staring at me.

Athenades said, "Can't you tell me anything about this new Aristophanes? I feel rebuffed, as if you did not trust me. And to tell you the truth I have already heard some things from Chaerephon, that our friend Socrates is one of the characters for example. Poor fellow. No doubt he will be mocked as viciously as the poet does everyone."

I much admired Aristophanes, having been taken by my father to see the *Acharnians* in a rural production of some competence. The play was critical of the state's confiscation of citizen's land for the uses of war, sentiments close to my father's own. It was said to be the first comedy against war, although Aristophanes later wrote two others that also were, *Lysistrata* and *Peace*.

Lygis said, "There is no use trying to hide anything from you, Athenades. Indeed Socrates is a character, and I myself am playing him. We've only had one reading and had hoped to keep it a closely guarded secret for a while longer. That Chaerephon!"

Athenades said, "But he had nothing but praise, and you know how loyal he is to Socrates. He thinks it will be the best of the three competing comedies, especially with you Lygis in the lead."

Lygis said, "In the theater, Athenades, flattery gets you everywhere."

I thought that Athenades much have heard about the play during Chaerephon's visit to the shop a few days before, although I had not overheard that conversation.

Simonides said, "Did he really say he thought it would be the best? Well that is good news isn't it Lygis? We have high hopes, high hopes."

Athenades said, "I have heard something else about it." He cast a mistrustful glance out towards the street as if spies were lurking by the door. "You know how much I admired the *Acharnians* but Aristophanes' work has been uneven since then, not at all filled with the same moral sentiments. But I hear that he gets off a few good lines about peace in the new play?"

Lygis said, "Ah yes, *The Acharnians*. Not to my taste really. You know what I think about all this ranting about peace over war. It is positively subversive, and worse, badly argued. In fact, I would have to say I found *The*

Acharnians trite, as did others in the audience because I saw many walk out."

Athenades said, "No actor I have ever known has any sense of politics."

Simonides added his say. "I think you both misunderstand Aristophanes. He is no advocate of anything and wishes to offend everyone. That is how he sees comedy. His play is worthless if someone is not outraged."

Lygis said, "I too am misunderstood. Arguing against war and the way it deprives the landowners of their land does not play well in the countryside outside of Hellas where three quarters of the population does not have the wherewithal to own their own land."

Simonides said, "For my part I liked *The Babylonians* a bit more than *The Acharnians*. No one in the city was daring to criticize our politicians for fear of being called a traitor, and along comes Aristophanes and does just that. I call that heroic courage."

Lygis replied, "Or stupidity."

"Stupidity? I think not. He shot to instant fame, after all. And think of the work he gives us!"

"I have nothing against making our politicians look like fools, but not in front of foreigners, which is what Aristophanes did. After all it's a crime just short of treason to denigrate our politicians in front of foreign audiences and he paid dearly for it, too, I warrant."

"How so?"

"Didn't Cleon haul him up on charges for being so roundly mocked in that play? And didn't they find Aristophanes guilty and fine him a pretty penny?"

Simonides said, "Yes, they certainly did and I should be the one to know because I paid his fine. But I also was repaid four-fold. It made his work all the more popular and the audiences larger. Which is probably what he was after in the first place. And anyway he had his revenge a year or so later don't forget. In the *Knights*."

The *Knights* had only just played the year before, and had won first prize. I had not seen it but knew it portrayed Cleon as the King of the Oligarchs, a dishonest and greedy man using his wealth for personal gain instead of the general good. Indeed, it called him worse that that too. Aristophanes was, if anything, a democrat, if one ready to lampoon the people when he saw the need. Still, his sentiments were clear. He abhorred the selfish use of wealth and position and wanted the best for Athenians, peace first.

Simonides added, "I would only say this among friends, but I hope Aristophanes' plays teach these politicians of ours to respect the comic arts as an alternate form of power to their mad lusts. After all when *The Knights* won first prize last year it was as much because it was so popularly received for lampooning Cleon as for its artistic merits, which, don't get me wrong, were considerable. The citizens have spoken, have they not?"

Athenades said, "Yes, I would say so too. That racket about *Knights* sent Cleon scurrying with his tail between his legs. But, Aristophanes might be, well, a little too mischievous for his own benefit. He knows his verse has the potential to undermine reputations if taken seriously. So, Cleon might have been on to something in trying to stop him, being no dullard when it comes to understanding power."

Simonides said, "Are you defending Cleon? It is hard to call a play like *The Babylonians*, or *Knights* for that matter, treason, don't you think just because a few in the audience have a little laugh? As I see it, it is litigation, litigation, and more litigation, that Athenian obsession. That is the problem. All these wars have made us lose our sense of judgment. Poor Aristophanes. All he wanted was a little freedom to spin a joke. Praise be Dionysus, we still have some freedom of expression in the arts, litigation or no litigation."

Athenades said, "Of course we do, of course we do. We are just talking among friends my dear Simonides." But he looked around nervously again, which set me wondering what the hidden life of Athens really was if political discussions made Athenades uncomfortable. His convictions were traditionalist, at least those I had heard him mutter. War was popular among the people, especially in the interminable conflict with Sparta. Athenians were still boasting of Xerxes defeat at Salamis.

Athenades continued, "But enough of this. Let's talk of other things. This *Clouds* that you are producing? It will be entered in the competition against Ameipsias' *Connus*, which is the favorite this year, because of Ameipsias' connections and lobbying. But *Clouds*? That doesn't give much away. Is it about the gods on Olympus then? When you mentioned that the rejected title was *Cloud Cuckoo-Land* it made me a little uneasy. The thought of Aristophanes taking on the gods, well, that would not sit well with some. Can you tell me in just one word what it is about? If you do I promise I shall stop asking you."

Again my hand paused over my work. I could not bear the thought of missing this.

Simonides said, "One word? What do you think Lygis?"

"Well…"

Simonides said, "I suppose if it is to be one word, then it has to be Socrates, doesn't it Lygis?"

Lygis said, "Well, perhaps, if not only." He suddenly declaimed, "Socrates! Hero of Potidaea! Savior of Alcibiades' honor! Pillar of Delium! Praised be his steadfastness!"

And Athenades added, not without irony, "Yes, he is at the height of his popularity isn't he?"

Socrates, I thought, so it is about Socrates. I could not wait to tell my friends.g about you."

This raised my suspicion that he had overheard my remark in the Agora that his poetry was not Pindar. I said, "Asking about me?"

"Who you are. Where you are from. Whether you are freeborn. Whether you show talent as a goldsmith, are even tempered or insolent."

Now I was convinced that he had overheard me and was abashed. I said, "Perhaps I have offended him. If I have I will immediately make amends."

"No, no. You have not offended him. He was impressed by you."

"Impressed?"

"He said that you had dignity and that your gaze reflected the light of virtue."

"Perhaps he caught me staring. I did not mean to, but Leagros told me he was a famous poet when we stopped to

115

hear him read one day."

Athenades said, "Not just staring but eavesdropping I might add. You did not want to miss a word."

I thought for sure that this was the reason for the talk and felt mortified that I had been caught shirking. "I am sorry. I will make up for it. I can stay and work an extra hour if you want."

"Don't be silly. I saw that you had finished your design. We can go over it later. I am only telling you what impression you made. In fact, it is probably my fault. I went on a bit about you over dinner a few nights ago; too much wine I suppose. I told Simonides and Lygis that you were not only one of my most talented designers, but that you played the lyre and sang beautifully. So now they've taken it into their heads that they might sway you to enter one of the competitions, and be coached by them."

I was not at all pleased about this. In fact, the idea horrified me. "But Master. I don't sing at all well. I know you hear me singing around the house to please Assur and the other metics, but I would never have the slightest chance of winning any of the competitions. Perhaps I might in Macedon, but not here in Athens! I could not. And think of what it will do to my lessons. I won't have time for anything."

Athenades looked surprised. "I thought you would be pleased. Simonides was talking about finding a role for you in the new Aristophanes. They need boys for the chorus. Of course, I said it was out of the question. Unless you have your heart set on being in the theater."

It was a leading question, I knew, and I said, "I do like the theater. I like it more than anything. But I never had

116

any ambitions about being a performer. Father called me the ideal spectator, because I loved it without wanting to join it."

Athenades breathed a sigh of relief. "I'm glad you said that. In fact, that is what I was hoping you would say if you are to be out and about with Simonides. It is already enough that you and some of the other boys spend all your pocket money on sweets and those appalling sausage rolls they sell in the Agora. I am sure your father would not approve of your being distracted by the theater too much. He told me that you had your enthusiasms and that you needed a little reining in."

I did not much like hearing that, but I knew enough not to try to contradict Athenades and I said instead, "Out and about with Simonides?"

"Simonides, as you can well imagine, is a very famous and busy man but he has made a very generous offer. Seeing how avidly you were listening to his theater shoptalk, he has asked permission to take you shopping and possibly to the Odeion in a few weeks time for the dress rehearsal of Clouds. As it is Aristophanes, and his sentiments are somewhat my own, well, I can't see what harm it would do or that your father would object; if you want to go, of course; and if I give my permission; and if Leagros can be persuaded to chaperone you. A lot of ifs in other words."

I was quite speechless with excitement, but calmly asked, "Does it mean I have your permission, Master Athenades?"

"Well. I'll talk to my father-in-law this evening. His legs are bothering him again, the poor man, so you might

117

have to watch over him more than he over you."

I said, "I can do that."

He smiled. "Yes, my boy. I am sure you can. But I promised your father I would protect you and, to tell you the truth, some of Simonides circle . . . Well, I won't gossip. Your father brought you up well, and you have your head on your shoulders. I will give you my final decision after I speak with Leagros, the poor old sod. Now let me see what you've come up with for Lady Aspasia."

In all the months I had been in his home Athenades had paid me few if any compliments. This was the closest he came to expressing affection. He did it so naturally that I do not think he noticed. My excitement should have been unbounded, but I dared not believe that Simonides' offer would come true. I also felt abysmally ignorant about the Athenian theater world, and feared that I would make a fool of myself. Had Simonides also produced The Acharnians? Was Lygis the chief of the four actors playing in Clouds? Was he playing other roles? How old was Aristophanes? Would Aristophanes really mock Socrates? Surely not! Weren't the two friends? Cleon, perhaps, but not Socrates.

If I had known how badly Simonides was already smitten, and how much it was in Leagros' self interest to chaperone me, I would not have tormented myself with any doubts.

5. 423 B.C. Simonides comes courting.

The Dionysia was still some weeks away. The seas were beginning to calm, making travel possible again. It would not be long now until the festivals.

118

Simonides waited a discrete time before coming into the shop again, on the pretext of checking on the progress of their order, but he did not approach me at my work desk, which would have but you and, to tell you the truth, some of Simonides circle . . . Well, I won't gossip. Your father brought you up well, and you have your head on your shoulders. I will give you my final decision after I speak with Leagros, the poor old sod. Now let me seehe first of a number of excursions with Simonides, or rather with Leagros, Simonides, and several of his slaves to carry our refreshments and Simonides' purchases in the Agora. He was a great collector: of spears and spear heads, antique shields, old coins and pots, statues, and most of all antique theater masks. Taking me to the dealers who supplied his collections was a clever way of getting to know my tastes, and me; by questioning me on my reactions to what we were seeing, asking *my advice o*n some old wooden thing he wanted to buy, whether I *though*t it well executed or considered it genuine. Leagros would allow me to spend time alone with Simonides, while he went off to drink. I would drag Simonides to the news-crier's corner, hungry for the smallest tidbit from the north. Most of the time they held forth on one or another of the latest scandals: an unfaithful wife caught by a husband, or a man with less skill than Dareios or Alcibiades caught in some wife's bed not his. Crimes of passion always drew the largest crowds. Simonides attitude to these interested me. He claimed that the practice of our vices taught us more about our nature than did the practice of our virtues, and that Socrates was wrong about this. It was a far cry also from Athenades' morality.

I loved these excursions with Simonides through the streets and markets of Athens. Caught in a sudden downpour, the water streaming from the various hillsides turning the streets into mud rivers, we would dash into the shelter of the nearest open doorwhe first of a number of excursions with Simonides, or rather with Leagros, Simonides, and several of his slaves to carry our refreshments and Simonides' purchases in the Agora. He was a great collector: of spears and spear heads, antique shields, old coins, vegetables, clothes, and goods necessary for daily life. He would treat me to the fresh warm sweet rolls we rarely had for breakfast at Athenades'; two would never suffice.

One day he was carrying a large bundle and when we stopped to rest he unwrapped it to show me. We were sitting in the Painted Stoa, under the mural of the Battle of Marathon by Micon, our favorite resting spot to take shade. It commanded the best view of the crowds milling along the Panathenaic Way, yet the bench where we sat along the colonnade afforded us privacy. His latest purchase was a very old mask from a dealer in antiquities we had visited the week before. I had thought the man much too shrewd to be honest, and had said so, but his masks were so rare as to be beyond resistance for Simonides. Most theater masks are of plain leather, and not particularly fine leather either. They are humdrum and uninteresting, but the one he showed me that day was superb. It was a hundred years old or more, he said, and purchased I knew for a phenomenal sum because it had been quoted in my presence to tempt Simonides to show off in front of "his boy". It must have been oiled a thousand times because it had a deep reddish brown hew. The oil had kept it from cracking, and had given it depth and charaay to await its passing, or take a meal; I ate twice my weight, he said. In early morning he would sometimes fetch me before the start of my duties. We would become caught up in the chaos of carts and hawkers setting up their portable stalls for the fruits It is remarkable isn't it? Do you still like it?"

He handed it to me and I was thrilled to hold something so fine. I said, "It's really better than I remembered it."

"Does it remind you of anyone?" I shook my head and he said, "It is a hundred and fifty years old at least, yet it's the image of Socrates, don't you think? Now you see why I wanted it so much. It will be a huge sensation at the opening of Clouds. We'll spread rumors about the mask before the performance. You know, people will come just to see such things."

I said, "I would myself. It does look like Socrates. At least I think it does. I have only seen him from afar in the Agora, but never close up. I don't think he's ever come in to the shop to order or buy anything, nor sent in a slave for that matter, at least not since I've been there."

Simonides said, "Socrates buying jewelry! Now that would be news for the hawkers. I can't imagine the last time he might have bought a trinket, gold or silver, or iron."

"Is he stingy then?"

"Oh no, far from it; indifferent perhaps. Buying such things is just not, well, him." He suddenly took the mask from me and put it over his face. Lowering his voice he said, mocking Socrates, "Virtue is the gold of the soul. Who stores up virtue has treasure indeed." I thought it irreverent but funny.

I said, "It looks a little like Zeus", recalling the face of the enormous statue of Zeus in His temple on the Acropolis.

Simonides now was the one to laugh. "Keep your voice down when you say that. If Zeus hears you say th It is remarkable isn't it? Do you still like it?"

He handed it to me and I was thrilled to hold something so fine. I said, "It is really better than I remembered it."

"Does it remind you of anyone?"

I shook my head and he said, "It is a hundred and fifty itive you are. It is why . . . " He put the mask suddenly back over his face and said, "You are dearer to me than Alcibiades."

It was the first time he had voiced his affection. Before I could react or respond he handed me the mask again and I turned it around and around in my hands pretending to study it more closely, but really to hide my conflicting feelings. In Macedon, my young Eleusinian tutor had courted me with some success. I wanted Simonides as a friend, but was not sure yet I wanted more. I hardly knew him, I told myself; but a niggling doubt was holding me aloof.

The mask did intrigue me. The eye sockets were bulbous and greatly exaggerated, the nose twisted. I knew that Socrates had protruding eyes, as everyone referred to them, but Simonides m it; indifferent perhaps. Buying such things is just not, well, him." He suddenly took the mask from me and put it over his face. Lowering his voice he said, mocking Socrates, "Virtue is the gold of the soul. Who stores up virtue has treasure indeed." I t was meant to suggest when it was made? A philosopher?"

Once again I had not intended a joke, but this he found all the funnier, perhaps because it relieved the erotic tension that had built between us.

"A philosopher! I must tell Lygis that one. Of coursat he looks like Socrates, I am not so sure He would like the comparison; nor Socrates for that matter."

"I did not mean to be disrespectful," I said for fear of being misunderstood, "I only meant it was imposing."

"Yes, yes, my dear boy. I forget how sense suffers in derision? In Macedon we revere them. At least my father does and that is what he taught me."

"Oh, but then you Macedonians have not had to put up much with our ridiculous Sophists."

"Why do you say that?"

"We hold the gods in high esteem. At least the politicians like to tell us that we revere the gods although the truth is less than that. And the gods were prey to passions that swept away all judgment and drove them to acts they might never have performed when in a sober mind. So I for one am skeptical of being too rational for fear it makes the gods remote. After all," he added looking at me, "Zeus did the maddest things when he fell in love. It rather endears him to us."

"Right now I'm a devotee of Apollo," I said.

"Well, he also lost his head over love, didn't he?"

"Yes. It is true he did."

He looked at me rather sadly. "Who would not? There is wisdom in the gods' mad passions and abductions.

123

Power that is never powerless is not true power and power that knows its own powerlessness is wise. To love once is to know that."

I did not like to talk of love and said, "Do you think Socrates is too rational?"

"Socrates? Good heavens no. He reads dreams, knows about love potions from Aspasia, and has too much experience of falling in love to be the dupe of rationality. And then there's that inner voice of his! God alone knows what that is! But take that Thales of Miletus, or Anaxagoras, for that matter. They were so solemn about simple things like water and air, and not serious enough about other matters such as having enough money in your purse."

I laughed, "I never have enough …" But I caught myself up, not wanting to seem to be speaking against Athenades, or to be suggesting that Simonides should give me money, which he would have in a wink.

Simonides patted my hand, "I know, my dear boy. I know."

I was holding the mask and now handed it back.

I said, "Athenades told me some things about Socrates. He seems very odd but I hope that I can meet him. Is it true he goes around barefoot everywhere, and wears only a thin tunic in cold weather?"

"Yes. He leads the simplest of lives. But you shall meet him soon enough. He will be at the opening of *Clouds*."

"But I shall never meet him there, not standing at the back with my friends."

"But you shall sit with me and my friends! And accompany me to the rehearsal at the Odeion the day

124

before. I was going to surprise you. I already asked Athenades and he said you could."

Poor Simonides. How bumbling he was at this seduction game."

I did not like to talk of love and said, "Do you think Socrates is too rational?"

"Socrates? Good heavens no. He reads dreams, knows about love potions from Aspasia, and has too much experience of falling in love to be the dupe o be your guest." I added awestruck, "But the Odeion!"

"Guest of honor, guest of honor. I have the rows just behind the High Priest, you know, right in the center. But Socrates will probably sit to the side with the other dignitaries and some of his students. In fact, you might get to meet him before that."

"How so?"

"The rehearsal at the Odeion in a few days? You never know. Socrates might just poke his head in to see how great the disaster is. I'm sure Chaerephon has wrested the whole text out of Lygis and promptly recited it to him."

"Then he must know he is in it."

"My dear, of course he knows. All of Athens knows, and that is an understatement. How else would we stand a chance of winning first prize? The buzz, dear Amyntas, the buzz."

6. 423 B.C. The Odeion.

The Odeion was a square, enclosed building used for kithara and flute competitions, for reading plays to the judges before they were selected for competition, and for rehearsals. It adjoined the right side of the older Theater of

Dionysus, and was still relatively new at the time of my youth, having been built by Pericles in the middle of his reign. Its conical, wooden roof sloped down from a central apex, and was considered at the time of its construction a radical, influential design, of Persian origin. The timbers were brought by Pericles from Salamis to commemorate the defeat of the Persians at one of Athens' greatest battles and victories, and so it might be said that the Odeion displayed Persian influence in order to flaunt Athenian might. If the building whispered war, words of peace often rang within its walls. It was also one of the most secure buildings in the city, having been built into the southwest slope of the Acropolis, perfect for secrecy. Guards could be posted at each door to prevent spying upon the rehearsals.

Simonides had booked it for the day for five hundred drachmas, five minas, an enormous price, nearly a year's wage for a skilled worker; my first inkling of his wealth. *Clouds* would command a singular advantage for having use of the Odeion prior to the first public staging next door. He arrived half an hour early to fetch me the day of the rehearsal, as excited as I.

No sooner were we out of sight of the workshop than he said something that shocked me. "Here, guard this, and give it to me when I ask." He handed me a large purse, heavy with coin.

"What is it?"

"Gold coins and gemstones for the judges, of course. Some of them will be there today. In fact, most of them I expect. I put the word out that I would come prepared."

I said, "But Simonides! You do not mean to bribe them

do you!"

"Oh you are an innocent. Let us say that our eponymous archon, Aminias, is particularly fond of rubies for his mistress." He rattled the bag and handed it to me.

To ensure fairness, the plays to compete were chosen by lot on the day of the performance, but this had become something of a joke. The choice was often made, or bought, long before. Nor was it difficult to falsify the drawing of lots. The names of all the plays were written on shards and placed in a jar, as with the oracles, one way among many that the Athenian theater resembled ritual. The judge drew three shards from the jar, the finalists, but the drawing could be rigged in different ways: by nicking or scoring the edge of the shard, or by drawing lines under the inscribed title, easily deciphered with the fingertips. Persuasion of the judges, Simonides explained, was no longer a question of whether *Clouds* would be included but whether it would win. This was "better negotiated in the secluded confines of the Odeion", he said, than in the open tiers of the Theater under the full glare of the bright Attic sun and citizenry.

As we trekked across the city, Simonides also explained the rather complicated machinery that was being used in Clouds, and that needed to be tested; cranes, hoists, lifts, and a large turnstile that could be put to good effect in the larger Theater to rotate scenes. Aristophanes needed to use as many elaborate contraptions, extravagant costumes, and superb masks as possible were he to stand a chance of winning, cost be damned.

I asked, "Is Clouds the favorite this year?"

Especially because Socrates, so recently the hero of

127

Delium, was a character I thought, but did not say.

Simonides said, "I fear not. The rumors have it that the dreadful *Connus* by Ameipsias is the favorite. It has big money behind it; probably Cleon's, more revenge for Aristophanes' insults. Cleon would use every opportunity. And Socrates figures in *Connus* too. But perhaps we can change the results yet."

When we entered the Odeion my first impression was of a pious hush. The interior was cool and dim. The stage area was at the far end; a few people milled about. I felt shy and intimidated. A cold chill went through me, and I trembled so much that Simonides looked startled and put his arm around my shoulder protectively, thinking that I was overcome with excitement. "Have you sensed a god?" he asked. When a god flits unseen across our path we shudder. At the time of Socrates' arrest the Odeion was being used to detain people, a far cry from the use for which Simonides had hired it. Socrates was there for a day or two before being sent to jail, and it was while he was there that his friends first began to plot to rescue him and whisk him away to safety.

The group of four by the stage were speaking and laughing. Simonides whispered, "There, that is Aristophanes over there, the compact one of medium height."

I already recognized him.

Aristophanes son of Philippos, was born and lived in the deme of Kydathenaion, a humble district just off the Agora, "within smelling distance of the sausage-makers," he said; they often figure in his plays. He made a sausage-seller the hero of one of his plays not only because their redolent products were familiar to everyone but also because the Athenian district in which he was born and raised was downwind of the sausage-seller's. The smells of childhood linger long. Kydathenaion abutted the Agora, on the threshold of the teeming life of the city. The curses and slang of the district also creep into his plays. He looked older, as we drew near, than I had thought but should have guessed. His sophisticated plays balanced complex themes in a sly yet wise way. He was rather coy about his age, an affectation that has always made me impatient. His first play, Daitales, was produced under a pseudonym four years before; and won second place. When Simonides asked him why he had not put his name on it he said that he had been too young to produce it himself, according to the rules of majority. That would have made him seventeen or eighteen at the writing of Daitales, or perhaps twenty if he had waited until immediately after his military service, and at most twenty-five now. But I think he was nearer to thirty at the time of Clouds, and that he had not used his name for Daitales because he had been insecure about his talent and its reception. He had a full head of black hair with no grey; his full beard tangled into wild curls like his humor.

He suddenly cried out, broke off talking to the group, and rushed across the stage shouting angrily at one of the carpenters who had let something fall with a crash. Simonides groaned. "Oh my god, there he goes again. He'll ruin everything." The carpenter seemed indifferent. He simply turned and walked away. Skilled slaves in Athens were a proud lot. There was a great demand for their labors and they were very highly paid. You did not alienate them. They were clannish and could put out the word that someone was difficult. It did not stop Aristophanes. He shouted all the more at the man's retreating back. It only served to inspire the other workers to walk off. Witnessing fits of rage intimidated me, perhaps because I was still uncertain of myself. My father had also raised me to govern such things, a bit of Temenidai snobbery perhaps.

Simonides said, "Amyntas, I am sorry. I had better try to calm him down or nothing will get done on time, not to mention the stacks of my minas that will scatter like bees from a burning hive."

He took my arm to drag me along, but I held back. He and Aristophanes were arguing all the time about who should play the producer's role, and accusing each other of wanting to control every aspect of the performance. I did not want to get drawn into the fray, and sought a bench near the front. Some of the workmen were drifting back, carrying fragments of scenery and paintings of backdrops; the chorus was gathering at the side waiting for their time to be called, in comedies, generally twenty-four men and youths dressed as women and girls. Some were my own age. They cast jealous glances my way when I entered with Simonides, and one of them now loudly said, "Oh so that is Simonides' latest tart." I was used to jealous remarks, and pretended not to hear.

There was not much lighting in the hall proper, but the proscenium was well lit by hanging oil lamps. The set had two doors in it and a curtain that was drawn. Work was being done on the backdrops that would then be taken to the Theater for the performance. There was some

130

confusion about this. Most of the backdrops stood haphazard against walls, or lay flat on the floor. Painters were off to the side finishing what seemed to be a bedroom, while others worked on another panel I took to be the outside of a school; they were drawing various scientific instruments on the sketched columns and part of a saying that began "Wisdom is the---of fools", the word being missing presumably because Aristophanes had not yet decided on it.

Several men were struggling with a tall wooden crane, three times my height. A leg had come loose threatening to topple the whole thing over. It tottered and I saw Aristophanes clasp the sides of his head, and Simonides put a hand on his arm to restrain him. If he lost the device, with such a short time remaining to the competition, it would have been a disaster. While three men held it steady a fourth banged the leg into position, the ropes and pulleys attached. In the play, of course, all this machinery would be hidden behind painted sets and only the effect would be seen, gods descending from the heavens; or flying, or changing into birds as Zeus transformed himself into a giant eagle in order to abduct fair Ganymede for his bed on Olympus. We mere mortals had to make do with machinery that did not always work. But the gods have no need of artifice to work wonders, a definition of the divine.

Simonides glanced my way and smiled. Perhaps he was not taking Aristophanes too seriously. Aristophanes was trying to justify his anger. "But, Simonides, you've only just arrived and have no idea how much has been going wrong. I tell you it is a bad omen, a bad omen, and I don't

131

like it. No one has learned their lines, those oafs may yet ruin my hoist and my play. And on top of it all, Lygis is so hoarse today he sounds like a lovesick frog, and Krioisos has not even shown up yet! Ruined! I tell you the gods are trying to ruin me."

Krioisos would play the lead of Strepsiades, as Lygis would play Socrates. I thought he must be one of the fleeting shadows I saw seeking refuge out back, not daring to venture out until the storm should calm.

"I'm sure it's not as bad as all that."

"Not bad as all that! It's worse than you think. Much worse. I'll be the laughing stock of Athens, I tell you."

"Oh please. Let's have a break. Come over and meet my friend Amyntas. And I also want to tell you about the rare mask I bought yesterday and which we can use tomorrow. It's a real knockout. We've also brought a good wine with us, guaranteed to take the edge off of your cares."

A wry smile attempted to break through Aristophanes' scowl. The storm was lifting. I stood as he came over to greet me. He said, "So you are the boy genius goldsmith I have been hearing about. I hope that you are not put off by my rant. It blows like the west wind but does no harm, I hope."

"I am honored to meet you, sir. I am an amateur and hardly a genius."

Simonides said, "Amateur! Just listen to him, Aristophanes. Why they are saying everywhere that he is already as good a goldsmith as his master was in his youth if not better, aren't they? Haven't you heard that too?" Aristophanes shrugged, and Simonides said, "And with a fine treble voice too, fine enough to compete in Delphi. He plays the lyre like Apollo himself."

I thought my voice reedy and thin and said, "Please Simonides. I don't sing well at all. Certainly not well enough to compete at Delphi. And my gold designs will never be the equal of Athenades'."

I was sincere in what I said, although too often protesting achievements is an invitation for praise. I learned later to have better graces. Despite my protests and the jealous glances of the chorus boys, who looked as if they might murder me, a lyre was quickly found, none too difficult that, in the Odeion. Simonides, as patron, could have hired me for the performance had Aristophanes agreed, so the chorus had cause to feel threatened. I was coaxed to sing a Macedonian lament, amid the hurly-burly of stage activity. The carpenters could not seem to make the turnstile work properly. It groaned and creaked. Stagehands were bringing a door to the center with a curtain over it. Two men were carrying a large wicker basket, for what purpose I could not tell. Bits and pieces of other scenes were piled here and there, a wall panel painted as a map, and a table on which there was a scattering of scientific instruments. Some precious masks had been left lying on top of a crate as if they were detritus. A slave hurriedly gathered them up before Aristophanes saw them.

Finally my agony, or song, came to an end, and just in time. Voices from backstage were heard practicing. I felt sure I recognized Lygis repeating the same line again and again, first as loud declamation, then as mere statement of fact, then as question, "I walk upon the air and delve the

133

sun's secret mysteries…I walk upon…."Again and again.

He suddenly poked his head out from behind the curtained door, wearing the mask designated for the Socrates character and that Simonides had shown me a few days before, and shouted out my name.

Simonides exclaimed, "There, Aristophanes, there is the mask. Isn't it superb?"

I broke out laughing. It was a good joke Lygis had played to get me to laugh, I thought. I would thank him afterwards. It eased my self-consciousness about the song I had sung and the attentions of Simonides.

Simonides was saying, "Well, what did I tell you? Doesn't he have a fine voice, and wouldn't he be perfect for our main song?"

There was to be only one main song in *Clouds*, if one of Aristophanes' most beautiful. I was horrified and said, "Please, Simonides, you are embarrassing me. My voice will soon break. What if it does at a performance?"

Neither he nor Aristophanes had the chance to answer. There was another loud crash and bang from behind the curtain. I glanced anxiously at Aristophanes thinking he would jump up and rush off in a rage, but he did not. He glanced slyly at me, and smiling said, "Don't worry my friends, I'll keep the wind in the cave this time around, but you'll have to excuse me." He went off calmly to deal with the problem making me wonder what his previous show of wrath had meant.

Looking as surprised as I, Simonides said, "Will wonders never cease. We may have a play yet."

I said, "What is all the machinery for anyway?"

He had refused to tell me too much about the play, so as

not to spoil my surprise, he said. He said, "Fishing for a catch?"

"Why won't you tell me? I know what you say, but surely you can tell me just a little. Besides, I am sure I can guess some already. It's about the heavens, isn't it? And the gods activities?"

"Perhaps."

"I know it is. I saw a caged platform being attached to hoists and that usually means a god is going to descend from the heavens, doesn't it?"

"Well, wait a bit. I brought you today because I thought you'd be amused by the scene they're rehearsing this afternoon, and I don't think it will spoil the play for you."

"But if I am only to see a scene how will I know how it fits in with the rest unless you tell me a little. You need to explain it all beforehand."

"So you can tell your mates tonight? Nice try! Well, all right then, a smidgen. Suffice it to say, some students are outside their school debating certain matters of the universe when the basket descends from the heavens."

He did not have time to tell me more. Signaling the start of the rehearsal of a scene, Aristophanes was ushering the workers and stagehands off to the side, leaving a curtained doorway at the center that also hid the machinery to the rear, although I could hear the creaking of pulleys and straining of supports. The doorway was at the top of two stairs but the curtain extended upwards beyond to hide the ropes from view.

Krioisos/Strepsiades entered, wearing his own comic mask. He ascended the stairs and pounded on the door to ask admittance to the school.

135

"Boys! Let me in. Let me in, my little lamby-poohs!"

A student shouted back, "Go to hell!"

There followed an elaborate joke about fleas jumping onto Socrates' crooked nose from one of his student's eyebrows and a funnier discussion about gnats farting, "smelly bug-trumpets," he called them. A mock-sophist discussion ensued, about how Socrates, lost in contemplation of studying the passage of the moon across the skies, mistook it for a lizard running across the roof that shit right in his face. This too made me laugh so much I lost some of the lines and only came to myself when the students and Strepsiades were studying a map, and fell into discourse about Sparta, which took my interest. As Strepsiades pours over the map he asks one of the students what that blob might represent and the student says that it is Sparta. Strepsiades says, "It can't be. It is much too close to Athens and that would not be that good for us. You better think that one over and get someone to change the map to make them farther apart or there'll be trouble, I can tell you!"

This too made me chuckle, to think that by moving a mark on a map the place would move was also a veiled criticism of the Sophists.

"Don't be silly," a student says. "We can't change a place by changing its mark!"

Strepsiades throws a fit and begins to beat the student with his walking stick, "You can't can you! Well, take that! And that!"

And just then the curtain parted further. There was the whirr of levers and the creak of pulleys. Descending from the heavens as it were, Lygis/Socrates was lowered on the

136

caged platform I had seen earlier. Bars prevented him from falling off. It swayed and listed to one side and he gripped the bars groaning. I feared that the ropes would break and spill him to the floor below.

Lygis was costumed most outrageously, not only in the antique mask but also in a very short chiton that might have proven obscene had he not been wearing tights beneath. It was stuffed with wads of padding to make Socrates seem grotesquely bloated, wherein he was muscular and solid. An enormous leather phallus threatened to topple him as much as the swaying cage. It was the same burnished brown as the brown of the mask, and with a huge bulbous, red crown resembling the great red, bulbous nose.

The pulleys whined and the caged platform tilted even further. In fact I jumped to my feet thinking I should spring forward to steady the contraption, only to be held back by Simonides.

He said, "It is all right. It is all planned."

Strepsiades says, "Socrates! What are you doing up there on a rack?"

Socrates declaims, "I float upon a rack/amid the clouds/to free my mind/from mortal thoughts."

The cage bumped to the ground resoundingly. Some of the ropes from the pulleys came loose and fell around him. Lygis/Socrates tried now to speak some of his lines amidst the turmoil, but not exactly those I had heard him rehearse earlier, his words sounding more like gargle. "I walk among the gods delving the sun's secret mysteries ...I walk amid the clouds to study the sun from above... I walk .. "

Aristophanes stopped him. "My God Lygis. You can't just put in anything you want. Not just my lines, but also all the variations we rehearsed! And that rasping voice of yours! I thought it would be better by today. Are you sure you want to go on?"

I whispered to Simonides, "Is it another joke?"

"Wait and see."

Aristophanes said patiently, "Now where is your copy? How about trying the lines I gave you. Shall we start over? Where on earth is everyone? I want that blasted thing pulled up again."

But Lygis did not respond. Like a monkey he deftly leapt over the bars of the cage onto the stage, cackling like a witch, "Walk on air! Walk on air" much to everyone's amusement. Rushing up to Aristophanes and doing a formal bow with a sweep of his hand he cackled like an old crone, "Gnats who fart! Gnats who fart!" Suddenly he stood straight up and whisked the mask off with great aplomb. Lo and behold it was Socrates himself making fun of Socrates being made fun of. I clapped and shouted. We all had a good laugh. Putting the mask down tenderly he and Aristophanes embraced.

This was my first real glimpse of Socrates at close quarters, and it endeared him to me at once, because he had gone through such trouble to show how graceful he could be when the brunt of such farce. And there was affection and respect for Aristophanes in his gesture too, and acceptance of his role as a public figure who could be mocked. In other words, there again was his ability to do many things with one act, one of Socrates' chief characteristics, the mark of virtue, too.

But I also have a terrible confession to make, something I have never told to anyone, until this moment telling this history. When Socrates tore off the mask, revealing Socrates, I thought to myself, "Oh that is a good joke that Lygis is playing on us. When he takes off the mask of Socrates underneath there is another mask of Socrates." I could not believe that anyone could be so odd and ugly looking. It took me a split second to realize that I was staring indeed at the real Socrates, and praise Apollo, I did not tell anyone I thought it was only another joke or I would have never lived down the embarrassment. I think the moment goes further too. Just as it dawned on me that it was the real Socrates, so too was my affection born.

Other impressions from that moment still survive my memory. Socrates looked younger than I had expected. He was in his mid-forties but had the body type of an Olympic wrestler rather than a philosopher. All philosophers should be ancient, I thought, not with the thick arms and strong shoulders of Hephaistos. They should not be made for the battlefield. My mental image had also been fashioned by statues of Zeus and the old gods, but the playful glint in his eye suggested more Pan son of Zeus rather than the father. The derangement of my stereotypes confused me. My mind was being purged of false images and I looked on him in wonderment. He was barefoot. I wished to discard my sandals. He wore home spun; and I would do the same. I glanced up at him and saw that he was staring at me. I was too shy to return his glance.

Simonides called out to him, bidding him to come over to join us but he did not seem to hear, lost in thought.

Aristophanes was saying, "That was a good joke Socrates! I shall remember it for another play. If I live to write another play after this one."

Was Socrates staring at me, I wondered? The question must also have crossed Simonides' mind, because he muttered, "One of his states I suppose. No doubt communing with that voice of his."

I glanced at Simonides thinking to ask him what he meant, but I saw one of those jealous looks I was already beginning to see cloud his face whenever someone or something came near me he thought threatening to his affections. I held my tongue and glanced back at Socrates and it was at that precise moment I had another secret thought that I have also not told anyone until now, but which has colored my view of Socrates since. He was not at all ugly, I realized. He was truly beautiful.

There is one last thing to say about that day. If Socrates was not shackled, he was encaged.

III. My Life in Athens: *Clouds* & the Banquet.

1. 423 B.C. Spring: The City Dionysia.

It was my first spring in Athens, and my first City
Dionysia festival, held in the massive Theater of
Dionysus, one of the largest in Hellas and one of the
glories of Athens. Pericles had replaced the timbers of the
open structure with stone, encrusted it with beautiful
friezes, statues, comic and tragic masks. It sits on the
southeastern slope of the Acropolis, or "Cecrops' rock" as
Athenians say, Athens being Land of Cecrops, the half
man, half serpent second god of the city, after Athena. It
holds seventeen thousand, or more depending on how
many squeeze around the top tier, from which the figures
on stage far below are like ants crawling along a distant
plateau.

The entrance fee was generally two obols unless you
were extremely poor, when it was one copper chalkous. At
the time eight chalkoi equaled one obol, and six obols
equaled one drachma. A drachma was an average day's
wage for an unskilled laborer, two drachmas for skilled.
But I rarely had an obol no less a drachma. Father used to
say, "Always have an obol for Charon, my son", but he
sent me very little pocket money, so as not to spoil me.
Besides room and board, Athenades provided a pittance
for some personal needs, hardly enough for the almond
and date cakes to which I was addicted. I would readily
have forgone these and everything else for tickets to the
theater. And then Simonides, in all his largesse, dropped
into my life. How clever of him to appeal in such an easy
way to this enthusiasm of mine; call it vanity.

141

Besides the rehearsal at the Odeion, I would be his guest at the opening of *Clouds* in the Theater a day or two later. He owned permanent center seats two rows behind the High Priest of Dionysus, who presided over all the performances. For the great procession and sacrifice of bulls at the start of the day Simonides had also purchased prized places for us, perhaps paying more that year than usual for the best because I was in tow and it was my first Dionysia. It seemed to me that everyone in Athens, freeborn and slave, Athenian and foreigner, had turned out for the festivities. The seas were by then free of winter or early spring storms and the festival was timed to take advantage of the sea calm, to encourage as many as possible to attend. I had never seen such a throng. Deafening cheers were raised for the parade of the ephebes. They would go into the next battle, already taken as inevitable, although there was a lull in the war with Sparta. Flowers were thrown before and over them. The parade of prisoners was more chaotic and met with greater merriment. They were granted amnesty that day, and their release they treated as an orgiastic opportunity. Certain women would hang a strip of wool from their window to invite a visit. The day was brilliantly clear, the air pungent with the smell of sacrificial fire. I was dizzy with excitement.

Simonides had insisted on decking me out. White was customary for the Dionysia, but this was not to suggest the trim and finery added. Father had made little of such things and whenever I was presented at court he had insisted that I appear in simple clothes with no elaborate trimmings or crowns. Simonides would have none of that.

142

He wanted to show me off. I had protested and told him of father's feeling that aristocratic arrogance had toppled many a throne and that the cultivation of modesty was the better path to a just life. But he had waved his hand dismissively as if those were the sympathies of provincial minds, although I used the example of Socrates to chide him. We settled on a compromise. He bought from one of the better cloth merchants a new white chiton of the softest Egyptian cotton, but I balked at a silk fringe.

On the day he came to fetch me he also gave me gold shoulder pins, which he attached himself, and a white cloak of fine Miletian wool. It was early enough in the year for cool winds to come down from the nearby mountain regions, but too warm for a cloak. It had a gold neck chain, "in the manner of Alcibiades", as they said in Athens, because he had made it fashionable when still in his teens, being fond of parading around the Agora to show off his beauty, aristocracy, and wealth. I felt self-conscious donning it and used the weather as an excuse to hand it to a slave. If Simonides would give it I did not have to wear it. We had a small argument. I said that the cloak would attract every thief in the Agora and that it would make the black market sellers in nearby Thebes very happy. He said this was an insult; I insisted it was a fact. Such already were our disagreements and tests of will, only to grow the more so. Poor Simonides. I was very stubborn, if the truth were told. The cloak made me feel dashing and I took to wearing it later to Aspasia's house, and a few times to meet Socrates, but I did not tell Simonides this. At least he had not asked me to wear short sleeves. In Athenian slang to call a man "short sleeves" or "cut sleeves" was to call him effeminate. Women wore short sleeves but men never. Men did not wear tassels either, and Simonides never asked that of me. There is as much tyranny in what to wear, as what not. I gave in that day to other of his whims: gold ankle and wrist bracelets. My sandals had brightly colored straps, but when he insisted on a laurel wreath I refused. The fashion that year was for long hair, started by sons of the aristocracy who liked to think they set the trends for Athenian boys, and generally did. The long hair was sometimes held with a band and sometimes not. I held strong opinions as a youth on certain customs and held head garlands in low regard. I wanted to let my hair grow despite being teased about it by Assur and the metics, but Athenades made me keep it short, so that strands would not spoil my work, he said.

We arrived for Clouds in the middle of the day, just as the performance of Ameipsias' *Connus* was finishing and well after the performance of Cratinus' *The Wine Flask*, which was to take first prize that year, as *Connus* did second. As we entered the Theater, I walked one step behind Simonides, and properly lowered my head when he pushed me forward to meet this or that dignitary. More people than I could imagine knew my father, or had heard of my gold design work for Athenades. Everyone knew everybody and everything in Athens. The greatest of all cities was a village.

Aristophanes' comedy would be at a disadvantage, performed last, late in the day. Apparently Simonides' bribery had not succeeded in having it scheduled before a fresh audience not yet restless or suffering "laughter fatigue" as Aristophanes later called it. As we paraded

144

conspicuously down to the front, we could sense the rowdy mood. The competition ran continuously from dawn to dusk and people were already passing us on the way out, only to be replaced immediately by those who waited at the gates. From their comments I had the impression that Ameipsias' play had been well received. Indeed cheers and cries were going up for the playwright as we entered. I also heard Socrates name often repeated, and calls too for his appearance. Socrates was mocked in Connus as he would be in *Clouds*. People were standing and milling about, and the crowd was too thick, or I was too short, to see Socrates in the throng. Aristophanes had misgivings about two plays in a row dealing with the same protagonist, but Simonides and Lygis thought that Athenian audiences reveled in their favorite themes, much as children do not tire of repeating a game or song that pleases them, a low judgment about such a sophisticated audience that may have helped to lose Aristophanes a coveted prize that year.

We found Simonides' seats easily; his name was inscribed on them. Wine was being passed around, fresh and dried fruits, it being popular to dry the fine Mieza apples and sell them for exorbitant prices at the Dionysia. Dates too abounded, this being my first inkling of their variety and scarcity, the best being reserved for the festival where they were meted out for political favors, a broad interpretation of refreshment. The foodstuffs might also become weapons in the hands of the audience. They often showed their displeasure not only by hissing and whistling at the actors, but also by pelting them, and the playwright should he be unfortunate enough to show his face, with

145

over-ripe oranges, rotten eggs, and spoiled fish. Violent disagreements often broke out over some interpretation or other, or at lines in the work attacking some politician or event popular at the moment. Aristophanes especially liked to make the world topsy-turvy; one of the definitions of his comedy might be turning reality upside down. Violence at performances was illegal and warranted imprisonment, but it did not prevent it entirely. I had hardly been able to sleep for nights in anticipation of the festival, yet I felt newly born.

As we took our places a great cheer went up and I saw Socrates entering down front to our right. He turned to scrutinize the audience, saw Simonides waving, and waved back. I saw, with some satisfaction, that Socrates was not wearing laurel either, as so many men and boys were. His tunic was threadbare; he did not bother with a cloak or sandals, although a chill wind blowing down from Mount Parnes almost made me put on mine. Macedonians believed that the cold hardened men and often sent their youths to the mountains for toughening, although thank God, father never asked this of me. When I shuddered and Simonides tried to wrap mine around my shoulders I brushed it off petulantly. Socrates was already more my model than Simonides.

It was odd to watch Socrates and his entourage threading their way across the front of the theater to their seats. They were all barefoot, without cloaks, and all wore threadbare tunics. Their unassuming air made them stand out by contrast with the preening audience and was itself a statement of the good life lived in simplicity. Socrates was solid but lithe, as was clear from his easy gait. Did the

146

Stoics, who claimed that leading the natural life was itself a virtue, influence them? Socrates had none of their solemnity. Some in the crowd chanted, "Socrates! Socrates! Socrates!" He had inspired two poets that day but I was not sure the shouts were accolades. His group sat in the section reserved for students and honored youths of the city, some of whom were poor and admitted through civic largesse.

Simonides also pointed out to me the tall, emaciated Chaerephon accompanying him. He had been one of Socrates' star pupils and was now a close friend. He was so thin and wraith-like that they nicknamed him "the Bat" and made jokes behind his back about his skeletal appearance. His gaunt face was very haunting and later, when I got to know him, I discovered that he was not thin because of fasting or some fastidious philosophical practice as rumor had it, but from disease. Aristophanes also made note of him in the play that day. We later went to Delphi together, the story of which I shall tell later in this history.

As I settled onto the bench for the play a disturbing wish flitted through my mind. I wanted to sit with Socrates and his students, and not with Simonides. They treated him with such camaraderie, claps on the shoulder and affectionate embraces. I could see that Socrates both inspired affection and gave it naturally, which do not always go hand in hand. They leaned on him, draped over his shoulder like over a pet pony; he did not either encourage or discourage it, but accepted the affection peacefully. At one point he amused me by hopping up onto a bench with great alacrity, showing he was in fine form, waving to this and that friend, to us again too, heartily. There was something playful about him, not the fool as some suggested, true playfulness being a gift given by Eros, and consistent with his deep seriousness. I dared to wave back and wondered if his greeting were meant for me as well, hoping against hope that it was. If at first I was drawn by his charm, or the vanity of being liked or merely noticed by a famous person, later I hoped that I might have virtue enough to please him.

Simonides turned and said to me, "Look Socrates is waving at you. Why aren't you waving back? He's quite taken with you, it seems."

Such statements from Simonides were storm warnings, and I elaborately replied, "Oh, I hardly think he is waving at me. I have stopped to listen to him in the Agora on the way to school, but we never so much as exchanged one word. I'm sure he was greeting you, or waving to someone behind us. If he had wanted to greet me he would have come over to us at the Odeion."

"No. You are quite wrong. He fancies you." I began to protest but he cut me off. "None of your false modesty today, Amyntas. Not today."

I was going to protest that my modesty was not false, but there was some sadness mixed with his chiding, and it made me hold my tongue.

Another clamor passed through the crowd. An elderly man was making his way proudly with long strides to his place at the front of the theater not far from where we sat. From the reactions of the crowd, derision competing with adulation, I understood that he must be a politician. The Archon presided over the City Dionysia, but he stood in

148

deference. He had pride of place among the notables.

Simonides saw me straining to look and said, "It is that rascal oligarch, Cleon." It was indeed, the same Cleon who was the brunt of satire in two plays by Aristophanes, The Babylonians and Acharnians. Cleon had sued Aristophanes because of *The Babylonians* and there was still bad blood between them. "He's probably here to see if there is any mention of him in the play that might be cause for litigation, certainly not because of his love of Aristophanes. He is so much of an egotist he will probably be disappointed not to be the center of the mockery today."

I said, "Aristophanes must hate Cleon if there was litigation in the past and he knows that Cleon is awaiting his opportunity for more."

"There is no love lost between them. In fact, Aristophanes makes no secret of despising Cleon as the sort of aristocratic tyrant that brings out the worst in democracy."

Cleon disdained both the derision and the acclaim and went directly to one of the seats of honor reserved for generals and politicians.

Cleon, son of Cleanenetus, was a wealthy tanner. As leader of the opposition to Pericles and Periclean reforms, he had accused Pericles of misappropriating public money, and Pericles has actually been found guilty of this ludicrous charge. He had recently become popular by tripling the pay for jury members, which had endeared him to the poor, and accounted for some of the cheers that day. He was a forceful speaker too. But his love of litigation seemed to win him the most popularity. Litigation, they

149

said, was the second greatest Athenian pastime.

The cheering had made me curious and I stood on the bench to get a better look at a populist tyrant. He had a great shock of white hair that made him seem wild and odd. Men seemed eager to speak to him secretly, leaning close to whisper things in his ear, to which he would often nod his head 'yes'. He must have been seventy that year but still vigorous. Yet his unkempt white hair and smooth skin made him seem effete. I did not like what I saw. This was to be Cleon's last City Dionysia. But it was not my last glimpse of Cleon. The next would be within the month, and unpleasant.

A murmur again surged through the crowd. Are the people a sea through which waves course unimpeded? I craned to see, and asked, "Is the play about to begin?"

Simonides pulled me down beside him and said, "Sit still. It is Aspasia. She is entering at the front and the traditionalists do not like it. "

A small section for women was set-aside at the far back, with its own entrance. Aspasia daughter of Axiochus of Miletus had been granted a special status in Athens, as the former consort of Pericles and mother of his only living son, but entering at the side with a small retinue would have been considered by some inappropriate.

I was about to ask Simonides whether she sought to disregard custom when he added, "She wants to make a show of her friendship with Socrates but takes a risk of earning civic displeasure."

A woman ready to break taboos intrigued me. She wore a magnificent silk robe that was perhaps the real cause of the murmuring. It was of rich reds and blues and embroidered with the labyrinths and mazes of Ariadne, wife of Dionysus. There were two slave girls attending her, at least I supposed they were girls. Their heads were covered. They were dressed as wood nymphs. From their contours I did not suppose they could be boys. The nymphs were the protectors of Dionysus. Everything that Aspasia did that day she did to honor the god of the festival.

I said, "She is beautiful and pays tribute to the God."

Simonides said, "And her own reputation as diviner and matchmaker. Now sit down again as I told you. She will be coming by here and will stop to greet us. You must not appear eager. She told me that she wishes to thank you for the necklace you designed. Now don't disgrace me."

I was about to protest on several fronts, but she was already drawing near and I recognized the necklace I had designed, my first real commission. I had put all my talent into it and Athenades had called it "fine indeed", which was high praise coming from him,. But seeing it on her I thought it wanting.

As Socrates later said to me, Aspasia put the contradiction to Pericles' famous statement that women should be loved but never mentioned, for she was loved and often mentioned, by Pericles, poets, and many others. Pericles was an unconventional man who tired of doing things the normal way. His battle tactics, his plans for Athens were extraordinary, but so was his relationship with Aspasia as his lover and closest adviser. Many called his dependence on her weakness, but I call it testimony to a creative, bold, and daring mind. He took to having her at his meals, for example, which Athenades would never have done with his wife; and after his death she held symposia. Pericles encouraged men to think outside the normal pattern of things; it became the mentality of Athens Golden Age. Socrates too might thus be described, Aristophanes, and many others besides.

Simonides stood to greet her, and I with him. Aspasia was in her late forties, a year or two older than Socrates, and at the height of her energies. She had a strikingly beautiful, chiseled face, with a high brow and aquiline profile, her black hair pulled back making it seem sharper; her deep black eyes assayed your nature. She had accumulated staggering wealth, begun before she ever set foot in Athens through inheritance, property and the courtesans she owned. She had a sharp business sense and bought and sold land shrewdly and at great profit; her holdings in Miletus were extensive. While she was with Pericles, she also wisely consulted his slave, Evangelus , who was reputed to be one of the cleverest men with money in all Hellas. I made use of his acumen when I set up shop in Scythia years later. He had kept Pericles' accounts and had turned Pericles small, inherited fortune into a vast one. It was his idea and not Pericles' to use the money left over from outfitting for war to build public buildings and works and make Athens the greatest of all cities. The city of free men would never have flourished without the skills of this slave.

Evangelus may have remained faithfully at Aspasia's side counseling her, but she developed her own skills too. She was not the sort of person to be dependent, or to delegate responsibilities without learning economies herself. I have often found women to have a better sense

152

of owning and managing land than men, my wife Eshe included who has managed our house and lands with great skill all these years.

Aspasia approached us now, the gold broach holding her hair catching the sun. She had invented a cream that kept the face free of wrinkles. She glanced at me and I shivered, as if touched to the core. Simonides was speaking to her and she bent close to him because it seemed to be something private, her eyes taking in him and everything around. She was not only Socrates' friend, but she had been his teacher, and so must have a nose for falsity, in speech or demeanor, I reckoned, or he would not have cultivated her. It was alleged that the evasion of a glance or the intonation of a voice could signal a truth or a lie to him. I reasoned too that Aspasia could not be the shrew that the comedians called her, not someone with her degree of dignity and power.

As she spoke with Simonides one of her slaves sidled closer to me, and none too discretely either. It was certainly a girl, I thought, a very attractive girl, but impudent. It was the wild Mania; she was roughly the same age as I. She had removed her headdress as she approached. Her eyes devoured me, the way a hungry, thirsty man eats a peach. They said that young girls had the power to turn you into a frenzied animal, so that you could not find your way back to being human again. Mania had chosen the name herself, whether to signify what she meant to inspire, or her own inner disposition, I was to discover when she set out, successfully, to seduce me some weeks later. There were interventions along the way, about which I will speak.

153

She edged closer now and asked me my name. I found it both bold and inappropriate, offended, intrigued, and excited. Why I told her I do not know, nymph of Dionysus or not.

She said, "Oh, you are the one who made the necklace!"

I said, "Yes, I did."

"But they say you are a genius!"

She said it with such astonishment that I took it for disbelief, and I replied, "Is that so hard to believe?"

"No. That's not what I mean. It's just, you're a boy and I thought from what they said that you must be an old man."

"Well, I am at least as old as you, or older."

She smiled prettily, "Do not be offended. I meant it as a compliment."

I had no further time to reply.

Simonides turned to me and said, "Amyntas, please let me introduce you."

Aspasia smelled of eastern spices and fragrances, of lavender and rose delicately combined and balanced, of her own mixing. My first impression of her was of some exotic place brought close.

She said, "So you are the artist who has made my necklace?" She put a hand to her neck. Her fingers were long, beautifully tended. She wore only one simple gold ring. I was looking down in deference but she raised my chin so that she could look deeply at me.

I said, "I did not know it was for you, or I would have done it differently."

"Oh? And how would you have made it then?"

154

Athenades had advised me to make something elaborate but discrete, and I had decided on a three-link, strap necklace that from a distance might seem humble but close up would reveal pure gold intricately wrought. From the twisted bands, each strand woven with many threads, were fixed a series of twelve, solid gold rosettes. Hanging from each side of the rosettes were solid gold seed pendants. Each seed pendant was intricately carved with raised folds of gold resembling drapery, and the edge of each rosette was rippled and embossed with rings of star like designs. Yet, if you saw it from afar you noticed only the glitter of pure gold.

All eyes were on me and I added hesitantly, "Well, I would have, that is if I had known it was for you, Lady Aspasia, I would have added black obsidian for your eyes, and instead of seed droplets, pearls of great constancy. But I would still have used as much gold because its beauty never fades nor tarnishes." Now, I only meant the comment about gold to be factual, and had meant to say also 'pearls of equal consistency' instead of "great constancy", but I was so befuddled by the attention and awed by her presence that I did not speak my intention, although the result must have been fortuitous because she laughed and clapped.

"So that is how you see me then?" She leaned close and put a delicate kiss on my cheek, obviously pleased. It was not easy to please her, Simonides told me later. She had seen everything, knew everyone, and was wary of flattery. But she heard in my voice that I was telling her a fact, and was innocent of manipulation. Perhaps the gods took over my tongue at that split second, because they had their designs on me when it came to Aspasia, and her role in fostering my friendship with Socrates. But Aspasia was constant, as all will testify who were her true friends, and I had, unwittingly, spoken the truth.

I did not think she required an answer, but shook my head in assent.

She said, "You will come to see me. I shall arrange it with Athenades. We shall have a better opportunity than here to get to know each other."

I noticed immediately that she did not say that Simonides should bring me. I said, "I would be honored."

"Good then. We shall ask the omens about your future, for I can see that there are bright things in store for you. I have a very reliable soothsayer who will read your signs better than the Sibyl of Delphi." She turned to Simonides. "You were right, Simonides. Your young friend does not deserve to be hidden away. Someone who puts such thought and beauty into his work is a rare creature. We must have a dinner for your kalos kagathos."

I watched her carefully as she departed, moving with that impatient hurried step of hers. I was curious to see whether an exception would be made for a woman who had shaped Athens as surely as had Pericles, and she would break custom to sit among the dignitaries, but she hastened up to the women's section, to my disappointment. I will tell one more thing. Before her retinue had departed Mania had suddenly whispered to me, "I will see you again." And she had dared provocatively to graze my hand.

Simonides had noticed Mania's attention. As they departed he said, "You seem to have been quite a success,

Amyntas, and not just with Aspasia. Be careful."

I said defensively, "And why should I be careful?"

"That Mania will cast a love spell over you and before you know it you will be spending every cent you have in order to free her from service. Or worse, to lavish gifts of her."

"There is no need to worry about that Simonides, not on the allowance Athenades and my father give me. I can't afford fish cakes, no less courtesans. Besides you always make too much of too little."

He laughed and said, "You are surely my path to virtue. But I warrant that Aspasia has not seen everything in you that she thinks she will see, or everything in you that she wishes to tell you for that matter, or she would not have invited you around. Few are invited to her house."

"If Athenades lets me go."

"Don't be silly, my boy. You have yet to learn how much Athenades' business interests are of importance to him. She is his best customer, after me. Or before me, for that matter! But tell me, what do you make of her? I am interested in your impression."

This was a question he would often ask me when together we met someone for the first time. He prized my answers. I thought carefully before saying, "When I heard her being spoken of I thought she would be frightening."

"Frightening? I've never known her to go around trying to frighten people. At least not now that she is mellowing with age and still mourning the loss of two husbands. Her last, the sheep-dealer Lysicles has just died you know. But then I never did know what she saw in him except that he was loyal to Pericles. But tell me why did you think she might be frightening?"

"They said she was the one who ruled Athens and decided wars, not Pericles, so I thought she might be…" But I was fearful to say the word that had come to me, not wanting to offend Simonides.

"What then? You can say it. It is just between us."

"Please don't misunderstand me. I don't think she is, but I was going to say devious."

"Devious? Aspasia? Is that how the stories portray her? How so?"

"Because she would have had to work behind the scenes all the time to exercise power. But now that I've met her I just think that she is forceful. And impatient with fools."

He laughed. "That she is! Yes, She would like the things you say. They are fresh, and that is no mean feat, and, yes, you will go to see her. I will put in a word too with Athenades, and take you there myself if need be."

"Oh, but Athenades will want to send Leagros along." I added in a whisper because Leagros was nearby, "He is my shadow."

Simonides said, "Of course, if you prefer the company of old men." He looked hurt.

I said, "I did not mean you should not go. Just that, well …"

He interrupted me, and held up his hand, "Never explain. The truth is Aspasia did not invite me. She would have if she had intended it, but clearly she wants to see you alone."

"But why?"

"How should I know? I long ago stopped trying to

158

divine the female mind, no less one as intricate and agile as hers. Of course, she is very much a match-maker and might like to find out how you feel about me."

He had never said anything so direct before and I was not pleased. I said, "I would never talk about you to her. I am not like that."

But he had no time to answer. The High Priest was standing and commanding the heralds to silence the restless audience. *Clouds* was about to begin.

It was not one of Aristophanes' successes and placed third in the competition. He revised it over the course of the following year and published, but did not produce, a second version correcting some of its mistakes, and toughening some of the remarks against Socrates. Despite the revision it never became one of the more popular Athenian comedies and was not to my knowledge produced at Corinth or elsewhere. I cannot call it my favorite play of his. This is *Lysistrata*, written many years later, one of the greatest anti-war poems produced in that most enigmatic of all cities. And then there was the role *Clouds* played at Socrates' trial. He referred to it himself in his own defense, as causing sentiment against him. But the mood of Athens in the year of *Clouds* was not the mood of Athens in the year of his trial, and what was spoken publicly then did not resonate the same later. How could Aristophanes be blamed for the fickleness of history?

I came to know Aristophanes well, and saw that my initial judgment was clouded with youthful prejudices. Later I became friends with his son, Araros, and produced Araros' comedies, following as he did in his father's

159

footsteps and also winning deserved first prizes. I did as a boy admire Aristophanes, if from afar. In all he did he strived for excellence, and stated sentiments in Athenian life that no one dared speak first, and did so in such a funny way as to make these sentiments palatable. He never ceased wishing for something better for Athens, a life without war being better than a life with war, as anyone can see. But who does? War is the breeding ground of tyranny, and in his peace plays he did noble service to a sometimes not always noble city. He became something of a hero to me, which is not at all the same thing as a friend. I tried to apply his commitment to my craft. Aristophanes knew creative success and praised the excellence of my work, that of a mere beardless boy awkwardly finding his way in a great city. But still I must confess that I have always had reservations about Aristophanes, stemming from *Clouds*; or at least about the power of comedy to transcend time and affect events far from their premiere. *Clouds* helped to sow feelings against Socrates that would bear disastrous fruit. We do not like to see those we love maligned, or the seeds of injustice planted by those we admire.

Clouds made mockery of many things that year. Athenians were fond of mocking their philosophers, and Clouds was not different in catering to this than other comedies. Poor Strepsiades has come to the Thinkery to learn how to argue his way out of debt. He is not interested in dialectic for the sake of truth, but only to learn how to use words to turn black into white, a good joke about Socrates' teaching methods, if more appropriately leveled against the Sophists. Simonides' grandfather too was

160

maligned, and Chaerephon was lampooned as effeminate, which he was a bit. Sophists were insulted, philosophers, politicians, debtors, creditors, reasoning and astronomy. Why bald men and even Athens itself were scathingly dismissed. And the list is longer, much longer, nor unusual for comedy. Why then did the mockery of Socrates linger so long in Athenian minds? The view of him in the play, both played and published versions, is much exaggerated, as most would recognize. Aristophanes' Socrates charges money for his teaching of rhetoric, music, and grammar, which was not true. Nor had Socrates relinquished his belief in the old gods, which was the worse that could be said, and was.

At the performance, at least, the winches and pulleys worked properly and Lygis was not thrown to the floor from the caged platform. The audience clapped and laughed loudly as Lygis/Socrates uttered his famous words, 'I walk on air to study the sun. I walk on air…' The idea of Socrates walking on air was ridiculous, and was met with great mirth and much stamping of feet, and 'studying the sun' also produced much name-calling and shouts of blasphemy and tampering with the realm of the gods.

As we were walking out of the play I lingered among the throng with Leagros while Simonides bade farewell to this and that acquaintance. We were waiting for Aristophanes to go to a celebration. Two gentlemen walking by me deep in conversation said things I noted.

The first said, "So, what do you think of his having a go at Socrates like that?"

The second replied, "The mores the better, as far as I'm

161

concerned. These philosophers are all so high and mighty. They all need taking down a peg or two, don't you think? You can't be too careful about giving them too much influence."

"Right you are. There's a heretic lurking in each of them. Remember our teacher, what things he implied about the gods?"

"Heavens yes. Aristophanes is right. They would all have us believe that the weaker argument is the stronger and than black is white. I don't trust any of them no matter what name they call themselves, be it Sophist, or Socrates."

The first had the last word. "And that Socrates? How can Athens trust anyone who says he relies on some sort of inner god that will not tell us his name."

But their voices trailed off and Simonides took my arm. "Are you ready to leave?"

"Yes. Are we going to your house now?"

"Yes. There is a party."

I knew he was quick to jealousy and had been put out by Aspasia omitting him, but was I distracted by the remarks I had overheard and said unwittingly, "Will Aristophanes and Socrates be there?"

"They are invited, of course, but Socrates often stays away from things like this. Are you disappointed?"

I said defensively, "No. I am relieved. I mean, I feel sorry for him after the scathing remarks in the play. Although it would be interesting to see if Socrates and Aristophanes shake hands when they meet."

"Don't be silly. Of course they would. Our comedy is not cruel."

"I know that." I turned to him and lay my hand on his arm. "I'm very grateful to you, Simonides, for taking me today. I shall never forget it."

I meant it sincerely, and he squeezed my hand, pleased that I was pleased and with him.

But one last thing more I will say about *Clouds*. Many weeks later, when I had come to know Socrates at the Lyceum, I was speaking with him about *Clouds*.

I asked, "But were you really not angry with Aristophanes?"

In his fashion Socrates asked, "Do you think I should have been?"

"Well I would have. "

"Then do you think I should?"

"No. I do not think it necessary. I was just wondering if you were or were not."

He said, "No. I was not. Sometimes, when I am with my voice, I suppose it can seem to other as if I were walking on air, but I do not think he meant it unkindly."

He was being self-deprecating, but I regret not asking him more.

2. Simonides courts me.

After the play several of us made our way through the festive streets to Simonides' house for dinner. The drunken crowds along the Panathenaic Way made me feel insecure, despite our numbers. Wine had passed freely among us during Clouds. Chaerephon, Lygis, and Leagros were all drunk. Indeed, Leagros was so far gone that he had to be propped up between us. He had chaperoned me a dozen times but I had already realized that by tempting him with

163

drink, or by showing I could hold my tongue about his serial affairs with scullery maids, cooks, married and unmarried matrons, I might do what I wanted. My own scruples would have to be my chaperone, but I was young. If wine had been passed around, I had not drunk much, nor had Simonides. The excitement of the day had overcome me, which was another sort of inebriation. When I was a boy and overwrought I talked too much. No sooner were we out of the theater than I began to chatter my way through the streets all the way to Simonides' door. He found it charming, which reveals the irrational state of his affections. No rational man could have found my hyperbolic drivel amusing, about the costumes, this or that refinement of the performance; who had recited his lines convincingly, and who had not; which acts of the play succeeded, and which not. The production was admirable, the masks stupendous.

We might have seemed a very rowdy group, and had the police after us if we had been the exception, but the streets were full of revelers. By the time we reached Simonides' door we had to linger to allow the others to catch up, staggering and swaying. I felt close to Simonides at that moment, so grateful for the day and still excited by it all. I had unselfconsciously taken his hand as we walked. At another point he had put his arm around my waist and as we stood by the door waiting for a slave to open the door upon which he had pounded loudly to make himself heard above the outside din, he placed his arm over my shoulder. I was of medium height and he a head taller. A moment was about to happen over which I have pondered much, if I understand it now.

Simonides stared down into my face with great affection and said, "It will be dangerous going back home through these streets tonight, Amyntas. And Leagros won't be fit to stand before morning." With great tenderness he wiped a speck of street dust from my cheek. "Perhaps I should send a messenger to Athenades?"

Of course, I knew he was asking me to spend the night. We were standing so close together anyone passing would have thought us in embrace.

But what did I say? I said without hesitation, "Oh I have to be up early in the morning to work, you know, so I had better not. Athenades might say yes, but he would still be grumpy all day tomorrow. Leagros can stay here but I can return with one of your slaves."

Simonides took his arm off my shoulder and said, "I would not want trouble for you, of course."

He was clearly upset and turned away as the door was opened by one of his household slaves. His gesture had not been disrespectful; nor was it entirely unexpected. He had given me hints enough in the guise of half jokes. Nor was I innocent of suitors, nor for that matter innocent. My young tutor at home, when his moment had come, had put the matter to me directly, and I had readily agreed. Yet something held me back with Simonides that night. In simple terms, perhaps I did not want to return favor for favor. The day had been magical, and I did not want to make a transaction of Simonides' beneficence. Free men did not do that, my father had taught me.

If Simonides was hurt by my rejection he accepted it with good grace. We went in to dine, and the good food might have sobered the others if there had not been more

165

wine, always the best at Simonides' table. I did not partake of that either. Was I, then, already under Socrates' spell, the new path of virtue and moderation, so separate from the ancient Dionysian spirit of the festival day? Socrates was a man of frugal habits. He was rarely drunk. I never remember him being so. Although in love with Alcibiades, he had refused Alcibiades' overtures. One of my classmates at school had mentioned this in passing, perhaps in derision or disbelief, and it had stuck with me. But if Socrates was influencing me that night, I most certainly did not know it. Rejection was never a final word for Simonides. He was not about to stop wanting me because of one refusal, nor did I necessarily want him to stop. The humors drove a boy's moods, as did whims, and whispers of the gods.

In fact, Simonides found an excuse to visit the workshop a few days after *Clouds*. A ring needed readjusting, or was it some trinket broken in the play? I forget. Athenades sat at the front of the shop as much watchdog as proprietor. They sat discussing the Dionysia and the various awards.

Athenades said, "I hope that Aristophanes is not depressed about placing third. It is a poor reception for someone of his talents and undeserved. Please tell him how unfair I think the prizes were. I had no idea that Ameipsias could offer such large gifts to the Archon, or I would have at least warned you."

"We think that Cleon is behind it, you know. I suspected him before the play and tried to, well, compensate."

"Of course, Cleon! I never thought of it but it makes

perfect sense. He would love to see Aristophanes humiliated and one way is as good as another. He has always been ruthless. Are you sure?"

"No. But we can find out. Lygis' wife's sister is married to the brother of the niece of Ameipsias. His wife will ferret out the story for us."

"You must let me know. If it is Cleon's revenge, or if it is someone else playing with the judges, we had best find out. For the good of Athens, of course."

"Of course."

"I myself think it was a superb play. But I heard afterwards that Aristophanes has gone around saying he will revise it? I don't think it is necessary, if his losing was Athenian politics as usual."

"I'll tell him of your sentiments."

"I know that Amyntas also liked it, did you not Amyntas? Come over here for a moment."

He took it for granted that I would be listening in, I suppose, as I was, and I replied. "Yes, Master Athenades. I did like it."

Simonides had not been staring at me, as I had warned him not to do on pain of "never seeing him again", because I did not want to be teased by Assur and the others. Our little "family" was close-knit, and everything about everyone commented upon endlessly. Now, however, he turned an adoring gaze on me. I was sure the others would notice, and they did.

Simonides said, to Athenades and not to me, although he continued to stare at me, "Actually, Athenades, I have an idea for a design that I wanted to show Amyntas, with your permission. Aspasia's birthday is soon, you know and

167

I have thought of a gift you might make for her."

Athenades said, "Of course. Come over here, boy. Why are you dawdling?"

He sometimes commanded me like a slave, in order to seem to spread his authority over his workers evenly. I went to look. As I stood next to Simonides inspecting an elaborate design, I thought was grotesque, and trying to figure out how to tell him gracefully, I felt his hand brush mine, and then again. He was trying to sneak a message to me, I realized and quickly took it from him.

He said, "It is only a crude idea, you know. You are free to correct it, or discard it and use your own imagination."

It was to be a pair of earrings decorated with rubies and pearls. I said simply, "It is a very good beginning." I knew it would please him.

I found out later from Chaerephon that Simonides interpreted "good beginning" to be a comment on our friendship because I had not said that "his design was a good beginning" but had said "it", leaving it deliberately ambivalent. Desire is definitely a form of madness. I did not have an opportunity to read his message until that night, by lamplight, before I slept. All of his messages, letters, and poems, every single scrap, I have kept, passions stirred by a boy, read with age.

My dearest love

O, do not be put off, if I address you so. Surely you know it is how I feel. I have spent the last nights sleeplessly for fear that my crude suggestion the night of the play has put you off. How could I not want this so desperately, and how much I should have respected the virtue of your restraint. But do not mistake my impulse for demand. Being with you in simple ways is my great joy.

Your eyes trouble my soul
Deep passions stirred
In silent longing calmed
As ships from war return
To safe harbors still waters.

I would take you out and about again soon and will ask Athenades. Perhaps in a few days for discretion, but no more, ostensibly to help me choose a bolt of Egyptian brocade to go along with Aspasia's earrings, so that you may design the raised, gold thread decoration and have it done in the workshop? That will win Athenades' approval. How can I eat or sleep or think until we are together again?

Your most humble servant
Simonides, son of Bacchylides

Of course I did not take his pledges of restraint too seriously. I put the small scroll in my secret niche behind a loosened wall stone. His attentions were flattering if too fearful. How earthy and forward my tutor had been! My father called him a farm lad, although he was not. He would whisper in my ear exactly what he wanted to do, arousing me. Simonides was more complicated. He made sincere pledges that he had no hope of keeping. He resolved to follow one path as he set his feet upon another. There did not seem to be a direct connection between his intentions and his feelings. But I fell asleep that night pleased with his message, written in good Attic Greek, I noted, with just a bit of a flourish, not rigorous and stiff as I had been taught. Eros swathed me pleasingly in dream that night.

Simonides was ever inventing reasons for seeing me. There was new construction on the Acropolis, and like most boys, I liked to see the various machines in use, the wooden towers, platforms, and pulleys needed to move the heavy blocks. We would go up there together when I had free time, which was not often, and admire the handiwork.

Many days had passed since the festival, but it was still spring I remember. On one warm day we sat in the shade on some discarded marble blocks, flawed in some way and unused, one with a deep crack that might split, another with murky discoloring. He had taken me to a spot beside the Brauron, the Sanctuary of Artemis. Dining rooms were being constructed on the stoa side. He was working on a new hymn cycle. It was not about my eyes praise Apollo, but about Demeter and her beneficence, for the Greater Eleusinian Mysteries held over nine days in the early autumn. The Archon Basileus himself had commissioned the hymns, Simonides told me proudly. They would pay honor to the Homeric hymns on the same subject, but add fresh meaning about the fertility of women and the harvest. He would be paid a staggering sum for the work, and he told me the figure quite proudly, seven minas. I reckoned that a farmer with five children might live comfortably a year on it.

It seemed to me that the Acropolis was always under construction. Yet, little wild areas were left untouched. Where we sat scraggly olive trees and pine brush still grew offering some shade. The city din rose as a soft murmur.

170

There was always enough wine and refreshments to entertain Leagros and the accompanying slaves. They left us alone.

Simonides said, "I wonder if you could do me the honor of reading aloud the hymns I have finished in the last few days. I have read them so often myself I cannot hear them any longer, and a fresh voice might highlight what needs to be corrected or added."

I agreed and he slid closer to me, to hand me the fresh scroll, draping an arm over my shoulder too.

He said, "Will you mind if I interrupt and have you reread a passage so I can contemplate it?"

"No. That will be all right."

I began to read, "I sing of Demeter, fairest mother of Persephone . . . " but he stopped me.

"Do you think I should mention Persephone so soon? Or at all?"

"Why not?"

"Well, it is Demeter's festival. I do not want to anger her. Read the next line. Perhaps it can be combined."

I read, "you of the golden scythe who relishes the harvest." I paused and said, "Well, you could combine those two lines and maybe change it a bit. What about this? 'I sing of the fair haired Demeter whose golden scythe ravishes the harvest.'"

"Why Amyntas, that is very good. Let me call for my writing instruments. Read on a bit further."

I said enthusiastically, "All right then. 'You, most generous of all the goddesses, wife of Zeus, pursued by Poseidon with amorous intent.'

Simonides interrupted, "Does that sound right to you?

171

It is not neglecting her attributes is it? Should they not also be placed first?"

I said, "No, that seems all right. Shall I read on?"

"Yes."

He was retelling one of my favorite stories about Demeter. She was searching for her daughter, who had been stolen from her by Hades and taken to the underworld, when she met an old poor man whose small son was gravely ill. I read, "She of great compassion/ bending low by bedside/kissed the fevered brow/pouring life from lips/returning son to father.'"

Simonides placed his hand on my knee as I read, which I did not miss. He slid his fingertips beneath the cloth, but I did not pause in my reading, nor when he slid his hand higher. I reached the end of the page and handed him back the scroll. Athenian clothing, hiding but permitting, permitting and revealing! But he could see it did not reveal what he wanted.

He kissed my cheek paternally, took his hand from my thigh and the scroll back, and said evenly, "You read beautifully. But I fear the hymn needs much more work. That last bit is crude."

"It is one of my favorite stories about Demeter. "

"Then we should rewrite it together. Are you willing?"

"Oh yes. I would like that."

"Where are those writing tools?."

This day on the Acropolis had great consequences, for me and for our friendship. Because he had not elicited a response in spite of his advancing caresses, it sent questions flying around Athens; I was to learn over the next weeks. It seems that no one was spared his doubts.

172

Was there something wrong with him, Simonides asked his friends, that he should be spurned? Was I an innocent who did not recognize an advance? Did I not like such things? Did I not like him? Had he offended me? Was there something wrong with me? Were such things different in Macedon? Had Athenades, a man who only liked women, been influencing me? Did I need some sort of love potion or spell? Was he offending some god? Surely that was it. He went off to see Aspasia, the wisest matchmaker in Athens they said, with Socrates.

3. 423-422 B.C. In Aspasia's study.

A number of weeks passed in which the unresolved tensions in my friendship with Simonides began to intensify and cause problems. Stifling summer was closing in on us. The still air was ripe with foul smells. Work was more enervating, my mood more sullen.

"Watch that Simonides," Leagros told me one day while walking me to school. "He can't hold his tongue for a minute. He was at Aspasia's last night bending her ear about you until midnight." Leagros boasted that he had a confidant in Aspasia's kitchen.

I was as thin-skinned as any boy, and was none too pleased that Simonides was discussing my hesitations behind my back, without having the decency or common courtesy to talk to me first. Leagros made light of my ire. "Love lives are as much a city sport as are the Olympic games, and far more enjoyable than the endless religious festivals. Simonides is only being a good citizen." Leagros was something of a cynic, and I was not sure whether he was making fun of me, Simonides, or Athens, or sincerely trying to console. I wanted for good advice, although this was soon to change.

My daily schedule was also absorbing me: work, school, schoolwork, more work, and every now and occasional leisure. Many days would pass before I would see Simonides again, although he found clever ways to send messages. He knew that Leagros did not mind his attentions, and would send a slave to intercept me on my way to school, slipping notes into my hand, to Leagros' amusement. "Oh my darling, I have not seen you for days. You did not answer my last note and so I send another. Please, please respond or I shall die." I shamefully would scan the rather elegant scrolls with their carved wood ends, and stuff them into my drawstring bag. I was happy to be invited out by Simonides and forge social bonds through him, but not in love. He was so afraid of losing my affection that I had complete control over him, and I am ashamed to say that I took advantage of it without wanting to hurt him. I did not have enough experience to estimate my effect on him, or his emotional pain.

Life lived in Athens never went long unexamined, ambiguous attitudes and actions doubly so, as if they were civic riddles not private dilemmas. The air buzzed with curiosity and philosophy, at least in the circles into which I was being drawn. If I had known this I would have been expecting the moment when Athenades, some weeks after *Clouds*, took me aside one day and said, "Amyntas, it seems that you are invited to Aspasia's house. It is a rare honor and before you go I will have to instruct you in the proper etiquette. It seems she is to sponsor a banquet for you."

174

He was frowning and I wondered if he entirely approved. But an invitation from Aspasia was an obligation for Athenades. Simonides was right about this.

I said, "When I met her at the theater she said she would like to see me again, but I thought she was being polite."

"You should have told me this. Aspasia is never polite for the sake of politeness. She does not have to be. I would have sent a messenger to thank her. There is so much you have to learn about Athenian life. Please don't let a slip like that happen again."

"I am sorry. Should I write her an apology?"

"Too late for that. We must, however, consider what gift you will bring."

"If you will permit, Master? When I met her at the theater I saw that her bracelets did not suit her and thought of something simple and elegant that might."

"Simple and elegant? Is that how you see her?"

I hesitated. "Yes. I suppose it is. Do you think I am wrong?"

"Wrong? Elegant perhaps, but is any woman simple? Certainly my wife is not, or her mother, or my mother either. And Aspasia? It is not how I see her, or most of Athens, but perhaps you are right. Tell me. Did you like her? Dislike her? Think her frightening, as some find her, or mysterious, attractive, or dull, or interesting?"

Aspasia represented an entire new world to me, about which I was very curious. But I was also afraid of her eyes. I was hiding my grief over the loss of my brother, over leaving father and home, hiding also my anger with King Perdiccas for being so drunken and mad, or my

175

confusion about Simonides, or my impulse now and then to run away when I was overworked and tired. There were so many emotional mists clouding my soul that the thought of being invited to the house of someone with her reputation for prescience frightened me. Yet I desperately wanted to go. Was I so ignorant as to suppose I could hide my troubled soul from her? I also knew that she could cast spells. At least, that is what Leagros told me.

I answered, "Much could be lost if I do not make a good impression so I am rather apprehensive about going to her house."

"Well that is being realistic. But we shall prepare you as best we can. Have you packed any finery in those two Phoenician cedar chests of yours?"

I assured him I had. Aspasia spent a fortune at his shop. I understood that he did not want to take any chances with that either. Leagros was as excited as I about going; he would chaperone me, and it seems that a certain fifty-year-old cook in Aspasia's household had caught his seventy-year-old, roving eye. He claimed that coupling rejuvenated him, as some sought youth through potions, or walking in the mountains.

When I mentioned that we were to go a little early, before the banquet was to begin Leagros said, "Banquet? You said nothing of that."

"The Master said that Lady Aspasia was sponsoring a banquet for me. To tell you the truth he seemed none too pleased."

"He is too much the traditionalist to be pleased. How many times have you caught so much as a glimpse of my dear daughter? Not many I warrant, the poor thing. I can

176

count on one hand my own encounters, and she is my blood. Half of Athens would have Aspasia locked away; the other half admires her effrontery. Let us hope her independence is not her undoing."

Soon after this conversation and before the banquet Simonides arranged to spend a free afternoon with me. I nearly refused, angry about the gossip. He arrived as usual with arms full of gifts: a new book, sweets, an ivory handled knife, writing implements which he claimed were for writing to my father but were criticisms of my silence. It was all very awkward. There was nowhere in my small room to store everything he gave me, and might create envy if I left it strewn about; envy is an insidious vice.

He was also invited to the banquet and was very excited about it. Doubts had, however, already arisen in my mind about whether the bracelet I was making was grand enough. He said he was taking me shopping and before we went off to the Agora I showed him what I had designed.

Simonides said, "But it is perfect! You do not want to be too lavish with Aspasia. She would find it vulgar. Just do it as you have drawn here and come out today and forget about it. I've asked Azelaeus the cloth merchant to put aside something special that just came in from Persia that I think will suit your green eyes. But that Macedonian country drawl of yours! I still think that you should consider speech lessons. Lygis is between plays. He could coach you."

He had brought this up before but I loved Macedon. Now and then when I was homesick a few "bar-bars" as the Athenians called them would infiltrate my Greek. Holding on to some Macedonian idiosyncrasies was

177

holding on to Macedon.

I said, "I do not mind people knowing where I was born. I am proud of our line, and proud of being raised in the country among my father's vineyards. Besides the poets tell us that the countryside can be superior to the city because it is filled with natural spirits, while the city is more the work of men."

He suddenly squeezed my hands between his, his face welling with affection. "Aspasia would adore that! I know you will be a success."

And we had another disagreement. I pulled my hand away and said, "Not if I let you overdress me. Really Simonides, I brought enough finery, and do not want to go to that cloth merchant today. We were just there and I am already being teased about it. What else do you have in store; sandals with gold straps, or the gods spare me, short-sleeves! I suppose we are going to stop at the barber too for some hair styling? Or curling? You would have half of Athens preening me if I let you have your way. Not to mention all the gifts you gave me the last time. I told you before that I had no more room for anything, yet here you are bringing more. I have half a mind to throw them to the beggars. At least that would put me in favor with the gods."

"Calm down, Amyntas. There is no harm in my gifts and it gives me pleasure. I'll take them back and keep them in a special room just for you."

I groaned. How could I win? Here he was already outfitting my room in his household. I said, "Pleasure indeed! You just lavished me with new clothes for the City Dionysia. I don't see why I can't wear those?"

178

"Stop being difficult. You are simply not aware what a great function the kalos kagathos banquet is in Athens. You have to have something special, including jewelry too. I thought something discrete, a thin gold strand for your neck perhaps to set off your lovely olive skin. And. as it is your birthday soon...."

"Soon! I won't be fifteen until late summer."

"Yes, summer, like your temperament. We shall celebrate it early, and again when it happens."

We went on like this as we made our way to the Agora, and I heard behind me Leagros chuckling.

Aspasia had asked that I be brought to her house early. She wanted a chance to speak to me on her own before the other guests arrived, she said in her message to Athenades. Simonides and I had finally agreed on one piece of jewelry, a shoulder buckle made from a rare ancient coin. It was very discrete and I pinned it on myself. Protesting his gifts had not stopped him. He bought me a silk, summer cloak and had me drape it over one shoulder, rather than have a slave carry it. He came by to inspect me before I left and insisted on walking me to Aspasia's door, although he would be there later.

As usual he made unwitting remarks that irked me. "Now let me see my handiwork" was one of them. "Your handiwork?" I replied. One thing he said I did like. "Without adornment, a boy is no better than a wild beast." When I asked him what he meant he said, "The statues of the gods are always painted and adorned." I took this to mean that we need to sacralize ourselves from boyhood on.

Aspasia was a foreign resident of the city, a metic, but the same laws governed her that governed female citizens. Women were not allowed either to buy or sell property for example, but Aspasia's skill I have already mentioned. In reality, she occupied if not quite possessed two houses, a villa in the country, along the coast near Piraeus, and a city villa in the crowded Koile district of the city, one of the five into which the inner city was divided. They were really the property of her son, Pericles son of Pericles and his sole surviving heir. When plague struck Athens Pericles two legitimate sons, Xanthippus and Paralus, died; Pericles petitioned the city to have his son by Aspasia declared a full citizen, which the child lacked because both parents needed to be so. This the city granted, and Pericles changed his will just before his death to make his son by Aspasia his heir. She was his guardian, and managed his properties until he came of age. At the time of *Clouds* the young Pericles was about ten; Athenians did not always keep birth dates exactly. I was very fond of him and we became close friends. When he reached his majority he provided for his mother, and there was never a question of her leaving the houses. There was love between them.

But Aspasia was also wealthy on her own merits, besides the wealth bestowed on her by Pericles during their few years together, in the form of jewelry, ancient pottery, statues, gold cups and countless other objects which were to prove of great value. Pericles was the first true patron of the crafts in Athens. He used his private money and not the money of the city to support artisans, and gave some of their finest work to Aspasia as gifts.

180

Despite Pericles' example, most Athenians did not decorate their homes or see such things as utilitarian pots as being of lasting value, and Aspasia's collection was not much noticed. It took a generation or more for Athenians to value the crafts the way that Pericles did. After his death she kept his gifts and the city considered them hers by default, pots were pots, no matter who had painted the decorations. One further doubt might have been raised about this collection. During Pericles reign, Aspasia had advised him on the city finances by consulting various signs and portents and by reading the stars, at which she was most adept. She was known not to take reward for this, but did it generously for the good of the city. It might have been asked whether there was not an exchange of services, objects for advise, and whether, therefore, her collection was liable to taxes, but I did not hear it was. Resident alien taxes were very high in Athens, double that for citizens, or more.

As we neared her house Simonides was more nervous than I about the impression I would make. But I think he also feared her influence. She saw through the problems that beset friends and lovers, and the truth of their connection. Her advice could be harsh, as reality often is. He did not want her to see our impossibilities, but only our possibilities, but he knew that she would see things as they were, a rare gift given also to Socrates. He fussed over my dress, my hair, over the color of my cheeks, pinching them, and I grew impatient.

"Honestly, Simonides, will you calm down. You'll have me a nervous wreck before we reach her door. And besides I don't want you there when the door is opened, as if I were a baby needing a nurse. Having Leagros in tow is bad enough. I'll never hear the end of it. Leagros can see me the rest of the way. It is only another street in any case."

Simonides said, "You are a brute sometimes. After all, it gives me pleasure to share in the excitement of your presentation banquet. It is an important event in your life, and an important step towards your becoming Athenian. Why should I not be excited for you?"

Of course, the issue was really his affection, and I answered feebly, "You're coming later, you know."

He respected my request, nonetheless, and left us at the corner to proceed on our own.

Houses in the Koile district were crowded in together; the streets twisted and turned; a teeming warren mostly devoid of greenery. Hers was in an alleyway on the periphery of the district. Beyond there was countryside and she had cleverly purchased some fields that she had enclosed, so that, from the back of the house, there was a peaceful, formal garden, and a view of the farms that helped to feed the city. She grew fruits and vegetables for her own table, and secret herbs for the aphrodisiacs and potions she was so expert in making. The country was my familiar element, and at Aspasia's I had the sense of a second home where I could be myself.

Her doorway stood out, graced by bay trees. Pillars were to either side of the door, and a statue of Zeus the Protector as at Athenades'. A slave girl greeted us with a basin to wash our feet, and ushered us into a spacious marble hall. I was to wait there until summoned, but Leagros was led off to some other room leaving me alone.

It was cool and quiet, filled with the pleasant smell of jasmine; bird song echoing from an aviary.

The entrance hall was flanked by two gigantic and splendid Panathenaic amphora attributed to Kleophrades Painter, quite as large as I was. They were decorated on two sides, one representing an athlete being crowned and the other Athena. I recognized a statue of Hera that our workshop had gilded, in front of which garlands were placed. In niches evenly spaced along the walls were statues of Artemis, Aphrodite, Pallas Athena, and Demeter,; her household was dedicated to the female deities.

From far rooms I could hear the tittering of girls, the bubbling of a fountain, and the screech of parrots. I was left to stand a long while and had the impression that eyes watched me from behind silken curtains threaded with silver, but it might have been my own self-consciousness playing tricks on me. I could see from the hallway where I waited the first courtyard and beyond that a second dining courtyard with a hearth. Athenades home was undecorated in the Athenian manner of the day. What adornments he had, and they were considerable, he had moved to his country house. But everywhere I looked at Aspasia's there was decoration.

Simonides had given me an explanation of some of the sculpture I would encounter so that I could appear knowledgeable. One statue especially caught my eye, of a young javelin thrower by Myron. His most famous work was of the great running champion Ladas caught in mid stride, but Aspasia's javelin thrower was quite as good. I stood before it deep in admiration. It seemed to be infused

183

with strength, yet had weightless poise. There was a great sense of liberation and freedom. As I turned my back on it to look at other things I had the eerie feeling that I was exposing myself to the javelin's throw, so real did it seem. There was also an owl with wings spread set on a stand, by Sophroniscus, Socrates' father. I liked its spontaneity and vitality although I do not think he was as a great sculptor, like Myron. Simonides had also told me that Pericles had befriended Pheidias, one of Athens greatest craftsman, and I supposed that some of the sculpture I saw were by him.

The facing walls were covered with murals; the floors covered in tiles decorated with geometric designs. On the left wall was a mountain scene, so cool and elegant I shuddered; on the right were hills covered with vines and green valleys with eagles hovering and resembling an area near her Miletian home which I later visited. Smaller murals were painted between doorways and one caught my attention, depicting a simple bunch of grapes on a silver platter so real that I felt I could pick them off the wall. The great Zeuxis had recently painted it. He was then at the peak of his talent. She had acquired many other things too; coins and objects belonging to famous Olympic winners, athletics and the crafts being closely entwined, and objects belonging to playwrights too, for she loved the theater. She showed me once Euripides stylus, and books in his hand. Several side rooms were adorned with antique comic and tragic masks, much the envy of Simonides, who coveted them. Most remarkable of all, Simonides told me later, was that Aspasia's private bathroom was heated.

I heard footsteps and the wild Mania came to fetch me

to take me to see Aspasia. I recognized her from the premiere of *Clouds*.

I said, "I remember you. Your name is Mania."

"Well aren't you clever. I know yours too. You are Prince Amyntas."

I had a chance to study her more closely now. She was half a head shorter. Her dress was held tightly at her narrow waist making her new breasts more prominent, their points showing through the thin cloth. She painted them. Her eyes were a lovely, pale blue and her hair black, streaked naturally with blond. She was very pretty, but not beautiful. Her energy infused her, and made her very attractive.

She said, "When you have stopped ogling me we have to go this way."

I blushed, showing my naivety around women, and said, "I was not ogling."

A courtesan with an expertise in initiations had been arranged when I was twelve, and there were episodes with a farm girl, but I did not know about relationships and interactions, the give and take of male-female lovers.

She said, "Well if you were not staring then I am insulted."

This confused me the more, but I managed to ask, "Does anyone win with you?"

"Do you want to, Simonides' boy?"

I thought her impertinent and annoying, and said, "I am no one's boy. And besides you're very impertinent for a . . . a girl." I would not disdain to call her a slave. It might have seemed a threat and I did not want to threaten her.

She was not to be put off. "I don't see why you should

185

take it as an insult. After all, he likes you enormously. Everyone is talking about it, you know."

I was mortified by that and said quickly, "Well you can tell everyone, whoever everyone is, that I belong to no one."

"Then do you want someone to belong to you?"

"You really are very annoying," I said. "Are you always this annoying?"

"You have not answered my question."

"Nor shall I."

"Well, if you won't answer then I shall suppose that the answer is yes, which would be very promising."

"You may suppose what you like but I do not see why it would be promising, or any concern of yours."

She laughed and said, "I like you. I knew I would when I saw you at the Dionysia, although I do not think you are quite as beautiful as the others think you are, yourself included I suppose. Your nose is a little wrong, you know. And you have such a naive look in your eyes!"

"I don't see what is wrong with my nose. And as for being naive, it is ridiculous. You hardly know me, so all I can conclude is that besides being impertinent you are stupid."

Of course, she was neither, for after all she had me talking to her. She laughed and said, "Well if you don't like me I shall like you. Not many boys can hold their own around girls, but I think you can. I rather like that. But I doubt if you will dare to be so blunt with Aspasia. Why she would eat you alive!" This image seemed to please her. Her lovely eyes danced with delight. She laughed loud and long.

I said, "I know my manners. I would never think of being blunt with Lady Aspasia. She is a great woman and you...well...you're just.... a silly girl." Still I did not say slave.

"A silly girl? Do you know that we have placed bets on you?"

"Placed bets? What on earth are you talking about? And who is we?

"The other girls, the maids, the kitchen help. Aspasia does not approve, of course, but I am sure you will not tell her."

"I won't tell her if you tell me immediately what these bets are. Honestly you are completely impossible."

"Well it sounds a little bit like a threat, but I shall tell you anyway. The bet is whether Aspasia will make you a regular here or not. I have bet that she will."

I was both complimented and confused and said, "I was only introduced to her in passing, and I have no expectations. But I am sure she is very busy and would not want to bother with me much."

"You have a low opinion of yourself."

"Not at all. It is simply that Macedonians are realists. Besides, everything goes according to the wishes of the gods, regardless of what we want. I thought you would know that."

"Do you think that you would be coming to Aspasia's house without the signs being consulted? I thought you would realize that you are here because the gods favor it. Well there you have it. I know much about you, and yet you know next to nothing about me. And about girls, you clearly know less than that."

187

"You are the one who knows nothing about me!"

"I know that Athenades thinks you are his most talented apprentice ever, and I also know that you are not at all vain or arrogant, nor are you stupid as are most of the boys whom Simonides likes. I know that your father sent you here to keep you safe, and that intrigue hovers around you like poison bees."

"Intrigue? I do not know what you are talking about. Anyway, how do you know all of this?"

"Do you deny it?"

"You have not answered my question."

"Perhaps I shall, and perhaps I shall not."

I said quietly, "Thank god not all girls are as difficult as you or there would be no marriages no less births."

She glanced at me, and saw that I was trying to hide a smile. She said, "Be careful. I think you are beginning to fancy me and I am quite a lot to handle."

Before I could object she kissed my cheek and sped away leaving me standing before a carved cedar door of exquisite design.

"Just knock." she said as she ran off, blowing me a kiss. I knocked as bid and a strong voice commanded, "Enter."

Aspasia was standing by a large table on which a map was spread. Her pet weasel scurried around my feet. It was very friendly and was an excellent mouse catcher. There were many large and small chests scattered around the room. The one next to her was open and filled to the brim with scrolls. She was barefoot and wore gold ankle bracelets. A small gold ring in the shape of two miniature, intertwined serpents was perfectly proportioned to her long slender fingers. I envied its design and she told me that it was the work of Athenades himself some ten years before, in the age of Pericles that would have been, so I realized that their acquaintance was a long one. She was nearly fifty but her hair was still black, with bold streaks of natural white.

As I approached the table she turned to me and said, "Well, Amyntas, I see that Simonides has fitted you out for the banquet, although the restraint I would say is your doing and not his. Come here and let me have a look at you." I did so, and she made me turn around, and said, "But why not wear your cloak properly? It suits you, you know."

I was hesitant to tell her how self-conscious I felt wearing it, for fear that she would think I was a country boy untrained in city ways, but I said, "I think it is too lavish. Simonides likes gold trim, purple linings and all that, but I do not."

"Then throw it there over that chair and have done with it tonight. Socrates will be wearing his usual rags, so you needn't wear all of this merely to please Simonides. Not in my house."

She herself wore the finest silk and lace, the finest of scents too, many of her own invention. Inventing perfumes was her hobby. They were quite unique. Her secret discovery was to mix animal fats and secretions with flower essences. If I had known what a privilege it was to be asked to see her alone, and how many would have given fortunes for this, I would have been less hidden behind the shyness of unknowing youth.

I said, "I don't want to hurt Simonides feelings. He's been very kind to me. It's just that…" I hesitated.

189

Aspasia said, "Come, let us sit, here on the sofa. Here, sit beside me. Now tell me everything. I've set some refreshments out for us. The banquet is not for a while and I know that boys are always hungry. Why you will have to meet my son, the younger Pericles. I think you will be friends. Another day perhaps."

There were dates and pomegranates; wine laced with orchid blossom; honey cakes and fresh Mieza apples, not dried. All of these were considered mild aphrodisiacs

When we were seated she said, "Surely you must like his gifts? I have never known a boy who did not like gifts. And Simonides is more generous than most. So generous that I worry about him sometimes. Generosity has many sides. If it were not for Simonides' generosity Aristophanes' plays would have never been produced. But love's passion can infect generosity, and lead to bankruptcy. Why not accept his gifts gratefully?"

I said, "I am grateful. Really, I am. It's just that...that..."

"Yes? You can speak freely here, you know. Our conversations are in the strictest confidence, one that is sacred."

"Simonides does not know limits. I resist his generosity, but the more I complain the more he does it, like those rivers in Macedon that overrun their banks no matter how high we build the embankments against the flood. "

She said kindly, "Do you know the Athenian joke about more fortunes being lost over a boy than over the horses?" I felt relieved that she had said this and felt more comfortable. She continued, "Aristophanes told me that in

190

Clouds he was going to make Strepsiades' son besotted with boys instead of horses but thought that too many people would think he was making fun of Sophocles, who lost his mind over more than one boy, quite recently too despite his old age, and he did not want that interpretation."

"I do not want Simonides to go into debt over me."

"No danger of that! You do not know Simonides. He calculates very carefully what he spends and takes great care of his wealth. Few in Athens are wealthier, you know."

"Yes, but being so wealthy does not justify his lavishing things on someone when they do not want it. He thinks it shows affection but it gives the impression that he wishes to buy it."

She said, "Perhaps it shows his anxiety? Let me ask you something else then. We have another saying. The fault lies not in pursuit, but in yielding easily. But never yielding, well, there must be reasons. Do your friends mock you?"

"Oh no. It's not that."

A slave girl entered to pour us wine and serve the cakes.

When she left Aspasia said, "Can you tell me why then?"

I wished to give her the right answer; she inspired that. I remember pondering how slender her hands were, and firm and fresh the skin. I had visions of jewelry I could make. But I said, "What bothers me is that when Simonides gives me these gifts I feel that he is seized by some false religious notion. As if he were imitating all

191

those stories of the gods and how they gave gifts to boys, you know, hoops and chickens and things. By lavishing things on me he makes me a divine object in imitation of the gods. And no matter how much I tell him that I do not want more gifts the next time he sees me you can rest assure that he will give me some article more costly than the one before. Why just the other day he was saying that perhaps he should buy a piece of land for me off by the sea that he heard was for sale so that when I was finished at Athenades' and was a master craftsman myself he might build a house for me with a decent prospect. Imagine! Buying property for me!"

She said, "By why not? I am still baffled. Are you afraid of being obliged to him?"

"No. I feel more put off than obliged."

"Are you sure that you are not secretly pleased?"

"Oh no. I am sure I am not. I feel smothered and displeased. He does not give me the chance to know my own feelings."

"And what are they then?"

"Oh I like him. I like him very much. But..." I lowered my head. I was grateful she was speaking about this because I had not been able to speak about it with anyone else. I added, "I simply do not want him in that way, but I know he is besotted. I do not want to hurt him, and I do not know what to do. Father once said . . ." I glanced quickly at her and saw that she was listening intently, and so I continued, "Father said that Macedonians were simple and direct, and that sometimes it is a virtue and sometimes a vice. I do not want to be the sort who takes and takes and takes, and then rejects. I think that would be terrible."

She patted my cheek. "You are not like that, Amyntas. But you do need to discover what your sentiments are and make them clear to him. We already know a few things, that you respect him and might like him more if he were more restrained and gave you the chance to breathe. Of course, restraint is not his nature."

"Do you think I should give in to him then?"

"Oh, it is not for me to say! We can read your chart together. That might help."

"I would like that but I would not make demands upon your time."

She raised my chin so that I might look directly at her, and she now took my hand not in one but in both her hands and said, "My dear, you have every right to put yourself forward. Indeed, there have already been signs."

I was taken aback, and said, "I did not mean for you to tell me what to do, only that I would welcome your advice. Father taught me that advice is only good advice when we make it our own."

She affectionately brushed my cheek. "Enjoy your friendship with Simonides; enjoy yourself. After all, he is not a bad person, and he can teach you a great deal about Athenian life that will be useful to you in the future." She was studying me. "But there is something else, some mystery between you and Simonides that has not yet shown itself."

I did not know what she meant and she did not give me a chance to ask. She stood suddenly and pulled me to my feet with a laugh, leading me over to one of the several large chests.

She said, "Enough about Simonides. Come over to the

193

table here and look at my latest map. I am very proud of it." It was the one spread out on the table, that she had been studying when I entered. She added, "Now tell me, what is the first thing that you see that is different about it?"

I took in immediately the extraordinary fact that it showed the world as a globe and that the land seemed but a small island surrounded by vast waters, which I said.

"Yes, you have it exactly right. It is a rare map, a copy of an original from the time of Anaxamander. I had it brought from Miletus as a gift for Socrates, so you mustn't mention it. It perfectly illustrates his own theory about Hellas as an island, and I wanted him to have such a fine depiction."

My Eleusinian tutor had taught me that astronomical works from Babylon, and those by Anaxamander of Miletus, had represented the world as a sphere but he never had found any maps to show me.

I marveled, "The land seems so small in the midst of so much sea. It must mean that the sea gods are greater than I thought. Father always suspected it."

"Yes, a Macedonian might notice that first whereas an Athenian might think that the land was the center and the sea the access to conquests. They say you Macedonians do not know the seas as Athenians do, nor particularly like it. Is this true of you?"

"I have not sailed much. When my father sent me here to Athens I came overland, on horseback. He said it was safer, but it was only because he did not trust the gods of the sea to deliver me safely." I suddenly felt embarrassed for telling her father's fears, and I added, "But father

194

respects the sea. He says that Macedon will only be a great power when it learns to rule the seas."

Aspasia said, "He is quoting the Phoenicians, of course, and they were right."

I said, "I think Socrates will be very pleased with your gift."

"Do you think so? Actually I think so myself."

She turned from the table. The evening was warm and the wooden shutters were open on her peaceful garden and the view of the countryside beyond. Just within the garden was a stone bench carved with fauns. "Come let's go into the garden."

I was struck by the faint perfume that she wore, attar of lily with a touch of musk. It was said to calm and soothe and I am sure she wore it to encourage me to be at my ease. There were lines at the edges of her lustrous eyes. They had none of the opacity of age. The skin of her arms was taut.

She clapped once and the same slave girl entered immediately carrying a silver fruit bowl. A pomegranate had been broken into segments. She said, "Your lips are dry. Take some. It will refresh you."

It was a fruit I particularly liked, and did not need coaxing. How could it be, I wondered, that I was sitting here next to Pericles' mistress eating fruit as if we had known each other a long time. I was too shy to study her except in quick glances, but I noticed that she studied me carefully. On her wrist was a bracelet. Like her ring it was two snakes intertwined, the snakeskin crisscrossed with minute raised lines. Two rubies were its eyes, a cliché I thought. The two I had made for her were better.

She caught me staring at it and said, "You do not seem to approve? You must make something that you think suits me. I shall arrange it with Athenades, of course."

"It will be the first time I am making something for a woman I know," I said, and then blushed at my presumption. I made things worse by saying, "I mean, I meant to say...not know...but.."

She placed her hand on mine with a smile, "Do you think you know me? Do not be shy. What do you think you know?"

"I spoke out of turn. I did not mean to."

"Oh come now or you will displease me. So what do you see in me? Besides, I am ordering you, you know."

I could hardly refuse and glancing up I said, "You have become what you are because you know far more than people think you know. In fact, you know far more than most of the people with whom you are speaking, and that is how you have gotten along so well in Athens all these years. You don't just know more, but you know when to let people know how much you know and when to keep it secret. So most people think you don't know as much as you know, but it does not matter to you because knowing with whom you can or cannot share your knowledge has given you great influence."

Aspasia looked startled. "Well!" I thought she was displeased, but she added, "It is no accident that you are here in Athens."

"I know. Father would have me safe."

"I am not speaking of your father's wishes."

In the hallway earlier Mania had spoken about Aspasia reading my signs. I did not wish to get her into trouble and knew I had to be careful, but Aspasia had hinted at this too. I said, "Before I came here father had the signs read and they all pointed to my coming here. It was not what I thought my life would be like, but we are taught that the gods have things in store for us that are different from our own wishes."

"What was your wish?"

"It will sound silly, to stay at home among the vineyards, and write poetry in the manner of Solon. It is silly, now that I hear myself saying it. I mean Athens has already given me more than I could hope for, and I have only been here a few months. I did not want to leave father, but I know he was right to send me here. Perdiccas is dangerous. No, father was right."

"There was more to it than that. Did your father explain? He consulted his friends here too, you know; and our signs."

I knew some things. Father had been complaining for a while that Perdiccas was in one of his mad phases again and had taken a trip to Athens, which was difficult for him. He was also sending regular messengers to Athens, and receiving messengers. I know that the King knew of his trip and the messages, and could easily fear that one of his princes was making a secret pact with Athens. There was a truce with Macedon now, but father had lost patience with Perdiccas and court politics. He wanted me somewhere safe, somewhere away from periodic threat where I could grow freely. This is what I thought.

I said to Aspasia, "Father told me that Apollo had commanded him in a dream. It was the God's will." I hesitated, not having told this to anyone. "And when father took me to our temple, the priest indicated that the God favored me. But I do not understand all of this. In Macedon I am only one among many. In Athens I am only a workman."

"My dear Amyntas, you are already a craftsman and you have hardly begun. And in Macedon you are the heir to the house of Temenidai after your father, and as such men could rally around you in years to come to seize the throne. It is time you began to see these things."

"But I would not have any of it; at least not the politics. I love the crafts though."

"And if the gods willed it? Could you resist? But I see that you have become distressed with all this talk. And tonight we are meant to dine among friends and enjoy life. It is your evening after all."

Indeed there were sounds of laughter already from some inner room, and the footsteps of a slave coming to summon us. The first guests were arriving and Aspasia had to excuse herself in order to prepare. Strangely, she did not ask the slave to show me the way, high if odd trust, trust with a plan. She told me I could find my way alone to the room where the others were assembling. I need go down a certain passage, past a certain courtyard and along it to the second door. This too had been seen.

4. I encounter Socrates.

Aspasia's conversation created mixed feelings in me. Discussing Simonides filled me with self-doubt. How was I conducting the friendship? Was I being too clever and selfish? Simonides wished to shower gifts upon me, but was that so wrong? Would things be in better balance were

I to relent to his gifts and advances? The mention of father brought brief flashes of home: the mad Perdiccas, the court intrigues, the duties and dangers of our house, father's concerns, and my departure. I found myself questioning my life in Athens. If I could, I would have sped home that very evening to father's embrace. Would he have welcomed me? The thought that I might displease him held me back. As I left her study and walked down the silent hall, I must confess that I also found myself resenting Aspasia a bit for stirring me up like some still lake roiled by storm. Was that not her intent? Afterwards, I would often take everything she said seriously, if sometimes too seriously.

A fountain bubbled in the central courtyard. From other parts of the house I could hear voices, too muffled to identify the speakers. Had Simonides already arrived? Birds chirped in cages as if resenting the freedom of their wild brothers landing on the outside of their bars to tease them. I felt moody, petulant, and not much like staying the evening, but that would have disgraced Athenades and Simonides, no less me. Nor did I know where to find Leagros. Would he agree to leave? The banquet was for me!

I was so lost in thought that I nearly tripped over Socrates; he was sitting on a wooden bench, half hidden by a pillar. At first I thought he was with someone; he was muttering to himself, and it took me a few seconds to realize that he was alone. Had Aspasia sent me this way knowing that he would be there? I am sure she did. The setting sun suffused the sky above the open courtyard with warm rose. I was ready to apologize when I realized he had not noticed me. Now and again he would mutter a word or phrase, but I could not make them out. Was he in one of his reveries I wondered, communing with his inner voice, or simply admiring the evening? A linnet had descended onto the scarlet bougainvillea and I thought that Socrates might be scientifically observing its actions and I did not want to scare it away. Yet when it flew through the opening into the outside air Socrates did not move or seem to notice its flight. Such was my state at that moment that I was immediately torn by conflict. If he were listening to his inner god I must not disturb him. But what if he was not, and I dared slip past him without so much as a greeting? Would it not be an insult? The hall was narrow and passing unnoticed would have been impossible.

The dilemma was easily solved. Socrates turned and said, the first words he ever spoke to me; "You are the goldsmith boy?"

I stepped towards him and said, "I am not a goldsmith yet, only a pupil in the workshop of Athenades."

"A pupil who is more than a pupil, from what I hear. He has adopted you into his household, hasn't he? And your designs surpass his?"

Because of the thoughts I was having, and the mood I was in, Socrates' mention of the word 'adopt' made me sad, and his praise confused me. I glanced at him and saw that his face was alert with interest and soft with concern. I wondered if he could possibly have understood my reaction. His eyes were askew, and this also disconcerted me. Was he looking at or beyond me?

I had seen him from afar at the Odeion and at the Dionysia, but close up he was indeed as ugly as they said.

Add to his bulbous, flared nose and bulging eyes, his deep furrows, and the sores on his bald head where a recent infection had left scabs, and you had an appearance as close to a lower demon mask as was possible; the Silenus was more beautiful. He was so ugly as to make boys laugh when they first saw him, as I would witness at school and in the Agora. Adults turned their gaze away. Masks are rigid, but his face was expressive, suffused with kindness one moment, with the light of insight another. I came to understand through his face the law of the opposites of extremes: the very ugly can be exceedingly beautiful, and the very beautiful extremely ugly; they can cross over into the other. Physical beauty was known to drive the lover to madness. The gods had suffered from this malady. No such threat to sanity could be charged to Socrates' face. Yet, again, I found it beautiful, perhaps because it was so odd.

He gestured towards the bench and bid me sit. "You look troubled, Amyntas. Do they use your title? There is time before the other guests arrive. Has something upset you?"

I replied hesitantly, "I...I am worried about father. I have not heard from him for several weeks. I wish I were home right now. Our King..."I wanted to explain who my father was, what our politics threatened, but words failed me.

Socrates answered for me, "Your King is a bit mad, but I am sure your father knows how to survive in Macedon. I know the situation. Aspasia and I supported Athenades' petition in the Assembly, to be your ward."

I did not know this and thanked him. I said, "The King

is ruthless. And father takes chances. It has been six weeks and three days since his last message. It is not like him. He sends them overland with a slave and a guard but anything could happen. They might have fallen into the King's hands."

"It is no use worrying. Your father is cautious and wise. He is a good man, you know. You are right to miss him."

This surprised me and I said, "You know him?"

"I had the privilege to meet him last year. He spoke fondly of you. The thought of sending you away was painful, but he must have thought it was best. I understand that he wanted to keep you apart from the politics and thinks that Athens will offer reasonable security, which I hope is not misplaced. Reasonable is not a word I would use for things Athenian."

He wore a thin chiton, not quite the rag Aspasia had called it but close. His color was ruddy and wholesome from eating simply for health, not indulgence. Having just left Aspasia, I was sensitive to fragrances. His was a trace of earth herbs such as sage. If he never washed, as rumor had it, how could his scent be so fresh? It seemed very attractive not to wash.

I said, "Everyone in Athens seems to know him, but he never discussed his contacts here."

"Aspasia likes to keep her house open to new ideas that challenge the old ways, in the spirit of Pericles. It was here that I met him. There is a small but growing peace party here, in Sparta, and more secretly in Macedon too. You know your father gives money to our peace party through Aspasia, and she through Nicias?"

I suspected that Aspasia had given him permission to

202

say this and replied, "I did not know this."

"Do you share your father's sentiments?" He added, "You do not have to answer, of course."

But I wanted to, and said, "I loved my brother more than anything, more than my own soul, and war took him from me. He was my friend; I told him everything and he listened. He taught me how to hunt and fish and was kind to me. I hate war. And father? War crippled him for life, and not just in body. Before Potidaea he was joyful, and afterwards sad, always sad. What is war anyway? Father calls it the vanity of vanities of vane rulers, at least so it is in Macedon. Today King Perdiccas fights with Sparta, tomorrow with Athens, a slave to the wind gods. He is a king but he is enslaved to war, and he enslaves Macedon with his wars. "

My voice broke and I controlled myself through silence. Socrates did not speak, and I thought perhaps I had offended him because he was also a soldier. When I dared to glance at him his eyes were closed and his head lowered.

I was convinced that he disapproved and gently slid my hand out of his, and said somewhat defensively, "I did not mean to offend you. I know that you have fought bravely at Potidaea and at Delium. All the boys at school speak about it. They pretend they have swords and are you. Please do not be offended."

He looked at me directly. "Offended? I take part in wars but I do not take part in politics. I try to lead the life of a good citizen, so long as my voice does not caution me against a course of action. I uphold the law and fulfill my duties as a citizen. This path follows on my voice. But if

203

war is your worry then you should rest easy. King Perdiccas has ambassadors here to negotiate a new alliance and there has already been one debate in the Assembly, with few objections. Cleon and his faction will support it, while it suits him or his business interests. For the moment at least things back at home should quiet down and your father need not have to worry, about himself, or about you here if your King and our Assembly continue to see reason."

"It is not only the King who is a tyrant. Some of his advisers sees conspiracies everywhere and encourage his anxieties."

"Athens has its share of autocrats and plutocrats. There is always a tension between those who want the state to serve their special interests and those who have the best interests of the people at heart. It is a struggle in the Assembly to keep the special interests from accruing too much power. They have and give so much money it overwhelms people's common sense."

"Cleon?"

"I see you are catching on already to Athens!"

"Simonides positively despises Cleon. I thought it was out of loyalty to Aristophanes, but Athenades does not much like him either and he rarely speaks against anyone."

Something in my tone of voice must have made Socrates pause. We fell silent and I found him studying me again. The early summer, evening air was very soft, the garden air fresh with the smell of scented roses. I glanced at him. His odd eyes were a deep brown and stared at you without seeming to stare. He once argued that if beauty were to be measured by use then his eyes were more beautiful than most because they could see better to the sides than others could, and his flared nostrils could smell more subtly than others so his nose was more beautiful too. There was a long scar on his neck, and smaller ones along the right arm and hand that wielded his sword. They said he was fearless in battle. I wanted to touch them.

Socrates broke the silence. "Athenades is very pious. Most of the Athenian rich are patrons of war ships. Cleon pays for several triremes and will almost certainly lead another expeditionary force if there is to be one. But Athenades uses his great wealth mainly to support the religious rites and festivals, and gives only enough support to the navy to fulfill his civic duties. If he did not give so generously to the gods he would be detested, but he escapes censure through his piety for fear criticism of him will be heard by the gods." He added, "Are you happy there?"

The directness of Socrates' questions would always catch me off guard and I replied, "Work, work, work! I work too much. Work and school and schoolwork and more work. Sometimes I'm so tired by the end of the day all I can do is fall into bed without eating."

"But I saw you at *Clouds*?"

"Only recently has he relented and allowed me to go to the theater more, ever since Leagros became my new chaperone. But I have no right to complain, I am just an apprentice, after all."

Socrates said straight out, "Don't be silly. You are not just an apprentice. He has adopted you into his household, and goes around telling everyone except you that you are the finest craftsmen he has seen in years. If you were only an apprentice there would be nothing you could teach Athenades, but of course there is. Is there not?"

"Well, yes, I suppose there is."

"What then?"

"When Athenades designs something he does not let himself see the whole thing that he is creating so that sometimes the parts do not harmonize with the whole. And sometimes I feel as if his creations have more to become than they have become, but he doesn't let them. He would also never let me tell him this though."

"Do you first glimpse your designs as a whole?"

"Not always. Most often it is just hard work."

"When you see as a whole, does a feeling spring from it?"

I mused, "A feeling? If there is then perhaps it is the same you get when you assemble one of those wooden children's puzzles and the last piece is put together making a horse. When it is my own design and I sense that the design has come together properly I feel energy and exhilaration."

"Where does this come from?"

"Come from?" I was about to say Apollo, and indeed the "A…" was already out of my mouth but I stopped myself and said, "I was going to say it comes from Apollo but it sounds presumptuous. It does not seem to come from me, but from beyond me. Perhaps the god secretly whispers to me and inspires me? Why do you ask?"

Socrates said, "I admire the crafts and their processes. They were looked down upon in Athens as the lesser trades until Pericles began to support them. Only Corinth ever honored them properly. Despite Pericles, Athenians still undervalue them, except for those who know better. Pericles found in the crafts knowledge of the truth more than he ever found it in politics and power. Why did your father decide on Athenades' workshop?"

"Father said I had to become self-reliant, because of uncertainties in Macedon. He made friends with Athenades on one of his business trips here to sell our wine. Athenades fancies fine wines. My stepmother weaves, and I offered her weaving designs. Father showed some samples to Athenades. He liked them and saw that some of them could just as well be adapted to gold filigree. So, I suppose that put the idea in everyone's head. Later father bought a necklace for his wife but I was critical of it and could see how it could have been more beautiful. This too made an impression on father." I paused and then asked as directly as I had been asked, "Is Athenades part of the peace group here?"

Socrates said, "Yes, and another reason for you to be in Athens and in his house? Is that what you are asking?"

I smiled sheepishly and acknowledged it was

He reached out and touched the coin brooch holding my robe. "You did not make this?"

Glancing down at the brooch, I managed to say, "No, it was a gift from Simonides. It is a lion's head and some two hundred years old. Simonides says it suits my temperament, the lion I mean, at least around him."

"Oh, a lion. I am not so sure that suits you. Are you?"

"I think he means I roar at him when I should not."

"Do you?"

"Yes, I do." A doubt made me hesitate. Should I speak to Socrates about Simonides? This reluctance may have been the first inkling of my affection for Socrates, but I nervously rattled on. "I like the brooch though. It is a little crude, and is not pure gold. It is an alloy of gold, silver, and some copper, but it is a very rare coin, probably Scythian, and I like its age and significance. I can tell what it is made of by tasting it with the tip of my tongue, or by softly scratching or rubbing it. I can feel the alloy. Pure gold does not feel the same way. This has a greenish brown tarnish in the crevices, whereas pure gold would not. It is a little like my friendship with Simonides, I suppose. Perhaps that is why I agreed to wear it, because it shows our friendship truthfully, that it not quite pure gold. I mean, as if the elements did not quite blend or harmonize and had a little tarnish to them."

"And it makes you sad today?"

"Yes. But I am homesick too, and worry about father. Sometimes...sometimes I would run away. I would run away back to the mountains of Macedon, my home. But I also like being in Athens, and I think I am doing well here. But is that not a betrayal of father, wanting to stay or wanting to flee?"

Socrates said, "Neither is." His tone lightened. "May I tell you about my own father?"

"I would like to hear about him."

His father Sophroniscus was a craftsman, a sculptor, and he himself had worked as a sculptor when he was young. His father had a workshop and would invite him to watch and help him when he was a small boy. They would talk about schooling or wrestling, and his father would describe what he was doing to the marble in a natural way so that without knowing it Socrates learned. Then one day his father handed him some tools and a block of marble and said that perhaps he might like to make something and he made a small dog that barely looked like a dog, which he was proud of nonetheless. His father's work could be seen in the friezes of the new Parthenon and on the Temple of Heracles. Some of these Socrates had a hand in carving when he was in his teens and early twenties.

He said, "If you like I can take you around the city one day and show you all of my father's work. We can make the grand Sophroniscus tour and I can show you which chisel marks are his, and for that matter which are mine."

"Oh, I would like that very much!"

If Athenades would allow it, I thought! But I did not say that aloud. Once, when Socrates' name was mentioned he had looked askance. I resolved to ask Leagros about this.

I grinned and said, "Then perhaps I should not run away?"

If this was the first time that Socrates surprised me, it was not the last time. He suddenly shut his eyes and fell into deep thought. For a minute or two that seemed like hours he held his silence before he said, "No, you should not run away."

He had taken my light question seriously, and had consulted his inner voice, because there were serious implications to my question. It was my first experience of his seriousness, and his voice.

5. Chaerephon's biting tongue.

A lute being tuned signaled the arrival of the musicians. I waited for Socrates to stand and lead the way into the banquet room, but he did not. He had closed his eyes again; his hands lay folded in his lap. Was he praying or communing with his voice? His breathing was deep and regular. My classmates had told me that at Delium his reverie lasted a day and a night. It was peaceful sitting there and I was reluctant to leave him. He might need protecting, I thought.

More guests arrived. I heard now Simonides distinctive laugh. He would toss his head back and roar, as do mountain people. The respectful thing to do was to steal away from Socrates, but I did so regretfully. Joining the others was to step into another reality, of noise and celebration, and not a little love turmoil. As I wandered into a reception hall Simonides greeted me warmly. He was with Chaerephon. I was surprised to see that they had both decked themselves out in the brightly colored tunics all the rage then. Simonides had also added vivid fringes. No wonder he had protested at my choice of plain whites.

Simonides said, "There you are Amyntas. I was told you were in the fountain court with Socrates."

Jealousy was a safe assumption, and I quickly said, "I was, but he seems to have fallen into one of his spells. I was not sure what I should do but finally I left him there."

Chaerephon moaned, "Oh god, not lost again! He might sit there all night and miss the banquet entirely. That voice! I lose patience sometimes."

Simonides said somewhat sarcastically, quoting Clouds, "I walk upon the air. Yes, indeed. It's a good thing you got away. That voice of his is a dangerous thing in Athens where the old gods are revered. Better not to be linked too closely with it, in any way. You definitely did the right thing."

I was going to defend myself, and Socrates, but Chaerephon spoke up, "You are too hard on Socrates, my friend. He does not spurn the old gods. He has written hymns to Apollo and might recite them for us tonight if we prevail upon him. I personally think that his voice is Apollo."

I was surprised by this and said, "Is that what Socrates says?"

"The most Socrates can say is that his voice refuses to give its name, nor when it might, if it might."

"But why will it not tell its name? All gods want to be worshipped. Doesn't Socrates say?"

Chaerephon paused to scrutinize me but only said. "Well…"

I knew that Chaerephon was one of Socrates' inner-circle, and renowned for his loyalty. He had accompanied Socrates on that famous visit to Delphi, when the oracle declared Socrates the wisest of men. His age was hard to determine. At first I thought he was in his middle or late forties, as was Socrates, but I later discovered that he was about ten years younger. He was very tall, thin, and wraithlike. His skin was sallow and he did not look at all healthy, as did Socrates. He must have been afflicted by the wasting humor, at least some of his symptoms were similar, such as shortness of breath, night sweats, and not gaining weight no matter how much you eat. When we later went to Delphi together, a hilly place, he found it hard to make any of the ascents and I often had to sit and wait until his chest pains subsided. Phthisis was a common ailment in Athens, and Hellas. Hippocrates considered it the most common, as I learned later from Philiscus. Chaerephon was of a nervous nature, constantly fidgeted, and never kept his hands still. His mind was quick, and he caught on to the meaning of what you were trying to say when you yourself did not entirely know it, or were speaking obscurely. He knew little magic tricks, with which he would entertain me, and I enjoyed his company.

He at last replied, "All that Socrates says is that if the god wished him to know his or her identity then the god would have revealed it, but the fact that the god has not revealed his or her identity is essential to the god's task. In fact, he says that it is all he can say."

I said, "I do not think I understand this."

Chaerephon did not, however, clear up the matter much. He said, "Nor do I. Perhaps it is not important."

"Why?"

"Because it has always told Socrates what not to do, and the advice has always been for Socrates' good, and for others when they ask through Socrates and follow it. That rather proves to me it is a true god and not some malicious being masquerading. We have been friends for a long time and I came to see that Socrates is very fortunate having his voice and that it is a fortune we all share. His voice could be said to lead us all when it leads him. It is generous, which also seems to me godly."

Simonides said, "I think his voice is just some sort of Pythagorean mumbo-jumbo and might well be the dead Pythagoras himself for all we know. And as for being for the good of us all, well, I for one find it just a little sinister to rely so much on a god with no name."

Chaerephon said, "Come now Simonides, you are

212

surely wrong and it is simple. Pythagoras was not always right, but Socrates' voice is always right."

"Yes, yes, if you interpret it that way. Socrates is in his middle years, so there is still much to see. "

I was about to add my defense of Socrates, but held back. Simonides outburst against his voice made me cautious. I knew jealousy from my Eleusian tutor's passion; it hides behind many masks, one being concern, and I would have to be careful what I said around him, about Socrates, or the voice.

The three of us stood together chatting in a hallway. The smells of dinner were already drifting out to us, whetting our appetites.

Simonides changed the subject. He put his arm around my shoulder, and said, "You look a bit peaked. Are you hungry? I hope you like game bird and fish?"

"What are we having? I am famished."

"Stuffed pheasant. It is very expensive, but Aspasia has an extravagant nature. Or boarfish from Argos."

"I've had pheasant at court but never boarfish."

"It's a great delicacy, and one of the specialties of Aspasia's cook. It is better than conger eel."

Conger eel was Poseidon's favorite. "It must truly be extraordinary, " I said, recalling a remark from *Clouds*, in which "fish-loving" was meant to refer to gluttony and Athenian decadence. I quoted it, and it pleased Simonides to no end, perhaps proving to him that I had been listening closely to the play, which he had produced, and that my attention might signify caring.

As he so often did, he then spoiled it. He said, "Did your mother or step mother not make these things for you at home? Of course, Macedonians know nothing of the sea."

I pulled away from him and said, "We ate simply according to my father's wish and belief, not decadently as some Athenians."

Chaerephon thought this was very funny. "He put you in your place, Simonides." He hastened to change the subject. He rarely argued and hated to see others argue, which was not to say that he did like a good discussion. No sooner did someone begin to argue for the sake of arguing than he would begin to fidget, look uncomfortable, or walk away. If he did not know the people he might listen a bit before offering a new line of conversation, but if he knew the person, as he did Simonides, he would interfere directly.

Chaerephon asked, "Was your step-mother kind to you or as terrible as Hera was said to be?"

"In general she was kind to me. She often made dishes she knew I liked, tuna and sea-perch. Mostly when father was away. He did not like her to spoil me. She said I was unusual because I could tell the differences between one fish and another."

Simonides said, "Of course, Amyntas, women serve fish to us for many reasons. It is said that some fish and some fish dishes inflame their husbands when desire wanes...."

"Oh I don't think she was after me, if that is what you mean, Simonides. She also made plain stews for me!"

"Oh, but I meant that if fish were her specialty..."

I could see that he was going to launch into one of his lectures, and my mind wandered. He thought, too self-consciously, that his role was to mentor me. Sometimes this became pedantic. I did learn a good deal from him, and should have been grateful, about the fish the Athenians preferred above all others, and which wines set the palate tingling, and which suited which food perfectly. Some fish indeed were tokens of seduction, and harbor aphrodisiac properties. Eros, after all, gave not just hoops but also fish to boys who enchanted him, and this made the god irresistible to boys and women. Praise Eros! The thought of Simonides coming to see me at Athenades' workshop with a fish made me chuckle to myself. Many things were ascribed to the gods that men could not do without seeming silly. Aspasia knew the ways in which eating could enhance intercourse, and how fish above all the other foods could be best prepared for this purpose.

Simonides said, "Now what are you laughing at?"

"At what you said about my stepmother serving me fish. But are we only to have pheasant and fish?"

"No, of course not. I had a word with the cook earlier and there will also be sow's uterus filled with wild mushrooms and braised thrush; pheasant, and cakes. No one in Athens will eat better tonight."

As we neared the door to the banquet room Mania crossed our path, which I knew to be deliberate, and coyly smiled at me. She was dressed in a myriad of bracelets and bangles for the dance. She would be part of the entertainment.

Simonides said, "There's a little sand-smelt if ever there was one. Be careful, Amyntas, she is after you and shall beat your dog in a thrice if you give her half a wink."

Here is a peculiarity of Simonides' jealousy. Women's

and Mania's attentions did not bother him, but we had many rows over other men and boys' glances. How odd is possessiveness.

I said, "Is she to be the main dancer tonight?"

"No, I am sure there will be others, along with a fine young cithara player from Sicily, more beautiful than Mania they say, and he sings like a dream, though not with as pure a tone as yours. Do you fancy her! I saw you grinning coyly back at her. If you fancy her I am sure it can be arranged."

"I did not grin back at her, coyly or any other way. And how could I fancy her? I hardly know her."

"Hardly? Then you've met?"

Simonides was always too quick, and I said hastily, "She showed me to Aspasia's quarters when I arrived. And she was with Aspasia at *Clouds*."

Chaerephon exclaimed, "Showed you to Aspasia's quarters! That is most unseemly! One of the old women should have accompanied you. My, my! So that is where you were coming from! And I thought you had come early to speak with Socrates."

Simonides and I looked askance at him. What did he know that we did not? I felt rather trapped. I had not wanted to emphasize my conversation with Socrates to Simonides, as much as I had not wanted to mention Simonides to Socrates, and here was Chaerephon referring to my meeting him in the courtyard as if it were prearranged, and of course it was. How odd and exasperating Athens could be. I relented, and said, "I was talking to Aspasia first and only came upon Socrates by accident on my way here."

216

Chaerephon made much of people's interactions. He was very fond of looking for motives. When he drank he also had a loose tongue. He said, "By accident? Did Mania accompany you again?"

"No. Aspasia said I could go alone to find the others."

"Alone? The evening gets stranger by the moment." He turned to Simonides and said, "You said nothing to me, Simonides, about Aspasia seeing him privately first. That's why you said earlier you had an errand to run. It was to bring him here!"

"Yes, I confess it was."

"That is highly unusual. I mean we all know she likes older youths. In fact, we are going to meet her latest Olympian bed-friend tonight if I am not wrong. But she must have taken a fancy to you, Amyntas."

Simonides said, none too happily, "He has many fanciers, this boy."

I said, "She meant to thank me for the gold work I designed for her, that's all. We just talked normally, you know."

Chaerephon said, "My dear boy, there is no such thing as talking normally with Aspasia and talking with her is seldom just about the things you discuss. She saw you at *Clouds* you say? I was sitting with Socrates and did not notice her talking to you. That is very significant. Very. My guess is that she is too much of a diviner not to have been struck by something within you. Perhaps we should ask her? What do you think Simonides? Do you know something that you are not telling me?"

"Only what she told me, that she respected your father, Amyntas, and would meet you, and that you showed talent

217

too. She has kept Pericles' practices alive, of supporting the crafts. That is about all."

Chaerephon said, "No, there is certainly more. We will have to be very circumspect to find out, but if we put our heads together…"

I interrupted, "Oh please don't. Then she'll know I spoke to you about her, and she might be offended. Promise me? Honestly, we only spoke about jewelry making and gold, because of something I said to her at the premiere, that if I knew her I would have made something different. She was curious to know what I meant."

Chaerephon said, "Think how much that remark of yours reveals. Aspasia is very curious about people, you know. It comes from long years of protecting her survival in the house of Pericles, not to mention now in Athens. You must take it as a high compliment too, or else you will miss the opportunity to befriend her in return."

"But I wouldn't presume to think of befriending her!"

Simonides said, "You will soon learn Chaerephon that the most exasperating quality of my darling friend here is his modesty."

I knew he was being ironic but Chaerephon laughed and said, "Oh I disagree. He thinks highly of himself, very highly indeed. Highly enough for … Well, never mind."

Simonides said, "Tell us. You won't offend me. Or him."

But Chaerephon would not. I found out many weeks later that he had meant to add the word 'Socrates" to that prescient sentence. He was not noted for holding his tongue. Perhaps Hermes restrained him.

Simonides said, "We will only say something about you

218

to Aspasia if she brings you up first. Is that agreeable to you?"

I knew this meant that he or Chaerephon would try their best to turn the conversation around to me, but I said, "I was only in her study a few minutes."

Simonides could see I was growing more and more uncomfortable and so changed the subject again, "But Amyntas has not told us what he thinks of this vixen Mania, has he Chaerephon? Perhaps he is cleverer than we think and has thrown Aspasia to us in order to put us off the scent. Come now, little mullet. Will you give her a wink when she dances for you tonight?"

Chaerephon said, "I hear she is quite frenzied and can drain you dry five times a night."

I said, "She's just a silly child. Like a little bird flitting around here and there, chirping this, chirping that, but with an empty head. Besides I would never think of making advances to Mania in Aspasia's house. Macedonians are civilized you know."

Chaerephon said, "And do you prefer fine wine to beer, unlike your countrymen?"

It was said that Macedonians liked beer because they were boorish. I said curtly, "My father makes some of the finest wine anywhere, and sells his best to Aspasia. We might be drinking it tonight."

Chaerephon had a biting tongue, more than any woman I met. He said, "Fine wine is the least of your father's connections with Aspasia."

If it was the peace party to which he referred it was all well and good, but if it referred to the services she provided as a courtesan, it was quite another. I did not want to give him the satisfaction of discussing it.

"I wouldn't know," I said.

6. Aspasia's Banquet.

Musicians led the three of us into the banquet room, as in ritual procession. I had imagined a simple meal and evening, and had been skeptical of Simonides' fussing over my appearance and his endless instructions, ascribing it to the disposition of those humors that exacerbated an already exacerbated character. Perhaps, by Aspasia's standards the evening was simple. We Macedonians did not make such a fuss over our kalos kagathos the way the Athenians did. I had been presented at court with little pomp.

The banquet room was large and square, but not so large as to lack intimacy. The entrance was to the side to allow for the most convenient arrangements of the dining sofas, sometimes pushed back against the wall and raised on a bed of pebbles and cement, or as now, with their heads pointing to the center of the room, permitting more intimate conversation. They were constructed of cedar decorated with silver, covered with Persian throws, and piled with large silk cushions. The floor was of fine tiles, the walls decorated with dolphins and sea scenes, and the ceiling painted as a starry firmament. Erotic statues adorned wall niches; carved tableaus of eating scenes were set into the walls. All the decorations, down to the smallest oil lamp and the cups and bowls, were of a high order.

The arrangement of the seven couches was uncommon, and of some importance that night. Aspasia had deliberately ordered them to be set this way. As I have said, they radiated from a center, in this case a round serving table, but they were pushed together in peculiar groupings, two groups of two, and one group of three, with gaps between the groups to allow the slaves to serve. Aspasia's couch formed the central apex of an arrangement of three, with Aristophanes to her left and Polydamus, her current lover, to her right. The remaining four couches formed two groups. Chaerephon and Simonides were next to each other; Socrates and I, that is, not Simonides and I, formed the last. Although our couches were all close to each other, the groupings were also meant to be distinct, if linked by the round table at their head. Pericles started the practice of having Aspasia at his dinners, and now she had us to hers.

When we were told where to sit I cast a glance at Simonides and saw that he was troubled. He tried to put a brave face on it and came up to me with a cup filled with a fine wine from Lesbos, which we were meant to test and criticize. Simonides advised me not to add water, as this particular wine was delicate and refined. Water in wine was a peculiar habit of Athenians, I pointed out, but not Macedonians. Lesbos was not a far sail from Miletus, Aspasia birthplace. She must have known these wines from an early age, and their growers. I began to see why she might have felt drawn to father, if Chaerephon's insinuation was factual and not cruel; they had a number of common interests. Father had kept his best, Mendaean wines for our own table and guests; they were light and fruity. The one from Lesbos I found too heavy.

As we waited for the others to arrive Simonides explained to me why the room had a marine theme. It was the smallest of her banquet rooms, and she used it only for intimate dining with friends she considered family. To these she also served her best fish dishes. The wine served could also produce the same effect as the sea, leading us into a vast expanse seemingly devoid of direction upon which we felt tossed by the gods. Conversation could do this too, and so the décor was conceived as a backdrop for good conversation. I wondered aloud whether she thought a banquet was more like a stage drama than a dinner. Simonides liked this and said I should ask her, but I never did. I also reflected silently that when talking to Socrates I had felt cast adrift on a deep sea and hoped his inner god would release him in time to dine with us. I wanted to see him again.

Slaves were milling about bringing food platters and wine vessels but we had not reclined yet. Suddenly, with no fanfare, Aspasia entered with her current lover on her arm, Polydamus of Skotoussa in Thessaly, whom Simonides dubbed Polydamus the Tall as he towered above us all. She had changed into a purple dress of finest Amorgas silk fringed with gold in the key motif. Athena was said to weave her own cloth, and this cloth was worthy of Her. She had also donned sandals studded with jewels, the straps threaded through gold buckles. She wore the bracelets I had made, as a gift from Athenades and myself.

She introduced Polydamus. He was still a youth of early beard. He had finished his military service a year or so before, so I supposed he was in his early twenties. He would compete in the boxing, wrestling, and kickboxing categories at the next pankration, and the year before had competed in boxing but had not won a prize. The trainers, and the Athenians who knew about these things, saw in him a bright future, and his life was already lavish with wealth and important friends. He had enormous strength, and many legends would be told of him for years to come, that he wrestled and defeated lions with his bare hands, as did Herakles; and imitated other of the god's feats. To demonstrate his strength and amuse us while we waited for the others to arrive, Aspasia made him dangle two servant girls from each arm, which he did so effortlessly that we were fooled into thinking they were weightless wraiths and not real girls. Or did he manage three from each arm or more if there was room? I do not recall. A few weeks later Socrates made a joke of this feat at the palaistra, but I will tell of that in good time.

Polydamus was very affable, the sort who likes to amuse. He said he would suspend me from his foot while he was suspending the girls but I did not volunteer. He was the pankratiast victor some fifteen years later, as is well recorded, but of his life in between there were certain mysteries. Certainly he accumulated great wealth, as many Olympic athletes did, but it was rumored that Aspasia used him to intimidate owners of precious objects so that they would part with them for her collection. This was impossible to believe. If Polydamus received some of his wealth from Aspasia it was because she was generous with her lovers. Simonides told me that he was much sought after by those courtesans and wives who cultivated Olympic heroes. He was reputed to have great stamina in bed and was a favorite of Aspasia's for several years, and so, I later mused, Aspasia had won the real Olympic prize;

223

well into her fifties.

When the fun subsided a bit, Simonides said, "I have been telling Amyntas about the fish we will be served this evening. "

"And did you tell him of my secret practice?"

"You mean your disguises?"

"Yes," Aspasia said, "Do tell him."

Simonides told the following, "Our dear Aspasia knows the ways of the city better than anyone, Amyntas, and if you need to know about anything going on you need only go to her and she will tell you every detail. But what she does not tell is how she gets this news through a simple ruse. She cleverly disguises herself as a slave woman and goes into the marketplace among the fishmongers pretending she is there to buy things for her mistress. She has mastered her disguises so brilliantly that some of the merchants in the stalls really and truly believe that she is the old hag she pretends to be."

Aspasia said, "I am afraid that I truly am guilty of this disgraceful behavior, Amyntas. If I want the best fish I have to go myself at first light to the Agora, or the Piraeus Road in the shadow of the Long Walls. I simply do not trust anyone else to choose. Of course, the fishmongers have not only the best fish but the freshest gossip and it is sometimes useful to have the first version of it before it is adulterated by repetition."

Aristophanes entered suddenly, unannounced. I thought he would be downcast and somber after the defeat of his play, but he was buoyant. His face and figure were bloated from too much eating and drinking, to celebrate his opening if not his success. I wished Socrates were there. I

224

wondered if there would be enmity between them over his lampooning, and I wanted to see how Socrates would handle it.

He said, "Gossip? What is this about gossip? Are you sharing gossip without waiting for me! How will I write my next play without the latest gossip? And did I hear you speaking about your gift for disguise, Aspasia? Have you told them how hard I have been pressing you to disguise yourself as a man playing the part of a woman in my next comedy, whatever that will be, as I have not conceived it yet, but would certainly include a part especially for you were you to agree. Come now, don't you all think it is an iconoclastic idea worthy of comedy, Aspasia as a man as a woman? Wine! Bring me wine! And tell me the latest, quickly."

I had heard that Aristophanes was a hardy drinker, and he would prove it that evening. Women could not appear on stage, of course, but I thought it a brilliant idea.

Aspasia said, "If you mean is there gossip about you, Aristophanes, there is always something to tell. The fishmongers were giving every detail about your drinking habits and how you were getting yourself into debt with a certain tavern keeper. The rumor has it that you were really writing about yourself in *Clouds*, and your penchant for gambling and debt, not that silly youth what's his name, Pheidippides."

"I hope that they are also saying that I am generous to a fault when I am drunk and treat everyone in the house to drinks, because to get drunk alone is to wallow in misery, but to get drunk in company is to partake in the revels of the gods. But what else are the gossip-mongers saying?

225

That my play should have taken first place?"

Aspasia said, "I am afraid they are silent about that."

"Unspoken gossip is as deadly as spoken. I need a drink."

Perhaps the wine loosened my tongue but I burst out with long pent feeling, "Those judges are completely corrupt for not giving you a first! I thought it was the best by far of the three. The other two were humdrum but yours was the only one with genius."

Chaerephon said, "Well said, Amyntas. Corrupt is certainly the right word for the archon and his ilk."

Simonides interrupted, "The sad truth is that the bribes of others were greater than mine, for which I hold myself responsible dear Aristophanes."

Chaerephon added, "Friends of Cleon out to do you in, I've heard."

Polydamus said, "I have to confess that this whole business of giving awards to plays is terribly flawed and open to corruption. In sports matters are simpler. If you come first you are first, or as in boxing, if you knock out your opponent you win. The standards are clearer, as are the rules."

Simonides responded, "Oh come now, there is corruption as well at the games. Why I've seen some stumble suspiciously not a hair's breath from the finish line. And boxing! Why that is positively rife with fixing."

Polydamus said, "You have been watching too many sports in the provinces. Here in Athens things are more transparent."

Simonides sniffed at that, "Well I wonder."

Chaerephon now exclaimed, "Socrates! There you are!

226

Come and settle this business for us, my friend. I heard you were in one of your reveries and was afraid you would miss Aspasia's banquet entirely. Aspasia, you will have to stop the music now!"

The doorway was behind me and I had not heard Socrates entering, so softly did he tread on bare feet. He did not like music at banquets, and the musicians filed out. I turned to glance at him, expecting him to look dazed or muddled, but he looked rested and alert.

He said, "From what I heard your question was: Which is more corrupt sports or the theater? But is it not more accurate to ask who sponsors both and how corrupt they are? In fact, do not often the same people sponsor both?"

Aristophanes said, "You will tie us up with questions when we are all parched and famished. I say eat and drink first, and philosophize last."

Socrates said, although I think he meant it affectionately, "Can we separate food for the body and food for the soul?"

Aristophanes responded, "Noble sentiments, useless first we faint from hunger. Why look at Amyntas there. He is positively white."

By drawing attention to me he was also drawing attention to the empty space on the couch next to me. Socrates was staring at Aspasia and when I turned to see why I noticed that she nodded subtly to him, and he came to recline near me. No one in the room missed this and I found myself blushing.

There was much laughter; an argument ensuing between Aristophanes and the others over the Athenian and Spartan desire for war, despite the recent truce, a favorite topic of the poet's. I was trying to listen, but was intrigued by the subtle exchanges between Socrates and Aspasia. As he slid onto his couch a slave girl suddenly appeared bearing a silver friendship cup, shared by two, and a vessel of wine. She took the cup from my place and set the friendship cup down between Socrates and me, one cup for us both.

Aspasia raised her cup and gave words of greeting. I did not know what to do until Socrates leaned close and whispered, "I think we are meant to share this cup tonight, Amyntas, if you agree?"

I nodded and said, "I agree."

Socrates again whispered, "I do not drink much but I hear it is a very good wine from Lesbos."

I replied, "I do not drink much either Socrates, so half a cup would be more than enough for us both for the whole evening."

Socrates said, "I toast you. It is your evening."

I glanced around the table, first at Simonides, and saw that he frowned. The sharing of the cup was the completion of the pairing of the couches. So had Aspasia's signs, dreams and oracles dictated, why I did not know.

Aspasia clapped her hands and Mania entered bearing something covered with a silken cloth. She was supposed to play the flute for us, if Socrates allowed. Simonides had coached me about this moment. A boy was "presented" at Athenian banquets, and given a special gift. Mania brought the gift over to me and when I uncovered it found a beautiful silver dish engraved with the image of a boy and inscribed, "Amyntas is beautiful". I also knew that it would say this and was very pleased.

Simonides now spoke, in a gentle manner, and I could see that he was sad, "You see, Aspasia, you have him blushing. He is a modest boy, and has other fine qualities, so yes, he deserves the gift. Let us raise our cups to Amyntas, Prince of the Temenidai."

Aspasia said, "You needn't blush, Amyntas. We are all agreed that your gold work proceeds from inner qualities reflected in outer form, are we not?"

There was general agreement.

I dreaded becoming the center of attention. But Aristophanes saved me from that fate. He was not too interested in boys, and said, "Tell us Socrates. If you have come from communion with your inner voice, has it anything to say about the recent truce with Sparta? And if not, perhaps you will tell us what you think? Will it hold? Will war break out again soon?"

"I did not ask my daimon, but I think I shall live to fight another day."

Indeed, his wish would come true before a year was over.

Chaerephon reached for a wine jar and exclaimed, "Well said Socrates! War honors the gods of Athens, and Athena smiles upon us for waging war in order to defend her city and democracy. Sparta does not share our faith in democracy, nor has it built half the culture we have made for the glory of Athens and our gods. They are barbaric in comparison and the clash is really a clash of two cultures, one civilized and the other barbaric. I pray every day that we prevail. Were we to go down to defeat so would all our values of the good and beautiful. I for one would lay down my life for Athens, Athena, and our democracy, even if you would not Aristophanes."

Aristophanes had served his military service and could have disputed Chaerephon about this, but he merely leaned over and poured more wine into Chaerephon's cup.

The truce with Sparta had only been signed some two or three months before. A great sigh of relief had gone up in the Agora. It was one respite of many in what was beginning to seem an interminable war with Sparta, in that year already some ten years old and destined to last twice that. Yet each time there was a truce, irrational fears of a Spartan betrayal, or in Sparta of an Athenian plot, would surge through the people like brush fires on the slopes of the nearby mountains. Athenians had learned through experience that hopes for a permanent peace were short lived. New battles were strung like rubies around the neck of time: Potidaea and Boetia, where Socrates had fought, Sybota, the Spartan invasion of Attica, that had brought its forces within a spear-throw of Athens, and all those before and after too numerous to mention. Did they not all serve the same purpose? Was not this war, Aristophanes wondered, draining Athens of its youth and resources in order to serve the vainglory of arrogant men?

Aristophanes ended, "My prayer, my good friend Chaerephon, is that our gods bestow wisdom, and show us options for war. War enervates Athens and will be our ruin. Protection of our values is all well and good, so long as there are youths to be honorable and good. But war is the attrition of our best youth and so it is an attrition of virtue. In the old days we excelled at diplomacy and our ability to reason was an example for others. But now all is war, war, war, and more war. I am tired of the bloodletting.

This war will end badly, as do all wars no matter the victor. It is draining our best energies, consumed in the fires of rage towards a perpetual enemy."

Chaerephon said, "But surely, Aristophanes, Sparta raids our lands, torches our crops, and spreads terror. War against terror is surely honorable and just?"

He replied, "That is unending, and unending war is the tool of tyrants. It has no virtue."

But Chaerephon replied, "This war is a mimesis of the old heroes and their heroic deeds. It does honor to the gods and to us all."

"It is our secret enslavement to death and the dark mysteries hidden from view and poisonous to life."

But Chaerephon would not have it, because this view would have made soldiers slaves of death and Athenian soldiers were free men, in the law, and in their souls.

Aspasia spoke up, "This time around the Spartans seem to want the peace more than we, and that bodes well for it lasting. At least that is the word we received from our ambassadors. The Spartans have thrown down a challenge to their citizens, that if anyone thinks the terms of this truce are unfair they should let their views be heard. Perhaps we would do well to invite the same here."

Chaerephon said, "Is this propaganda, or a rumor spread by the invidious Alcibiades? Can any good come from Sparta?"

Aristophanes replied, "The Spartans are making the point that this truce is a just truce and advantageous to them. If anyone disagrees then they can speak up, but no one has. Perhaps we have not had enough debate in Athens to decide whether it is equally advantageous to us? There

231

are those among us who have every hope that this will be the permanent peace we have all awaited."

Chaerephon said, "According to the terms it is only for one year, and at that, a very shaky year."

Aristophanes said, "Powerful forces are aligning to make it last, here and there."

Socrates said, softly, as he often did when posing a disagreement, "I am afraid that you have been so preoccupied with your production, Aristophanes, that you must not have heard the news. The Phocians and Boeotians are already challenging the truce."

"What is the latest? Those idiots."

The Boeotians and Phocians controlled the land routes to Delphi and the north. I was hoping to make a pilgrimage to Delphi, to the Temple of Apollo in order to pay homage to my favorite god. But if there were the slightest hint of danger father would never give his permission. Socrates' response confirmed my worst fears.

He said, "The Boeotians are threatening to block the land routes."

Aristophanes replied, "To show they still have power? That is exactly the kind of vice and childishness that war brings out in men. In fact, I am better informed that you think, Socrates. I too have heard that there our delegation is in Boeotia now discussing it, and if it is handled well and with wisdom the way to Delphi should be clear for some time to come. But I take your point too. This truce is shaky at best. We need to find more permanent means to establish peace. If we do not, any truce is bound to fail. Powerful forces in Sparta and Athens want perpetual war. It will be a struggle."

Chaerephon asked, "Are you a realist or a cynic, Aristophanes?"

Aristophanes replied, "Well, look at the facts. After all these battles the terms we negotiate are never meant to end war, but only bring that battle to a close. To end war itself, it will take much more. We should have had enough of war and yet, the terms of this truce only show that we wish a respite before going back to the slaughter again. Why yesterday, in the Agora, I heard countless discussions about replenishing the fleet. Just walk by any of the forges. They are working overtime churning out new weapons. The lust for battle is sometimes weak and sometimes strong but it is never banished from our soul. It makes the peace, any peace unstable."

I groaned aloud without realizing and suddenly attention was upon me. Aspasia said, "Well, Amyntas, Aristophanes makes you groan? Is it with agreement or disagreement?"

"It's just that I had wanted to make a pilgrimage to Delphi, and if the truce is unstable my father would never permit it, nor Athenades."

Simonides suddenly leaned over and said quietly, so the others could not hear, "If the gods will it and you are so disposed I would be honored to accompany you there."

I glanced around the room to see if others had heard, but they were going about their drinking. The meat course was being served. Large platters were being placed on the table, the one in front of me heaped with uterus and spiced lamb.

Polydamus said crudely, "I'm surprised you're feeding the boy lamb, Aspasia. I would have thought you would

233

have chosen choiros instead." This was a very crude pun on the word for "pig" and women's parts. He had a certain directness and naivety that I came to appreciate. "Do you not fancy a taste of that my boy? Or a large feast?"

The others laughed, while I grew red, from the sudden attention if not the allusion. I glanced over at Aspasia, to see if she were impatient with his remark. Her hand was on his strong thigh and she was looking at him fondly. He did not hold his wine well and was rather drunk after only a cup or two. She signaled a slave girl to pour him more. In fact, his remark led to a misunderstanding on my part, concerning Mania's designs.

I was trying to think of something witty to say, but the room was filled with music, dancing and loud conversation. It had grown warm because of the closeness, and I felt a bit dizzy too. Because I was silent while the others spoke, I was the first to realize that not all the commotion was coming form the dining room. At first I thought that a quarrel had broken out among the servants, which would have brought disgrace upon Aspasia. I turned my head towards the door to listen, and Aspasia was the next to notice this, and suddenly was calling everyone to silence. Indeed, as I turned to look, her household guards rushed past the doorway and I heard women screaming. "Thief! Thief! Intruders! Intruders!" There was more screaming, more rushing and suddenly Aspasia leapt from her place and rushed to the doorway to issue commands. She turned back and shouted to Polydamus, "The boy! Polydamus! Quickly now!" Before I could blink Polydamus had seized me around the waist as if I were a sack of rose petals and was carrying me out of the room, running with me down a long corridor and into a distant room. He set me down.

"What on earth?" I said breathlessly. "What is happening?"

"Probably nothing. You stay here, little man, and let me see. Do not show yourself."

Confusion seemed to reign but I managed to piece together some words from some speakers, one rough male voice especially rising above the others. "Bring him out! The traitor! Let him come out and fight! Traitors! Traitors all! Mincing peace girls! False philosophers! Heretic! Let him come too and take his due!" I paced the room impatiently, but it was several long minutes before Polydamus returned.

He smiled at me, "Well, it is nothing really, certainly nothing for you to worry about. Just that old fool Cleon and some of his cronies showing up drunk at the door to bait Aristophanes and Socrates is all. Aspasia wants you to stay here a bit until it all calms down and she decides whether you should be taken home or stay here the night. Of course Simonides is incensed and wants to take you home right away, but we are afraid that the drunken fools might linger in the street nearby for a good part of the night."

"What will happen now?"

"I am afraid Aspasia will have to put an end to your banquet. She is seeing if that old chaperone of yours Leagros is sober or awake. He would not be much in a fight though, drunk or sober, even against that old fart Cleon. Of course I would be happy to see you home, lad. I can slip you a knife and we could handle ourselves well, I

235

warrant."

The evening had hardly begun, and I wanted it to go on until dawn, but there was still much shouting and confusion and it took many more minutes for it all to calm down. Polydamus stayed with me, which I appreciated, although I made a show of saying that he should be at Aspasia's side protecting her.

Aspasia came to find me, full of apologies for something not her fault. She said what I had already surmised, that drunken Cleon and his cronies had come to pick a fight with Aristophanes. They had drifted off now. The streets seemed quiet but I had best stay the night. Would that all of Athens had been there to see his drunken stupidity. If they knew what a sot he was the Assembly would not have listened to him so eagerly, as it later did.

***

Aspasia herself and an elderly slave woman brought me to a comfortable room looking onto the walled garden garden, to remind me of Macedon and give me peace from turmoil. I assured her I had liked the excitement. She left a lamp burning on a small table near the door and said that a guard would be close at hand should I need anything.

Aspasia was not gone for many minutes, and I was already settled in bed and half asleep, when a scratching at the door frightened me. I was ready to cry out when Mania slipped through the door. She put her finger to her lips and came to the bed. Her dress was made from thin Amorgos cloth, so thin as to reveal all the allurements beneath, yet cover them too.

I whispered too, drawing myself into her plot, "What are you doing here?"

"I came to see if you are all right?"

"What do you mean? Of course I am all right."

"Lady Aspasia was so worried about you."

"She needn't be worried. I am fine and you had better go."

"Go? Really? Do you really want me to go?"

She sat down on the edge of the bed and slid her hand under the coverlet. She said boldly, "You see. You are glad to see me. I have also brought you sesame cakes as a treat." She planted a kiss on my lips; wrapped her hand around me; and what a skillful hand it was.

I said, shakily, "You must not. I would not want to offend lady Aspasia. I am a guest in her house."

"Oh come now, you silly boy, do you think anything happens in her household without her knowing it? And I made the cakes just for you."

"I am not a silly boy."

"Then prove it."

I was filled with too much fine wine, good food, and delicious sesame cakes to resist in more than a token way, and indeed acquitted myself three times that night, driven by her extravagant versatility. But it was to be pleasure steeped in consequences.

If the night were not odd enough, one more oddity visited me in dream, in fact, the first dream I had of Socrates.

I dreamt that I lay sleeping, that is, a sleep within a sleep. I awakened in the dream but did not actually awaken, to find Socrates standing by the bed. He said,

"Awaken." I suddenly truly awakened. Mania was curled asleep next to me, the household quiet. Morning birds had not yet begun to sing so it was well before dawn. A deep, tangible peace filled the room, and me. I prayed to Apollo for Socrates.

IV. My Life in Athens: War to Peace.

1. 423 B.C. A warning.

After the banquet at Aspasia's I was eager to return to her house, but my life was too filled with responsibilities for this to be easy. I was also a little afraid. Her command of politics, logic, magic, and divination awed me. But fantasies of Mania threatened to betray me at work or school, in fact, at any time of day or night. And there was the curious matter of the friendship cup Aspasia had set between Socrates and me, and what that might bode for my relationship with Simonides. I hesitated to ask Simonides about the evening. It had not gone the way he would have wanted. How could I possibly expect him to arrange another meeting with Aspasia when she seemed to be signaling another course? My life was so work-centered and routine that Cleon's intrusion was welcome excitement. I had liked the way Polydamus had swept me off to safety like a bag of feathers. Yet, surely Aspasia, or Simonides, would report the intrusion to Athenades. Would he in turn inform father, and if he did would it have consequences for my stay in Athens? Whereas prior to the banquet I had felt homesick, afterwards I would be struck unawares with panic, that I would be forced to leave Athens when, I reckoned, my life there had hardly begun. I wrestled with so many questions and doubts. Was Mania eager to see me again? Did the friendship cup augur a god-ordained friendship with Socrates? Was his inner voice Apollo? His voice intrigued me, but it did not intimidate me as it did others, especially if it could help me sort myself out. For weeks afterwards I felt as tempestuous as a storm-tossed sea, and the days did not pass quietly into summer.

As a matter of fact, it was some time before Athenades took me aside to talk with me about Cleon and the dinner, so many days in fact that I had nearly forgotten about it. The delay might have been because, right after the banquet, Leagros informed me, Aspasia had taken advantage of the good sailing season to make her annual voyage to Miletus, with full retinue. Before work one day Athenades asked me if I wanted to go up to the Temple of Herakles to assess some damaged statues we had been hired to gild and retouch, and to pray with him. This must have been just after the Herakleia in August because I remember him berating the citizenry for their "impious carelessness" during the sacred festival. No sooner were we clear of the shop than he said he wanted to discuss the Cleon incident with me. He looked angry and all my dread boiled to the surface. Had Aspasia sent him word from Miletus? I doubted that. Had Simonides told him? I did not think so. It was more likely one of his spies in the war camp of Cleon who told him; or Leagros for one of his complicated reasons, or loose-mouthed Chaerephon.

"I heard about what happened that night," he said. "I am angry with you for not telling me yourself. You should have come to me immediately. I suppose you liked all the excitement, but what am I to tell your father?"

"Does he need to know?"

"Of course he needs to know."

"Why is that?"

"He shall hear whether I tell him or not. Don't you know that? Are you being impertinent?"

Indeed, I was not being impertinent. I was fighting for my right to stay and was determined. I said forcefully. "No, Master Athenades. I did not tell you because I did not think it was worth telling. After all, everyone thought it was just a bunch of drunken men acting foolishly. Besides neither Cleon nor any of the other intruders knew I was there."

"Yes, well, that is what we are trying to find out now, isn't it? Cleon was not alone and we have to be certain of everyone's intent. At the moment it just looks like drunkenness and nothing more."

"That is what Aspasia herself told me."

His ire boiled over. "Aspasia! She should have told me about this before she set off. She really should have told me! And been more mindful of your security. We should all have been more mindful. I am inclined not to have you go there again, at least until the whole matter is sorted out. Arrangements will have to be made if she does invite you again."

"Arrangements? But Master! I mean no disrespect, but there are her commissions to consider for the autumn festivals. I may have to go to her house for fittings as soon as she returns."

"I'm well aware of that. It's a big mess."

"But I don't understand. Why is it such a big mess?"

He was still very angry and said, "Do you really mean that I have to explain this to you? Cleon and his cronies hate the truce and are already plotting to overturn it. They have a vested interest in making sure the arms makers and merchants are kept busy."

I protested, "But I know this. I knew it all along. But

surely Cleon was just trying to bait Aristophanes that night? That is all any of us thought it was."

"Well, answer this. What if Cleon did know you were there, as he surely must? Do you think that he is unaware of your father's interest in the peace, or his influence in Macedon? And are you not your father's son? Do you wish to disown that?"

"Please do not say such things. You know I would never disown father, or Macedon."

"So?"

I was crestfallen, seeing my chance to return to Aspasia's evaporating before my eyes before it had had materialized again. I said, "I doubt if Cleon was at Aspasia's door because of me. I respect what you are saying, but I really cannot believe he would care what a boy thought one way or the other."

"I do not think he cares one jot about you or what you think, but he may have meant to send a message back to your father's faction in Macedon. That is exactly the matter we have to ponder. I am responsible for you, after all."

I said sullenly, "Polydamus would have defended me."

"It should not have been necessary. None of it should have been necessary."

I was still defending my freedom, and replied angrily, "Well it was and there is no use exaggerating it, least of all in upsetting father too."

But all he would say was "You are very impertinent. Very."

The rest of that day I worked morosely and silently at my table, hardly daring to look up when some customer or delivery boy would enter. If Athenades made good his promise to inform my father I feared that father would want me to return home, or worse, hide me away among the falcon breeders in the Sicilian mountains. Yet, the more I thought about it, the more I wondered why Athenades was as angry as he was. There seemed something else behind it. He had seldom showed us his anger, having left that first to the terrible Plator, and then to the new overseer. Indeed he was even-tempered most of the time. Not for the first time, and not for the last, I found people's behavior inexplicable and half wished that Simonides would appear at the door and whisk me away for the day to the countryside, as he had been promising to do.

Reassurance came from where I least expected it. Later in the day Leagros found me sitting by myself in one of the courtyards making drawings of designs for the autumnal corn feast of Demeter, the Eleusinian. He said, "You have looked quite upset all day. Has that pompous son-in-law of mine been blowing things out of proportion again?"

I felt relieved by his question and smiled sheepishly. He was grinning back at me as he might at a co-conspirator, which was not far from the truth. That evening at Aspasia's he had lain drunken and had never roused. I asserted, "He means to inform father about that night. Father panics when it comes to my safety and I fear he shall send me away from Athens."

"I doubt that wastrel son-in-law of mine will do that. It is not in his own best interest to lose his best designer right now, is it? At least, not until he finds out exactly what

243

went on and who was at the door with that rapscallion Cleon."

"What do you think happened?"

"More than a bunch of drunken louts, that is for sure. But whether it has anything to do with you is quite another matter. Cleon and his ilk like to see traitors everywhere you know, and anyone mentioning the word peace is considered a traitor to them. The city has been fomenting since the defeat at Delium. Aristophanes, and a few others think there is an opportunity for permanent peace with Sparta, but those around Cleon want more war in the name of full security, and revenge. The two sides are always at loggerheads. I heard that some of the people with Cleon were cousins or nephews of the fallen General Hippocrates." He came closer, so as not to be overheard, "Let me tell you something else. That son-in-law of mine is more inclined to peace and supporting the fledgling peace party than he makes out publicly, or would want anyone to know. He's afraid he'll lose business, you see, but let's just say there's more money passing between the Athenian and Spartan peace factions than can be explained by lofty ideals."

I said, "I will tell no one." Leagros was not known for his veracity, and I only half believed what he said about Athenades. I added, "I don't understand one thing Leagros. How could Cleon know of the banquet? It seems strange his appearing at the door like that." I hoped he would not answer Simonides, but feared he might, knowing what a gossip Simonides could be. That would complicate matters the further between us. His answer surprised me.

"My guess is Chaerephon. Rest assured, we shall find out."

"You don't think it was someone else then?"

"Chaerephon is the best guess. He's been bragging in the barbershop about his connections. It would be just like him. But it will all come out. Things in Athens do not stay hidden for long." I knew that already. "Anyway, I can see that the excitement did not exactly put you off. "

"No, not exactly. You missed it though. You could have joined us." Despite his being my chaperone, as a freeman Aspasia had invited him, but he had declined and I now found out the real reason. He had pleaded tiredness and age, but that was not it at all.

He whispered conspiratorially, no doubt needing to draw me into his own plans for when he was out and about with me, "Aspasia's chief cook is very generous with me, not too mention she is very ample, which I like in a woman. Besides offering me certain privileges shall we say, she also tells me everything that is going on, and serves me the best wine and the tastiest morsels of fish. It was like having my own private banquet, with fringe benefits." Now Leagros was a most unlikely lover, I thought. He was in his mid-seventies, a bit toothless, bald, and with blotchy skin from a bad liver. His ears were hairy and the backs of his hands scaly. I was amused by his lust for life. He added, "I had my own party the whole night, and more treats at breakfast. You will keep this between us of course?"

"Don't worry about that." Athenades would have found me another chaperone in a flash if he knew all that was going on that night.

"I see that our arrangement suits us both then?"

"Yes."

"You are not to be underestimated, I see. They've talking about you in the kitchen, you know."

"About me?"

"Yes. Mania had her heart set on seducing you for weeks after seeing you at the Dionysia. The cook told me they were laying bets on her long before, well, she succeeded most grandly, from what I've heard. Well done my boy! I could arrange a few more trysts if you like, as a return favor for your discretion?"

I was not sure I liked being wagered over and said, "Te tell you the truth, something bothers me about this Mania thing."

"Now what is that? You did not finish too quickly did you?"

"No, no, I held my own. It's just that she said that nothing goes on in Aspasia's household without her knowing about it, but Mania seems to me capable of saying anything in order to get her way. I am not sure she was telling the truth. Or, rather, she may have been telling her truth and Aspasia might not know. I have enormous respect for Aspasia and would not want to defile her hospitality or be defiled."

"Well, all of that sounds just a bit too high-minded, if you don't mind my saying so. But before you go off getting offended, I think I can find out for you what Aspasia knows or does not know. "

"From your cook?"

"And other sources in her household too. Leave it up to me, will you. I do respect what you are saying; you want

246

Mania, but you do not want her to be an occasion of defilement, and so offend Aspasia. Seems clear enough. I am sure you can have both."

I said morosely, "All of this might be moot. Athenades may never allow me to go to Aspasia's again, and if he informs father I may be in some remote outpost in a month's time. What if he sends me to Cyropolis!"

"Don't be so fatalistic. Don't you want to go to Aspasia's again?"

"Of course I do. It would be more important to me than just about anything. If you could arrange that you would have my true gratitude."

"And Socrates?"

His question seemed to come from nowhere, although it was calculated, and surprised me. "Socrates?"

"Come now, I heard about the friendship cup. What Aspasia did was very odd. Putting you and that old goat Socrates together like that. After all, Simonides has broadcast his love affair with you all over Athens and what does Aspasia do, she places the friendship cup between you and Socrates! There were certainly things said about that in the kitchen. It is another reason for you to be having Mania, by the way. She'll keep you informed, while you perform."

It irritated me to be the source of so much speculation, and worried too that it would further complicate my stay in Athens. I said sharply, "Are the kitchen slaves placing wagers about Socrates and me too? Or about me and Simonides?"

"Of course they are. Don't be so thin-skinned. Simonides or Socrates, Socrates or Simonides? The odds as of yesterday were very much on Socrates. So it would seem Aspasia thinks too. She is a formidable diviner, probably the best in Hellas, and she seems to have had some sign of a friendship between you and Socrates. That may prove of greater significance than any desire Simonides might throw your way. Otherwise she would not have so openly arranged the seating and cup as she did."

"Is that what the cook said? I would not presume to know Aspasia's intentions, at least not until she makes them known to me herself."

"Yes, yes. Aspasia sees things in the future, you know. Don't you fancy Socrates? They say you do."

"I hardly know Socrates. I had one conversation with him. And a friendship might prove difficult. Athenades does not seem to approve of him. At least I think he doesn't from some hints he's dropped. So there would be obstacles."

"Well you are a smart one to pick up on Athenades' ambivalence towards Socrates. My pious son-in-law has doubts about Socrates' voice, but he agrees that it is divine and does not close his mind entirely. And none other than the Delphic oracle has declared Socrates the wisest man anywhere, which he accepts. It is the contradiction of his piety, you see. On the one hand Socrates' voice is something he himself does not experience and cannot worship, yet if it is a god speaking through Socrates, then he feels that he should not close his mind to the voice either. But as for Aspasia, if she has seen something about you and Socrates written by the gods across the stars then what my son thinks or does not think does not matter one jot, not if it is written. Do you want another meeting with Socrates?"

I said. "If Aspasia has seen something then the fates are arranging it already."

Leagros said, "Perhaps. Rest assured, Aspasia will arrange it. I'll tell you this time, but next time you will have to figure this sort of thing out for yourself. Do nothing and Aspasia will summon you. Mania or Socrates may be another matter, but Aspasia is special. You must wait patiently. I could have lied and taken the credit when she sent another invitation, but let's just say that this advice is payment in kind. The things hovering around you intrigue Aspasia. She senses that the gods have intentions for you. No, my boy, she will summon you again upon her return from Miletus, and sooner rather than later."

"I hope you are right."

"And one more thing. Cleon may not have been much of a danger for you that evening, but there are dangers for you in Athens and you yourself must give more thought to your own safety. Cultivate allies Amyntas; cultivate allies. A great deal will depend on it, your future livelihood for sure, but your safety too."

I said, "I too have a question."

I knew that Simonides' was at best apolitical, but when pressed declared loyalty to Athens. He had served his military duty at a time when there were no battles, and had not been tested in war. He did not consider himself above political matters, but simply did not give them much thought. It was Socrates who confused me.

Leagros replied, "Well then"

"Simonides I understand. But Socrates I am not sure of.

Harsh things were called against him that night. Cleon shouted traitor and heretic."

Leagros said, "Oh Socrates! There is no love lost between Cleon and him, or should I say between him and Socrates' friends, especially Aspasia, whom Cleon hates almost as much as Aristophanes, if not more. Cleon would judge Socrates by his friends, and if that is the case then Cleon and his loyalists have many grievances against Socrates." He added, "Socrates' friends may get him into trouble sooner or later, but I doubt you will be one of them, Amyntas, if that is what you are worried about?"

It was not what worried me, but I did not say this.

2. False friends.

Simonides did not come into the shop again for a month or two. They said he had gone upcountry to Corinth to read at the festivals, but I wondered if he were not taking time to think us over. Nor had I heard from him since Aspasia's dinner. He was very sensitive and I was apprehensive that Aspasia's flagrant pairing of me with Socrates had made him angry or depressed. The least criticism of any aspect of his poetry would send him flying into self-doubt.

He came to the shop that day ostensibly to talk about their forthcoming theater tour. Aristophanes was already revising *Clouds*. If he could finish a new version in time, they were thinking of trying it out in the provinces, they hoped with better success. They never did and the revision remains in book form to this day. Some of the finer decorations that they had used in the Dionysia Simonides wanted to store in the guarded cave at Athenades' country

250

villa; they would only need meaner objects for the tour. Simonides had mentioned my joining the troupe at Corinth, but I had not taken it seriously. I noticed that several times he whispered something to Athenades. I still imagined that everything centered on me, and felt sure that the whispering was about the tour. It would prove to be about me but not about the tour.

Soon after they left, without Simonides having approached me, Leagros came to tell me that we would leave a little early for my classes at the Lyceum. He had errands to run. But as we neared the corner of the Agora he nudged me and I turned to see Simonides' most trusted slave following us. He approached politely and said that Simonides was waiting by the Stoa, apparently with Leagros' collusion. I steeled myself for an argument. We had agreed that he would never walk me to school although he wanted to every day. I did not feel like being teased that day by my classmates. Yet when I saw his face light up with pleasure as I approached, relief swept over me. How complicated my feelings were for him. With Eshe and Alexis they have always been simpler, and perhaps truer, so simplicity might be the better indication of lasting love than complexity. Riddled with youthful insecurities, I longed for reassurance, and knew Simonides would give it.

He had brought me gifts as he always did, but simple ones. Boys were sporting a new sort of flaxen, draw string school bag that season, to hold their writing implements and snacks, with a thick band sewn into the seams so it could be slung over the shoulder; I did not have one. It was a very inexpensive object, and better for it. It felt

251

heavy and when I looked inside there were some of my favorite date cakes, and an orange. We had argued so often over his showering me with expensive things that I saw in these simple gifts genuine effort.

He noticed that I was glad to see him, smiled affectionately and said, "Amyntas, I had heard that you were worried about the incident at Aspasia's." Had he heard it from Athenades or Leagros, I wondered? "I know you do not like me to walk you to school, but I thought I had better talk to you about it so arranged to meet you early." Was this the new Simonides, chastened by Aspasia's signs? "I also wanted you to know that Athenades told me that he was considering sending a letter to your father about the other night, but I told him it was nothing and urged him not to. You saw us whispering?"

"Yes. But did he believe you and agree?"

"I think so. Besides, you are his most valuable designer, and he would not want to lose you."

"That is what Leagros says." I turned to have Leagros confirm this, but he was some feet away to give us privacy. All of it must surely have been planned between them. We were just below the new Stoa. They were already calling it the best place in Athens to talk, which said something because there were so many. Hellenes liked to talk, but they also liked to sing as they walked, especially out in the countryside. We proceeded along the busy street, keeping our voices low.

Simonides said, "Actually, I have some news about the intruders and thought that we could stop at the Stoa so I could fill you in, and have a bite together. I brought some special foods for you. You don't eat enough these days and are looking a little thin. I promise to have you on time for your first lesson."

It was a fine day with a little wind dispersing the sickening smells of refuse ripening in the hot sun. The Stoa of Zeus Provider had already become one of the most popular meeting places in the city, near the Herms and the Altar of the Twelve Gods, and within a stone's throw of the best food stalls. It was just to the northwest of the main road junctions and was built in the style of the Propylaia on the Acropolis, with that attention to harmony that so characterizes Athenian buildings. A saying later became popular in Athens, "to meet at the Stoa", meaning to discuss politics because it was built to commemorate the victory over the Persians and was dedicated to Zeus as deliverer of democracy and preserver of freedom. His statue stood in front at the middle. There had been a great feast to unveil and dedicate it, but this was before my arrival. The subject of the mural in the central section was also political; it depicted King Theseus, son of Poseidon, slaying the Minotaur; he was called the founder of Athenian democracy and was the first to unify Attica. The murals were fresh and suffused the colonnade with color.

The Stoa was still under construction and we paused to watch the workers moving large stone slabs along log rollers. The central portion and the colonnade were finished but the north and south wings were not. Simonides had sent some servants ahead to secure a place for us to sit and talk quietly, just off the middle but within sight of the murals. We could look out onto the city from there. Sounds of bustle and braying animals filled the air around us.

253

Simonides said, "The city is filled for summer already. I don't like it when it is so crowded and look forward to the march up country, despite the danger from brigands. Verse comes easily to me on the country road."

I thought he might be trying to entice me to join him again and said cautiously, "Your departure is approaching quickly."

"We won't leave until after the Greater Eleusinian so there are some weeks yet. I am reading my own hymns during the festival you know."

"Are they finished then?"

"No. I have only drafted them. In fact, I brought them with me. If you will indulge me I could read some excerpts, but it is not why I wanted to talk to you."

He meant to cajole me into joining the tour, or he meant to discuss our friendship, I thought, neither welcome topics. I said, "I am not sure there will be time to hear your poems. I don't want to be late for grammar or I shall be punished, have to stay late or run laps, and miss my evening meal. Besides I have decided not to go on the tour with you. My father would never think it safe enough, especially if Athenades gives him the least hint of trouble. I simply do not want to ask father. I am sorry, Simonides."

"I had reconciled myself to that already. It is not what I have to say. I saw Aspasia yesterday. She is just back, you know. In fact, I am rather angry with her. I think she was too casual with your security and I hope that she never makes the same mistake again. Her spies have been busy."

I doubted whether he was really angry with Aspasia, and said, "That is a harsh thing to say of her. I was never in any danger. Polydamus carried me off like a sack of

254

feathers while the intruders were still at the door. He's as strong as three gods. It made me feel like a little infant though. In fact, I wish she had allowed me to stay. Cleon and his bunch never got past the door. But I liked the drama. What do her spies report?"

"I am sure you liked the drama! But anyway, Aspasia had her spies frequent a certain bar known to be the haunt of some of Cleon's cronies. Well, the story is quite simple, in fact. You see, one night a few weeks ago, that is just a night or two before your banquet, Chaerephon was drinking in the same bar. With the right prompting and a few too many, he started bragging about the banquet he was attending for a certain kalos kagathos, and the whole plan for the evening spilled out, including the guest list. The very night of the banquet Cleon was in the bar boasting how he and his cronies would disrupt a certain you know what party and teach Aristophanes and his ilk a lesson or two. They were very merry by the time they left, and bought several jugs of wine to take along with them on the walk to Aspasia's, so heaven knows how much they had had to drink by the time they reached there. Well, that is the whole story. It was really all the fault of that blabbermouth Chaerephon, and had nothing to do with you, except perhaps make you a poor darling victim of circumstance and on your special night. Anyway, I wanted to be the bearer of good news."

"But Simonides, this is wonderful. Will Aspasia write this to my father, do you think?"

"If need be, she said she will. And the best thing for you to do is forget the whole matter and get on with things."

"Oh Simonides! What a relief! It means that father will not send me away!"

"Yes. I wanted you to know."

I was so overcome that I threw my arms around him, as he must have hoped.

He patted me comfortingly and said, "There there. Still I would have Aspasia protect you better, though it goes without saying. Apparently Cleon's intrusion was preordained, so it would not have mattered how many guards Aspasia had posted. But I am sure she will tell you all of this herself. She wants to prepare new charts for you but she needs you there to do it. Look for an invitation soon."

"Cleon has hatred in his heart. I could sense it in his shouting."

"Of course he does. Does it surprise you?"

I had not dared to bring up Socrates but now thought that I would. I said tentatively, "Perhaps not against Aristophanes, but against Socrates?"

Simonides said, perhaps too bitterly, "That inner voice of his. It reeks of false gods for some of us. If he were to name it, well, it might put the whole matter to rest."

His "us" made me angry, sad, and wary. I had stirred his jealousy, and more, I realized. I said, "If the god has not told Socrates its name he cannot simply name it himself. It would be arrogant, and wrong. There must be some purpose behind his voice not naming itself. If he has not told us its name than the God has not told him. And if the God has not told him then the God has a purpose."

He looked askance at me, and said, "Did he tell you that? I myself find it hard to believe, as does half or more of Athens. Every god wants devotees and a god that wants none seems strange indeed. Have you ever heard of a god that did not want a shrine? Come now. Of course, that is also not Cleon's chief complaint against Socrates." Staring over my shoulder he muttered sarcastically, "Friends, his friends, if they are his friends."

His tongue could be serpentine. I wanted to ask him what he meant but did not dare pursue it. I turned to see what he was looking at over my shoulder, and saw that Leagros had made his way over to a group of men who were looking in our direction. One of the strangers broke off from the group and began to approach with Leagros. He was in his late twenties, I thought, and strikingly handsome, lithe and compactly built, like Polydamus, although not quite as tall. His hair was aristocratically long, his carefully trimmed beard light brown. He had striking, pale blue eyes, restless, sharp, and intrusive. His hands were long and more restless than his darting eyes.

***

The stranger said, "Simonides! I thought it was you sitting there in the shade with your friend. Enjoying the new Stoa are you? It seems as if everyone is heading here these days."

"Well, well. Alcibiades. You are right. They are already saying that if you sit here long enough you will see everyone you know and here you are. Will you join us?"

"If I am not interrupting? In fact, I was on my way to see you when I spotted you from below. I heard you might be walking your friend to school today."

257

Simonides said, "Village Athens. Our friend Chaerephon or Leagros over there should have been town criers."

"Yes, everyone knows everything in Athens."

"Not quite. I had heard you were at your family's villa, still resting from the battle at Delium, but I had not heard you were back in the city. If I had known you were back I would have invited you to dine. When did you return? Surely after Aspasia's dinner or you would have been there. Come sit. We have some refreshments. Have you met Amyntas?"

"No, I have not but I have heard much about you, young man, and thought it might be you from Aspasia's description."

Alcibiades had known Aspasia since childhood. Pericles became his guardian after his father Cleinias died, and so he lived for a time in Pericles' household when Aspasia was already mistress there. Alcibiades' mother was Pericles' cousin, and she belonged to his house, the controversial House of the Alcmaeonidae. There were rumors that Alcibiades and Aspasia had an affair when he was seventeen or so, but half the rumors about Alcibiades were of sexual escapades, and exaggerated. The others, of his political intrigues, were mostly true. He divided his time between scheming about war, and the pursuit of physical pleasures. He was a great beauty in his youth, some said the greatest there ever was in Hellas, and was still very handsome.

He counted Socrates as his friend, and stories were rife of his unsuccessful attempts to seduce Socrates. This much I knew from Simonides.

I said, "I hope what you heard was good?"

"The reports were glowing. And if anything, Aspasia was too restrained."

We made a place for him between us.

Simonides said, "Amyntas does not have much time before his classes start. We don't want him having to run a hundred laps because of us, now, do we?"

Alcibiades said, "Then we shall walk him! That is the solution. If you do not mind, Amyntas?"

Simonides' answer surprised me. He was very protective of me around other men. He said, "You two go along together. I have other things to do." As I was to learn later on, he loathed Alcibiades and avoided his company. Simonides could not know this but I had for some reason taken an instant dislike to Alcibiades, one of the few instances in my life of dislike at first sight.

Simonides added, "Then you've seen Aspasia since getting back, and have heard about the Cleon episode?"

"I was at her house a night or two ago, and heard the whole story from her."

But the sundial clock near us told me that it was time to leave. I called to Leagros, at the side drinking already, and thanked Simonides again for his simple gifts. As Alcibiades and I set out from the Stoa to the turn off for the road to the Lyceum grounds it was clear from the smiles, waves, and greetings of those we passed that Alcibiades was held in high esteem. Yet, there were many smirks, his latest exploits in and out of bed being the subject of much gossip in the Agora barbershops. His Eros was mischievous, Simonides said to me later; it could also be malevolent. During the walk, he revealed another connection to Aspasia, which would surprise me.

Alcibiades was saying, "Well, and what did you think of the hubbub the other night? I hope you enjoyed it?"

"I did, as much as I could. Polydamus whisked me away before I had a chance to see a thing."

"Yes, I heard that from him."

I said, "Cleon is such an old fool." I caught myself up short, worried that he and Alcibiades might be friends, and so added, "I should not criticize. I know he is revered by many Athenians."

"Not in your circle my boy. Besides you are right. When Cleon is drunk he is an old fool. Beating down Aspasia's door like that, well, who would approve of that? Although I've been known to do some pretty silly things when I am drunk. So, perhaps I should not criticize either?"

I did not know him but he spoke frankly with me, perhaps feeling familiar because of Aspasia. Nevertheless I was astonished and said, "But you're not a drunk are you?"

"Well! You do get right to the point! Macedonian bluntness is it? Not too drunken to acquit myself in battle and bed I'll have you know."

"Oh but I didn't mean that. Everyone talks about how Socrates saved you at Potidaea and how bravely you fought at Delium."

"Schoolboy chatter, you mean?"

"Not just, Simonides too. And people in the marketplace. " Indeed, Simonides had praised his heroics, if with qualifications. "They say you are a great horseman and one of the most daring in a cavalry charge."

"When you fight in battle you have to exceed yourself because you fight not just to win the battle or war but for the glory of the city and to inspire your cohorts. Remember that when you are of age to serve. The future of Athens depends on its prowess in war."

"You do not share Aspasia's or Aristophanes' peace sentiments?"

"Hardly anyone does. To me peace is a form of unconditional surrender, far from the ideal of the total defeat of the enemy that brings real peace. After all what is peace if not the liquidation of an enemy? Aristophanes is a fool. Or rather he plays the fool to win an audience. Poetry makes for easy sentiments, hard to believe in the reality of politics. Do you not agree? What are they teaching at the Lyceum these days?"

He was treating me with some disdain I felt but I answered politely, I hoped. "I am not sure I agree with your definition of peace."

"Oh? What then?"

"Well, peace might just as well be called the negation of war, not its opposite. It is a separate reality."

"Well, I wonder. Is Simonides instilling these ideas in you? Surely it is not Socrates. Or is it Athenades? I was never quite certain about that goldsmith's politics. Too much piety can confuse your loyalties you know."

It was a privilege to be seen with Alcibiades, but I did not like his company. I said, "I can think for myself."

"Of course you can; of course you can. If you have strong ideas about peace and war then you may be interested in knowing that there are rumors going around about negotiating with Sparta for a permanent peace, something I am sure Aristophanes and Athenades would support. Can you keep a secret?"

"Of course I can."

"Well, I was just in Sparta and know for a fact myself that the rumors are true."

"But that is good news!"

"For Macedon too. And something that Cleon would die to prevent. Another reason for his appearance at Aspasia's, would you not agree?"

"Well, yes I would." After what he had said I wondered aloud, "But would you welcome such a peace?"

"I doubt I would. I am too much of a realist. I do not see peace treaties serving any long-term purpose. They just delay the inevitable, so to speak. There is too much enmity on both sides towards the other and both have powerful enemies in each other's camps. Let me give you some advice. Never underestimate or trust the enemy. A treaty can just as well undermine as establish a peace."

I wondered if he did not caution me about himself, but I said, "I don't agree. War takes everything away and leaves us desolate. But for what? Father says that war is a struggle between two competing vanities."

"Doesn't that belittle the great heroes? The most I would grant you is that war can become tragedy, something fated, grand, and of the gods. War is the fight to the death of equal truths."

"Yes, it is tragedy. And it does make heroes. You are one of them! And Socrates!"

He said, "Oh Socrates! Your face lights up when you say his name. Did you know that?"

"No. I think it does not."

262

"Oh come now. Aspasia told me about the portents, and her placing of the friendship cup according to the signs. It seems to have surprised her as much as it did everyone else. Or should I say horrify, in the case of Simonides? What about you? Are you ready to bond with Socrates? Or, is there already a bond between you?"

I looked down shyly, my face hot. "I could not presume."

"Aspasia sees the possibility, and she rarely gets these things wrong."

I replied, "She sees the future but the gods constantly interfere."

"They always do, don't they?"

"Yes."

"Do you want it?"

"I do not understand."

"Socrates' embrace?"

"I would value his..." I stopped myself, distrustful of Alcibiades, and said, "I would never presume. They say that Socrates is the wisest man in Hellas. The Delphic oracle proclaimed it, and I trust that. I trust Socrates."

This seemed to annoy him and he said, "Leave it up to him? Is that what you are saying? Well, that is simplistic. I would say it depends on that infernal voice of his. If it tells him not to do something, include take you to bed, he won't, no matter what seductions you try."

Of course, Alcibiades tried every wile to get Socrates to bed him, but Socrates would not. Was it his inner voice or common sense that told him to abstain? Alcibiades was a wild boy, and used the bed for vanity. It defied everything Socrates believed about the middle way of virtue.

Alcibiades also had a sharp tongue, and he added, I would say deliberately, "Well, at least while you are waiting around for Socrates' voice to make up its and his mind you can satisfy yourself with Mania."

I was angry that Mania must have made it common knowledge and said, "Is she gossiping already? I suppose she is! Honestly, she goes too far. Has Lady Aspasia said anything to you too?"

"Let's say that Mania is pining over you, won't eat, and says that no one has evoked her ecstasies as you."

"Did you hear that from Aspasia or Mania?"

His answer took me aback. "Let's say that Aspasia would not want one of her girls ill and nothing happens in Aspasia's household that she does not know about." It was the answer that Mania herself had given me. Had she learned the line from him?

Alcibiades now told me something unexpected, "Aspasia and I are related not just through my mother and Pericles, you know, but also through marriage. Her eldest sister married my grandfather. My family helped arrange for Aspasia to come to Athens when she was about twenty, and they later introduced her to Pericles. When Pericles took her as his mistress it was a family liaison with complex political and social implications. In any case, I tell you all of this so that you will not underestimate our connection or her acuity. It has brought her to where she is."

"I do not think I do."

"If not then you should stop playing the fool."

The remark offended me but I had no time to reply. We were in sight of the school. Some of the other students, seeing me approach with Alcibiades, ran out to greet us crying out his name. In a moment, boys surrounded us shouting questions, taking his hand, and dragging him right into the palaistra, all those strictures against strangers not being admitted quickly forgotten by the guards when they saw it was Alcibiades.

For that day, and a few days afterwards, I was the center of attention. How did I come to know the cavalry hero Alcibiades? Had he told me about his battles? Would he return to school and regale us with his heroic exploits? I was not sure I wanted to be counted his friend. Alcibiades baffled me. He seemed to have more complicated motives than Simonides, and that was saying something. Simonides' intensity was childlike. If he did wrong because of it this was not because he intended malice. I could see that Alcibiades also had a passionate nature, but his passion was more deliberate and calculated. It might be the stuff of generals, but it was also the stuff of traitors and I mistrusted him.

3. Visiting Aspasia.

If it was stifling mid-summer, the city was already preparing for the autumn Eleusinian, honoring the Corn Mother, and celebrating the autumn sowing. The festival lasted a week, and attracted a huge crowd to the city. The city stenches made people fearful of plague again, and the heat frayed tempers. Fistfights could break out over the pettiest of matters, the price of a chicken, the ripeness of a lemon. Leagros commented that you could receive more lewd looks and proposals on one summer day than in two weeks of winter.

265

Commissions were again pouring into the shop, for sacrificial cups and bowls, ankle and wrist bracelets for the girls who would dance in the procession, clasps and chains for the musicians' robes. We were working overtime, which I welcomed. There was no time to brood over friendship or politics. Simonides would be going away in a few weeks, and I harshly speculated that the separation might do our friendship good. Thoughts of seeing Aspasia or Socrates again were forced to the back of my mind, by the sweat pouring from me as I worked or studied, or by my sheer exhaustion at the end of a blistering day.

In the cool of one early morning, as I prepared my table for work, Athenades brought a new order from Aspasia. Girls from her household were in the dance procession and would need the usual finery. Was Mania one I wondered? Aspasia ordered for herself an "innovative sapphire and gold necklace", by which she meant to tell Athenades that I should be given free reign. I was determined to outdo myself. Fine gold strands wound together formed the chain from which were strung sapphires encased in gold pendants, increasing in size on each side to a central, large sapphire set in elaborate filigree. She had also requested that I bring it myself, "in case any adjustments needed to be made to the fittings." This intrigued me, and seemed something of an excuse as I had her measurements. I hoped it meant she would read my charts. Would I see Mania again or was she at Aspasia's country property, or worse in Miletus? Perhaps the heat of summer did encourage the excesses of Eros.

When the necklace was done, and approved by

Athenades, I went to her house. Immediately I was shown into Aspasia' study and she greeted me warmly. Several girls rushed in too, to see what had been made for them or their friends. The atmosphere was festive. She served me fish cakes and they became my instant favorite; the version in the Agora did not compare with those from her kitchen. There was great excitement as each object was unwrapped. The girls were delighted with what I had made for them and showered me with kisses. I had fashioned each piece to honor Demeter; the bracelets like twisted grain stalks, the broaches like apples, grapes, or grape clusters. Aspasia had also ordered cups and bowls and these I decorated with tableaus of scenes from Persephone's life. At the last minute I had added to her necklace seven rubies set in gold to signify the magic pomegranate seeds Hades tricked Persephone into eating before she left the underworld, so that she had to return to spend seven months a year with him. It was all a great success. I would have taken more delight had Mania been there, but she was not.

The house was full of music and laughter, an enormous contrast to the serious, somber mood at Athenades'. The girls' spirited chatter echoed through the halls as they departed. In all the years that I was to know Aspasia, she was always impeccably dressed and coifed. I have never been able to judge the age of women very well, but with Aspasia it was harder than with most. The Persian creams she used smoothed away the wrinkles from around her eyes. Her skin was healthy, from caring for it on a daily basis. I studied her face for those qualities Pericles or Socrates valued in her and caught her staring at me.

She said, "Were you upset by the intrusion at our dinner party?"

"Upset? Not at all. I liked it. Athenades keeps such a serious household it is sometimes a little gloomy. All I do is work, work, work, it seems. I felt as if I had been thrown into a cold mountain brook. Lord that Polydamus is strong! He tucked me under his arm as if I were a puppy. No, I liked the excitement."

"Cleon and his men were foolish. Do you know he sent around an apology a day or two later, and some fine wine from his own cellar? As if that were enough."

"No, I did not know that. And not to Aristophanes you mean?"

"No. He would never do that."

"Then it all seems a little calculated to me and was certainly not enough. First he disrupts your banquet; then he apologizes to you but not Aristophanes; or Socrates for that matter. He makes it too easy. He should apologize to everyone."

When Aspasia laughed she laughed heartily, her head thrown back. "Cleon apologizing to everyone! I do wish my dear Pericles were alive to hear that one. He would have enjoyed it to no end. And perhaps apologize to you too? After all, it was your evening that was disrupted. And you worried about your father finding out. Are you still worried?"

"No. Everyone reassures me he would not find out, but in the end I decided to write to him myself and tell him the whole story. It is too soon yet to have had his answer, but whenever I have trusted father he has repaid it with trust in return."

"That is a surprise. I had meant to reassure you myself today, but there you go and do the right thing."

"Before I left Macedon father asked me to promise him that I would take nothing for granted and would keep him informed, so all I was doing was keeping my promise. Father also warned me that King Perdiccas could use my presence here in some way if he thought it would further his ambitions in Athens or Sparta. He told me to keep my eyes open and be on my guard. His latest letter said that things had died down again in Macedon, now that we have decided to respect the latest truce." I paused and then said, "May I ask you a question?" She agreed and I said, "Did Chaerephon really blab to Cleon's men the details of the banquet?"

"Yes, I am afraid he did. He is an old gossip when he is drunk. Everyone becomes his friend and he will tell anything to anyone."

"I shall remember that. And may I ask something else?"

"Of course."

"Cleon shouted terrible things against Socrates. Why does he hate him so? I can understand his enmity towards Aristophanes, who makes no secret of his peace sentiments. But Socrates? I do not understand that."

"Cleon thinks in simple ways; that Socrates, for example, cannot be trusted because his voice might serve gods who will in time bring harm to Athens. He does not trust Socrates choice of friends either. Alcibiades is his ally right now, but he is suspicious of Alcibiades and Socrates influence on him, and of me, for that matter. Cleon hated Pericles and brought a successful lawsuit against him, which was overturned on appeal. He thought that Pericles' military strategy of turning Athens into a naval power, fortifying the city against siege, and building the long walls to Piraeus, were the wrong choices. In other words, you could say Cleon has always been consistent. He identifies his own judgment with what is best for Athens, and puts his own judgment first. Those who disagree are traitors. But enough of Cleon! You've shown the girls their things but you have not shown me the necklace you made for me."

I had wrapped it in white silk and laid it on a table by our reclining couch. She unwrapped it and held it up. "Oh, but it is splendid! You are a genius! Surely Hephaistos himself must have had a hand in directing you towards this craft." She went on in this fashion, and added, "Now, come over here and fix it around my neck so that we may see if it fits properly." She turned her head aside and held up her hair with her left hand. Her neck was long and firm; she smelled of lavender. I could see the swell of her breasts and feel her attractiveness.

I said, "It does not need adjusting. It fits perfectly."

She seized my hand. "I knew it would. It is worthy of Demeter and Persephone. Now sit back down here next to me and tell me, do you have special devotion to these gods or another?"

She had an ulterior motive in asking me this, but I did not know it when I answered her, "To Demeter? I do not think so?"

"And to Artemis?"

"Not her either, not really. She spends her time alone in the forests and mountains hunting. Although I envy her strength in solitude, it is far from the way I would lead my life. I like to be surrounded by others and, at home, I did not care much for the hunt. She is also the finest of archers and I never could string a bow properly or hit my target. Apollo speaks much more to my life as I am and would be."

Her next question made her intentions clear, and startled me. "You do not see yourself as Hippolytus?"

"Oh!" I said, seeing what she implied. The youth Hippolytus, son of the Amazon Hippolyte, was devoted to Artemis and remained chaste, a rare virtue in Athens. She was alluding to my abstentions with Simonides, and wished to see if there might be a pious motive.

Aspasia had made no effort to be circumspect and I said, "I am no Hippolyte, nor do I wish to be, except perhaps with Simonides. I share my bed some nights with Assur, one of the other apprentices. He is very thoughtful towards me. I have kept it from Simonides so as not to hurt his feelings."

I had the opportunity then to mention Mania but did not take it. If Aspasia knew then she did not say.

She said, "The signs do not suggest a physical bond between you and Simonides but they do not suggest an explanation either."

"Like Socrates voice! It tells him what not to do but never tells him the reason."

"Perhaps. Poor Simonides. It is not the first time that he has become enamored of someone who resists him. None of the others have stood by him as you have. He can be very exasperating, can't he?"

"Very! Sometimes he is so sweet, and then he goes and spoils it! He mentions private things without my

271

permission, which I hate. And I wish he would stop giving me things. It is so embarrassing. Knives, and robes, and capes and sandals; head and wristbands, buckles, and bags, food, and spending money! There is no end." She clapped her hands and started laughing. I said, "Oh, I'm sorry. I did not mean to sound ungrateful."

She said. "But my dear boy, Simonides is one of the most exasperating persons anyone could know. And yet he is also dear. I would never want to see him hurt."

"I would never hurt him. But he is so . . . so excessive."

"He would never harm you."

"But that is not what I mean."

"What do you mean?"

"I fear that if I do not insist on restraints then there will be no restraints. But I also fear that if he were to stop giving me things, it would be over between us, so I accept them as part of knowing him. But it is sometimes degrading."

She said again, "And yet you are neither an Hippolytus nor will you have Simonides. Tell me about this friend of yours at the workshop? Are you in love?"

"Not in love; he is a friend. He watches over me. There is not much to tell. It started soon after I arrived because I was homesick and cried at night. He overheard me one night and came to comfort me. Things are simple between us. He makes me laugh and learns magic tricks to amuse me."

I might have mentioned Mania at that point, but again I did not.

She said, "And Simonides? How do you characterize that friendship?"

I took some time to reflect before saying, "In a word, reality." I could see she was about to ask me to explain this and so I added on my own, "The desire to share myself with Simonides is simply not there, and so I don't, because it would be false. If it changes then I shall."

She said, "That is so Macedonian: practical and direct." She surprised me again. Taking my hand, she asked softly, "And Socrates?"

Her hands were large and strong, and mine fitted easily in hers. Her question confused me. I did not know how I felt about Socrates and said, "He is the wisest man in the world and I am just me."

"And if it were written?"

That only confused me more and I did not answer.

Aspasia broke the silence. She rang a bell for more refreshments. They were brought not by a slave as I had expected but by a boy of some ten or so. His hair and eyes were jet black, but his skin was a pure white suffused with health. He had the beauty people thought I had; Aspasia's beauty.

Aspasia said, "Come my darling Pericles! There is some one I want you to meet. Put the tray down and sit here between us."

Pericles son of Pericles, from that day, was to be my friend. In adulthood he was a great general but was condemned to death by the Athenians as unjustly as was Socrates. Telling this history now, I feel inclined to lay aside this narrative in order to write Pericles' history, because it parallels in so many ways the mystery I am trying to unfold of Socrates. Why did the Athenians, enervated and demoralized by war, sacrifice one of their

273

finest citizens, to their eternal shame? Why was the wisest man in the world persecuted and condemned to death? I lost two friends to democratic madness. The conditions of those two deaths were already there in my boyhood, namely war, litigation and putting conflict over reconciliation. If I must stay the course about Socrates and see this history through to the end, still I mourn Pericles too.

***

I was to see Mania again that evening. A slave left me at the end of a corridor, where Leagros was to join me to take me home. But no sooner did the sound of the slave's sandals fade away than Mania appeared silently on bare feet.

"Quick, in here," she said, unlocking the door to a pantry with a key hanging from a string around her neck. She had come earlier, I saw, to arrange a pallet on the floor. She threw her arms around my neck, "Oh, at last!" She pulled off her tunic and mine too. She was wearing one of the new cloth breast supports that my classmates had whispered about. She asked me to unfasten it, which excited me greatly.

4. The Way to School.

Besides my duties in the workshop I attended classes with a Master who held his lessons on the grounds of the Lyceum. Pisistratus had commissioned the original structures, but Pericles had rebuilt and enlarged them, as part of his great cultural renewal. It was outside the city walls, off the road running past the Temple of Zeus Olympeion; I would stop there to pray for the day's blessing. The Lyceum grounds harbored several small buildings and a small palaistra not as grand as the Taureas, which I would also attend later. We did not have the formal gardens or sacred groves that some gymnasium had, but several ancient olive and plane trees gave us shelter enough to have our classes in the shade on the hottest days. I could retreat there also to do my grammar assignments, a better place than at the workshop.

The compound would have been no more than half an hour's walk, if it had not been for Leagros. We had to leave more time than that if I was not be late and incur some horrible punishment; several runs around the palaistra track, a hundred repetitions of some exercise, or more studies. He liked to linger to take a drink or gossip, or have a friend walk with us leisurely. Athenians loved to walk, but walking was always more than walking; it was a pastime, a hobby, or a form of community. They thought nothing of a jaunt to Piraeus, an hour at a brisk pace, to lunch at the seaport or visit the temples before returning home. The two-hour trek to the hills for a picnic I did many times with Simonides. We met hordes along the way going and coming. Walking forged the Athenian polis.

I looked forward to the walk to school, pausing to inspect new leather wares, stopping by the toy vendors at the corner of the Panathenaic Way, or by a slight detour at the bookstalls. The way home was more amusing, along the eastern wall and up around past the Ceramicus and through the tavern district, the "disgraceful parts of town" as Athenades called them, instructing Leagros not to allow me to venture there, although we did two or three times a week. Male and female prostitutes haunted the Ceramicus day and night, teasing us with their catcalls and taunts.

Most days we proceeded straight along the main route to the first fork. The left road went all the way to Marathon, and was nicknamed Victory Way. The right road led directly to school. At the fork there was a cluster of food stalls selling sweets, drinks, and those Athenian sausages made of heaven knows what crude animal offal; Aristophanes had shown me one day which one sold the best. Their acrid smell could not, however, overwhelm the stench of the foul tanneries also nearby, and the source of Cleon's wealth. I came to associate Cleon's character with foul smells, which is symbolically accurate if unkind. This bias I later carried over to Anytus, one of Socrates' accusers, who also made his fortune through tanning and was an oligarch tyrant of the same stripe as Cleon.

The sausage roll was a foul food, but we ate it with relish; the Athenian diet, and especially our workshop and school diet, was vegetables and fruit. We could also buy small rolls, cakes, and pastries along this stretch of road. Honey was one of the chief products of Athens, along with certain cheeses, wines, barley and a delicate olive oil. The best honey came from the slopes to the north. The cakes were made of a mixture of dates, figs, ground mountain nuts, and this honey. They were my first inkling of what the gods might have eaten and I was addicted to them. When I taste them now they seem sickeningly sweet, but then they were nectar. I would have eaten them at every meal instead of the bland barley cakes Athenades' cook served up.

As we paused at the fork one morning to buy a snack, I was involved in an altercation. Two men were arguing about the price of an old mule. A crowd had formed and was blocking the way. As we attempted to pass the men accosted me.

"Hey, you there, boy. You must be going to the Lyceum and have smarts enough to solve this for us."

"I would like to stop, but I am afraid I shall be late."

"Come now, it will only take a second or two. What better education is there than real life?"

This appealed to me and so I stopped and said, "I shall risk punishment, but all right go ahead and tell me the problem."

The first man said, "I sold this mule to that rascal in good faith and for only thirty drachmas. He was to pay in two equal installments but I have never received the second half, and so I want my mule back."

Thirty drachmas was a month's wage, which seemed more than fair, if the animal worked hard enough to pay back its cost.

The second man said, "I have only paid him half because the mule is lazier than this thief said and works only half as much. What I paid is what it is worth. However, I am willing to return the beast."

"If you are willing to return it then what is the problem?"

The first man said, "I said I would take it back gladly, and give him his fifteen drachma to be rid of him. But he wants me to pay him thirty to return the beast when he has only paid me fifteen and owes me fifteen. Can you imagine the gall! First he complains about the animal and

277

the price, then he won't pay me in full, and now he wants to return it for twice what he has already paid! I warrant I'll give him a good beating, that's what I'll give him!"

Indeed, if the first man's friends had not restrained him there might have been violence, and it did strike me that this would have been justified.

I addressed the second man, "Why do you want more than you have paid if the animal is so worthless? As I see it, by rights, you should pay him back his fifteen and have done with it. Indeed, he could add a surcharge for user's fee, so you are lucky."

And now we reached the heart of the matter. The second man said, "Ask him what the price of mules is today in the Agora?"

It was rumored that a delegation of farmers from Euboia was looking to buy work asses because some plague has afflicted theirs. A demand for work mules had more than doubled the price overnight. The crowd began to speak all at once but as nearly as I could reckon the second man had also been caught taking the mule to the animal auction where he meant to sell it, pay the first man the remainder he owed and keep the profit. Friends had run to find the first man and this is when I came upon the scene.

Someone shouted at me, "What do you say to all of this Master Lyceum Smarty-Mouth?"

I said, "Well, the situation is clear enough. Let us suppose that both parties acted initially in good faith. Now, if that is the case, then the second man has not yet fulfilled his share of the bargain, which is to pay in full. He meant to do this only after auctioning off the poor beast, but it can be asked whether or not he had the right to do this if the animal was not yet fully his." There were many shouts all around both in agreement and disagreement, and when it subsided I said, "The first man, the former owner, does not quite own the mule anymore either because he accepted the installment already paid." I was interrupted again by fierce arguing on both sides and had to shout to be heard, "Let me finish!" Finally there was enough quiet to be heard and I said, "It seems to me that the mule now has two half owners, so I think the poor animal should be taken to the Agora and auctioned off. If what you say is true it should fetch at the very least thirty drachmas and most likely much more. Now whatever it fetches the income should be divided this way. The first man should receive the first fifteen, so that he has now been paid his full thirty. The second man should now receive the next fifteen to reimburse him what he has paid. And the remainder should be divided between the two. Thus, let us say, sixty is received at auction. That means that they would divide thirty between them or fifteen each."

I thought this was an infinitely fair and clever solution, but some in the crowd liked it and some did not, and the two men positively hated it. They saw the flaw in my reasoning: that the mule was an old nag and might fetch less at auction than thirty, and then what? They began to argue all the more bitterly. I was already late, and as I sneaked off through the crowd and looked back I saw that a fistfight had indeed broken out. The first man was shouting for his money again.

Leagros had been watching the whole affair, letting me

drown, as it were. He took my arm and said, "Well, now you have had a real dose of Athens."

I don't think I did very well with my first effort to be a judge, did I?"

"Let it be a lesson to you. Do not try to solve Athenian's problems with reason, until you understand Athenians."

"What would you have done then?"

"Thrash the second man until he paid the second half and then thrash the first for being such a fool as to sell in a low market. A good thrashing is not ideal but it works."

I glanced quickly at him and saw by the glint in his eyes that he was only half serious. The admonishment to mind my pride had been serious, and I took it to heart.

***

Another experience, of another nature, happened near this same fork in the road. When walking home I would often grow impatient with Leagros for wanting to linger and have an evening drink here and there along the way, sometimes from the wine flask he always carried with him, but most often in one of the numerous taverns. He especially liked the tavern haunted by Chaerephon. I would simply walk on ahead alone and wait at one of the book or toy stalls. Their wares changed almost daily. I could not afford the books, but their very touch thrilled me. A simple toy was within my means, a yo-yo for example. I could practice until the old man caught up with me.

I was browsing toys one evening when a crippled

soldier approached me. His left foot was covered in thick, dirty bandages. He used a stick to hobble and I was not sure he still had his foot. He did not seem much older than I, his beard being very light, and so I knew he must have been wounded in the recent Battle of Delium. He was gaunt but handsome.

"An owl or two for food?" he whispered. If the merchants overheard people begging they chased them away. His face was tight with pain, and yet his blue eyes were bright and lively.

"I do not have an obol," I said. "But I can give you whatever small change I have from buying this." And I gave him what was left from the yo-yo.

"Then give me your gold bracelet there?" he said.

It was a gift from Simonides and so I said, "A friend gave it to me so I could not part with it."

He leaned still closer to my ear and said, "We could go into the graveyard. There is a private grove there. I could satisfy you for the bracelet. I'm very good. You would never forget the things I do to you. You cannot believe how much I can teach you. Tell me what you like?"

He went on in an obscene fashion describing various acts with his hand, mouth and otherwise, until I broke into laughter. Sex and laughter are rarely compatible. I said, "I have these sorts of friends and do not need to pay."

"You have no pity."

"But I am sympathetic. Were you wounded at Delium?"

"Yes."

"The city gives the wounded the means to live. Do you have to beg?"

"They give, but barely enough to survive and not

281

enough to pay for the herbs that fight the pain." He added bitterly, "And we nearly died for her."

"I am sorry." I suddenly slipped off my gold bracelet and pressed it into his hand. "If you take it to the Sign of the Argos there is a merchant there who will not cheat you and give you fair exchange."

But he said, "Is this out of pity?"

I shook my head. "My beloved brother died at the Battle of Potidaea. I know the pain of war."

He said, "You are beautiful in face and soul. Please, let's go in the shadows. As a favor."

But I saw Leagros hobbling towards me. "Tell me your name," I said. "We might meet again."

"Demetrios."

The matter does not end there. A few weeks later, at one of the many public funerals for fallen soldiers, I paused to ask the mourners who was being honored with the sacred rites and they told me it was a boy named Demetrios from a poor free family. It was a common name, but still I wondered. Should I have afforded us both a little pleasure?

***

I told the story of Demetrios to Simonides, thinking he would be sympathetic about the death of someone so young, and that he might compose an ode for the family free of charge. He had been hard at work on finalizing his entries for the Eleusinian and I had not seen much of him. His friend, Antiphon, a wealthy book collector and Socrates' friend as well, had a villa on the coast half way between Piraeus and Ephesus. Simonides went there to write and, he said, inspirational solitude; I sometimes thought that he made more of being a writer than the writing, because of his Dionysian, theatrical temperament. When I told him, rather excitedly, my Demetrios story, he was furious, not at me but at Leagros for being so lax with my safety again, and threatened to chaperone me himself too and from the Lyceum. I heard this first as threat, then as treat. He could buy me those sweet date pastries I liked, but could only occasionally afford. Of course, he knew this very well.

We were standing at the bookseller's stall when we had that conversation. Some of my schoolmates spotted us and stopped to greet us. I had wanted a small edition of the hymns to Apollo but Simonides had not decided whether to buy this or something else, and was to the side talking with the bookseller.

One of my classmates hailed me. "Amyntas! Fancy seeing you here! We were just talking about Alcibiades and when you might bring him around to school again?"

"I do not know him well enough to ask him such a thing just like that."

"Oh come now, surely, you can arrange it."

"Well, I suppose I could try." I was hardly taken with Alcibiades and told myself I would not try. They had been coming from an odd direction through the Agora, and so I asked, "Where are you coming from? The food stalls are the other way."

"Oh we were down in the blacksmith district. You have to get there as soon as possible. This one smith has designed a new breastplate that is really fantastic! It is lightweight but impenetrable, a real wonder. Have you

283

been down there recently?"

I had not. The new breastplate design was another sign that war was always in the air, no matter what agreements were scrawled on parchment. I did not like this, but did not comment. Simonides was approaching, a book in hand, and I introduced him. My friends looked askance at the book under his arm.

One of them asked slyly, "What have you there? A new treatise on wrestling, or perhaps something we might like?"

Simonides said it was a volume on the herms and love spells, and one of them quickly said, "Oh, herms to oil, Amyntas?"

I did not laugh, and knew it was not the last I would hear of it. To make matters worse Simonides came right out and said he was intending to buy it for me. He might at least have lied and said it was for some priest or other. I was furious but did not show it. I said that I would accompany my friends to school now with Leagros, and Simonides took the hint that he was not to go further.

Later that day, as I went into the palaistra yard for training, one of the boys that had spoken to us in the Agora called out to me, "Hey, Amyntas, what about a match?" He was a year older, taller and heavier, but I was agile.

"Very well," I said, knowing it had been planned, that there was little chance of my winning, and that I could not avoid it.

We were already oiled. Our arms locked, hands on shoulders; one of his friends would referee. The rule was simple. You wrestled standing and the first to fall lost the round. There were usually three rounds, but my opponent had declared a "winner take all" round. I will say in my favor that I tried my best and made him work and sweat for his victory. As I weakened under the exertion he suddenly kicked my knee from behind and I sprawled backwards to the ground so hard so that the wind was knocked from me and I lay stunned. As I did not move, one of the boys watching took fright and ran to call a trainer. I had hit my head too hard and felt dizzy and dazed and was told to rest in the shade until I felt better. The trainer kindly took me there himself, berating me for accepting a foolish challenge.

I was not angry with my classmates. I had expected something to happen when I had seen jealousy in my classmate's eyes for being the special friend of someone known to be as wealthy as Simonides. It was Simonides I was angry with. Yet it was to Socrates that I wanted to rush, to tell him everything and have his consolation. It was as if some strange leap of the emotions had happened that day between the bookseller and the palaistra yard, something altered that was bound to alter and needed only some token reason, an emotional detaching from Simonides but a bonding with Socrates. Yet I hardly saw Socrates. He went nearly every day to the Taureas palaistra, but began to haunt the Lyceum only later. How could I see him then?

A few days later one of the same classmates provided a plan. We were practicing for a match with the Brauron palaistra, much the better team, and did not stand much of a chance. Our trainer was Demetrios of Chios. We liked him well enough, but as a trainer he was mediocre and lackadaisical. If I had been so summarily dismissed by the older boy and I were to wrestle against anyone from Brauron, I would fall instantly. We could all see we needed more training before we were ready for the competition.

One friend said downheartedly, "If we had Hippothales as our coach we would win hands down."

I did not know who he was and asked, "Is he at the Brauron?"

He scoffed, and said, "You dumb Macedonian. Of course he's not. He's the head coach at the Taureas. And none better."

I replied, "Couldn't we at least have a class with him?"

"Just listen to him. If you were good enough you might, but you couldn't throw a puppy, or one of us, no less a Taurean."

Another boy said obscenely, "Of course, Hippothales could teach you a tumble or two. I'm sure he'd fancy doing that." At tumbling and leaps I was better than most, although that was not his innuendo. He added, "Why don't you ask your precious Simonides to bribe Hippothales to take you as a student. Your poet would in a flash just to please you, I warrant."

He was my size, and his remark might have led to a fistfight had not one of our teachers called us in for rhetoric. But the plan for seeing Socrates was drawn. I did not know how, but I would arrange a class at the Taureas, not to prepare me for a competition, but to be nearer Socrates again.

5. Socrates in the Palaistra.

The class with Hippothales at the Taureas was easier to arrange than I had expected. I asked Athenades' permission to write to father seeking his approval, hoping that father would readily agree. Father had often warned that I was too inward. More exercise balanced me. I was a very good gymnast, which he also encouraged, so the matter was really decided before the formality of writing to him. I owed him a letter; it went with a messenger that week, a positive answer coming back straightaway.

A few simple questions among my classmates also let me know that Socrates went to the Taureas most every day at the same hour. Mornings he was in the Agora giving lessons and advice. He taught for free, contrary to *Clouds* where he asks for money to teach. The Sophists were the real brunt of Aristophanes' joke, as the audience of that year would know, but later audiences would forget. After a small lunch of fruit, and in the hot weather, a rest, he would arrive at the palaistra for the late afternoon classes, I discovered. He had kept this routine for so long, were he not to show up it could be seen to be a sign of the decline of Athens itself, so steadfast was he. Scheduling gymnastic classes in the late afternoon did not conflict with my duties at the workshop or studies at the Lyceum.

I was very curious about Socrates, and especially his voice. If I had other motives, I was not ready to own up to them. Socrates was as skillful a matchmaker as Aspasia. I rationalized that I could ask him for advice about Mania if not Simonides. My curiosity was also whetted by remarks I regularly overheard about Socrates in our local barbershop, the true center of news and information.

287

Indeed, news seemed to reach the barbers before the news criers cried it at dawn in the Agora. There were, of course, many barbershops in the city, each catering to a specific clientele. For example, Simonides, Lygis, and his theater friends went to a very elegant one in the arcade at the top end of the Panathenaic Way. The one we frequented was around the corner from the workshop and popular with artisans, athletes, and gymnasium students. Aristophanes went to still another near the Odeion where the poets and producers met to discuss new plays.

Ours was very modest, a neighborhood affair run by the same family for several generations, really only a large square room you entered by parting a noisy, beaded, cobweb of a curtain. Crowded, waiting-benches ran along two walls. You had to ask, "Who is the last?" and take your turn after him, becoming the last. At the back there was another doorway into a smaller room where certain ghastly surgeries were performed, praise be Asclepius, never on me. There was no masseur as there was in the luxury establishments. It was always very crowded, and conversations often overlapped, one person interrupting a conversation with someone to his right to add a remark to a conversation going on with someone to his left. Never was the climate more filled with rumor and gossip than when a group of boys gathered there. Boys' gossip shamelessly. How simple it was to turn the conversation to whatever topic you wanted without anyone noticing, especially if it had to do with sport's heroes, food, or sex with courtesans.

Haircuts and hair fashion were diverse that year. Athenades made sure that we went weekly. He said that short hair was the mark of a free man, and that long hairs could spoil the jewelry making. During the long war with Sparta, Athenian boys wore their hair short; Spartan boys wore theirs long. The exception was boys from the aristocracy, for whom long hair was not so much treasonous, as a token of social standing and privilege. Their long hair demanded expensive coiffing. Slaves often had their heads shaved, or at least cut short, but Athenades only demanded that we keep ours trimmed, that is, be neat and clean, which he placed high among the virtues. There was also a set time of day when we were to go to the barbershop, usually we four freeborn workers going together, the oldest acting as chaperone. It was in the hour just as the sun touched the horizon, so it changed week by week with the seasons. This was the hour when the schools closed, but was before our evening meal. The news of the whole day would all be known, and the discussions lively.

Socrates was a public figure, more so after Delphi, Delium, and *Clouds*, and now and then, if not often, the topic of conversation. I can remember one discussion of him at this time that I turned into advantage, if treacherous memory does not compress the many into the one. One of the barbers was discussing some scandal that particular day, one that had taken place a year before but was controversial enough to provoke outcries and disgusted remarks as fresh as the day the scandal first broke. The winner of the boxing event at the last Olympics had been the great athlete, Cleomachus of Magnesia but he had begun brazenly to cultivate effeminate men. That afternoon as I sat there with some friends waiting our turn

289

he happened to pass the barbershop door with one such friend and that was all it took to revive the discussion.

The barber said, "Did you see that! There goes that filthy Cleomachus with that mincing fairy he's taken up with! Why they should strip him of his Olympic honors they should!"

Men who affected female ways were held in contempt in Athens, as were men who preferred them. In other places, these men-women were often given sacred tasks, had the power to prophesy, and could divine the intents of the gods. They made excellent priests, dream interpreters, and healers. But in Athens they were detested, perhaps because the Athenians thought their survival depended on prowess in battle; in Athens if you wished to find a reason for something you rarely had to guess further than war. It was also a great transgression in Athenian culture for free men to lower their status in any way. The rights and privileges of free men were among the greatest achievements of the city. To mimic women was a denigration of the role of free men, a deliberate desecration of the city's meaning and achievements among its neighbors. These men the Athenians called, cinaedus and cinaedi and Cleomachus' offense—some would have it a crime—was to take up with the most notorious one of all, one who tried to recruit others to his "cause". A militant cinaedus was thought by some to be the worst enemy of the state, although the body politic had not banned them, at least if they were freeborn. Cleomachus was being seditious, according to some in the barbershop that day by taking up with a militant cinaedus.

Many remarks floated around the room against the

290

boxer: "Revolting! Disgusting!" but it seemed to me that the criticisms had mostly to do with his flaunting certain sexual preferences over moderation. When he had passed, not only was Cleomachus imitating the mincing steps of his cinaedus, but on his other arm he had a prostitute who was famous for training men to satisfy other men's lust.

I heard someone say, "If he had conducted himself in private as an experiment that would be one thing. But to go out and about like that, and an Olympic champion to boot, makes a disgraceful politics out of it!" And I heard this too, "He has no self control. Or if he does he would wish us to believe either that he does not have any or that it is his to discard as easily as bending over." And another, "His crown should be taken away from him. Take away his crown!" And finally, "Right you are! He is no Socrates for sure! Indeed, you could call him the quintessential opposite of the philosopher!"

My ears perked up at that. When my turn came I was filled with questions, and took my place eagerly on the low stool, set before the long gleaming steel mirror. Aristodemus the barber knew everything, and sharpening the razor he used to trim the hair, he greeted me by name, "Are you well today Amyntas?"

"I am, Aristodemus."

"And your hair neat, but not too short as usual?"

"Please. But not too long to offend my Master."

"Don't worry. I know what he will and will not accept. And I know what you do and do not like!"

We had this conversation most every time. As I bent my neck to the slaughter, and I watched the gold strands fall, I worked the conversation to my true topic. "I have a

291

question, Aristodemus."

"And it is?" His sharp razor went cut, cut.

"I just heard it said that Cleomachus was the opposite of Socrates. But I do not understand this."

"Oh, of course, you would not." The barber thought all foreigners had defective intelligences. I was seldom doubted when I played the role of the Macedonian ignorant of Athenian ways.

He said, "Socrates is known for his self-control and abstinence. Of course, in his love for Alcibiades he came close to losing his mind, but they say he resisted Alcibiades wiles successfully, and Alcibiades knew more wiles than most. He was a wild boy, you know, and a wilder man. To any man I'd say, send your wife to the country before having Alcibiades for dinner."

If he wanted to talk about Alcibiades, I quickly turned the topic back to Socrates. "Do you think Socrates really did resist him, or is this just another legend? I have met Alcibiades and he is still very handsome, and they say he was the most beautiful boy ever known in Athens, so maybe his beauty made him irresistible."

"Well his kind of beauty is a matter of taste. Alcibiades was too wild and vain for some. Socrates can see right through physical beauty! You weren't in the city some fifteen years ago when their friendship was at its height. Why Alcibiades was so pitiful to see. Going all over the city moaning and groaning about Socrates denying him. Oh no. Socrates is a virtuous man, if you call that virtue. I suppose he thinks that philosophers have to show the rest of us how to live, but what's the sense of example if it isn't practical. I would have given that Alcibiades a good go."

I said, "Then what do you think? Is Socrates virtuous or stupid, pious or vain? Do you admire him? It sounds as if you do not find him sensible."

"He is, if you can follow his example. But most of us are led by the nose by some god or other and can get carried away by this or that passion like those fevers that sweep periodically through Athens."

Cut. Cut. Trim. Trim. I began to worry too much was falling. "Not too much, Aristodemus."

"Don't worry. Don't worry."

I felt that it was time to get to my point. "But everyone says that Socrates is a good teacher. Some go to the Taureas palaistra just to study with him."

"Yes, that is true. My nephew goes there and says they flock around him when he arrives, mostly the younger boys who like his war stories and the new games he invents for them. They also say he does magic. That Socrates has something of the trickster about him you know. Did I see you at *Clouds* a few weeks ago? I thought I did. It's a terrible play, quite the worst of all of Aristophanes' plays. But the best bits for sure were the lampooning of Socrates. Got him to a tee. By the way have you heard the latest joke, about the man who hated his wife and pretended to be sick to avoid having to satisfy her? His wife said, 'My darling, if anything happens to you I shall hang myself.' And the man answered, 'Why not do me the favor now?'"

I laughed at his joke and asked, "But why would the Taureas allow Socrates access every day when he is not a paid teacher?"

"Socrates is famous. The Taureas attracts boys whose tribes expect the best and harbor ambitions for their line. The school knows which hills hold the silver."

I said, "It sounds as if they do. Still, I heard that Socrates was there most every day at some time or other?"

Now if they are anything, barbers are worldly wise. The razor paused mid-air for a moment and I thought, the gods forbid, that he had found one of those nasty creatures that lurk in your hair, but he had not. He had guessed the course of my questions. Lowering his voice he whispered in my ear, "Socrates is at the Taureas late every afternoon two hours before sunset. Why didn't you just ask?"

***

Soon after this conversation I went to the Taureas for an interview, a mere formality because it was a forgone conclusion that I would attend, given my status in a royal house of Macedon and the letters of recommendation from my new connections in Athens. What immediately impressed me, besides its immense size and grandeur, was the elegance of the changing and oiling rooms. The walls were covered with Persian tiles and the benches were of cypress wood. The statues in the niches were of bronze not of plaster. The bowls and oil jars were decorated with Olympian gods and contests, not plain or with simple vine or key motifs. The inner halls and rooms, including those where classes were being conducted or boys were changing or being oiled, were spotlessly clean, and quiet, all a far cry from what the Lyceum offered. I thought of temple compounds, of sacred rituals, but I was not reminded of the rowdy Lyceum.

The rooms were off a colonnaded walkway giving onto an enormous open yard, so large that a class or game at one end did not disturb one at the other end. Here in Paraetonium the custom of boys to go naked at training has never proven universal; some still wear loincloths, whereas in Athens it was the rule. The first thing you did when you entered the palaistra was to discard your tunic. From the shouts and warnings of the coaches out in the yard I could see that the training was demanding and rigorous. Some boys were waiting for class, or their turn for oiling, and were playing knucklebones, or blindfold; a boy is blindfolded and tries to tag any of the others who taunt him. Another was practicing his tortoiseshell lyre, the fair sounds echoing under the archway where he sat. Athenian boys followed a peculiar custom that I remarked often in the palaistra and Lyceum, and often practiced myself. Two friends would be walking together, their arms draped over each other's shoulders, whispering in each other's ears. Usually it was sex gossip, who might be with whom, or who might have left messages for whom for an assignation, whether someone had glimpsed his sister, and what he could tell. Sometimes it would be about a master, how strict he was, or how he had taken the rod to someone, and how we must take revenge or stay clear him. A boy-oiler had gone too far; he might lose his position. A stranger had been seen loitering by the entrance, taunted to enter, a high crime if he entered without permission. The real life of schoolboys was shared in warm whispers, lips brushing ears. In Macedonia we did not do this, nor here in Paraetonium have I seen it. But in Athens, where so

295

much was public, the whisper protected many private things. There were whispers about Socrates too. His inner voice caused much speculation among us, and many hypotheses about its origin were put forward, some respectful, and some obscene.

On my first days at the Taureas, the new boy starting midpoint, I had intended to make my way cautiously and keep Socrates at a distance, politely not to take advantage of our previous meetings. I noticed him instantly, at one corner of the enclosure talking to a class curled around him on the grass. He was expounding on the need to dedicate learning to the gods Eros, Hermes, and Heracles. Eros presided over friendship and love and taught us through example to be pure and not weighed solely by physical desire, which we were meant to transcend. Hermes, one of the most mysterious of all the gods, helped us through the transitions and transformations suffered between childhood and adulthood, and inspired us with intelligence and eloquence. He was the god of wrestling and rightly venerated at the Taureas, Socrates said, pointing out the life-sized ring of herms on pedestals around the yard. Hermes bestowed cleverness, guile, and swiftness. Heracles on the other hand inspired us to build outer strength as a compliment to the inner strength of virtue; we would never know when we would need the double strength in battle or in the performance of our duties as citizens. To worship all three from an early age was to cultivate unity of soul. They represented the three chief aspects of the whole man, spiritual, intellectual, and physical, without which there was no true citizenship, nor good citizen, nor warrior. The worship of the gods was the life of the city. These are the things I heard Socrates speak about that day and many days afterwards, too numerable to count. He meant to instill virtue, and it is a lie that he corrupted.

As he taught I witnessed his skill at teaching. Some of the boys were restless, poking at each other or whispering. Socrates was standing, four square of frame, and suddenly interrupted himself and held out his arms straight to the side. "Who would like to test me?" he said, meaning to imitate Polydamus for my sake, although I did not know he had noticed me standing at a distance, nor had I realized he had seen Polydamus' game that evening at Aspasia's dinner. Immediately two boys jumped up and proceeded to hang from each arm as if his arms were tree limbs. "Come now," he taunted, "only two?" Two more leapt up to test his strength. Socrates called out, "And you Amyntas? Will you not join in?" Everyone turned to see whom he addressed and I sheepishly went forward but did not dare test his strength myself.

I said, "Your strength in or out of battle is legendary, Socrates. There is no need to test it."

Socrates laughed and said, "Spoken like a true gentleman! It is not a lack of faith to test human legends. Come now and join us."

And so I did. One of the boys dropped off his right arm and I replaced him, holding my feet aloft to dangle, amazed that he could hold two aloft on his right, and two on his left. His arm was as solid as an oak limb. He feigned exhaustion and dropped us, part of the game, amid much merriment.

The boys did not disperse and still demanded attention.

They had an easy relationship with Socrates, not as other teachers permitted, and felt free to admonish him. "Come on Socrates! You promised to tell us of the battles today, don't you remember? There is still time before class."

"Of course I remember," Socrates said, brushing himself off. He alone was clothed, in his customary thin wool robe, loosely draped. He turned to me and said, "I have heard that you would start today, Amyntas, to train in Hippothales' class, but you are early. Perhaps you will sit here in the shade and join us?"

In these ways he made me feel at home there on my first day.

He seated himself on the ground. Boys leaned against or on him as if he were a large doll or family dog. The easy familiarity I now know took much wisdom, virtue, and discipline. He told these stories, speaking with great animation, sometimes throwing his arms about, making boys duck, or he would jump to his feet spilling them on the ground to show the swordplay or spear thrust.

"I would tell you today of the terrible loss at Delium against the Boeotians. Indeed, before the battle there was much praise of the Boeotian general Pagondas. Many said that none were more brilliant or innovative. Imagine, boys, a line of our best, painted shields raised thus to take the full sword's blow, thrusting and parrying too. Your shield is not just friend in battle, but father protector too, so that your flank will never feel the cold blade come to drain away your life."

Cheers greeted this and the chaos of boys in mock battle. When they had calmed, he continued.

"We were already headed home, but encamped only a

298

few minutes outside the city, where General Pagondas would array his troops against us. His first brilliant tactic was to argue better with his men than our General Hippocrates did with us. We were told that to defend the line here was to secure Athens against northern assault, and so we were defending the city and our freedom as citizens. But Pagondas told his men that to be defeated was to become the slaves of Athens, and his men were in sight of their own city and stood on their own land so his appeal was stronger than Hippocrates could make to us when Athens was still so distant and we so longed to be their among our family and loved ones. To defend your home, or to long for it, do not weigh equally on the battlefield."

"But did not Pagondas use a new tactic?" one boy asked.

"He did. His hoplites and ours numbered the same, some seven thousand. It was in all battles the custom to array your hoplites six to eight deep. This spreads them wide and at the same time keeps the line strong enough to withstand frontal onslaught. But Pagondas surprised us. He gathered his hoplites on his right flank twenty-five deep and this risked exposing his left. Indeed, it almost did not work. Imagine us charging fiercely his left and finding it under-defended. It drove us mad with the lust of conquest and we easily broke through and would have routed him."

"What happened? What happened Socrates?" came from all sides.

"If Pagondas had one brilliant and new idea, then he had two. Calculating that his left would be vulnerable to the assault of our right wing and permit it to break through, he arrayed his specially trained Theban allies to intercept our charge, while sending his cavalry secretly around behind our left flank now attacking his twenty five deep right flank. Suddenly behind us was a rage of charging horses and our line panicked and broke. In the confusion all our lines erupted into chaos. We were routed."

Socrates fell silent and the story seemed to be drawing to a close. He shaded his eyes to look at the sun. Boys will do anything to escape class, and some immediately cried out the question I feared that someone would ask. "But what of Potidaea, Socrates? You fought there too and it was there that you saved Alcibiades fallen from his horse. Surely it is not too long ago for you to tell us now?" From all around came the exhortations. "Tell us about that too, Socrates! Tell us about that!"

I did not want to hear about this because of the pain it brought me and prepared to leave to look for the part of the yard where Hippothales might be holding his class. Just as I stood up Socrates also stood.

He said, "It is enough for today and the hour grows late. Now all of you back to class. Off you go!"

But he came to me and took my arm.

"Come Amyntas, Hippothales' class is this way. I shall show you."

I could see some boys casting envious glances our way, and wondered if his attention would not bring me teasing as with Simonides, but I was too happy to care.

Socrates surprised me by saying, "A few days ago I came to the Lyceum to watch you at gymnastics class."

"Oh, but I never saw you or I would have greeted you. You must think me impolite."

"Not at all. You were concentrating and I knew you had not noticed me. I liked it that you took what you did so seriously. I did not see anyone do your flips or spins any better. You are a worthy pupil for Hippothales."

We approached the colonnade. Socrates asked a boy to fetch us a cool drink and we went into the changing room where you left your tunic and bag upon arriving, at the moment deserted but soon full. The boy-oilers were busy in the next room. Spirits were high and with Socrates there I felt secure. He had a simple flax bag with him, such as Simonides had bought for me.

He knew that I would be there that afternoon, having heard it from the headmaster, and he said, "I have brought you something." Reaching into the bag he took out a book, the Homeric hymns. I had heard that there were copies of this available from the bookseller in the Agora but I could never have afforded it. He handed it to me now. How it thrilled me to hold it.

Socrates said, "This is the first compilation, you know. I have heard you have a devotion to Apollo and his hymns are particularly beautiful."

I said, meaning it too, ""But it is the best gift that anyone has given me!"

Socrates made a joke. He said, "Even Athenades would approve of such a gift."

I laughed, "Yes, he would wouldn't he?"

"Is Leagros here with you today? I did not see him."

"He is at the lodge talking to the gatekeeper."

"I should have guessed!"

I said, "Yes. He likes to befriend the gatekeepers and maids. He tells me that they like cheap wine but that he prefers it because it is so strong. He does not water it either. He also learns more than anyone about what is really going on in Athens."

Socrates said, "He is a legend in Aspasia's household."

"I imagine he is."

Socrates was studying me carefully and said, "Of course there are legends and there are legends."

I heard his note of caution but was not ready to discuss Leagros and the things he was leading me into. I picked up the book and started to leaf through it. Socrates did not press the matter.

He said, "The Apollo hymns are worth memorizing. But you could start with those to Dionysus. They are shorter."

"I know some of those already. My tutor at home was a devotee of Dionysus."

Socrates took the book back from me and said, "Here, let me see it for a moment. I was reading them again this morning and found one to Pan I particularly liked." He unfurled a bit more and read, "'Son of Hermes/ of the woodland deep/god of shepherds/protector of lambs/bestow your freedom/of bird and field/ of pipe and flute/on kalos kagathos Amyntas."

I was touched that he had included me in a prayer, and said, "I do not think it says that Socrates."

He handed the book back to me. Going to the top of the scroll I noticed that he had inscribed it "to my friend".

He saw me staring at it and waited. Finally I said, "I am very grateful for this gift, Master Socrates." It was my

302

awkward way of paying respect.

He laughed heartily, "Master! My slaves refuse to call me that! Especially my faithful Nubian!"

They say that Socrates did not worship the old gods, and that he did not laugh, but that day, one among many, he proved both rumors false. In order to change the subject I said, "When we sat together talking, on the wall in Aspasia's garden, you said that you wrote songs to Apollo. Will you recite one now?"

Socrates said, "I do not think there is time today, but I shall write them out for you and give them to you tomorrow when you come to class. Will you come tomorrow as well?"

"Not tomorrow but the day after. I am to train three days a week. It is not too much work for you to write them out?"

"No. You will have one of the only copies."

"The start of a collection" I said. "Along with the Homeric hymns. I will be another Antiphon if I am not careful."

"Oh then you know him? Of course you must. Through Simonides."

There was noise from the yard. Socrates said that the deep voice was Hippothales calling his boys together. We went to find an oiler, making conversation along the way.

Socrates said, "At the Lyceum I saw you doing Cretan leaps over a bar. Can you tell me what you feel when you make such a leap? You seem so free."

"I try to imagine myself like one of those leaping dolphins in the murals at Aspasia's house."

Socrates said, "Aspasia sees the spirit of gods breathing

in souls."

Did he mean me, I wondered? I said, "What do you think she means?"

"Oh, it will take a long time to give a proper answer to that my friend, and your class is about to start. God forbid you are late for the first one. Perhaps, on another day."

I ran off, excited with the prospect of seeing and talking with Socrates another day.

6. Political intrigue.

The Athenian year began in mid-summer, in the month of Apollo, a custom that no one else followed. In Boeotia, for example, just across the border from Attica, the year began mid-winter. We Macedonians changed our year in the month of Zeus, that is, mid autumn, and so, the New Year began for me rather in the middle of things.

Indeed, there were many calendars in Athens: the festivals, the political meetings, and the farming seasons, each in its own right played a dominating role in Athenian life and were used to mark people's lives. Then too, every four years there were the Olympic games, and you often heard Athenians speaking about being born in the year that so and so had won first prize at boxing, or the stadion. As in many other matters, multiple ways of marking time was another example of Athenian exceptionalism; or imperialism, depending on your loyalties. The prevailing sentiment during my years there was that Athenian democracy was the be-all and end-all, the culture that everyone should emulate, and that should set the standard for everyone else. If you had Athens you did not need anything else. Socrates rarely ventured outside the city. I

304

asked him about this one day and he said, "Every day here the life of virtue is challenged." It was an Athenian sentiment, as strong as faith in Athena. Calendars were one more adjustment that I had to make in moving there. Adjusting to new things challenges us and brings an understanding that habits restrict. It is one reason for breaking habits and starting new things. In Athens, I began to note my life by the occurrence of the religious and theater festivals more than the changes in the seasons, and the time since or to the next Olympic, but certainly never by the name of the month.

Measuring the year by public occurrences helps me now to date this period of my youth, when strange forebodings crept in, and strange men began to appear in our shop to discuss secret things. I am certain that this was after *Clouds* and the dinner at Aspasia's, but before the end of the year Assembly meeting, the one that approved the Truce of Laches and gave us all a little breathing room.

The weather was very hot. I was beginning work early when it was still cool and my sweat did not fall on my designs nor did I have to wear a headband. Two men entered one day just as I settled at my bench, and greeted Athenades in whispers. They could not have been customers because Athenades did not bring new orders to our worktables, nor was he shouting at us to get busy because the work was piling up. They stood close to him, whispered things for a few minutes and departed. A few days later there were two more who did the same. The other apprentices speculated that they were investors, and that some sort of land purchase was under way to extend Athenades' country villa, or that they were money lenders

305

and Athenades older son had accrued gambling debts again, like Pheidippides in *Clouds*. His son was a wastrel whom Athenades kept far away from his business, and finally disowned because of scandal; he tried to steal to pay his debts and was caught. I myself suspected that the strangers were members of Athenades' peace fellowship, and it all had to do with Cleon and the recent treaty with Sparta, already in danger of being broken. If they were coming and going so frequently something ominous was afoot. I did not voice any of this to the other apprentices because it would have revealed more knowledge of Athenades' affairs than I should have had, and led to more questions than I was willing to answer. I had also overheard one of the strangers speaking with a Spartan accent, and knew from Leagros and Simonides that Athenades had secret connections with the Spartan King Pleistoanax who was making hints about a permanent peace. Was one of the men Pleistoanax' agent?

If I had any doubts, Leagros quickly dispelled them. He did not approve of his son-in-law's politics. One day walking me to the Lyceum I said that the shop was busy that morning with a lot of strange men and hoped that there would soon be many orders. Leagros muttered, "That fool will cause his own downfall if he isn't careful." I considered Athenades a paragon of conservative values and could not imagine him causing his own downfall. I thought that perhaps they must have had words about Leagros' endless affairs with cooks and housemaids. Might Athenades begrudge Leagros his "health regimen" as he called his love antics? They had been going on for so long that Athenades must have been use to them by now.

To draw him out I said, "Is Athenades on at you about your drinking again?"

"That too! Thank you for reminding me. Fuel to the fire, that is what it is, fuel to the fire."

"But does he disapprove of your drinking or its excess?"

He thought I was being impertinent and said, "Not you too! What is all this talk in Athens about virtue, virtue? I say live to the hilt; that is what I say. He shouldn't go around trying to tell me what to do. After all, I am his elder and not some slave. Besides, he knows that sex and drink keep me young."

I glanced at him to see if he was being ironic, but he was not. Perhaps a compliment would inspire confidences, and so I said, "You are very young for your age. Is sex and drink your secret?"

"Secret? There's no secret. When you are seventy-five and then some, as I am now, you have to consort as much as possible to keep yourself in shape, but not so much as to weaken your reserves. It is all about finding limits. None at all will make you shriveled and bitter, and too much, haggard and prone to fevers. I have worked it all out very carefully you see. I 'cavort' as that wastrel son of mine calls it, three and sometimes four times a week, if I am not suffering from wind or stomach cramps. But the other days I rest, eat well, take walks around the city, and have a massage at the barber. Pleasure with gusto but within limits is one of the luxuries of experience and old age. Pleasure drives you young people crazy, but by my age most are past the crazed stage and can enjoy it as the true gift of life that it is."

"You walk me to and from the gymnasium. That keeps you healthy too."

"Yes, walking is a good way to keep toned, you know. They have Olympic games for running the hundred-meter race but not for walking three thousand meters, which is just plain stupid. I shall propose it if I serve on another Council, which I doubt I will."

"Mania told me that you were a great favorite in the kitchen and that you told the funniest gossip of anyone."

"Mania, eh? So, has she crazed you yet? There is a little wildcat if ever there was one. Be careful of that one."

As soon as he warned me about Mania all else went out of my head, as it will with a consuming passion, "What do you mean, be careful? I thought you approved."

"Of Mania? Of your having affairs for sure. I started at your age with courtesans. But Mania? I am not sure what I said to you about her but I doubt if it was outright encouragement."

I was stunned by this and stuttered, "But I thought..." I paused and gathering myself, said, "Well then what do you think about her?"

"Cook tells me that Alcibiades uses her to gain information and I believe her. Be watchful of what she asks you when your heads lie sweetly together on the pillow and you are spent and lazy."

Mania had just been Mania to me but I realized that I did not know the name of her father or where she was born, no less any of her other associations including one with Alcibiades.

I exclaimed, "Alcibiades! Alcibiades and Mania? And what sort of information? He does not like young girls I

308

am told, or boys for that matter, so I doubt if he has much interest in either of us." Father had so instilled fear of the King in me that I wildly added, "Alcibiades has also not been recently to Macedon so far as I know. Aspasia would have told me. Or father would have sent word. I don't know what you are talking about."

"Lower your voice or you will draw attention to us."

We had already reached the first stalls of the Agora on our way beyond the walls to the Lyceum. It was a shopping morning but the streets were not as crowded as usual because of the heat. I was very agitated, and thought, rather wildly I must say, that Leagros had heard that Alcibiades might be plotting something with King Perdiccas. The mad King was a constant, if remote, threat, so my irrational fears had some basis in reality. I also disliked Alcibiades from the moment we met by the Stoa, and was ready to believe the worst about him. That kindling of dislike must have been the first inkling of my deep feelings for Socrates. I was jealous of Alcibiades. But that was something I did not recognize for many years.

I lowered my voice and said, "I do not see how schoolboy secrets or what I do in bed with Mania would interest him."

"Come now. Either you play the fool or are. Now consider this: your father is one of my son's peace associates and so an enemy of Cleon; you have been granted a special place in our household; your work table has been set right at the front so that you can see and overhear everything; you have been coming and going in Aspasia's household, and word has gone around that she sees something special in you; you are having her favorite girl, who is had by some famous men, which allows you to spy for the peace faction; that Simonides of yours has taken you everywhere, right into the Odeion and God knows how much actors gossip you have overheard! And Aspasia sees an inkling of the gods in a friendship between you and Socrates. Need I go on? Isn't that enough to make you interesting to Alcibiades, someone who cultivates others for information, someone with strong links to Cleon and his faction? Alcibiades loves power. He loves it more than he loves love or his brothel orgies."

"Then he will grow quickly tired of me because I know nothing and anyway Mania has shown no interest in asking me about anything political. You make a good case but it is far-fetched."

"Give Mania time and she will turn the pillow talk to politics. After all, consider where Mania is from, and then ask yourself whom Alcibiades cultivates the most these days?"

When I looked blank Leagros exclaimed, "You do not know where she is from! Or whom Alcibiades cultivates!"

I stuttered, "I ... I.. no, I don't know."

"You are hopeless! Absolutely hopeless! Mania is an Argive. This very day there are those in Argos plotting to undermine the peace between Athens and Sparta, with Alcibiades' encouragement. He and his aristocratic friends want war and more war. You know, of course, that Alcibiades has family ties with Sparta through his grandfather? The family made show of cutting those ties, but there are many, myself included, who believe that the ties were never cut. It suits Alcibiades and his family's oligarchic ambitions to encourage Athenian imperialism, if

310

it is not disguised self-interest. Now are you catching on?"

I said, "I really doubt whether Alcibiades cares much about me."

"Well, Athenades' tribe has the Council next month, you know. With Nicias' support, Athenades is planning to use the Council meeting to introduce a resolution calling for a permanent peace treaty with Sparta. It will be the main topic on the agenda for the following Assembly of all the people." The Councils or boule, rotated between the various tribes in order to give all equal voice in the democracy. The Council could propose laws and resolutions, which would then be voted on by the full Assembly. Leagros added with a flourish, "Alcibiades is an ambitious soldier. There is no doubt he will support Cleon's faction in the Assembly, and has all the more reason to spy on you through Mania the next time the two of you wrestle your way to exhaustion. "

I said, "Mania may be ambitious but she is also transparent. I am not worried, especially as I am now forewarned. In any case, she has been more curious to know about Simonides and his efforts to seduce me than anything political."

"Oh that rubbish. I suppose women would find that interesting. As far as I am concerned you have missed a fine opportunity of having a fortune thrown at your feet and enjoying yourself in the bargain. You Macedonians have peculiar ways all right. Praise Eros that you are not playing the same game with Mania. Granted she is ambitious. She would be your wife if the law permitted. Having title suits the ambition of a slave."

Leagros had a way of irritating me more than anyone,

and I said, "My friendship with Simonides is not rubbish. And as for Mania, she knows that marriage is out of the question. Besides, she is too wild to make a good wife. She just seems interested in sex."

"Oh, what did you say? Wild? Well that really alarms me, more than the rubbish about Alcibiades, which is just speculation after all. I mean what if she has a case of female displacement? Aspasia called the doctors in recently you know. I wonder if it was about Mania. I'll have to find out for you right away."

"Female displacement?"

Leagros sighed, "My dear boy, you know nothing. It is a common female complaint. The female womb becomes displaced and floats around the body until it finds a comfortable spot. The most common place for it to lodge is in the throat, which leads some women to become crazed with that sort of sex. Has Mania shown signs of this?"

"Well no, not really. I mean, well, once or twice. She prefers to have me on my back and straddle me because she says I am beautiful when aroused and she can see my face. Is there no cure for this... this displacement?"

"Of course there is a cure, a simple one too. The doctor puts foul smelling things to the nose and sweet smelling things below where the womb should be, and as soon as the womb gets a whiff of the sweet smells it immediately heads for the sweet smells and returns to where it should be. It is that new doctor on Cos who discovered this, you know. Now mind you, if Mania starts obsessing about using her throat on you, be very careful. It is a sure sign of a displaced womb, and everyone knows that a misplaced womb can cast an evil spell over the best of men."

I said, "Perhaps that is what happened to Alcibiades."

He saw that I was joking, but he also warned me not to be too open in my dislike of Alcibiades. But I would not have. We were nearing the Lyceum. I was already drenched in sweat and hoped grammar class would be out of doors under the shade trees. How much self-interest was there in what he was about to say?

Leagros said, "One last word of advice. If Alcibiades has no interest in you through Mania, perhaps you should have an interest in him through her. Information can be of value to you. Who knows, perhaps your little wild vixen will tell you Alcibiades' secrets if she is not milking you for your secrets. The bed works both ways you know. Time you were a real Athenian, and woke up to the advantages and ways of bedroom politics. In any case I imagine you'll have the opportunity soon enough. Cook tells me there is a matter that Aspasia wants to discuss with you, so you should be invited back soon. You seem to be becoming one of her regulars, so perhaps you are cleverer than I think."

"Is it about Socrates do you think?"

"Socrates? How should I know? Now why would you ask that? Be careful! There I am, saying it again. Just don't get involved with a philosopher. That is worse than a poet. Look at poor Alcibiades, after all. He pined away his teen years unrequitedly for Socrates, and now tries to make up for lost time with prostitutes. I would never want the same thing to happen to you. I'll give you a good thrashing first."

I said haughtily, "Aspasia says the gods have given

313

signs. Would you impede the gods' designs? I don't think Athenades would."

Leagros said, "Socrates may be the only thing that Athenades and I agree about. We doubt a philosopher who takes directions from a god who will not tell the people his name. Have you ever asked yourself this? Is his voice a god, a demon, or the delusion of an arrogant man? You should at least make an effort not to be taken in."

"Then I challenge you to show me any instance when the advice his voice gave him led to harm and not good. I have asked this of many, and no one has ever been able to point out one instance. That alone would indicate a god."

"Listen to me, Amyntas. Socrates' voice has told him not to be a politician. Yet, is it not the duty of every citizen to be ready to hold office? If it is, then has his voice not told him to be a bad citizen? I don't want you corrupted by this voice of his, or him."

I was indignant and said, "His voice has told him to be a philosopher, and that serves the city better than someone like Cleon who calls himself a servant of democracy but abuses his power. Is Socrates not also a hoplite?"

Leagros was angry and said, "Prince or no prince you are impudent to your elders, Macedonian. No doubt Socrates will be at the next Assembly in a couple of weeks, and then we shall see whose side he takes, whether it is Cleon's or Nicias'; war or peace. Let him speak, and let the catcalls tell how the people feel about him, as they did at *Clouds*."

I thought it best not to argue any longer. Indeed, Leagros had raised his voice and we were near enough to the entrance of school for some of my fellow students to

314

be looking askance at us. I replied meekly, "In any case, how can I see for myself at the Assembly? I am not of age and cannot attend."

Leagros answered, "Don't we ridiculous. All the boys sneak in through the west gate of the Pynx, which is never guarded. Just ask any of your friends over there in the schoolyard. They will probably go with you. If you approach the Pynx Hill from the side there is an entry into the Ekklesia just at the base of the hill. If you stand far at the back you can still hear and be hidden. You do not look of age, of course, but if anyone asks you they would be more interested in taking you home for a turn, or knowing whether you have citizen status rather than what your age is, and your special status in our household protects you. If you want I can be at the back to make sure no trouble comes to you. Unless war and peace does not interest you."

He had been harsh with me, and I said petulantly, "If I decide to go, you shall have to chaperone. Now it is getting late and I had better get to grammar."

"School indeed! Maybe it will dispel some of your ignorance, but I doubt it." Suddenly he laughed, "Better to have Mania instruct you, than the Lyceum or Taureas. She'll sap some of that insolence."

7. The Assembly: Cleon & Laches.

Many have wondered if any form of government were better than the Athenian democracy? I have seen none better, and yet it was the worst. In the year of *Clouds* it was said to be at its apogee. But ten years later, demagogues would overthrow it, and in twenty there

315

would be civil war. Was the collapse brought on by war, and the exhaustion of war?

Athenians seemed to me insecure. They longed for strong generals, or demagogues, to reassure them. They were fickle, governed by passions, and easily swayed, but when aroused by injustice they were fearsome, if not always right. Aspasia once quoted Pericles to me. "Let tyrants beware the wrath of the people. Nothing is more terrible." Their wrath came to pass years later in the overthrow of the Thirty and in the prosecution of the generals, including, unjustly, Aspasia's son, Pericles son of Pericles. She paid a high price for living in a democracy, the life of a beloved son. Must a democracy embrace tyranny before it can return to its roots? If Odysseus' return was uncertain to him and his men it was not uncertain to the gods; he did return. When the democracy fell, there was no guarantee that it would be restored. Democracy is more fragile than an individual life, and that is very fragile.

As a schoolboy I loved the democracy for all the wrong reasons, chiefly because it was good theater, a display of the broad spectrum of human grandeur and failing that informed Aristophanes' comedies. Fistfights regularly broke out in the Agora over politics; rotten fruit, and vegetables were hurled; men paraded their ideas and partisan loyalties the way they did their finery. What was Alcibiades' next move? Would he trot his horse across the podium at the next Assembly as the rumors suggested? At a previous Assembly some two or three months before, a madman had presented his backside to the people, farting his displeasure. The Agora still laughed over it. Political discourse was not of much interest to schoolboys but it took little to convince my school friends' to sneak in, as Leagros encouraged. They relished a risk, and the theater might be obscene.

There was a more serious reason for my curiosity about the Assembly. My remaining in Athens might depend on the peace, or at least Macedon's alliance at the next outbreak of battle, the longer deferred the better. If father supported Athenades and Nicias against Alcibiades and Cleon, King Perdiccas might shift with the winds. At that moment he was with Athens. Would the House of Temenidai be safe if Perdiccas were to abandon his current treaty with Athens and shift sides again?

In the day or two after Leagros' cautionary remarks about Mania my first reaction was to call them completely farfetched. Yet there was no harm in my informing myself through her. I refused to believe that I was being naive about a sexual adventure, or that being in Athens exempted me from the responsibilities of our House. Information was power, and survival.

Matters of friendship also compelled me to attend the Assembly. Leagros thought that Cleon might attack Socrates for not engaging in politics. Attacking Socrates was the sport of the year it seemed, encouraged by the mockery of *Clouds*. How would Socrates defend his life as a citizen? Would he voice his support for Nicias, or Cleon, for peace, or war? I went that day with high hopes and expectations, but I left shaken.

***

The Assembly started at dawn and lasted until sunset. It rarely ran more than one day, or past the morning, especially in summer. Thunder and the threat of rain, were signs from Zeus not to hold it, or to end it abruptly. Leagros did not come to fetch me until an hour after daybreak. I was already working at my table and thought he had forgotten. I was anxious about missing the main speeches, but need not have been. When we arrived in the Agora a huge crowd was milling around eating and drinking but hardly anyone showed any urgency about making their way to the Pynx in the western section of the city. The police were milling around too, but I saw no sign of the red stripes the police painted on those not attending, stigmatizing them for the day, nor did I see any of the Executive Committee either, the delegates from each of the Athenian ten tribes. They usually led the procession from the Agora to the Hill.

I said to Leagros, "It doesn't look as if there will be an Assembly at all."

"I forgot it is your first or I would have warned you. It's always like this. That's why I took my time this morning. Everyone comes as late as possible, but they will end up coming, most of them showing up at the last minute and then rushing to the front to get the best seats. You'll be better off standing at the back. No one will notice you in the hubbub."

I found my school friends near the stalls selling sweets. We were all in high spirits. It was late morning before the crier and the police holding the red thread appeared. Some ten or so police would hold the line between them and walk through the crowd as if scaring game bird. If you did not get out of the way of the rope, and make your way to the Assembly, you were marked red for the day and disgraced.

We waited a few minutes while most of the crowd filtered off and then made our way to the quiet west gate. By the time we reached the upper rows at the back where we would stand the suckling pig had already been paraded, purifying the area where the speeches were given, and the opening prayers and curse had already been delivered. I glanced around, reassured by the extra contingent of Scythian archers deployed for security that day, perhaps because the discussion was about treaties and war. These archers were chosen for guard duty only after proving their marksmanship.

One of Cleon's supporters was speaking. I think it must have been Cleonytus because he was being booed for dropping his shield in battle, a disgrace many years old but never forgotten. The amphitheater seated some five thousand; it was packed that day because the discussion was about war. I looked for Socrates but could not spot him among the throng, but I recognized the Executive Committee parading to the front rows. Some farmers threw rotting vegetables at Cleonytus; they were shouting for him to leave the podium. The more he tried to speak the more they jeered. He finally threw his hands up in disgust and stomped off.

A sudden deafening cry went up, half cheer, half jeer. Cleon entered with a large retinue. I added my hisses and foot stamping to the jeers. He strode across the podium throwing his robe over his shoulder or off his shoulder, any gesture that would gain attention. Would not Nicias,

Athenades, or their spokesman have the floor first? It was their resolution that was being debated. Payments could be made; the podium monopolized at will.

People were stamping now, begging him to speak. Rhythmic shouts of "Cleon! Cleon! Cleon!" rang out from the Pynx to the corners of Athens. Strutting back and forth he held up his arms to silence the people and slowly they subsided, only to erupt into laughter. A comic-masked actor, sporting a large leather phallus, suddenly jumped onto the podium and made lewd gestures behind Cleon. The rumors later flew that it was Aristophanes himself, although he would not have shed that much dignity. Cleon silenced the crowd enough to say, "Our comedian would rape the air. Perhaps he is a philosopher?"

That elicited another uproar from the crowd, and again it seemed to me that those who agreed with Cleon outnumbered those who disagreed. The actor, or drunk, jumped from the podium before the police could catch him, and rushed off through one of the front gates, but not before slapping his backside to the crowd, to much amusement, and only a few shouts of "desecration".

Cleon walked back and forth nervously, and now raised his hands for silence. But cries of "Nicias! Let Nicias speak first!" threatened to disrupt proceedings again. The Archon moderator came onto the podium to restore order and announce that Cleon had been given permission to speak first. Cleon stepped forward to the edge of the podium again. He used dramatic gesture well, learned from the rhetoricians.

Cleon said, "My opponents have chosen to let me speak first, because they think your memories will be too short to remember my arguments for war long enough to influence their pleas for peace. So let me tell you now what Nicias and his kind have come today to propose, and how they mean to win your support, for it is a simple matter, easily disposed of here in the sacred Ekklesia. They would put to you today the argument that a permanent peace with Sparta is in the best interests of Athens. " Cries of "No!" and "Never!" were heard throughout. Cleon continued, "But I ask, can we trust Sparta when it has so often betrayed a truce and shown itself a treacherous foe ready to use every trick against us including peace, and peace treaties? Has Sparta not raped and pillaged Attica? And are we such fools as to think it would not do so again? But I tell you that there are many more reasons for rejecting peace, not least of which is that to spread our democracy we must have a strong military at all times ready to make war, not just for the spread of the empire, but for the preservation of security at home. For are we not quite simply the single greatest force of justice, the exception to the surrounding tyrannies of Sparta and Persia? Nicias, I say, is naive, and his naivety endangers Athens. Nicias and his kind underestimate our foe and their determination to destroy all we hold dear. We must not let down our guard, and today we must be more resolved than ever to dig into our purses to support our military. Our navy is second to none, and the glory of our empire. I today pledge three triremes to Athens, and other of my friends, the true friends of Athens, pledge three more. Here is what I say, peace with Sparta is a delusion, and to harbor this delusion risks losing all. I and my friends would protect Athens through ever ready military

321

might." He paused to throw his robe over his shoulder again. There was an impressive silence and when he continued he hardly needed to raise his voice, "We must ask ourselves today: Do we love Athena and her ideals? And if the answer to this is, as I know it will be my friends, a resounding 'Yes!' then you must reject calls for appeasement of an enemy set on our destruction and enslavement. We must remain the bulwark of freedom through a strong military. I cry unto you today: "Long live Athens! Long live democracy!"

The crowd leapt to its feet and there were many minutes of bedlam.

I now expected Nicias to take the podium. I did not know that the fellowship had decided that, not being a strong speaker, he must not represent their side in the Assembly debate. This task fell to another aristocrat member of their group, General Laches son of Melonopos. He had recently gained popularity by regaining two of the Athenian strongholds in Sicily, redeeming the failure of his other Sicilian campaign some three years before, a great disaster for Athens. Laches had been prosecuted for negligence of Athenian interests, and the man bringing the charges was none other than Cleon. The lawsuit against Laches had split the aristocracy. Each side was convinced that the other was the greater danger to Athens. Now here is another revelation of the mood then. The year following *Clouds,* Aristophanes premiered a new play at the Lanea, Wasps which was to prove much more successful and enduring than *Clouds*. Indeed, *Wasps* has come to be seen as Aristophanes most perfect play. It satirizes the Athenian love of litigation, and its subject is this lawsuit of Cleon against Laches.

So it was that Aristophanes now strode onto the podium in order to introduce Laches. Besides the revision of *Clouds*, Simonides had told me that he was hard at work on a new play, but did not know it had to do with Cleon and Laches.

Someone in the crowd shouted out, "Where's your leather prick now? Or would you rather show us the real?"

Aristophanes raised his hands and shouted above the din, "Calm yourselves now. My body is less exciting than the business at hand."

Someone again shouted, "Business at hand? Oh you use your hand do you? One only?"

Again there was much jeering and shouting, and it took much effort for Aristophanes to silence the crowd. At last he could speak in calm. I thought he would make a long speech, as he was not known for brevity. He said only, or rather shouted with great aplomb, "I give youAthens' one true General, our own hero, General Laches!"

Thus did he introduce General Laches and slur General Cleon in one breath.

Laches came to the podium. He was about fifty, and very fat, which did not endear him. He wore extravagantly colored robes and was not one to hide his wealth. He was rich, if not as rich as silver mining had made Nicias, or tanning had made Cleon, rich nonetheless. Like Athenades he gave generously to the rituals, but unlike Athenades he gave equally to the war effort. I thought he was an unlikely ally for the peace fellowship, but his piety was so great that he came to agree with Athenades that war siphoned off funds best spent on the temples and gods.

I was looking down on him from where I stood at the top of the amphitheater, but his bulk and bearing were enough to recognize him as one of the men coming and going in the shop the last few weeks. Well, well, I thought, this Athenades does move in high circles. I was very much concentrated on the proceedings, and not paying much attention to my surroundings. In fact, as Laches came onto the podium I am ashamed to say that I joined my classmates in their catcalls. Laches' stomach was too good to pass notice. I hardly felt a hand brushing my backside, not an uncommon, if annoying, experience in Athens. I turned in order to see if one of my classmates were making overtures, but three strange men had blocked me off from my friends. They looked rough, not simple citizens attending an Assembly. It was hard to believe they could care much about me. None of the Scythian archers were near enough to me, a mere boy, to intervene.

The one closest to my side suddenly gripped my left buttock so hard as to cause sharp pain. His mouth was near enough to my face to smell his breath fouled from rotted teeth. I saw the other two trying to converge on me, but managed to break away and back among my friends. I was shaken. Scouring the crowd, I could no longer see them. I was trembling and upset and searched for Leagros so that I could leave, but could not see him near. Behind us there were pillars, a wall and some shade. I stood there to collect myself, pretending to be a bit overcome by the heat.

Laches was already speaking and the crowd had gone quiet so that everyone could hear. Random shouts of "Quiet" were still heard here and there. I do not remember

324

much of what he said, but the speech was later published.

Laches said, "...and so you have heard Cleon speak with his customary eloquence about what is in the best interests of Athens, but that is not to say, my fellow citizens, that what he says is in the best interests of Athens. We must ask ourselves: Is there anything new in what he said? And the answer is clearly: There is nothing new in what he said. War is war. We all know its consequences. But what he did not say is that in the proper conduct of war, not just battle or retreat can be the best strategy, but also truce. My point is simple. We are a noble city depleted of resources by war and the plague which have taken the lives of half our citizenry, and drained our coffers to care for those left without family, wives, or children. The war has made terrible demands on our resources. Is it not eminently sensible to argue that those who say war should be waged without end until there is total victory do not plead reasonably? A truce can heal and restore. What then a lasting peace? We are not cowards and we have proved this many times to our enemy. A truce with Sparta will worry the Spartans, and it will be difficult to get them to agree. They will argue amongst themselves that it will give us time to regroup and build our military. And they would be right. They will argue that it will give us time to retrain our youths, and to churn out more shields and train more horses for the cavalry, and they would be right. They will argue that in one year we can build twenty new triremes and in this they would be wrong. We can build thirty. I have come today to plead for a truce with Sparta, a year's truce, one year only, so that we may rebuild and heal."

I was sweating profusely and feeling dizzy. My friends were ready to leave, disappointed that there had not been at least a fistfight. Cheering and booing in equal measure still disrupted the speaking. I looked back one last time, still fearing to catch a glimpse of the three men. There were too many vendors crying, too many people standing and shouting, or chasing dogs that had wandered in, to see anything distinctly in such a muddle. Democracy was a messy, inefficient thing. As thick a crowd was waiting to enter as was trying to exit. My friends and I pushed our way through.

Suddenly my way was blocked again. A friend had me by the hand, and when I stopped abruptly he lost his grip. The bad-breathed Charon grabbed a fistful of my tunic and hissed into my face, "We know you, Macedon." That was all. He shoved me away, and was gone. It happened so quickly I hardly had time to react. My friend as suddenly found my hand again and pulled me through the last of the crowd to the exit.

"Come on!" he said impatiently. "Let's get cakes in the Agora. I have a new game and want to see if you can do it." He pulled out from his bag an intricate wooden puzzle cube. It came apart in twelve pieces. Who reassembled it the fastest won. We huddled together trying it as we walked along but I could not concentrate, fumbled with it, and he took it back impatiently lest I drop it.

We had left too early to hear the end results of the meeting, which I heard from Leagros that evening. The debate had gone on to the edge of evening, the legal limit. When the vote was taken just before sunset, an

326

overwhelming majority voted for the peace resolution of Laches, Nicias, and Athenades. By the following week it was being called the Truce of Laches.

As I lay in bed, I did not think of the meeting but only of being accosted, those men like some malevolent spirits breathed up from foul depths. I could not understand it or sleep. I went to find security beside Assur, but did not tell him what had happened.

V. My Life in Athens: Peace to War.

1. 422 B.C. The New Year. Know Thyself.

If the Athenian year ended and began with the Truce of Laches, everywhere there were still signs of war and the preparation for war. The Agora was still teeming with beggars. Some farmers had tried to return home to sow their autumnal crops only to find their house and land scorched, and their families facing starvation. They sought refuge and sustenance within the walls, many reduced to beggary, as Aristophanes would decry later in his play Peace. Discharged soldiers prostituted by the Herms or in the Ceramica; the lame and disfigured were reduced to humiliating penury, so recently crowned as heroes. I came to loathe the culture of death engendered by war, so antithetical to the creative vitality of Athens. Were war and peace the two faces of Hermes? Were they contradictions, opposites, or negations?

Despite the new truce, the ironmongers were still churning out an endless stream of spears, shields, and arrows, and there were still weekly if not daily parades of military contingents. Hatred of the Spartans and discussions of new battle strategies were heard everywhere, in the doctors' offices, in the barbershops, and in the Lyceum where so many of my fellow students yearned for battle. If the Assembly had agreed on a truce, the same Assembly on that very same afternoon had approved funding for new warships, the wealthy falling over each other in their rush to appear the best of best citizens by spilling their purses at the feet of bloodlust Ares. The tragedy was that Athenians needed an enemy.

What was best for Athens? A truce was far from peace.

War had made our workshop busier and Athenades wealthier. He profited from war if he discretely opposed it. Gold and silver objects were given as offerings to the gods for protection of a farm or household, or for the safe return of a cherished son. Bribery with gold artifacts could also curry favor with allies in the hope of tipping the balance against Sparta. Morning, noon, and night our shop had been busy with sacrificial gifts for the war effort. Yet, Athenades argued that war prevented the unrestrained expansion of Athenian business interests to the further reaches of the Great Sea, meaning his own interests. I once heard him pray before the household gods, if not at the public rituals, for "a hundred years of peace that my business might flourish", but he made most of his fortune during the long war.

As the truce began to hold, Athenades also one day mentioned a city name I had not heard for a long time, and that raised the old homesickness, a name that would come to evoke in one breath both war and peace, although it would take many months for anyone to know this.

He was speaking with one of his agents who purchased our gold supplies and said, "Now that there is peace again and an alliance with Macedon we should take advantage of it. You should go right away to Amphipolis and secure a gold supply for us."

Amphipolis! I was startled, and he heard me catch my breath.

"Do you know the town, Amyntas?" Athenades asked.

"Yes, Master. As a matter of fact, father took me there once or twice. It is not far from our home. Less than a day's ride."

Athenades said, "Do you have relatives there?"

"No. Father thought there might be opportunities for his wine trade in the new town. It was only a few years old then, built on the ruins of the old, you know."

"Yes, I know. I was there myself just before your arrival. It may have been new then but it has grown rapidly since."

"Father has told me how large it has become because . . . " I paused, not wanting to offend.

Athenades finished the thought. "Because General Brasidas and the Spartans have a garrison there? I am sure they brought prosperity with their tyranny. Did you not know that some of the gold you work comes from the Pangaeon mines just north of Amphipolis?"

I shook my head, embarrassed by my ignorance, and said, "I knew our gold came from Thrace, but not the Pangaeon."

The river valley was treacherous, for its fevers, and I remember being taken ill on one of our visits. Father had pitched our encampment on top of one of the highest hills so that the cooling breezes could restore me. In the northern distance was the snow capped Pangaeon. Father was often mother to me and I remembered his care nostalgically.

I went back to work, but later in the day, as he often did when we were alone, Athenades stopped to speak with me. He said, "Do you know if your father retained a business agent for his wine trade in Amphipolis?"

I said, "I think he did. Before I came here I helped him with his accounts and remember payments to someone there."

"I am glad I asked. It could be important and I shall write to him at once. If you have a letter for him you can send it with the same messenger. Amphipolis is of growing importance, you know. What can you tell me?"

The surrounding hills commanded the river valleys and father had told me that anyone holding those hills could control the trade routes eastward to Persia or westward to Sparta and Athens. I added, "Father called the region of Amphipolis a strategic knot and he said that knots could make or break ambitions, just as Thermopylae or Salamis had broken the Persians."

He frowned, and said, "Yes, it is what I thought."

I was beginning to worry and asked, "Is there growing tension?"

"Let us say there are rumors of Spartan conspiracies. But then there always are so you need not fear. When was the last time you were there?"

"It must have been a year before I came here. It is beautiful there and father liked to combine business with leisure time together." I rarely spoke of Macedon or my family in the workshop for fear of being teased or bullied by the others. Yet, that day I felt moved to do so, and I added, "Father liked to take me there because there are family connections with the site."

He looked puzzled and I explained that a great great uncle, King Alexander I, had defeated the remnants of Xerxes' army at the estuary of the Styrmon River near Amphipolis. I was named after his father and my great uncle, King Amyntas. The victory was after Xerxes had sacked Athens, and been defeated by the Athenians at

Salamis. The retreating Persian army was laid siege to at Plataea as it attempted to return home across the plains of Amphipolis. Alexander I was ruthless. He ambushed the Persian force of forty five thousand and slaughtered every last one of them mercilessly. I never thought he was one to emulate and was glad I was not named after him.

Athenades said, "I am afraid I did not make the connection. Your ancestor's feat is legendary here, you know, for giving the final blow to Persian ambitions. It has protected us since."

I said, "Father says King Alexander's defeat of the Persians consolidated Macedonian independence, but it also bound Athens and us together. We exacted your revenge, for the Persian sacking of Athens."

Athenades agreed, and said, "Who defeats our enemies becomes our friend. Your father and family seem to have more of an identification with Athens than I had thought."

"Father thinks so."

"Perhaps one day years from now if the peace holds we shall have a branch of our workshop at Amphipolis, to be near the gold and silver supply at Pangaeon. It would be a natural place for you to manage."

I was excited by this prospect, if it was but a distant dream.

***

It was after this conversation, about two weeks after the New Year and weeks before the autumn Eleusinian, that Simonides made a remark that upset me. He was walking me to the Taureas that particular day, having just indulged

332

me with another gift, one I particularly liked. He was leaving on his theater tour after the festival and was trying to be extra sensitive, not overly indulgent but considerately so, according to him. I had mentioned to him that the latest rage at the palaistra was basketball, my shameless way of eliciting gifts that I disapproved of his giving. That day he had given me a new basketball. The ones we used were cheap pig's bladder; and easily burst but this was cured leather that had been rubbed with oil and heated for sealing, to make it stronger. We were tossing it between us playfully as we walked. By then my resistance to his gifts was token, so long as they were fewer and none too extravagant. I was eager to show my schoolmates the ball and toss some hoops in the ring set up at one end of the palaistra yard. A board has been stuck haphazardly into the ground, with a hole at the top some three or four my lengths high.

Simonides tossed the ball and I caught it.

I laughed and said, "Look at that Leagros! He is lagging behind us again. He can't keep up with our moderate pace."

"I know. We had better stop over there to wait for him." We could not have been further than the turnoff to Sunium, with still a long way to go.

I said, "He's like that every day. And he's very fit too. If he makes me late again I shall never forgive him."

Simonides said, "I know, I know. Just look at that! He is not stopping to catch his breath. He is stopping to take another mouthful of that cheap wine he imbibes."

"I will have to do three laps of the yard! See what I have to put up with? Can't we run ahead?"

333

"Calm down. You will not be late. If I were not going on tour soon I would propose chaperoning you. With your agreement of course."

He dared only say this because he was leaving, so I knew he meant it for the thought. "Are you still leaving after the Eleusinian?"

"Yes. I imagine you will still not go with us? We would all enjoy your company and you would be very popular with your looks and that singing voice of yours. Lygis talks about you endlessly."

"Please! My voice is thin and reedy. You know that. Anyway, I have not changed my mind and if I did want to go I would not dare suggest it to father."

I had said this before but he had never reacted. He must have been preparing an answer. He said, "Why not? After all we are going westward and north, not eastward towards the trouble spots. Your father might approve."

"My life is here, Simonides. I don't want to leave school for the road. And Athenades sees a career for me as a goldsmith. Father wants me to make my own way in the world. That was part of the plan for sending me here. You know he thinks Macedon is too unstable to count on for my future."

"Yes. But you underestimate yourself and your potential in the theater."

"You exaggerate. I haven't the slightest talent. You just want me near you."

"Is that so wrong?"

"I did not say it was wrong, just transparent. Let's not talk about it. Besides, if you are so eager to be with me and do something, then there is something we might do

334

together."

"What is that?"

"You can help with a class assignment. One of our masters said that Cleon was scheduled to speak in the Agora about Spartan ambitions in Amphipolis. He wants us to try to attend and make a report for class. Athenades was also talking about Amphipolis in the workshop a couple of days ago and I would like to stay informed."

"When is it?"

"In two days time."

He looked surprised that I had asked and said, "Yes, of course I will do that with you."

I was still somewhat defensive around him and so I explained our family connections as I had to Athenades. The truth was that I was afraid to go with Leagros after the experience at the Assembly. He was so neglectful that it was as good as going alone.

I said, "Will you really? And afterwards, the Taureas is playing one of its ephebike rugby matches against the Lyceum. I have friends on both teams so I can't miss it. If you are free for that as well of course. I hope you do not mind my asking."

Simonides exclaimed, "Of course I am free!"

We were nearing the Taureas by then, with Leagros still lagging behind. Friends were already running for the school gate. This distracted me or I would not have said what I did. I had never told Simonides about the man seizing my tunic at the Assembly, but I now off-handedly said, as if he knew the whole story, or I had told him, "I hope nothing like what happened to me at the Assembly happens at Cleon's speech. But of course you will be there and not Leagros."

No sooner was it out of my mouth than I knew it was a mistake. True to form, at that inadvertent moment, Leagros caught up with us and overheard my unwitting remark, "Well, I am glad you're telling him about that, Amyntas. I always thought you dismissed it too lightly."

Simonides said, "Told me what? What happened? The Assembly? What have you to do with the Assembly?" He caught my arm before I could run off.

"Please, Simonides. I'll be late."

He would not let go. "Then tell me quickly."

And so I was forced to tell him, and so he threw a fit, first at Leagros for encouraging me to sneak into the meeting in the first place, and then for not being with me at every moment, and then at me for being so foolish as to sneak in, and for thinking that I could go unaccompanied, and lastly for not telling him. I tried to protest that my friends were with me and that nothing had happened, but his ranting was too far advanced. I really should get out of this city! I really should go with him! He would talk to Athenades. He would talk to Aspasia. If need be he would ride all the way to Macedon to talk to father.

Leagros saw what a mess it was, took Simonides arm and said, "Come over here, Simonides and have a drink to calm down. Let us talk about this. And you, young Master, you had better get to your gymnastics class."

I needed no urging. I ran off leaving the two of them to sort it out.

A couple of days later Simonides took me to the speaker's corner in the Agora, but made only passing reference to the incident, and I did not dare bring it up.

I wrote to father about Cleon's speech which was long and full of bluster as usual. Few of his remarks were about Amphipolis and those he did make were predictable warnings; that his spies had brought word that the Spartan General Brasidas was conspiring to undermine the Athenian strongholds in the surrounding plain's region, and that Athens had to begin now to prepare itself lest it lose its grip there. To lose its enclaves would be to lose protection from the Persians, and safe passage for Athenian businesses along those trade routes, Athenades included I supposed. Athens could not afford to let down its vigilance, to safeguard its economic interests, or its democratic freedom.

As we were leaving the talk and walking to the school match, I asked Simonides what he thought of the speech and he said, "Cleon would say what he did. He wants more triremes to be built and more battalions to be outfitted, and has ambitions to be a general again. But his spies are reliable and he is often right."

It was this remark that upset me. If there was conspiring in the regions so close to our home what would King Perdiccas do, and expect father to do? Would Brasidas and the Spartans risk the renewal of the war? And Cleon? How would he and Athens react? How eager were both sides to fight? Would the voices of peace raise a chorus loud enough? I had best write to father later that day to tell him what I had heard, and to beset him with a thousand questions.

That day the Lyceum took a terrible beating at the rugby match with Taureas, scoring no points at all! It was very awkward at both schools for a while because I went to both and received taunts and teases from all sides. I tried to bear it all with good grace and somehow survived that too.

***

As I ran off to class that day, leaving the none too reliable Leagros to sort it out with the highly emotional Simonides, I was myself distressed by Simonides angry, fearful response to the incident in the Assembly. It forced me to consider what I had lightly brushed off. Say what I will about Simonides he cared about me. Surely being accosted by those men was a coincidence? I was so insignificant anything deliberate hardly seemed likely. Yet the question broke the seal on Pandora's jar releasing the darker things in me. At least, she had sealed the jar in time to save hope. If the man with the foul breath had lurked in the crowd waiting to assail me he must have been sent, but by whom? My classmates hardly seemed candidates for such a malicious joke. The man had called me "Macedon". To say that my mates had the minutest interest in anything Macedonian would have been an exaggeration.

And as I dashed off I turned back for a moment. Leagros and Simonides were still lost in conversation and a dark thought assailed me. I had told no one about attending the Assembly, not even Mania; Leagros had been the one to suggest it. What if Leagros had hired the thug to threaten me? I had told Leagros as soon as it had happened. He had shown concern, but he had also sworn me to secrecy, I thought so as not to earn the disapproval of Athenades. But why would he expose me to danger?

338

Did he wish to tighten his grip on me by compounding secrets between us? I could not understand that at all. If I was so naïve as not to protect myself, and lay myself open to danger, then my dangers were my responsibility. Yet, if it were Leagros what did it mean about my affair with Mania? He had taken me back there thrice more so that I might have my pleasure with her, and hers with me. Was Leagros living vicariously through my lust? He hardly seemed to need it. As if through a slow progression of steps downward I reached darker and darker questions. What if Aspasia knew nothing about Mania and me, as I had always suspected in my heart of hearts. Neither Leagros, nor Mania, not Alcibiades for that matter, had claimed outright that Aspasia knew. Perhaps Leagros did have a reason. He was very angry with Athenades for disapproving of his drunkenness and carousing, not to mention his peace activities. Was I being used in some way to satisfy his rage? None of it made sense.

I crossed the palaistra yard to the changing and oiling rooms, looking for Socrates, but not seeing him. Socrates the Wise! How ready I was to flee to his side. He would have answers. At gymnastics I could not concentrate and made such a mess of my tumbles and leaps that for the first time Hippothales castigated me in front of the others. I told him I felt unwell, which was half a truth at least, and he told me to sit in the shade until I collected myself. It was there that Socrates found me.

"You look a mess today," he said, sitting next to me. It was a rightly chosen word and I nearly burst out crying. "I am a mess. It's a terrible mess!"

"As bad as that?" I hung my head and could hardly

339

speak. "I'm sure we'll figure it out." His hands were large and could encompass mine. "I feared something might be wrong. You've seemed so restless and moody lately. I thought it might be the change and that imbalance of humors boys suffer at their first emission time, until everything balances again. I heard your voice crack the other day, you know. But it is more, isn't it?"

"Yes," I said. He did not press me for the story, but waited patiently, as he did when he fell into one of his reveries and I wondered if he were not waiting for his voice to confirm he should listen to me. I leaned against him, and began tentatively to tell him, of the dinner at Aspasia's, where he was present, and the meeting afterwards with Mania, of the conversation with Alcibiades, of Leagros and the Assembly. As the story progressed in fits and starts it quickened, all of it finally spilling out with much emotion.

Socrates had closed his eyes, and for a long time he said nothing. I was worried that he might be thinking of a way to blame or punish me, little understanding his ways.

He said, "I think you know the answers to your own doubts and questions." He turned my hands palm upward. "Now close your eyes and try to calm yourself." We sat silently for a bit and I felt my troubled breathing harmonize with his. It was cool in the shade where we sat on the ground together. I noticed the birds, the cries of my classmates from across the yard.

Socrates said, "Now try to tell me what you think is going on."

"I...I think Leagros is an old drunk and likes to create dramas. There seems to be hatred in his drunkenness, so

340

his drunken dramas can be dangerous. He started making dramas as if I was a character out of Sophocles, and I let him. Mania was very agreeable. Athenades is so strict in the workshop. Leagros used me but I used him too. But I forgot myself and that it might be dangerous. Our enemies can control us through our passions. So lust has its foolish side."

"And Aspasia?"

"I don't think she knows. She has seen something special in me and I feel I have defiled her trust."

"That is too strong I think. We can go to her together if you like and you can tell her all you just told me. She has always surprised me."

I felt my heart sink but I said, "Do you think I am right that she knows nothing about Mania and me, or that she chose to turn a blind eye?"

Socrates said, "Aspasia is very open and direct. You must not make her too scheming as she is not."

"Oh Socrates, I did not mean that she was scheming. You see? I am so confused! I've made a terrible mess of things haven't I?"

"Not so bad it can't be sorted out."

"Do you really think it can?"

"Yes. You must go to Aspasia as soon as possible. It is very important that you do that. There are elements of your story that are troubling and that she should know of. We have to sort it all out."

"The man at the Assembly? You do not think Leagros hired him?"

"Whoever sent him, one thing is clear, and in this I am sure Simonides and I will agree, Leagros has done a terrible job; no matter what conclusions we draw, I can't see how he can continue to be your chaperone. But Aspasia will know what to do about this too."

"But Socrates. I am afraid to see her. Won't she be more furious than Simonides is today? And Mania? Will she beat or banish her? I would rather not tell Aspasia than see Mania punished."

"Aspasia is not a cruel person. You must see her."

I sighed and said, "How complicated life is in Athens."

Socrates said, "I think what you mean to say is, how complicated we make our lives in Athens."

2. False Friends and True.

Socrates did not wait long to talk to Aspasia and she soon summoned me. I went to her house this time with great trepidation, but she greeted me warmly. The scent of her exotic perfume again struck me as I was shown into her study chamber. Each time I saw her I tried to guess the unusual combination of scents she mixed herself. Was cinnamon added to lily, or sage to musk rose? She revealed to me years later that when the secretions of animal glands were blended with plant extracts they enhanced the smells. This made her cleverer at her craft than the Egyptians, I concluded. She wore one of the simpler everyday bracelets I had made, a small but reassuring gesture. Her everyday dress was homespun wool, in the manner of her student Socrates, the teacher taking from the pupil. She was barefoot and I had removed my sandals at the door. As I entered the study I again felt that she was the most beautiful woman in Hellas.

She turned, came and kissed my cheeks, "I have been

meaning to send for you. Pericles has been asking after you and I promised I would invite you."

Socrates had told me that he would leave it up to me to tell my story, and would say nothing himself. I tried to thank her for inviting me but my mouth was so dry with fear that when I opened it nothing came forth. To confess subterfuge, if undertaken innocently, to a woman who was my hero was one of the most painful moments of my youth.

She said, "Oh, but you are troubled. Socrates said you wished to see me over some serious concern. Come, let's sit here together and you can tell me. Take refreshments and tell me. We shall not be disturbed." She took my hands in hers, as Socrates did. "It will be all right."

Not one sip of wine had passed my lips before the whole story spilled out, of Leagros, Mania, the meeting with Alcibiades that day, and the incident in the Assembly. I rushed to the end and stopped, hardly daring to glance at her. To my horror I saw she was angry; it terrified me. Was she angry with me, with Mania, with Leagros, with us all? Would she beat Mania, or banish her? Would she refuse ever to see me again? It was one of the longest moments I have had to endure.

She finally patted my hand. Regaining her calm she said, "I have known that things were amiss here in the household. There were signs in the readings, and the girls were whispering among themselves. But Mania lied and apparently has her allies. It takes time and energy to unmask lies."

"Then you suspected?"

"The portents showed trouble. As with Socrates' voice,

or the Delphic Oracle, they tell but do not explain. The trouble might have been political. There is argument among the gods over this endless war with Sparta, some for Athens, some for Sparta, as much as there was over Achilles. There is so much at stake for Athens, more than I have seen since the death of my dear Pericles. The peace is fragile. I doubt if the truce signals the end of the war, or that the quarrels among the gods over our fates is settled."

"But am I being used? Unless…"

Aspasia seemed to know what I was thinking, as her response confirmed, "Don't try to outguess the gods. All we know is that a stranger accosted you at the Assembly. At the very least it should remind us of our responsibility to keep you safe. Leagros was not a good choice to chaperone you, but Athenades wanted him out of his hair and thought that the responsibility would temper his drinking, but it appears it did not. Leagros uses people and that is dangerous."

I said, "And Mania?"

"She is an initiate at the Eleusinian. Did she not tell you? It is a great honor and she must be here for the ceremony if there is not to be a scandal. But afterwards, well, I have been thinking of making some changes in my staff, perhaps with a certain head cook as well. I transfer staff regularly and it would not be noticed if some were sent to my villa in Miletus. Leagros may not like being suddenly deprived and, of course, it will be impossible for him to come here again. It will have to be handled delicately because of my friendship with Athenades, and my ties with the peace party. Most of all, Amyntas, you will need a new chaperone, one who can be trusted not to lead you off the middle way. That too must be handled delicately. If we go to Athenades with the whole story he will certainly send you back to your father. I do not think that is the best thing for you right now with the truce so fragile and Amphipolis on your doorstep. Your future here is bright. The signs tell it. You have a genius for goldsmith work. We shall consult the gods together and they shall guide us. Trust the gods, dear friend. They will favor you, you will see."

One phrase of hers stood out. "The peace is fragile?"

"The rumors are not good. But you are so young, and in Athens. You should enjoy your youth. It is important that you put cares behind you and get on with your life. It is a great privilege to be here. If I may give you some advice?"

I said meekly, "Of course."

"We must sometimes rid our lives of false friends in order to know true. If you are to have a happy and secure life here you must distinguish better between these. Nourishing the soul is a sign of true friendship. You have to be ready to discard, or at least hold in perspective, those who interfere with inner progress."

I suddenly felt a wave of anxiety and burst out, "And Simonides then?"

Aspasia laughed. "He tells me your saga continues."

I replied, "He wants to take me along on their theater tour north and I have told him that I won't go."

"Take you along! That would be impossible and he is impossible. How could he dream of taking you away from Athens and your apprenticeship? He will be gone for months you know?"

"Yes, four or five at least. I told him that it was

impossible."

"He is quite mad, which I rather like. He must be dreaming of marrying you. Some remote tribes up north have secret rituals, and across the Great Sea in the desert too, said to forge stronger bonds in war, like the Thebans. Simonides is quite capable of wanting anything." She sighed, "Simonides, Simonides. With anyone else I would say that if he were gone for so long he would forget you, but not Simonides. More likely, he will brood over you and the absence will fire his ardor all the more. At least that is his pattern. The more unattainable you make yourself the more in love he will be with you."

"But that means if I throw myself at him he will quickly tire of me! Perhaps I should do that? It is my fault anyway. I do not want sex and I do not want to lose him as a friend. He is my bridge to so many things Athenian. He introduces me to so much. And yet I find him impossible."

Aspasia said kindly, "It cannot go on like this. He suffers too much and it gives you too much conflict. Love is never static."

I said, "I do not like choices where choosing one thing means rejecting another. "

Aspasia said, "A choice is always a rejection."

"Yes. I suppose it is. Do you think then that I should end our friendship now?"

"Oh, I cannot tell you that."

"Yes, I know. Growth in love demands acting wisely and I have to learn that for myself."

"Will you see him again soon?"

"Yes. He has written some hymns for the Eleusinian, along with twenty more odes to my eyes besides the twenty he has already written. He wants to read them all to me before he leaves. We usually go up to the new Stoa when he is to read new poems to me."

"You inspire his poetry and that is good."

"Can you give me no advice?"

She looked at me quite closely. "I might make a suggestion."

"Oh please do."

"Wear an oversized chiton that covers you well, perhaps something ugly, one of grey flax or coarse wool, one that falls well below the knees. No gold chain around your neck either, and those sandals with the decorations, well wear something with a broken strap and let your feet get dirty and smell a little. If Athenades will tolerate it, don't go to the barber for a while, look a bit ragged."

I thought that this was extremely funny and said, "Oh, I see what you mean. I am making myself too attractive!"

"Yes. It is a way of flirting, you know. You are one of the kalos kagathos, as much as Alcibiades was at your age, so it is quite a coup for Simonides to have you on his arm."

I said, with a glint, "Of course, if I stink a little and have bad breath it might cool him off."

"It is worth a try. You have tried honesty, and it has failed, so a little trickery might work, so long as you don't go too far the other way."

I laughed again, "Yes, if he thought that there was a street urchin lurking inside a prince he might find me all the more interesting. Street urchins will get up to anything, won't they?"

"Yes. I think that you are catching on to the love game.

347

"

"I can flirt and seduce, but I can also repel."

"Exactly. And both with the same means."

We were interrupted. Polydamus burst into the study carrying the young Pericles on his shoulders. The boy had tied a blindfold around Polydamus' eyes and was guiding him by his ears. "To the right. No, stop! To the left! Stop!"

Aspasia laughed and said, "Call this house Kaos."

***

I was envious that Mania would become an initiate, but bitter. Initiates have proven their innocence and I felt betrayed. Perhaps I was too harsh. She had honored me with her abandon and I have had few more passionate. I came to see that she was truly smitten by the fever that besets us all, and view her kindly now. But I do not think that Leagros' supposition was correct, that she suffered from some womb displacement. I was not sure I wanted to witness the Eleusinian ceremonies and was half-tempted to run off with Simonides, to his eternal delight. The Gods stopped me from this foolishness at least. Simonides sent word that his festival hymns were finished and could we meet. Hints that the worst heat of summer was already over were in the air; the first chilling drafts creeping like spiders along the workshop floor over my bare feet. "I shall be among the 'red bearded tribes' soon," Simonides wrote to me secretly. "I would enjoy your company as much as possible before my departure to hold every memory of you I can within my heart for so long an absence."

348

The Eleusinian marked the interruption of war each year so that the autumn crops could be sown. Simonides had told me that his hymns would reflect the double blessing of cessation and truce, "the double peace" as he called it. The archons objected to his announced plans. They would not scorn the gods with mortal concerns, nor neglect Demeter or Persephone. They would not turn a sacred feast into a politics, but, of course, they did. We would meet again by the Stoa but I did not know what he had finally decided his new verse should be. He said only that he had made a draft and wanted my advice. When my free day came and I was to set out to meet him, quite suddenly there was a large Nubian to accompany me. He was my new chaperone and a relative of Socrates' eunuch; they were from the same village. He towered over me, and most every Athenian male. I did not dare ask how Aspasia or Socrates had managed it with Athenades, and was never told. With someone like this by my side, no one would meddle with me.

When we arrived at the Stoa, Simonides was already there waiting. He was in one of his hyper states that I found more difficult than his depressed. Everything was hyperbole. When he saw me he said I looked more beautiful than he had ever seen me, that the day was the finest there had been in months, that the new and fragile truce with Sparta was the finest peace so far signed, and the greatest opportunity for both states in decades. It was useless to argue. Either he would not listen, or he would disagree so angrily so to raise the Agora patrol. I did not like him in this mood, and regretted I had agreed to come.

Excitedly he unrolled a sheaf of his verse but I found it

too derivative. "I sing of Demeter and the fair Kore/torn apart by Hades/for his pleasure in the underworld...." It was nothing but the usual yearly hymn rehashed, I thought, but could not say so. "Her daughter lost/a mother thrown in mourning/she scours the world unceasing/in vain, in vain/aided by loyal Hecate/Helios faithful too/alert to Zeus' ways..."

I said instead with crafted enthusiasm, "But you told me you were worried about pleasing the Council and I am sure that it will be acceptable."

"Are you sure? You have only heard the first few verses, but there are fifty more. Wait, there is something else I want to read to you, something different that I had first intended."

As he pulled from his bag more scrolls, my heart sank. I was afraid that he would try to weave praise of my eyes into the Eleusinian hymn. I said, "Is the rest about the feast itself and how the gods favor it?"

"Well no, not really. Do you think I should?"

"I don't know. I am not a poet."

"I only meant did you have any ideas about what content should shape it?"

"Well, you could say something about the new peace being sent by Demeter as a sign to Athens that the city was in her favor. You know how sensitive Athenians are since the plague about being punished by the gods. They still think it was brought on them because of Apollo's disfavor. I do not mean to tell you what to do, but I think this is really the first opportunity since the truce was signed to sing how favored of the gods Athens is. It could restore some confidence."

Simonides jumped to his feet and began pacing, "The archons be damned! That is a brilliant idea! Absolutely brilliant! I knew we should have met today. You have changed my life! I don't know how to thank you. Of course you are right. I should have seen it myself." He suddenly burst into loud song. It was very odd; as if he had not listened to me at all, took inspiration from what I had said, yet produced something completely other.

Simonides sang aloud: "O sacred drink/ Demeter's brew/ Once drunk opening Athens underworld/ O birth and death/Beginning and end/A hero's dieing be our lot."

I muttered something about that not being what I meant at all, but said he should write it down. I dared offer no criticism.

My Nubian looked anxious, and I also was afraid that his bellowing would draw too much attention, but he stopped as suddenly as he started and said, "Where are my writing tools?" And at that he suddenly knelt at my feet. I saw the Nubian lurch forward to interfere, but held up a hand, use to Simonides spontaneous ways. He took my hand dramatically and said, "You have been sent by Apollo himself to guide me and I pledge to you all my love if you will have me. Come away and all our days will be devoted to praising the heavens, you who are the light of my life..."

He pressed his cheek to the back of my hand very ostentatiously, and fell silent, his head bowed, waiting for my answer. I did not know what to say, and after a moment or two, I slowly withdrew my hand and he looked up at me in silent sadness.

It was the end of his dream about me, but when he

351

returned from his tour several months later we began cautiously to build a friendship, which lasted with difficulty for many years, until his sudden death on Samos when I was by then in my forties.

3. Prince Argaeus of the Argaead.

Father had written that he might attempt a trip to Athens for the Eleusinian despite his incapacity. My former tutor remained in our household, as teacher to my younger half brothers; he also wanted to visit me and could nurse father along the way. I was very excited about seeing both of them. It was a year since I had left home, not having been back since because of the dangers father saw along the way, and at home. As the feast drew near, and the city began to fill with devotees and visitors, every day I awaited news from either, every day at bedtime disappointed. How exciting then that day, as I was gathering things together for school, was the arrival of a messenger. Athenades took the message without telling me whom it was from, and only handed it over when I was ready to leave with my Nubian for the Lyceum; he would never allow anything to interfere with my work or lessons. I can also date this quite precisely. It was two days after the conversation with Simonides that I have just recorded, and two weeks before the start of the Eleusinian, in other words at the end of summer just as I turned fifteen.

Athenades said, with feigned indifference, "I am glad I caught you before you left for the Lyceum. There is a message for you. Your cousin is here in Athens for the Eleusinian. He will be coming by tomorrow to take you to lunch and will accompany you to the Taureas afterwards."

"My cousin? Which cousin is this?" I had many.

He still held the message in his hand and studied it. "It is signed, Prince Argaeus. He has been here several days it seems."

"Is there trouble at home? Does he say?"

"He only requests permission to see you. But if there were trouble at home I would have heard from our sources."

"He said nothing about father?"

"You are impatient and full of questions. Here read the message for yourself. I haven't time for this."

He thrust the scroll into my hands, but it did not enlighten me much. It only said, "I shall give you the news when I see you."

Athenades did not walk away as I read the message but waited for me to finish it. As I rolled it and tied it again with the blue silk band, he asked, "Do you know why your cousin is here? He is an official in the court, isn't he?"

Prince Argaeus of the ruling house of Argaead was my father's cousin, which did not actually make him mine. He was in his mid-thirties, fourth in line for the throne and one of the closest confidants of King Perdiccas. He had been near the throne for some ten years; had survived attempted coups and assassinations, and the King's bouts of madness, none of which were mean feats. I could not imagine why he was in Athens, nor why he particularly wanted to see me, except out of politeness. But of course everyone flooded to Athens for the Eleusinian, the last large festival before weather closed the sea routes again. As I went off to school that day I felt annoyed that the social obligation would only add to my already long list of

353

responsibilities.

If the fates had willed it, and if I had wanted it too, the meeting with Prince Argaeus would have been a turning point in my life, but was not. A turning point that is not a turning point is in some ways a turning point, I suppose. I knew the Prince at a distance, from my court obligations on festival days as page or member of some entourage or parade. He was to me inscrutable, and I thought he must be ruthless to ride above the internecine politics and not be assassinated himself. How many died at his hand to further his ambitions I do not know.

The next day he arrived promptly, with four bodyguards, drawing a good deal of attention in the street and workshop. Argaeus himself commanded attention. He was large and thickly built, but without an ounce of fat. He had Polydamus' broad shoulders, and wore a heavy sword on his right hip, as if in the city for battle and not worship. There were grey streaks in his chestnut hair and beard, and he looked a bit like one of those northern tribesmen that Simonides was about to entertain. They too had a reputation for brutality, as did Argaeus. We went to a tavern where he had secured a room so that we could talk privately, and to make sure, posted his guard. He had brought me lavish gifts from home, and some simple things too that would make me nostalgic, our special mountain honey and cakes, and a purple tunic with gold trim.

"I have only these for you," I said, presenting him with wrist and ankle bands I had been given permission to make for him the night before. "I did not know you were coming or I would have designed something special."

"We have heard at court of your talent, and I have left a commission from the King with your Master, some things for you to design. They say you have genius and have done well in Athens. Better a Macedonian design for Macedonians."

"I am sure Athenades will be grateful for the work, but I would not call myself a genius, more a slave of the gold. It commands me rather than I it."

"You have your father's modesty, the modesty of the Temenidai, and their beauty and talent, it seems."

I thanked him but I was very nervous. This was not a usual visit, and I could see that he hesitated and had a purpose. An Argead with a mission was a dangerous companion, but my Nubian had not left m side. I said straightaway, after our greetings were over, "Are you here because of father? Is something wrong? There was not much in your message."

He was consuming too much wine, and this also worried me, having seen drinking cause Dionysian havoc in Chaerephon and Cleon. He said, "I saw him a month ago and he was doing well. I am only here socially, and for the feast, of course. I had business in the city and thought it would be a good opportunity to become acquainted."

I felt this was disingenuous, but I said, "It was kind of you to make time to see me. I shall tell father of your kindness and I know he will appreciate it."

"And I shall report back to your father how well I find you. You seem to have thrived in Athens. I have heard from many that you are not only well regarded but have also made influential friends. Aspasia. Simonides. Socrates. Why, Alcibiades tells me that you have had an affair with a courtesan vixen named Mania? I am impressed."

I did not like his nosing around my affairs, nor that it had come from Alcibiades, and would now become common knowledge back at the court in Aigai. I said, "Yes, well, Mania shall soon be in Miletus, so it is over."

"Come now. Don't be modest. It seems you have a genius for more than gold. At least, as she tells it, you acquitted yourself splendidly in the bedchamber and have acquired a reputation, for, well, artistry shall we call it? Are you fifteen yet?"

"Yes, just. My birthday was two weeks after the start of the Athenian New Year."

We did not keep birth dates too closely in Macedon. We celebrated births with rites of beginning, and marked our years from the rituals.

Argaeus said, "Oh yes, those Athenians and time. It is one more example of their imperialism. But a mistress at fifteen! Perhaps we should raise a Herms to you back home."

I did not like his sarcasm. It reminded me a little of Leagros. "Mistress is a little grand for what it really was." My annoyance was growing because it was clear he was taunting me, and so I said, "I know you are a busy person, cousin. Surely there must be a reason for your wanting to see me."

"Yes, as a matter of fact there is. Like your father, you get right to the point."

"It is then?"

Now I saw his eyes narrow in the way I had seen at court, and that father had so often warned me about. I glanced up and felt relieved to see my Nubian move closer. When I met his eyes he raised his chin ever so slightly so as not to be seen by anyone else, and yet reassure me. I could count on his knife.

Argaeus said, "There is a certain politics that goes along with your position as heir to your house, as you well know. Ninth in line for the throne, are you? And your father eighth? Or is it tenth and ninth? And a fine man your father, although he plays too much the peace card for the benefit of Greater Macedon."

Greater Macedon was not a term I had heard, or liked, and I said, " Is not our interest best served by peace?"

"So your father would have us believe. But no, I do not think it always is. He has certainly convinced enough people at home to secure his influence. But it is not the only and perhaps not the best position to take for our interests."

This was a bold statement, not quite accusing father of treason, but coming close. I said, "My father holds his opinions passionately. He prays over them and sacrifices to the gods so they might favor Macedon through his convictions."

"I have no doubt of that, no doubt at all. But as I said, there are other positions, other gods to sacrifice to for the future of Macedon. Your father's views and mine diverge about this. Indeed, you could say that in Macedon and Aigai there are only two views, your father's and mine. I am sure you know your father's, an alliance with Athens and the struggle for a lasting peace, but I do not think that mine has been sufficiently laid out to you."

"I know that your strategy is the same as the King's, to

shift alliances to fit the circumstances. Much like Alcibiades, although that is in his own interest and not Sparta's or Athens'."

"But there is a purpose in shifting alliances according to a given reality. Do you not see this?"

I did not think he meant me to answer, and if I had I would have guessed the purpose it served was greed, or power. He did not wait for an answer and continued, "They say that King Perdiccas is mad, but he is not mad. He is a visionary, and his vision is fixed on Macedonian greatness. From a distance Athens and Sparta do not look the same as they look close up. From a distance what we see is an Athens close to exhaustion because of the plague and the cost of war, torn by dissent, and so self-absorbed as to be exhausting its resources because of an interminable obsession with the enemy and security. Athens needs an enemy too intensely, the way some need drink or intercourse, in an exaggerated and not in a natural way. You have been living here. Do you not agree?"

"Yes, I would say that I would agree with this."

Argaeus said, "And then, of course, there is Sparta. They have found the perfect foe, so to speak, in Athens. The Spartan life from birth to death trains for the fight. And along comes Athens and provides them with a citizenry obsessed with having an enemy. They have made a kind of mad marriage. By locking horns they are both wedded to war as if one woman took two husbands who then had to fight constantly over her. War found its perfect spouses, in Sparta and Athens, and is quite ready to exhaust both. Their villages are burned. Their best and brightest die in battle. Are either victors?"

I asked, "And Macedon? Does she not side first with one and then with the other? And is this not an obsession with war and not just the court's whim?"

"Policy, yes, whim, no. It is in our interest to supply just enough assistance to see both exhaust themselves. Continuous war, you might say, is necessary if Macedon has any chance to rise and dominate. Their endless war is our war of attrition. It is in our best interests, and the best way to prepare the way for Greater Macedon."

I searched his eyes to see if he were serious, and saw that he was. I said, "Others might think the same, Persia and Corinth for example. And then your policy would all be for nothing. I think I prefer my father's way of peace alliances. Your way tempts the fates and is too uncertain."

He was very angry at my words but replied coolly, "Your father's way? And you think that is why he sent you to Athens? To train you in the ways of peace at the home of that eunuch Athenades?" Calling my Master a eunuch was unforgivable, but he went on, "After your brother's death you have become the eldest heir of the Temenidai. That is why your father wants you out of Macedon, as if Perdiccas' reach did not extend to Athens. Your father would protect his heir and tribe. That is his first concern, not Macedon, or Athens, or peace, or any high ideals, but blood-line."

I was outraged by this and said angrily, "I do not think that there is a difference." Again I glanced at my Nubian. He could not have understood our Macedonian dialect, but his hand went to his knife. I lowered my voice and said, "So have you come here to tell me that I am in danger?"

"No! I have come here to enlist you."

"Enlist me?"

"It is time you put aside the things of boyhood and assumed your responsibilities for Macedon.

"Even if it means disloyalty to my father?

"Disloyalty? Then tell me this. Do you share his peace views? Are they also yours? Can you really look me in the eye now and say that they are? Swear an oath to Athena, whose city you honor with your designs."

In the silence that fell between us now I saw that he hated my father and this might be because of family blood rivalry, jealousy, or some grievance to which I had not been privy. I might learn the full story some day but I knew that if I affirmed my own commitment to the peace faction that I would now be drawn into the circle of my cousin's hatred, and that he might wish this too. What good would that serve back at home for father or for family, I wondered, as the silence grew and the seconds passed? I had to say something, or my silence would be construed proof of my doubts; in this Argaeus would rejoice.

I finally said, "War begins in heaven among the gods, and so it seems to me the destiny of men. I do not think that any individual can change the overall fate of men. But we can tell the gods we wish something different for ourselves, and hope they listen. In Athens I have seen that war has brought exhaustion and corruption, so wishing for a time of peace, for restoration and renewal, to rebuild the roads and sewers, to re-sow the crops and rebuild the houses, to finish the temples and renew the public works, all of this seems to me a sensible wish. Perhaps the Athenians will see that so much is accomplished in times of peace that they will become attached to it. I know that this is what Athenades, Aristophanes, and others hope, and so do I."

A look of contempt and disgust swept over Prince Argaeus' face and he said, "The words of an idealistic boy, not yet a man. I see I have come too soon to Athens. Too soon."

I did not respond. He leaned back and downed another cup of wine. His disdain might mean that I was safe. But I must write with all haste to father and relay the conversation as fully as possible. Consequences could follow upon my denial of Argaeus' will. Consequences would follow upon my informing father.

I said, "If we do not agree let us at least toast Macedon."

He looked pleased at this suggestion. We raised our cups. I said, "To Macedon." He said, "To Greater Macedon." We did not toast the same thing.

4. Interlude: The Oracle of Delphi.

My cousin accompanied me to the gate of the Taureas. As I left him
I puzzled over his intentions. The conversation took me back to my court visits, and father's endless warnings about being "alert to the nuances", in this case hardly a nuance. The Prince had made me angry; his efforts to enlist me were insulting and dangerous.

I was seething when I went later to find Socrates. He was as usual teaching under a tree and I waited until he was free before approaching him. I immediately broke into a rant: against Perdiccas, the Argaead, Macedonian pride, and everything else that was pent up inside me for so long; Simonides' persistence, and Leagros selfishness. There were too many expectations made of me when I wanted to be carefree, it being Athens after all. He listened, but not as others did distractedly, thinking of their wives and mistresses, or war, or making money while they pretended interest. Socrates listened with all of himself, focused and intense, completely present, as no one ever listens, or he did not listen at all.

When I was finished extolling everyone's faults, Socrates said simply, "You have been wanting to go to Delphi have you not?"

It seemed not to follow. I was startled but said I did indeed.

He replied, "I can arrange for you to go. Are you here again tomorrow?"

"In two days."

"Good. Come find me after class and I should have it arranged by then. But tell no one and leave it all up to me."

In a flash my soul shifted, from feeling overwhelmed and morose, to feeling excited and liberated. Upon my arrival in Athens nearly a year to date, I had vowed that I would make a pilgrimage to Delphi, Navel of the World, as soon as possible in order to thank Apollo for the opportunity he had given me by inspiring father to send me here to study and learn the arts of self-sufficiency; but that was a boy's wish unseasoned by politics. War had made the routes northward dangerous and impassable because of Spartan intrusions, and their alliance with Corinth and other of the northern states, but now the truce opened them for the first time since my arrival in Hellas. As I went home that day it struck with full force. The road to Delphi was open! Socrates would arrange my pilgrimage! I would have my wish.

But Leagros seemed to take undo pleasure in dashing my hopes. He had been sullen since being replaced as my chaperone, and for "being banned" from Aspasia's household, his phrase if Aspasia's deed. His sulking fits would often make him cross over nothing, and yet I sought his company, perhaps feeling more responsible than I should for problems of his own making.

When I arrived home I went to find him, and asked, "Now that the road to Delphi is open again, do you think that there will be opportunities for pilgrimage?"

This was the wrong question to ask him. It did not quite break my word to Socrates not to speak of it; I was not asking Leagros if I might go. But he answered sharply.

"Delphi! What interest do you have in Delphi? There are rules you know, rules; Athenian rules, Delphic rules, Council rules, Assembly rules; rules, rules, rules. Just put it out of your mind."

I tried to protest. I had heard that the priests of Delphi had fallen on hard times because of a decline in worshippers due to the war. They depended not just on Athenian but on Lydian and Spartan offerings too. Perhaps it was a propitious time for Athenades to send gold and silver?

"You know nothing!" Leagros said dismissively, and took to explain.

Consultations with the Oracle were rare, if you were not Spartan. An exception was made for them.

Descendants of Zeus, father of Apollo, they were allowed to have two emissaries standing by at all times to ride with all haste to the oracle. For all others the consultations were held nine months a year; the other months Apollo was away on vacation. The Pythia Oracle proclaimed one day a month and only for a few minutes. The Delphic High Priest designated specific days to the various delegations, including Athenian, and limited it to a certain number of delegates. The demand for consultations numbered in the many hundreds, more in years such as this when access had been restricted for so long. Spartans, Athenians, Persians, Scythians, Egyptians, Lydians, and everyone else who could, wanted to rush to the greatest of all the oracles. But all of these had second rights to the citizens of Delphi themselves who could consult first. Every single person who wanted to consult had to be approved by the priests, with the High Priest holding the final decision. Politics influenced priorities, which alliance might profit Delphi most, or who might ensure its safety and independence. There were rumors of bribery and graft, but there was also obedience to the signs, portents, and dreams.

Word from the Agora was that a delegation had already been sent to Delphi to negotiate a visit and word was expected back any day on whether or not Athens would be granted oracle rights soon, or much later in the year. There was anxiety over this, as Cleon was already agitating for war, and access would be closed again. Brigands and rogue raiding parties also made the journey perilous. Word had arrived from spies in Sparta that they had sent a delegation to Delphi, not to mention those scores of others. If war had interrupted our access to the gods, peace had restored it, but that peace was fragile and riven by competition.

Leagros finished his diatribe, "Well, now do you harbor delusions?"

I shook my head and went to bed that night disconsolate, convinced that Socrates would fail. I do not know why I so glibly sought the wrong person to ask a good question, or allowed Leagros to have so much influence over me. Thanks to the fates, Socrates would be the right person to ask the right question, the sure antidote for such folly.

The day of my next Taureas class I found Socrates sitting under a tree reading, in the school olive grove. Earlier in the day I had stopped to ask one of the news criers if there was word about an Athenian delegation to Delphi, or any news of Delphi at all, ready to pay him the half obol he would have asked if he knew any. But he said there was no news about Delphi that day or indeed that week. Everything was about the delegations arriving from hither and yon for the Eleusinian, what they brought as offerings, what new fashions they wore, and what gossip they had of their own lands. Of that there was much to tell, he said, but I hurried on uninterested. Socrates, I noted as I slid down next to him, was reading a work by the Ionian philosopher Archelaus on first principles. His theory was that air is the principle of everything and that Mind is composed of air which is why thoughts are ever moving and restless. He also held that motion is caused by hot and cold separating. In his youth, Socrates had studied with him. They were also friends and had visited Samos together. It was because of his association with some of these nature philosophers that Aristophanes could lampoon Socrates in *Clouds*. He was glad to see me, which made me feel hopeful, and asked me to join him in the shade so long as my schoolwork was done.

I said it was and asked, "What is the work about?"

Socrates said, "It is quite charming. Here, let me read something to you." He read this passage, "'For Matter is only air, and Mind is only air. So they are the same and not two.' I was thinking of this when you came."

"I am sorry to interrupt."

"Not at all. But tell me. Do you agree with the passage I read you?"

"It is clever. Perhaps it is true. It would help explain how the gods can move among us as air and enter us through mind."

I was thinking of Socrates' voice, but did not want to question him about it directly.

He said, "But I do not think you want to talk about philosophy, do you? I was at Aspasia's last night, to discuss Delphi with her. We needed to consult her oracles."

"Were the signs favorable?"

"Yes. They all told the same thing, that your visit would be well favored by Apollo."

I was overjoyed but said morosely, "But I have heard that it is impossible to go, there are so many rules. And our delegation has not returned from Delphi yet has it? Nor would many want to go with the festival in a few days time."

Socrates said, "That is all true. The city is preparing for the Eleusinian. Everyone is occupied with that and not

366

thoughts of oracles."

"Yes. Then it is not the right time. I understand."

"You are too eager to be negative. You see; it makes it the right time. There has been no Athenian delegation to Delphi for many months and the priests there need money. So Chaerephon is going privately with a small group of devotees, and Delphi has approved. I spoke with him last night as well and he said in joking that, well, he would have need of a young servant to accompany him. If you do not mind being called a servant, or going with Chaerephon."

I said, "Mind! But when is he leaving?"

"A few days before the Eleusinian. He does not like large crowds and flees the city for some of the big festivals. Given the travel time there and back, plus the stay, I am afraid it means that you would miss the festival. That might suit Chaerephon, but would you mind?"

"I thought father might be coming for the feast days, or my old tutor who studied at Eleusis, but I have not heard from them, and think they would have told me already if they were coming."

"If they do come we can detain them until you return. I am sure Aspasia will welcome your father as a guest, or your tutor. Or they could stay with me."

"Has Chaerephon permission to consult the Oracle? Will he ask about you again?"

"He does have permission but he will not ask about me. The Oracle answers in riddles, you know. One Delphic riddle in a lifetime is quite enough."

"But the god saying that you were the wisest man alive does not seem like a riddle."

"The Pythia always speaks in riddles and so I had to ask myself what the riddle was and I decided that God was not saying that I was the wisest of all men but that I was only as wise as my knowledge of myself, and that depended on knowing what I do not know. But that is true for everyone. I know what I do not know. Of course, riddles also command us to seek solutions, which is why I go everywhere asking everyone if someone is wiser."

I wondered if knowing nothing, or what he did not know, and having an inner god with no name were not in some way connected. Knowing what you do not know was for Socrates to be possessed by God. Perhaps that was also a definition of being wise?

But I said, "This oracle frightens me."

"It is an opportunity. Do you have a question for her? You could not put it yourself, but Chaerephon could put it for you. Of course he might put one about you without asking you, so be careful when you say you will go with him!"

I said, "I think I will be too frightened to ask the Oracle anything. I love Apollo and only want to bring sacrifices to his altar. If I ask anything it might be about my father. I worry about him. But I am not good at riddles and think it is better if I do not ask anything."

Socrates said, "Is this wisdom?"

It was an example of his sense of humor and self-deprecation.

Chaerephon came to see me the next day. There were many plans to make as we were leaving so soon, and I had to clear my desk of work. I had not seen him since the dinner, and he seemed as emaciated as ever, much as he was described in *Clouds*.

We went to lunch, or rather he took me to my favorite fish cake stall, berating me for my bad taste, and I him for eating nothing while I ate three.

He said, "I consulted my own diviners last night and they said it was propitious to bring along a kalos. I also saw you in a dream, walking along a path through hills, and recognized it as the road to Delphi. Shall we sit by the Herms? Do you want something to drink? The seller over there has fresh fruit juices that are the best in the Agora. I'll have one too."

The worst heat of summer was over and the first autumn winds freshened the air. There had been a rain the night before, or a Zeus as they said, the first in many weeks, and the air was cleaner if the streets were muddier. Fresh flowers would that day be laid before Zeus' statue on the Acropolis. We walked under the shade of the numerous plane trees, passing one of the numerous fountains. The crowds had come out in force in the good weather, and I enjoyed the hubbub unlike Chaerephon.

He sipped at his juice as if it were fine wine. "Socrates said you did not have a question for the Oracle. Are you sure? I could put it for you, if it is worthy of the God."

"Thank you, but I don't as yet. Athenades is excited about my going to Delphi and had me working until midnight on his offerings. I am also bringing my own gifts for Apollo, so I've been too busy to think much about a question."

"You will have time along the way."

"It is kind of you to let me come."

We had continued to walk, and were by the fourth

369

Herms, an area of doctors' shops and he suddenly said, "Wait! I must make a quick stop by my doctor."

He was ill, but also a terrible hypochondriac, and to be his physician must have required infinite patience. I did not like doctors' offices, though some preferred them to the barbershops for news. The herbs being blended sometimes burned my nose and eyes, or made me nauseous with the thought of how they must taste, and did. In the last two months I had been given several different potions to calm the nausea that had suddenly begun to upset me late in the day. It was the first sign of the poisoning disease that would afflict me for years. I also could not stand the crying children, or people being bled, but Chaerephon left me no choice. He took my hand and dragged me in with him. He always looked pale but now that we were stopping by the doctor's I wondered whether he was not more pale than usual.

I said, "But are you sick today?" I was wondering whether our trip would be cancelled.

"It is just a routine visit. I have purges to clear bad humors but they exhaust me and so I have them here. My doctor is also putting together a sack-full of remedies to take on our trip and I have to pick them up."

He was greeted by a student Asclepian priest and led to a couch in a curtained alcove. If he is this thin, I thought, what is there to purge? Of course, now there are better methods for balancing the body. He asked me to sit near him until the doctor came, so that we might plan our trip. I asked what reason he had for consulting the Oracle.

Chaerephon was ever eager to disclose secrets. He leaned over, cupping his hands over my ear. I noticed his breath was thick, if not precisely foul, as if he were breathing away body matter. He said, "Let me just say, the questions are from Nicias, Athenades, and the fellowship, not from me. I shall tell you more when we are on the road."

"Oh, of course!" I said loudly, and then looked around sheepishly to see if I had drawn attention, which I had. He would ask about the peace. It needed no explanation and explained why he was going unofficially, while Nicias' great wealth explained why the High Priest at Delphi had agreed so readily. Things were never at rest in Athens, I thought, like Heraclitus' river.

***

And so I was not to be in Athens for the Eleusinian. It was a forewarning from the goddess; I had already left the city by the following autumn because of the outbreak of hostilities at Amphipolis.

My Nubian and I met Chaerephon and his party at dawn by the Painted Stoa. We were making the journey on foot, as did the more devout. The extra effort and endurance would gain favor with Apollo before a consultation. Since the plague seven years before, still painfully vivid in the Athenian memory, it was paramount of the city to seek the good graces of Apollo; it was popularly thought that He had brought the plague down on Athens through displeasure with its many impieties, although Socrates and Aspasia disagreed.

When I arrived at the Stoa, expecting a handful, I came upon a teeming crowd. It was the first Athenian trip to the

371

shrine in many months and there was some hysteria about our visit. True to form, Chaerephon had leaked word that he had been granted audience and the Council had secretly convened to propose some city questions mixed with a handful of private ones: whether the truce would hold, or a more secure peace would follow; whether Apollo favored Athens again after the plague, or still harbored displeasure; whether the Persians would pose another threat, as the rumors had it; whether a favored son would die in a next battle already presumed, or a mistress continue her favors, an illness find healing? Would the silver mines, upon which so much of Athenian wealth depended, continue to prosper? Would the seas remain calm along the trade routes another month? One aristocrat told me around the fire one night that he was seeking advice about an unfaithful wife, another about boils. Every possible concern was to be aired it seemed, and it was extremely generous of Chaerephon to offer to ask a question for me, although I had none.

Chaerephon was easy to find; he towered above the city officials and aristocrats. He was organizing the mules, packhorses, and slaves carrying the bedding, foodstuffs and offerings, and shouting at the thirty private guards. When I pushed through to greet him I was overjoyed to find Socrates there despite the dawn having not yet broken.

"Socrates! Are you going to join us?"

"No. I have come to see you off."

I wore a thick wool cloak, but he none. He was as ever barefoot while I wore walking boots. He had brought me two gifts, a wide brimmed hat to prevent sunstroke, and a gold brooch of Apollo, which he fixed it to my tunic. He said, "The God watch over you and bring you back safely." He touched my forehead with his affectionately, and I thanked him, noting too that Simonides had not come though he was still in the city.

He walked us to the outskirts of the city but as the city walls gave way to the first farms he turned back. The sun had risen now and the air was still and peaceful, the land freshly plowed for the autumn sowing of the Eleusinian. We were taking an indirect route to Delphi rather than the direct way leading through Eleusis, calculating that the eastern road would be quieter. The narrow dirt road, one chariot wide, was still very crowded for the festival and we often had to stand aside to let long parties file past.

Half a day's walk northwards, the ravages of war began to be apparent. Olive groves and vineyards had been cut down. The charred remains of a farmhouse, and further north a whole village, reminded us of Spartan cruelty and thoroughness in plundering. More distressing was the destitution of those who came out to greet us as we passed. Many farm men and youths had missing limbs or walked with sticks. They waved at us, brought us refreshments, but we were loath to take too much from them when they seemed so needy and gave them what we could. It was as if the heroic stories of valor and friendship that I had heard in the Lyceum were like a bright sun that blinds you to what lurks in the shadows.

The eastern route took us through Boeotia, no friend of Athens. The Boeotian army was as ruthless as the Spartan, their cavalry merciless. If they had also agreed on the truce it did not guarantee that marauders would not swoop

373

down on the unaware like falcons on prey, or that some Boeotian, hearing of an Athenian delegation to Delphi, might seek independently to revenge past grievances. We posted guards at all points from the moment we pitched our tents to the moment we broke camp. There was only one incident on both legs of the journey. One night our dogs took to barking and awakened us all. There were arrows fired and shouting but no one was seen. The next morning we found fresh horse tracks. There had been at least twenty men stalking us, probably bandits, but they must have deemed us too formidable.

While the work of men made havoc in the land, the landscape in contrast was of great beauty and drama. The tree and grass covered slopes of the hills were emerald green set against sand colored rock outcroppings. There was plentiful game to eat. We scared up frightened flocks of partridge and quail into screeching ascent; scared rabbits bolted into brush. In the mountains there was some danger from bear, and wolves we heard too, but they dared not trouble our large party. The air was cool and sharp, acrid with wood smoke from settlements, and pungent with the mountain herbs used to flavor the honey. Destruction and natural beauty in opposition, added to the approaching might of Delphi, awed us. At night too a heavy silence descended over us, random coughs from the camp, the cry of an owl or night prey bitten, echoing loudly. From high resting places along the inclines, the beauty disposed us to the gods of song and love. If the truce had given us a chance, along the way there were countless reminders that our first task should have been to pray and ask for a lasting peace. The raven call of Apollo

374

reassured us of our purpose. I often touched my pendant to remind me of Him, and it brought Socrates close.

As we entered the hills on the approach to Delphi Chaerephon called me forward and took me to a rise well off the road. He blindfolded me, and took my hand to lead me through the pines, their dried needles snapping under foot raising a fine sweet smell. When he took the blindfold off, there was my first glimpse of Delphi and the great Temple of Apollo spread out before me, resplendent against the green hills.

"Chaerephon! We are there! Thank you." I could have wept with gratitude that I had come to honor Him.

Delphi was many sacred and profane towns compacted into one, flowing along a ravine and spilling up over the slopes of surrounding hills. At the base was the white Lower Town, the din as we approached promising a bustling, thriving place. Despite the war having dragged on already several years, and despite the plague having decimated Athens and halted for a time its generous offerings, Delphi was still the richest city, richer than Athens, Aigai, Memphis, or Persepolis. Everything glistened with gold and silver. Entering the town we had first to pass the Siphion Treasury, a graceless building housing the finest silver collection anywhere. We paused to pay homage at the golden statue of Pallas Athena, three times life-sized, and given as thanks by Athens upon the defeat of the Persians. She was seated on a palm leaf strewn with dates, all of the finest gold. There too was the enormous statue of a lion given by King Croesus of Lydia, made out of pure refined gold. They say it weighed as much as ten horses.

375

Hovering over the town was the Acropolis of the sanctuary, the Temple of Apollo, the houses of the priests, all painted in dazzling purple, and vermilion. The clear air added to the sharpness and luminosity, the dazzling greens and blues of landscape and sky like ground, distilled gemstones. We entered at the town's lowest point. The main road had been carefully laid out to impress. The bronze statues lining the avenue alternating life-sized and twice life-sized, towering over us as we walked among them towards the guest house district beyond the Delphi Agora. Everything was sloping here and as we ascended we had prospects out over the valley, but upwards too of the magnificent theater, and, staggeringly beautiful in its domination of the town, finally a full view of the Temple of Apollo, a building worthy of Him I thought, calm, majestic, perfectly proportioned.

Chaerephon had been able to secure a private audience with the High Priest for the following day at the College of Priests. He was chosen for life from among the Delphi elite upon the death of his predecessor. He was more of an administrator than a seer; his managerial skills were a prerequisite for the position. His quarters were near the Temple, connected by a colonnade, or through an underground passage shared with the Oracle, through which she could enter the temple and sanctuary without being violated by pressing crowds. As we were admitted I noted that the High Priest's spotless house had little adornment, except for the painted and gilded wooden ceiling of the audience chamber. The shutters of the large windows were thrown open upon a view more breathtaking than the exquisite murals in Aspasia's house;

the gleaming town buzzed below, the mountains serene beyond. We waited standing for a long time before he entered, a man of about sixty, wearing a simple tunic gathered at the waist by his gold sash of office. He was accompanied by one of the lesser priests, or hosios, and slaves who might receive the gifts from our hands. Chaerephon was asked to recline, and brought refreshments.

The priest said, "Tell me the news from Athens."

I stood behind Chaerephon, and was offered nothing, in keeping with my role as servant. But as Chaerephon told him the news and how the city rejoiced to return to honor Apollo, I saw that the priest was not so much listening to him as glancing at me. It was not a look I recognized, having had many, from forthright lust to fleeting longing, envy to hatred; Simonides' annoyed glance at some boyish pretension, or Mania's feverish glance; Aspasia's frown, and Socrates' recent affection. The high priest's glance was of a different order, not desire nor hostility or curiosity, and I did not understand it. His questions were straightforward. He wished to know how the truce progressed and whether or not there were rumors already in Athens about breaking it. He did not trust the peace, as much as we did not.

Our gifts were to be presented and I had been coached in the formalities of the presentation. I would hold them cradled in my arms, my head lowered, approach when bidden, and kneel holding them aloft. There were several bundles of gold objects, wrapped in blue silk, and I presented the first.

As the priest took it from me I did not dare break

protocol and look up at him, but he said, "Yes. You are as I saw you." He set the bundle on a table to his side, rather than hand it to the slave as he had done with the other gift offerings.

"You are not a slave," he said to me, but I was not sure it was a question. I remained kneeling with my head lowered, and did not answer. In fact I was quite frightened as I often was in the presence of the sacred.

Chaerephon was annoyed and said sharply, "He is asking you Amyntas."

"I am sorry, your Holiness. I was not sure you were asking." I glanced up at the High Priest towering above me but again could not read his glance. I said, "No, I am not."

The High Priest laid his hand on my head and said, "You will attend the Oracle."

Chaerephon said, "He is not of age your Holiness."

"He will go."

Chaerephon did not seemed pleased, and I was thrown into confusion so that the rest of the meeting, although we stayed another half hour or so, is a blur. They must have spoken about Athenian politics or the needs of the Delphi treasury. All I could think about was the Oracle. I had no question, and for the life of me could think of none.

As we left the priest's rooms Chaerephon saw that I was pale and took my arm. I said, "What does it mean Chaerephon?"

"I have no idea what it means. But if the High Priest has ordered you to attend then you shall attend."

"It frightens me."

"I know, I can see that it does. But you must not always

think that the worst will come from things. Sometimes the best comes."

"I know, but I am still frightened. When is your consultation?"

"First thing tomorrow."

"First thing tomorrow! I shall never sleep. May I sleep in your room tonight?"

"Yes, of course.

It seemed a lifetime before morning broke. I had not slept and was sitting by the window looking at the dawn but dreading the day when his slave came to awaken Chaerephon. The night before leaving home for Athens had been filled with apprehension, and excitement, but this was different. We stand in dread before the gods. They infuse us with awe. I dressed reluctantly, but could not eat, and when it came time to leave I dragged my steps.

Chaerephon was bubbling, and full of pride to have organized and be leading the delegation. As we made our way from the guesthouse to the temple precinct he babbled on about the Pythia and her reputation. He had consulted the same Oracle before.

Seeking reassurance, I asked, "Is she frightful?"

His answer did not calm me much. He said, "The Pythia? Well, not frightful, but certainly frightening. Are you still afraid? She does or says nothing that harms us, you know."

"I was told that she saw our vices and could call on the heavens to punish us."

"Who on earth told you that?"

"My stepmother, when I was bad. She threatened to send messages to Delphi."

Chaerephon thought this was very funny, and his laughter made me feel better. He said, "They should ban stepmothers from the earth."

"Oh no. She was very good to me. She cooked better than anyone and took care of my clothes."

"And terrified you with bogeymen, it seems; simply to get you to obey, I suppose."

I said, "But why do you say the Oracle is frightening? Was she so terrible when you saw her before and asked about Socrates?"

"Well, it is the whole ambience, you see, the strange mists that rise from the ground, the smells, the hiss like snakes."

"Oh Chaerephon, I really don't want to go! Can't I stay behind?"

"I would have said yes, but after all the High Priest more or less said that you must."

"But I don't understand."

"I know. Neither do I. But calm yourself. Let me tell you a little about this Oracle. After consulting her about Socrates I asked around about her life. She's not from Delphi, you know, which is unusual, and is a commoner with hardly any education at all. She was chosen through dreams and signs, and had to prove that she was physically fit enough to endure the rigors of trances and divination; I have heard of oracles at Dordona who died from their trance seizures. Her ritual training was very brief, for only a year. She serves for life, sometimes alone and sometimes with one or two others, but alone right now. She dresses as a virgin for the rites, but was allowed to marry and lead a normal married life. Before the God she must be pure and

380

be seen to be pure by the devotees. She is also allowed to accumulate wealth, and this Pythia is particularly wise with money and owns considerable tracts of land, and also houses in Delphi that she rents out through an agent. Before I consulted her I was told by nearly everyone that she always answers in hexameters, but I found out that this simply is not true. Sometimes the priests answer for her, and they rather, well, dress up the answers, but most of the time the Pythia answers in riddles that are usually very succinct, but remarkable nonetheless. In my opinion she deserves her reputation."

"But she sounds very ordinary and nothing to be afraid of," I said.

"Well, perhaps, until you consider she has the ability to fall into a sacred trance and be visited directly by Apollo."

I asked, "It is like Socrates, is it not?"

"Shush. Don't say such things. Socrates makes no claim for his voice, which is what you mean, I suppose."

"But is it not Apollo?"

"It has no name."

"I know that, but…"

"Hush now. It is a matter of some controversy in Athens and I would not speak of it. Besides, you must pray now, and put yourself in the right frame of mind for the Oracle."

I wished he had not reminded me, and said, "I have fasted since last evening and prayed at dawn."

Chaerephon said, "That is good. A prayer to Apollo at the crack of dawn has the best chance of being heard."

The rest of our delegation was waiting for us at the entrance to the Temple, joined by our local guide. No one could consult without a freeborn citizen of Delphi being present. We presented the gifts he could accept for his service. Among his many tasks he also had to check the devotees to make sure their dress was appropriate and that they had brought tributes which were worthy enough to set before the altar. Not until all of this was in order were we conducted to a special spring-fed pool to be purified, as was required of all who would consult. This was not the sacred Castalian spring, reserved for the Pythia herself. Holy Castalian water was sold in the Agora. It was illegal to traffic in it, but it was taxed and there was no effort to suppress it. Before returning to Athens, I bought several small flasks to give as gifts. It was said to cure sore throats, blisters, and other inflammations; a few drops on the tongue would cure a cough.

After the purification we sacrificed the goat kid we had bought the afternoon before, slaughtered on the great altar standing just outside the Temple of Apollo. This lasted an hour or so, attended by the priests and a chorus, and was performed with great solemnity. Along with our sacrifice, private offerings of other visitors were being offered as well. In solemn procession we were led into the sanctuary, the corridors resplendent with the proportion of the spoils of the war always set aside as offerings to Apollo. Both the Spartans and Athenians reserved the first trophies for Delphi, which accounted for the plethora of Persian shields, cups, jewelry and the like. There were simpler offerings too along the corridors, stacked on small tables, or hung from pegs: ears of dried corn among the gold, or sticks the lame had miraculously discarded, and the bandages of the wounded. We descended down a long stone stairwell, ill lit by torches casting eerie shadows and filled with an acrid smoke, into a square stone chamber, pausing there to pray at the great omphalos stone, the navel of the world. The walls sweated earth water, and it became colder and colder as we descended. By the time we entered the consulting room I was shaking uncontrollably and Chaerephon put his arm around me and whispered encouragement. Why was I there, I wondered?

The room was of medium size. Thirty people might stand there in comfort but not many more. Being so deep, and with access only down a twisting stairwell, it was cut off from the sounds of the town above. The sputter of a candle, a cough, the shuffle of bare feet echoed. A pillared archway led into the tiny holy sanctuary where the Oracle presided. She could be seen but no one could transgress her space. Chaerephon was determined to get as close as possible, and pulled me with him. I could readily see the high, three-legged bronze stool with a bowl like seat on which the Oracle sat. The shape is meant to direct the Oracle's prophesies upwards to the God as much as downwards to devotees.

We pushed to the front. There was a strange hiss coming from the Oracle's chamber. I thought it might be a cage of sacred snakes, but could see none. We all were hushed with awe. A pungent, acrid smell made me dizzy and slightly nauseous, yet vividly aware of the proceedings.

Chaerephon whispered to me, "Come. I want to be right at the front."

He had a tight grip on my hand and pulled me to the pillared entranceway, nearly at the foot of the sacred tripod. The smell and hissing was worse here. I passed anxious moments wondering whether I would fall.

From a hidden corridor came the sound of women chanting. Four women escorted the Pythia into her chamber. I had imagined a slender, perhaps emaciated woman but she was large and imposing, white-haired, some sixty, tall and straight-backed. Her eyes were dark, and her face thin and long, not at all beautiful as was Aspasia, but stern and sharp. One of her priestesses put a stepping stool down so that she might ascend the tripod. Irreligious men said that she was often intoxicated in order to assist the trance, but I saw no sign of this. I did notice that the hiss came from a thin fissure in the floor at the base of her tripod. It was a jagged slash as of black lightning, and reminded me of the Pytho snake that Apollo had slain. At either side of this fissure there were large brass holders into which wavering torches were fixed, giving the impression that the fissure was emitting a gas, like vapors of thin steam. But I could not feel it.

There were more prayers and chanting, the voices of the women echoing in that small stone chamber. I was feeling panic, as if I might faint, and sweating profusely although it was cold and damp. The God wished me there, I kept thinking, but I felt dizzy and hardly aware of the proceedings. Would Apollo strike me down for dishonoring him with my stupid silence? I feared punishment or death, and as the chanting ceased and the Oracle gave ready to receive the first questions I hid behind Chaerephon so that I would not be noticed.

Chaerephon had agreed to allow some of our other delegates to ask questions first. Would the God favor

Athens again? Would there be another plague, or more war; would we be victors? Would Persia rise again? I knew the questions by heart that would be put, but still had none myself. His turn came. He bowed and stepped forward. Nicias had asked him to question the longevity of the truce and whether Apollo favored Athens again.

He waited for the priest's or Oracle's signal that he might speak, but it did not come. She raised her palms, her head tilting back, her eyes closed. She muttered unintelligible prayers then fell silent, muttered more prayers and fell silent. This went on for several minutes while Chaerephon waited. I saw that he trembled from the strain; being high-strung to begin with, sweat dampening his robe. Again she bent her head far back as if to shout to the heavens, but again nothing came forth. There was no sound except the shuffling of Chaerephon's sandals on the stone floor, as he grew tired standing.

Several minutes passed. A frightened silence fell over the room, including among the priests, whom I saw glancing anxiously at each other. The Phythia raised her right arm very slowly, and pointed towards the shadows where I stood, half hidden now by a thick column. Her mouth opened wide but at first nothing came forth; and then, still pointing my way she uttered a long, loud shriek.

The High Priest rushed over and pushed me forward. "You, she means you!" he said.

She pointed and shrieked again.

The priest said, "Ask a question. She wants you to ask your question!"

I tried to object but he pushed me to the very edge of her chamber. Chaerephon was suddenly at my side, gripping my arm. He whispered, "For God's sake, Amyntas, ask a question or she shall strike us all down."

But I had none. I had no questions, none at all. I fell to my knees ready to plead for my life, but when I opened my mouth and tried to speak nothing came out.

Chaerephon said again, "Ask it. Ask it."

I felt so dizzy I thought I would fall. Indeed, I felt in something like the trance you can fall into when you have high fever. And suddenly, as if possessed by gods, I looked up at her and said in a loud firm voice, "Is Socrates' inner god, Apollo?"

She threw her hands into the air, her head back but did not at once answer. There was dead silence. She slowly lowered her head. Pointing at me again, she deliberately shrieked a long, false, forced laugh, "Haaaaa! Haaaaa! Haaaaa!" She slumped forward as if she would fall from her stool and her slaves rushed forward to catch her.

I knew nothing else, until I was awakened with cold water and scents above ground. Chaerephon was hovering over me, rubbing my hands and looking anxious. "Amyntas, your lips are blue. Are you all right? Are you all right?"

I opened my eyes and was sure I saw a raven sitting on a branch above where they had laid me in the shade, although I am not certain of this now, so delirious was I then.

"Water," was all I could say.

5. Socrates' voice.

Upon my return from Delphi I found a great deal changed. It was a week or so after the end of the

Eleusinian and the city seemed empty. The first autumn rains had cooled and refreshed the city. I was accustomed to seeing homeless farmers and their families camping in various squares, but as I walked along the Panathenaic Way one morning expecting to be accosted by the usual beggars, none were about. The beginning of the truce and the end of the festival heralded the promise of normalcy for a time, and many farmers had gone back to the land. For the festival, the Assembly had also authorized a cleanup, for appearances sake. Athens natural state was order mixed with a good dose of chaos. Peace would focus attention on repairing the long wall to Piraeus, finishing the Stoa, putting the city in order.

There were changes in the workshop too. The next large festival, the Dionysian wine festival, was not for many weeks. The generals and aristocrats needed fewer gold buckles to adorn their cloaks, less silver for their battle swords, fewer objects to appease the gods. Athenades was cutting corners. Two Ambracian slave boys had been sold. They sang good songs, played a fine lute, and told well their country's fables. I was sorry to see them leave. When I made enquiries, our manager told me they had fetched a good price, as if I were asking about that and not about their welfare. He knew of my station, but he made haste to warn me that I had best work harder than usual if I wished to remain. I could not imagine working harder than I did, but it proved no idle threat. One morning, abruptly, one of the other apprentices was gone and his work divided among the rest of us. He had been sent to organize Athenades' new shop in Scythia, but thank God, it was not Assur. There was less work, I quipped, but shared among fewer there was more.

As I sat at my usual workbench at the front of the shop, the air stirring beneath the curtain hinting at winter, I found myself in the same instance missing Simonides, and wanting to see Socrates again. I had not been at the Taureas for nearly three weeks now, because of the trip to Delphi, and mentioned it one day to Athenades. My training was being neglected, and he pretended not to have noticed, although I was sure he had. I went eagerly that afternoon but Socrates was not there, nor was he the day after, and I began to wonder whether I should have run off with Simonides, a fleeting regret. Two or three days later, I noticed Socrates Nubian speaking with mine. Socrates was never without him and I was anxious that something had happened to him. As the Nubians were cousins I also thought that perhaps they were talking of some family matter. Socrates was generous, and gave him a good deal of free time.

I was in the changing room getting ready for a gymnastics lesson and waiting for the oilers, when his eunuch Phaidon came to find me, and said, "Socrates has invited you to dine at his house tomorrow. I shall come for you just before sunset. It has been arranged." I raised my chin in assent.

***

I had never been to Socrates house but had been told often enough that he lived simply. It was in the Alopeke district, to the south just outside the city walls. He had inherited the house from his stone carver father, Sophroniscus, who

388

had helped to build it and give it added graces, otherwise he could have never found or afforded a property in this the most desirable of all Athenian quarters. Socrates had the right to call himself a descendant of Daedalus. Many city and religious officials lived here. The streets were wider and lined with bay trees. They gave the air a fresh smell after a rain or when a light breeze stirred them. The houses were wider than usual too. Many had gardens, a luxury for Athens, unless you had Aspasia's resources and cleverness.

Socrates lived with his mother, Phaenarete the midwife, who also excelled at herbal remedies and potions of various sorts, including rare love potions that Aspasia might have learned from her. She was a quiet, pious woman, and had encouraged Socrates from an early age to think of the moral consequences of his actions. He was not yet married to Xanthippe. His oldest son was also called Sophroniscus. He was seventeen at the time of Socrates' death, twenty-three years after these events. So Socrates must have married Xanthippe six years after I left Athens.

As I knocked at the door it burst open and an odd man with an untrimmed beard and very long matted hair rushed out nearly knocking me over. He was muttering a lisping, rhythmic Greek. His right eye wandered and though he looked at me, he did not. "Ah Amyntas! Go in. Go in. Socrates is waiting. Can't tarry. Can't tarry. Go in. Go in. Don't tarry." He spoke like Aesop, I thought. He had several precious scrolls tucked under his arm that seemed about to tumble onto the ground, but before I could help him secure them he had rushed away without losing any.

The carved wooden door stood open but I hesitated to

389

enter, as there was no slave to admit me and wash my feet. My Nubian knew the ways of his household and whispered, "You may go in Master. It is all right." Still I called out. An elderly slave shuffled out to greet us. I was shown into a room adjoining the center court, where Socrates reclined, reading. The house I had noted was extremely neat and clean. I might have expected statues by his father or studies at least, but unlike Aspasia's it had no decoration. A small garden had been planted in the courtyard, and a huge crimson bougainvillea had been trained to spiral around a column up to the roof. It must have been planted at the time Socrates was a child in order to have reached such girth and height. Pots had also been planted with flowers or scented herbs; the household gave more of an atmosphere of garden than most. The rich smell of stewing tomatoes made my stomach rumble.

His study was very simple if quite large: two sofas, a chair and a small writing table with a few writing implements arranged neatly and seeming small in the large space. Most notable were the number of scrolls. They were everywhere, piled on the floor, stacked carelessly so that they tumbled into disarray, on tables, on the floor, in corners, on special shelves along one wall, at the end of his reclining couch. The walls were bare, except for one niche with a statue of Apollo carved by his father, again showing that Socrates had respect for the old Gods and a love of Apollo. The floor was of stone, not marble, nor was the ceiling painted. He reclined half propped on one elbow, barefoot, dressed in the simple wool I came to expect. It was from this visit that I began to adopt his simple dress, but it took some doing to become accustomed to being barefoot in winter. I have kept these simple habits until today. But here in North Africa there is not much reason for more dress or sandals in sand.

He was reading from a thick scroll. Several more lay around him. He said, "Ah Amyntas. Come in. Come in. No, come over here by me. I want to show you these. They have just arrived and I know what a book lover you are. Did you see my friend Antiphon the Athenian as he left? He is a great book collector you know. Simonides must have introduced you."

"I have heard about him but we never met."

"I am sorry he could not stay. Here, sit beside me and let me show you what he brought me. It his own work." He pushed away some scrolls to make room, and I sat close to see what he was reading. "Look there. He has numbered them and this is the first; nothing less than his life's work, and I am one of the few with a copy. What a gift! Here, can you read it? His writing is not always legible."

At the top of the sheet was written "Antiphon/ The Meaning and Sacredness of Dreams".

Socrates said, "Antiphon's is the first scientific dream book. The Egyptian have such but they are sacred texts. He has been collecting dreams for years from anyone who would tell him, and compiling as many interpretations as he can assemble by talking to as many soothsayers and priests as possible, but also to people in the Agora. You see here in his introduction he describes his categories: "Divine Dreams", "Animal Dreams"; "Sexual Dreams", but also "Nightmares", and "Sea-demons". He thinks that dreams can be logically classified. There are bad dreams, good dreams with simple meanings, such as finding a lost object, and prophetic dreams in which the Gods speak to us of sacred, hidden things. Here. This is the section I was mulling over when you came in. Antiphon has just returned from Kos, and from speaking with Hippocrates, and the priests at the Temple of Asclepius. During the plague, you know, they started to set aside rooms where visitors could sleep and dream. Antiphon was curious to know if dreams really could heal. Let me read what he writes. 'The priests vow that Asclepius Himself heals by breathing directly into your soul. Through the laying on of the priests' hands the God also passes into the body to heal... ...'"

"And they do heal like that?"

"Antiphon thinks they can. His evidence is compelling. In the dream chamber the God reveals to the dreamer what is wrong and what the priests must heal. But sometimes Asclepius heals the person directly, and when they awaken they are well. He heard of countless examples of this."

I said, "But if the person is healed then it must demonstrate that God really can visit us in dreams."

"Yes, but Antiphon has set out to provide the evidence for this. It is quite interesting." He pushed the scrolls aside. "But I am a terrible host. It is a warm day for autumn and you must be parched." He rang a bell and a few minutes' later drinks and small date cakes were brought in by the same ancient slave who had come to the door. His slaves came to his household young, and stayed until they were old, well cared for and content. He often asked their opinion about politics or some social scandal making the rounds, and they in turn kept him informed and did not lie to him.

Socrates said, "These cakes are your favorite are they not?"

"Yes. It was kind of you to remember."

I sat shyly next to him. He did not smell of pomade, as did Simonides. His tunic was threadbare at the shoulder, and the wooden shoulder clasp was cracked. I wondered why his mother did not sew the tears, or buy clothe for a new tunic, but, of course, either she saw the moral significance of his ways, or she relented to his ways.

We were leaning against each other and still reading together, a pastime we repeated many times afterwards. I said, "I am not sure I want to believe what Antiphon writes."

"Why is that?"

"It is disturbing to think that gods and demons can move in and out of our sleep like that."

"Disturbing? It disturbs you?"

"Yes. What if we do not want to let them in? I would not want a visit from the Sphinx! I would die of fright just to glimpse her and would be terrified she would ask me something lest my answer displease her. She would strangle me!"

"You could always awaken to escape her. You're a practical person, aren't you?"

"Well, yes, I suppose I am."

I was not always sure when Socrates was joking, but this time I think he was being literal. In the back of my mind, of course, had been the horrible shrieking of the Oracle, which still reverberated in my soul.

We had fallen silent, but Socrates was watching me

393

carefully, and I glanced into his eyes. They were very disconcerting as they stood out from his face and were one of the marks of his ugliness, as was commonly said by fools. It took skill to meet his gaze.

He said, "You were really speaking about something else, not the Sphinx, were you not?"

"Yes." I paused a moment and said, "I meant the Pythia."

"She frightened you?"

"Yes. I fainted dead away. At least, that is what Chaerephon told me. I don't remember fainting, and it might have been a trance."

"How much do you remember? Do you want to tell me?"

"I remember I was very dizzy and felt very odd, as if the room were swimming and I were there but not quite there. Real things were bending and waving. I was trying to hide behind Chaerephon and a pillar, but she saw me and when she pointed at me and asked me to come forward I felt resigned. Then there was the terrible shriek. And then nothing."

"And the question? Had you planned to ask about me? You do not have to answer."

I suddenly turned to him to protest, "Oh but I want to! I did not plan it. You must not think that. It was the exact opposite. I had no questions, none at all. I don't know how much Chaerephon has told you but when the High Priest said the day before that I was to go into the sanctuary I was already frightened because I had no questions and thought that it would be sacrilegious not to ask something."

394

"And when the Oracle asked you to come forward, you still had no question?'

"No. It was exactly the opposite. I was dizzy and my mind was completely blank. You must understand. My mind was blank, completely blank. I was horrified when I asked her whether your inner voice was Apollo. I had no intention whatsoever to ask that. I could feel my mouth opening and words coming out but I did not know where they were coming from. You must believe me, Socrates."

He put his arm around my shoulder. "Of course I believe you. You don't have to be upset. It's all right. I was just trying to understand where the question came from. And she threw her head back and laughed?"

"Well, no, not really. She feigned a laugh, which is not at all the same thing."

Socrates said, "Yes, feigned a laugh. And three times?"

"Yes."

"Feigned a laugh from Apollo for a question that did not come from you. And it was not the response to a joke?"

"No, definitely not."

"Did you have the impression that the Pythia was mocking your question, or me?"

"No, not at all."

"And yet it was not quite laughter, or divine laughter, or the God laughing, but feigning." He paused and then said suddenly. "So it is a riddle then. What is a laugh that is not a laugh?"

I said. "I don't know."

Socrates replied, "Neither do I. It is a task that the God has set us, to find out."

"And you do not believe that I meant to ask about you? I would never want to disrespect you or hurt you."

Socrates said simply, "I trust you."

I felt overwhelmed. I was trembling and it took me time to recover my voice, "As soon as I asked her I wanted to take it back."

"Perhaps you did not ask it."

Was he joking or serious? I scrutinized his face for signs but could not read it. I said, "If I did not then who did and what does it mean? And if I did then what does it mean?"

He said, "Precisely! We shall now have to set ourselves the task of finding out together."

"Then you really don't know?"

He shook his head, "No, I honestly don't." He stared again into my eyes in that disconcerting way of his, but put his arm around my shoulder reassuringly. "Do you feel better now?"

I could not speak. His presence excited me. The thin Athenian tunic betrayed my state. Socrates was if anything an observant man. I did not try to adjust the cloth to be less obvious. I turned my face up to his.

He said, "They say the kiss of a beautiful boy is like the sting of a poison bee."

I said, "Oh, but I don't think I am beautiful. You can kiss me then!"

He looked startled. And paused; listening to his voice? He took my hand and said, "But you are beautiful."

Simonides had wanted me more than anything and that had gone unrequited. I wanted Socrates but his god did not agree. It was as if a circle had been completed; or perhaps a journey, to the center of Athenian mystery. Because Simonides' desire was unfulfilled we drifted apart but remained friends, if distant. But Socrates and I grew the closer.

6. Winter. Alcibiades on war.

The sudden appearance of Alcibiades at the Taureas marks the first signs of a return to war. Winter was already upon us, my feet numbed at work, my hands breaking into chilblains. My admiration for Socratic hardiness doubled. We had heard from our trainer that we were to have a guest, and that classes would be suspended, reason enough to rejoice, but if I had known it was Alcibiades I would have stayed away.

Why my dislike of Alcibiades I wonder now? Was I jealous of his close relationship with Socrates, or did I sense that he was jealous of me? I had no more than circumstantial evidence that he had used me through Mania, but the perhaps unfair suspicion was enough. As a boy I was idealistic if not moralistic, disdaining those who used others. Alcibiades had a beautiful wife, Hipparate, daughter of the wealthy Athenian, Hipponicus. I heard from Leagros that she wanted to divorce him because he made no secret of consorting with prostitutes in some of the more sordid brothels. Her petition was turned down on a technicality, but I wondered whether Alcibiades did not have it blocked to demonstrate publicly who held the power in the marriage; it would have been like him.

A crowd of excited boys was gathered at the end of the yard, jumping about flailing their arms and mimicking battle. What general had the school commissioned to nourish fledgling warriors? I hoped it would not be Cleon. When I pushed through my sweaty, smelly classmates fresh from wrestling, there was Alcibiades holding forth on Potidaea, a story I had heard many times, always painfully, and did not want to hear again. He had not seen me, and I was about to slink off when the chant of, "Delium! Delium! Delium!" went up. For Alcibiades to speak of Delium was for Alcibiades to speak of Socrates; and this I wanted to hear. Where was Socrates, I wondered? There were a hundred or more clamoring boys surrounding him, along with our teachers, trainers, and staff trying to keep a semblance of order, but no Socrates. I slipped as close to the front as I could and still remain hidden. It would have been like Alcibiades to single me out, pretending to honor me with his attention but embarrassing me.

Delium was a rout for Athens; their defeat had encouraged them to negotiate the prevailing truce. Alcibiades had fought with the cavalry, not with the hoplites as had Socrates. His horse, a black Arab stallion, was nearly as famous in battle as he. It was tethered across the yard, much fawned over, a high-strung creature with lightning responses. He could make it rear, pawing the air fiercely, and wheel on hind legs. Some boys were baiting Alcibiades to give a demonstration of his horsemanship.

He raised his hands for silence and received an instant hush; he motioned for us to sit and we did, the envy of the teachers, never so well obeyed. His dress was trimmed with elegant, white silk bands that caught the sun, deference to his aristocracy. I had to grant that he was handsome: tall, broad of shoulder, narrow of waist, his

398

hair fashionably long, sandy colored with a few streaks of white blond; his beard naturally curled. He wore a thick gold chain around his neck. His dress had just enough refinement to remind others of his birthright, but not too much to seem crass.

So often did my classmates retell his story that it must have been committed to a hundred memories?

Alcibiades said, "In fair Boeotia, there so close north to us, they say their warriors can transform themselves into wolves at night and haunt the mountain slopes to prey on lone travelers. And this is not merely to frighten us into staying at home here behind our safe walls, extended to the sea and safeguarding us from siege. Their hoplites snarl as wolves and throw themselves on you in battle with daggers sharp as lions' claws. Grrrhhhhh"

He screwed up his face ferociously, growled and pretended to attack the boys at the front, who screamed in delight and launched backwards upsetting the rest gleefully.

He said, "That day as strong a land force as Athens has ever known, brave men and true, marched from our wives warm arms, our children clinging to us tearfully, to put an end once and for all to enemy arrogance. Our great general Cleon rallied us with stirring words. Had the Spartans, he said, for the first time not surrendered to him and the brave Athenian force he commanded at the island siege of Spachteria? And was this not a sign that the Spartan yearning from birth for war was waning and the time now ripe for total victory, giving no quarter and risking all for the greater glory of fair Athena?"

Again he was interrupted, boys leaping to their feet in

great excitement to mimic war as actors mimic other tragedies. Again he raised his hands and as if by magic there was instant silence.

"How willing we were to fight, fair lads, you can well imagine, you who bear the future of our great city upon your shoulders as you will bear armor and shield! We answered the truly great Cleon with ringing assent. 'Yes!' we shouted. 'Yes! Yes! Yes, we shall fight!' and marched out alongside him once and for all to slay the foe as the minotaur was slain, thirsting for heroics to set beside the old stories. Would you, brave boys I see here now, have shouted some meek 'no' or would you as with me now have shouted your 'Yes! Yes! Yes!'"

Again he caused bedlam. A roar rang out so loudly it might have been heard to Piraeus.

As he roused us instantly, he calmed us instantly, clay in his hands, and continued, "The Spartans had lost their will, this Cleon knew, and victory was ours before we marched. This we all believed. But fate would not have it so. Why is this you may ask, and who among us does not ask, what went wrong? Yes, what went wrong? And I will tell you now. Our spies let us down. There is nothing more dangerous in war than knowing half-truths about the enemy. The intelligence information we received from Sparta was flawed. Sparta was in disarray over the surrender of their men trained to die honorably in battle but never yield. This was true. The time was ripe for victory and to add to our territory in order to buffer us against future Spartan betrayals. Had we not suffered too many? This was true. Then what went wrong?"

There were cries and murmurs of assent, but none dared

tell how the great Themistocles and Pericles had warned about territorial ambitions as a means to peace. Had they not insisted that Athens must be primarily a naval power? They understood the Spartan prowess on land, and for all the years of war Athens had held out because its navy was superior to none. But Cleon led a land force. Was Pericles not Alcibiades' uncle yet was Alcibiades not siding with Cleon's arrogant judgments? I wanted to jump up and shout my disagreement but I held my silence.

Alcibiades said, "I shall tell you what happened, and mark my words, for you shall hear many versions of this from as many as can tell it, but I shall tell you the true story. Our intelligence network let us down because they did not inform us that the Boeotians, eager for revenge and lusting for conquest, were secretly gathering a massive army to launch full scale on us. And when they descended screaming upon us in numbers far greater than we had ever seen, we realized that they had been warned of our invasion and were well prepared. But we had not been warned of their buildup. Yet, outnumbered we fought fiercely, slashing to left and right, braving the downpour of arrows, the forest of spears to take back glory home through courage in battle."

There were shouts of "Show us! Show us! Mount your horse and show us!" I could bear no more, and was about to sneak away hoping to find Socrates, when the thought of him set me down again. I leaned over to a friend I knew who was boisterous and bold and whispered, "Ask him about Socrates. Go on and ask him. I dare you. Unless you are afraid?"

He pushed me away with disgust and said, "Of course I

am not afraid." Cupping his hands to his mouth he shouted, "Socrates! Tell us about Socrates. Socrates!"

Alcibiades commanded silence. "I hear a bold question being asked, but a right one too, lad. If you had left me to it I would have told you of my own accord, but you are right to remind me. There! Across the yard there you see my faithful horse. Astride him I could cut swathes through the shouting Boeotian hordes, as easily as farmers cut through wheat with their sharp scythes, saving friends but sparing no enemy. But suddenly, there in the midst of writhing chaos, what did I see? Can you guess? Can any of you guess? Two strong men stood calmly alone in the midst of savagery! Can you imagine this? Two Athenians brave and true, so commanding in their presence that the enemy dared not attack them but chased only those running from the fray. Hundreds surrounded them, yet they stood unharmed, an awesome sight, these two hoplites standing off the enemy by calmness and courage. It sent a shiver of respect through me such as we feel when face to face with hero or god. Their helmets obscured their faces and I swathed a way closer to see who they were. It was Socrates, and Laches shielded by him. Why were they not slaughtered, I wondered, cut down at once by the teeming mass of enemy around them, as if standing in a pit of striking snakes, unbitten? Why was it? What was their secret? I shall tell you. Socrates was calm and cool, entirely self-possessed, and yet he was fierce. He had discovered through experience in battle the secret of the perfect warrior, inner calm and outer ferocity. In battle he was completely focused, never losing himself to fear, rage, or the blood lust. It was the way of the true hero, he of whom Homer sings. The enemy was chasing and cutting down easily those who fled, but these two they left alone."

I half-crawled back through the other boys to be alone. The story greatly moved me. My brother did not know this secret, I realized, and he had died. My father did not know it either, and was maimed for life. But Socrates knew it, and Socrates was still whole. What then did war mean? Was it as much a path to the soul as peace?

I felt greatly confused and went off to find Socrates.

***

I could not find him immediately, and thought that he had simply gone home, perhaps guessing that Alcibiades might be called on to speak of Delium and not wanting to be the center of attention. But my Nubian said he thought he was still there and we finally found him at the opposite end of the yard as far away as possible from where Alcibiades spoke. He was sitting on the ground by a plane tree peacefully playing knucklebones with some of the younger boys. At least, he was playing a version of the game. The usual way to play was to hold back one bone as a jack; this you held in your hand. The others you scattered on the ground within easy reach. You tossed the jack. While it was in the air you seized a bone from the ground and caught the jack with the same hand. This you continued until all the bones were picked up, you missed the jack, or failed to seize a bone during a toss. The bones were numbered and each successful toss scored you points, the total on the total bones seized being your final score. If you did not throw the jack too high, so that catching it was easy, you were booed and hissed, but if you threw it too high so that scooping up the bones on the ground was easy, then you were also booed and hissed. The best players could seize several bones on one catch, swooping them up gracefully. Bones were very cheap to buy. They were only one tenth the cost of the fig and date cakes I liked, and everyone played.

There were many versions of knucklebones besides the one I have given, but Socrates liked to make up new ones to amuse us. When he saw me, his face lit up; it gladdened me. He bid me join in.

"If you do not mind playing a new way," he said. "Who wants to explain our rules to Amyntas?"

Several boys cried out at once and hovered around me. First the knucklebones were tossed on the ground; then the boy to toss the jack was blindfolded. The rest of the rules were the same but, of course, it was nearly impossible to catch the jack and pick up any bones while blindfolded. This had caused much excitement.

"Let him try! Let him try!"

It seems that boys were also wagering, because as soon as I agreed to take a turn bets flew through the air, how many I would catch, none or any. Although blindfolded, I managed three successful tosses, with two bones picked up for a total of nine points. Apparently that was the highest score so far of "blind man's knucklebones" as they had named it.

I said, politely, not meaning a challenge, "Have you tried it Socrates? What was your score?"

There were shouts of, "Yes! Socrates! Try it! Try it!"

I said quietly to him, "I did not mean to embarrass

you."

"It is all right."

He agreed to try, folded his legs beneath him, and sat up arrow straight. The bones were tossed in front of him and I saw him study them carefully. The rag was tied tightly around his eyes. Boys waved hands in front of him to make sure he could not peek. He held out his palm and the jack was placed in the middle. I saw also that he took deep breaths, his breathing calm and regular. He tossed the jack, high and straight and scooped up a bone; then a second, and a third, until they were all gone. There were shouts of glee and gasps too. He took off the blindfold. Had he really not been able to see through the black strip of cloth? He assured us he had not. There was no trick; it was only a matter of understanding simple natural laws. If you threw something straight up it came straight down, and at a certain rate if there was no wind to distract it, which there was not that day. The bones also lay at angles to his knees, which he could see in his mind when his eyes were shut. But try as the rest of us may that afternoon we could not duplicate his feat. I was next best.

As I sat there playing knucklebones with him and the others I made a vow not to speak to him of war, despite or because of Alcibiades' stories, and despite or because of my confusion. This may sound like a contradiction. But I was happy that afternoon, although such games might seem beyond my age and my peers were already taxing their muscles for battle. A simple life free of conflicts was something I craved and needed. As well, Alcibiades' warmongering I also dismissed. He was a poseur from whom nothing else could be expected. I wanted to get on with things and not be concerned with history. A week or so later, in a fleeting moment, I found myself thinking a darker thought. I did not want Socrates to die in battle. I could not bear it. It was an admission of bonding as much as of fear.

And yet I finally did ask him, but the question was not posed because of any special fear or circumstance. It must have been weeks later, well into the winter, and perhaps by then I already knew the answer.

"Socrates, why do you go to war?" I asked straightforwardly enough.

And he answered simply enough, "My voice does not tell me not to serve."

"But why?"

"As with the Pythia I do not always understand its counsel. Perhaps it has something to do with my calling as a philosopher and citizen. So much is clear from the things my voice prevented me from doing. I must meet my civic obligations and so I volunteer for service, but as a hoplite because it is not for honors or vainglory. My place in war is to be a hoplite among hoplites. In a way it is an extension of being a philosopher."

I said, "At Delium, Alcibiades thinks you were in touch with your soul and this made you a feared warrior."

He threw up his hands. "Oh Alcibiades. Battle has nothing to do with it. It is the way we should always be."

His voice alwys struck me as being as much of a puzzle as the Pythia. And was it a mystery to Socrates, or a friend?

7. Spring. Simonides returns.

Simonides returned overland to Athens in the early spring from his northern tour. He had written to me several times, he said, but only one of his letters ever reached me. Upon his return, he might have tried to rekindle his ardor had fate not intervened.

A Persian delegation was in Athens to discuss new trade alliances. They had also come overland, through Macedon in fact, so I knew of their advent. If Persia had suffered a decisive defeat at the hands of the Athenians decades before, they had never fully accepted it. Any arrival of a Persian delegation was met with suspicion. The Agora was buzzing with speculation about ulterior motives for "expanded trade", the ostensible purpose of their visit. Everyone had an opinion, or a suspicion. The Persians, as did the Spartans, Athenians, and Macedonians for that matter, acted in their own self-interest, but they said they were in Athens to renegotiate their silver contracts. If it was ostensibly true, it was not the whole truth. They brought a large delegation, guards and retinue, and soon the city was teeming with the sibilance of their pleasing language and ablaze with the color of their garments. Many banquets were to be held.

Now it happened that the Persian general, at the head of the guard accompanying the delegation, had brought along his fifteen-year-old son. In the barbershop I heard rumors of tempestuous love affairs and a suitor in Susa killing himself. Such stories had not whirred around the Agora since Alcibiades' youth. Several soothsayers also claimed to have had dreams of two storms converging, and seen other signs interpreted to mean two grand passions.

407

I played a small role in this story. At Aspasia's one day, I came upon a haggard Simonides sitting forlornly alone in the courtyard. We had seen each other twice since his return but I did not know he would be there that day. I took pity on his sadness, thinking vainly it was over me, and stopped to ask him how he was. He was never much of a one to hide his feelings, and so the whole story about this Persian boy spilled out, how they had met at a dinner, and how he had taken him off to his home for a delirious night, and how the boy would now not return his messages. He was bereft, desperate, was ready to throw himself off a parapet.

I felt sorry for him but sighed privately with relief and said, "An idea has come to me, if I may give you advice."

"By all means! I have run out of ideas."

"Send him a simple love gift, nothing extravagant, but something symbolic, a rabbit, such as the old Cretan stories of abduction tell is sent by a man to a boy. Woo him with modest symbols."

Much to my amazement he followed my advice, and it worked. Simonides sent him a pet baby owl, which he found for sale in the marketplace, with a note saying it was a token of Athena and something to remind him of Athens. The boy found the gift charming and it softened his heart to Simonides' wild eccentricities, to which he himself was no less prone. I fell into the role of adviser comfortably and it gave new life to a friendship that might otherwise have been lost. I harbored no jealousy for the boy, never having fancied Simonides in this way, and having now a bond with Socrates. The Persian delegation was not long in Athens, before continuing on to Corinth, Sparta, and other of the states. Simonides held out for a few days, but it was too much for him. He came to me one day in tears. Should he follow his love to Corinth, back to Susa and Persepolis, to the ends of the earth? It sounded as if they both needed extravagant gestures to channel their love madness. I said that I would miss him but I saw no reason he should not.

I asked, "Shall I see you again?"

Simonides said, "Of course you shall."

But he said it half-heartedly and I realized that I might not and was overcome. No matter how difficult he was and the pressures he put on me, he eased my introduction to Athens, brought me new friends and the riches of theater.

I spoke with Socrates about my feelings for Simonides soon afterwards.

"I am sad he has left. Is it wrong?"

"Why should it be wrong?"

"When we have something we do not think we want and lose it, then suddenly we think how much we had and how much we shall miss it. Does this mean we wanted it all along?"

Socrates said, "Will you miss the whole or the part?"

"I don't know. How can I separate them and know?"

"If he were suddenly to come back in a week would you stop resisting what you resisted for the sake of the rest you had?"

"No. It would still be the same."

"Then what will you miss?"

"All of the rest I think. Along with his wanting me so badly, and my ability to refuse while holding him. But I think we can still be friends."

409

"And what will you not miss?"

"Not miss?" I thought for a while and said, "I do not think his passion proceeded from what he wished best for me, but from something ungovernable in him that would have what it would have."

"What would you have been giving in to then?"

"Ungovernable passion. I would have accepted it, in some way, into my heart."

"And you will not miss that?"

"No. I shall not miss that. It, well, exhausted my spirit." And then thinking I had misrepresented Simonides I quickly added, "But he gave me many things that were good. It was he who introduced me to Aspasia, and she introduced me to you. It was also Simonides who took me to see the rehearsal of *Clouds* at the Odeon, which was also my first glimpse of you." I suddenly caught myself, because I heard how I was trying to justify myself to Socrates, and how unnecessary that was. "Well," I said, about to be tendentious, "friendship is...."

He waited and said, "Yes?"

I had been about to say, "complicated", but I suddenly realized that my friendship with Socrates was simple. I blushed and was disconcerted. I glanced at him and saw he was staring at me with full concentration. I said nothing, fearing to seem the fool, and only took his hand. We walked on hand in hand in silence.

8. 422B.C. War.

Within weeks of Simonides' departure for Persia, but still in the spring of that year, Cleon and his friends began to circulate petitions in the Agora agitating for war, the preliminary step towards debating it in the council chamber and putting it on the agenda for the Assembly. Wild flowers covered the mountain slopes, and the first warm days were well upon us, but the main spring festivals had not yet occurred. Sudden rains would sweep over the city, turning the streets to mud but settling the dust. My school friends and I would wait under the Stoa for the squalls to pass, crowding together under the archways to make fun of the speakers.

One day it was Cleonytus' turn at the speaker's corner. He had received word, he said pompously, of Spartan machinations on the eastern frontier. They were trying to take control of our ally Scione and block our grain supply. The city take heed. Athenians had suffered the threat of starvation before from a Spartan burnt earth policy. Any interruption of food shipments was feared almost as much as the plague. Sparta could starve out the city by controlling the eastern frontier. His voice was raspy and easily mocked. We would not believe him. "A frog croaking through gravel" one of my friends shouted derisively, met with much laughter. I was as shameless as the others and fled as fast when the Agora police headed our way to control us.

An encounter with Athenades I can also date to this time. I was usually the first into the workroom, not because of ambition or diligence, but because I was so busy it was hard to fit everything in without being punctual and orderly. Virtues dictated by circumstances were virtues nonetheless. I found Athenades one early morning, standing in the doorway looking at the hard rain.

He said, "Come and praise Zeus." I went to stand next

411

to him. The rain and air still had a touch of coolness. He added, "There are changes coming. I can feel it in the rain. But not only. The city is restless too. The Persians made us uneasy. And now…"

He did not finish the thought. I could feel it too, and I said, "Cleonytus and Cleon are saying in the Agora that we must be ready again for war or risk starvation."

He did not answer this directly. He held out his hand, and let the rain pour over it. Looking sad he said, "The gods know." He withdrew his hand but oddly did not wipe it on his tunic, as if he wanted Zeus to linger on his hand. He said, "I came early to speak with you. I had several messages from your father. One is for you. I'll give it to you now."

This was unusual as he usually waited until the end of the day. I said anxiously, "Is he well?"

"Yes. He is well. But things are not good on your border. I told you I would write to him about Amphipolis. I am afraid he has sent our peace fellowship bad news, of a Spartan plot to take over our enclave at Scione. If they establish a base there they can use it to destabilize our other enclaves. "

This confirmed what I had heard in the Agora. Scione was next to Amphipolis, and less than a day from my home. The town had long been more or less divided between loyalists of Macedon, Sparta, and Athens, but the balance was unstable and rarely equal. I knew that if it were true that the Spartans were conspiring to take control of Athenian enclaves it could only mean war.

Athenades said, "Your father writes that a Spartan garrison has already taken up position in Scione, aided and abetted by the Spartan faction. We are waiting to see what the reaction will be from the rest of the town, and the towns around."

I said, "Then Macedon will become involved."

"Yes. I am afraid it will. I am sorry. Your father thinks King Perdiccas will side with Sparta this time."

"Sparta!" I wanted to add a torrent of verbal abuse against the king but held my tongue.

Athenades said, "Your court thinks Brasidas is a better leader of the Spartans than Cleon of our troops. Perhaps they are right too. Brasidas is a gifted general." He wiped his hands now and went to his desk where he took a scroll out of a locked box. "This is for you."

Father's letter left no doubt that war was in the air. And if war were in the air, was it already when Argaeus visited me those months ago? Father thought the drift of events confirmed that the intention of Argaeus' visit was to demonstrate Argaead authority over our House, or as he put it in his letter, "to let the Temenidai know the reach of Argaead power." He also told me a story. It gave the flavor of events in our area of Macedon.

"Spartan marauders disguising themselves as local sheep herders have been stealing supplies earmarked for Amphipolis and the other Athenian enclaves: pigs, chickens, and the like. For many weeks now there have also been Spartan troop movements all along the coast and throughout the peninsula between Scione, Akte, and northward to Amphipolis. At an inn in one of the villages some of our friends were able to get a band of these marauders drunk and they bragged about what Sparta would do to Athenian allies if they had not learned their

413

lesson from the earlier Spartan victory at Amphipolis some three or four years ago. They are intimidating the villages and some have already acquiesced and installed village heads friendly to Sparta. At the rate that they are converting governorships, again in violation of the truce, they should have installed their allies in every strategic town along the plains and foothills within a matter of weeks. The drunkards bragged that Sparta would now finish the job of securing every inch of Thrace, left unfinished in the last battle there. Scione might fall to the Spartans within days. And war?

In the barbershop that week, and for successive weeks, the gossip was of war. I did not tell what I knew, but everyone seemed to know anyway. Cleon had petitioned the Assembly for more triremes. At least thirty would be needed, but he had only raised pledges for fifteen. The forges were back working overtime, and I often thought how right my classmates had been about the new reinforced breastplates.

War debate also began to disrupt classes at the Lyceum and Taureas. One day I nearly had a fistfight. In a fit of impatience I had asked our teacher. "What good is Amphipolis to Athens? Why can't it be left alone?"

There were shouts and replies from all around. "Fool! It's the key to the entire eastern sea network. Our food supply, dumb-ass! Our food supply! If we don't control the eastern sea Sparta or Persia certainly will! Then where will be?" There were cries of "Down with Sparta!" But praise God not, "Down with Macedon." The teacher explained that Persia used its western coastline, from

Lesbos south to Rhodes, as a staging point for mischief in the entire region. We would be pressed from two directions. Persia! And where was Simonides now?

I was irritated with it all, dreading the consequences for myself, and burst out, "It is all arrogance: imperialism and hegemony."

One of my classmates was ready to do battle. "And who shall Macedon serve this time, like the whore it is. And you, Macedonian, where are your loyalties? Would you rather have our women raped and all of us enslaved! "

I should have known better, and held my peace. Athenians were just xenophobic enough to harbor suspicions under a veneer of tolerance, like thin sheets of gold hiding worm eaten wood. I said, "No, that is not what I mean. With some sense peace can be maintained."

It was the first time I had dared declaim any of my own sentiments and they were not received kindly.

My classmate had an easy reply. "How can there be peace when your own king is ready to betray us to the Spartans at a crow's cry?"

He was right about Perdiccas. He was no better with his grandiose notions of Macedonian ascendancy than Brasidas or Cleon with theirs about Athens. One tyrant can make a war, I thought, and two tragedy.

If my apprehensions were not great enough to cause me sleepless nights, father added to them in another letter I received around this time, raising an ominous possibility, "It is certain now that the Argaead will wholeheartedly assist Sparta again if war breaks out again, as it increasingly seems it must. Be on your guard. It might be wise for Athenades to double your chaperones. I shall write to him with such advice, and consult our household oracles."

Father was right. Consulting the signs was imperative. I must go first thing to Aspasia and seek consul from her and her diviners.

And Socrates! If anything the transit of history was more absorbing to me now because Socrates had told me that he had given notice that he would serve again. When we walked together in the city some of his fellow hoplites would greet him, eager for the fight. "We shall trod them underfoot and mingle their blood with the dust, hey old friend?" or, "Dusted off your shield yet, Socrates? It won't be long now." They made reference to me as well, "Your young friend here does not seem old enough to be another Alcibiades to save on the field of battle, but he can keep your bed warm at home and give you something to fight for."

But would I still be in Athens by the end of another battle, or indeed by its start? If I had any doubts about the direction of father's thinking, the next letter settled it.

"Dearest Son. Perhaps you would be safer deep in Africa, at least for a time, until we can plot a better place for you..."

How utterly bereft I felt reading those words. I asked permission to send a message to Aspasia that I must seek her counsel as soon as possible. Athenades could see my distress and would not deny me any longer access to my friends.

***

Aspasia greeted me warmly. She and Socrates had dispelled any lingering fears about the Mania affair. She had been out of the city for some time, having chosen to return for some weeks to Miletus to attend to her households and property. Persian military maneuvers and rumors of war so near to Miletus, raised anxieties about the safety of her households, there and in Athens. She had her own alliances to consider. They said she owned so much land in and about Miletus that she could start her own kingdom. She led me into her study again, her and my favorite room in her house. The weasel lay asleep on its pillow in a corner. I do not know why but it comforted me. I asked to see one of her rare maps, of eastern Africa and the lower Nile, in case father "exiled" me there. She brought out a map that showed an area so remote from Athens as to seem Hades itself.

She saw my sadness and said, "You mustn't be sad, or try to outguess the fates. We'll consult your charts and the signs to see if there is any indication of travel. Besides I have a surprise for you. I have been working on it for many weeks. But today was indicated as the day to tell you."

"But what is it?"

"Actually, it is someone I am taking you to meet. He has a proposal to make. In fact Polydamus is there already and will join us."

Mentioning her lover made it the more intriguing.

I said, "But what is this surprise then? I have not seen Polydamus since the banquet. I liked his company very much. It will be good to see him again. Is that the surprise?"

417

"He speaks often of you. But no, he is not the surprise. I do not wish to sound coy. I am taking you to the house of the sculptor Polykleitos the Elder. I commissioned him to do a statue of Polydamus and he came up with the wonderful idea of depicting him as diadem-bearer. You know that his statues of athletes are considered the finest now that Phidias and Miron are dead?"

"Oh yes. I had heard this from Socrates. He tells me all about sculpture and sculptors when we walk together on the Acropolis. He knows everything there is to know, because of his father, I suppose. He also showed me his own chisel marks and calls himself "one of the eighty" meaning, I suppose that there were eighty sculptors working on the Acropolis?"

"One of the eighty! That is good. It also happens to be true, at least figuratively if not literally. There may have been seventy-five or eighty-seven, so he was one of many, the last thing one would think of Socrates."

I agreed and said, "But you did not tell me why Polykleitos wants to meet me. "

"I shall let him tell you himself. First let us read the signs and see if remote regions lie in your future."

She had old charts of mine from other readings stored on wooden shelves and could use these as the basis for charting the star path of new beginnings. There was a great surprise, if one that led to more mystery. We leaned together over the instruments. I loved the way she worked, so quietly and authoritatively, smelling so exotically. To think that orchids and pig urine could meld and intoxicate! If she had fancied me I would have benefited by being her lover. As I stood beside her while she consulted, serenity

418

overtook her and she seemed to become more beautiful.

I said, "Is it terrible news?"

"It is, well, odd. There is wealth. I can see that clearly, and an eagle hovering. Yes. All the indications are of things celestial."

She called one of her priests to bring fresh livers and entrails, and when she had read these too, she did not speak immediately but cleared everything away and called for refreshments before we were to set out. I thought that it must mean terrible news and dreaded what she might say.

Aspasia finally turned to me and would only say, "I can see a path but it is shrouded. It is very peculiar. Have you had any dreams? Perhaps they will have a bearing."

For many months she had asked me to record my dreams and so I was ready to tell one. I said, "I had this one a night or two ago. There was a giant feather that scraped its tip along the earth, but no bird. Do you think it means father will send me to Africa?"

"Perhaps it is the feather of Zeus writing a fate for you, in other words a blessing. You must trust Him. I know you are distressed by the thought of being sent away again."

"More angry than sad. I know that father is concerned about my safety. He has my good at heart, and he also has the responsibility of securing our line. Still, sometimes his anxiety makes me boil."

She said, "I am sure his judgment is taken in consultation with many. But, I do not think he will send you to some remote place. He will show consideration for your talents as a goldsmith. Of that you can be sure."

Did she know more than she was saying? She always did. I opened my mouth to ask what she meant but she cut

419

me off before I could.

"But enough! It is time we went across the city to Polykleitos. He is waiting for us, and we would dishonor him by being late.

***

After the death of Phidias, some seven or eight years before these events, Polykleitos was recognized as the greatest living sculptor. If he was not as gifted an architect as Phidias, his statue "The Amazon", in Ephesus, was considered the equal of anything that Phidias had done, and some thought it superior. His statues of athletes excelled at depicting pent energy with no sacrifice of lightness and grace. I was curious to see how he worked. We had never met although his studio was not far from our workshop, also "under the eyes of Herakles" in the craftsman district. I knew him by sight. Simonides had introduced me to him one day when we met by chance in the market, not uncommon in village Athens. He stopped to greet us, holding up his hand in greeting. I was struck by its massiveness, still capable of refined work: a burly, bald man older than Simonides but not Socrates. Sculptors and painters seemed to be of a more outgoing and active humor than goldsmiths. Polykleitos was restless and forceful. After meeting him, Simonides had pledged to take me to Argos to see his statue of Hera at the Heraion, but it was to be some twenty years before I saw it on my own. Simonides had also lent me Polykleitos' treatise on sculpture, The Kanon. He thought I might find something in it relevant to my own craft and I did. Polykleitos was a

420

follower of Pythagoras and had worked out a sophisticated system of proportions that he applied to his cast as he worked. He would draw mathematical formulae on it. Thus, arms and arm muscles had to be a certain ratio to the construction of legs and leg muscle. Pythagoras applied the ratios to music and harmonics, but Polykleitos to marble and bronze. In fact, they said that he worked harder at his cast than at the bronze, and that once the cast was right then the bronze would follow like a perfect bud opening to a glorious rose. He had written in his treatise, "Let the clay under the thumb be the real work", and I had taken this to mean that my designs should contain the hardest work, and the execution would follow. I was glad that I had read his treatise so that I might not seem naive, but I was also a bit sad that I had not gone with Simonides to Argos. How little of Hellas I had really seen since arriving nearly two years previously, and now there were intimations of war and leaving.

I was reflecting on all of this when Aspasia startled me. She had assembled a large retinue of slaves to accompany us, as befit a woman of stature. I insisted on carrying her sunshade. She said it was beneath me, but was pleased by my attention. The streets were crowded, although we had taken back ways to avoid the worst. We were not ten minutes from her door when she whispered, "Someone is following our party."

It was a shock and I felt a cold chill. "Who would follow us?"

She summoned two of her slaves and I saw them dissolve into the crowd. She said, "We shall know shortly. Pretend that all is normal."

"Is it one man, or more?" I thought it might be the same man who had accosted me at the Assembly. I had told Aspasia about this.

She said, "I saw one, a youth, tall and thick-set."

"Is his hair black and in a braid?"

"No, I think not, but I did not get a good glimpse."

This would have fit the description of one of the men guarding Prince Argaeus. Had he been left behind to watch me? If so, he was conspicuous enough to be spotted.

I said, "If it is who I think it is he wants us to know he is following us."

"Yes, I had that impression."

"Should we go back to your house? Or should I return to the workshop? We are near there."

"No. We shall continue as we intended."

In a minute or so her slave was back, whispering something to her.

Aspasia said, "When my man accosted him the fellow said he thought he had caught a glimpse of you and that he was just a school friend, from the Lyceum."

"A school friend? What was his name?"

"Before they could ask he slipped away into the crowd."

I breathed a sigh of relief. "Then it was nothing."

Aspasia said "Apparently."

I felt so relieved that I seized her hand, an uncommon liberty, and held it all the way to the sculptor's door.

Her lover, Polydamus of Skotoussa, was indeed there, standing nude on a dais as Polykleitos molded his cast with fine wooden tools they said he made himself. How beautiful Polydamus was, and how right for Aspasia to want his beauty captured at its peak. When I had met him at the banquet I had thought him a little too rugged, chunks of muscle here and there in obvious display, but nude he seemed lithe and supple, the fat refined away to a delicate sinew of flowing line. He held the long diadem ribbon above his head, the symbol of athletic victory, and the pose made him seem all the more stunning.

He groaned as we entered and said, "Aspasia, at last! I have held this pose for hours and even my agony is frozen. And Amyntas! How good to see you again. Please, Master Polykleitos, can we not stop for today?"

Polykleitos laughed and said, having greeted us, "He has been complaining for over an hour, Lady Aspasia, and I have turned a deaf ear. All right then, let's stop for the day. I shall have the masseur come to rub you down. We don't want your muscles to burst into flames."

The masseur set his table up in our midst, so that Polydamus could partake of our company. Refreshments were brought and we chatted idly about the mellow tone that had descended on Athens since the truce began, palatable as light wine, or fragrant as incense. I was eager to know what surprise Aspasia had concocted, but had to bide my time until she was ready to broach the matter with the sculptor. Polykleitos was watching me closely I noticed, but then he would have scrutinized everyone as a model for some work.

He said, "You have a fine face, Amyntas. I have been working on this idea of a group piece called, "Boys playing Knucklebones" and you might make a good pair with another boy I am using. He should be here shortly. If you can stay a while, and that is permissible, Lady

Aspasia?"

"Prince Amyntas is to dine with me this evening but we all might linger a short time." I had not been told I would dine with her and was glad to hear this. Aspasia continued, "Perhaps, Polykleitos, you might tell Amyntas why you asked me to bring him here. It is not only for knucklebones, of course."

Polykleitos said, "Oh no, not at all only for knucklebones, although the more I look at him the more I think he would be perfect. But it is for something else. As you know, Amyntas, after the supreme Phidias' passing, I was given the contract to complete certain work on the Parthenon and other temples on the Acropolis, and as you also know the great Phidias was particularly fond of finishing certain features with gold, such as Athena's shield. But the gods took him before his plans were complete and there is need for much gold work. Athena holds the goddess of victory Nike in her hand, some four cubits in length, but the gold used was not pure, and some of it has come away. Phidias intended to change it to pure gold, but he did not live long enough to fulfill every wish he had for the Athena, his greatest creation. We would like the entire Nike re-gilded with pure gold, and some refinements added to her robes as befits a goddess."

Aspasia had grown impatient and said, "But you have not asked him what you want of him! The surprise Polykleitos, the surprise!"

"Oh, yes, sorry. Of course, well, what I was saying, I mean, well, you see we, that is the committee of the Parthenon, yes, we would like you to be the official goldsmith for the Nike project, yes, you know, come up with a design and all that, oversee the work, yes, get paid, of course, get handsomely paid I might add, and well, Lady Aspasia has told me you share some of her own, well, sentiments about peace in Athens, so honoring Nike, I mean, it did strike all of us that you were the man, not quite, the boy, well you see, the person for the job, should you, were you to accept, of course, and a great honor, and all that."

Aspasia interrupted, "Isn't it splendid Amyntas!"

I was stunned to tears. I could not speak. It was as if the whole city of Athens had made love to me at that moment, as if I had entered into unity with her. Aspasia came over and kissed me on the cheek, "You have made the boy speechless, Polykleitos. You deserve the honor you know. We have never seen in Athens anyone with such talent as yours for working gold. You must have a part in honoring the gods with your work."

I was still unable to speak. Athens had been so good to me, so good, and yet the specter of leaving haunted the room. I put my arms around Aspasia and burst into tears.

I finally found my voice amidst my sobbing and said, "May the gods protect us."

9. My last days in Athens.

Word spread through the Agora that the Boeotians were raiding the northern farm districts again. The official delegation to Delphi was stalked along the way and lost one of its food wagons to brigands. Upon their return, I crowded into the Agora with half the citizenry to hear their frightening story; thankful it had not been me. Corinth was making threats again. The sense of unease was palpable;

425

tempers flared. Cleon and his war party encouraged the fears, and did nothing to soothe them. In the barbershop one spring day, everyone was talking about Alcibiades' aspirations to lead Cleon's faction, and the divisions among Cleon's allies about the role Alcibiades would play should war break out again, before the summer or New Year, it was now widely predicted. Any division in the war faction was an opportunity for peace, I wrongly thought. I buried myself in work and school, Socrates and friends, in order to forget politics. But war was tinder to the blaze of Athenian gossip. I wondered whether deafness was not a boon sent by the gods rather than the bane it was thought.

One more painful reminder of shifting history hit me one day at the Taureas. After training I went to find Socrates at his usual spot by the plane tree, but was told he was not there but in the training field at the other end of the city. The hoplites were being called up for maneuvers, including Socrates; they trained on the Academy grounds. I went there later that afternoon, along with a hundred other boys excitedly crowding the sidelines to cheer on heroes, stirred for future battle. I admired his sword and spear play, his rugged fitness, the quickness of his movements, but went away filled with dread and doubt. Was it the gods' will to lose those I loved to war? I desperately wanted to deny its inevitability, but it was on everyone's mind, and lips, and weighed heavily on my heart.

Nicias and his entourage from the peace party were visiting the workshop quite openly now. There were proposals to be written for the next Council meeting, lobbying to be done among the citizenry for the next

426

Assembly. He was angry, I could tell, from his wild gestures. "I shall open my purse to everyone," he said, and his purse was as deep as the deepest well, or the silver mines from which it was filled. They said he was wealthy enough to own a thousand slaves and brought a whole retinue for protection when he came to the shop, concerned about Cleon's spies, hovering like birds of prey over tidbits of carrion. There were shouting matches in the Agora between the two factions, but I could not imagine any of their invective harsher than that Aristophanes, born and bred amidst the banter of the street and the master of invective, had already leveled against warmongers in general, and Cleon.

I was spending more and more time at Aspasia's house, and met Aristophanes there one day. Aspasia's house was my refuge, my haven of civility and artistry. Her son, young Pericles, had also formed an attachment to me. He had no brothers and I served this purpose, being only five years older than he. He had some of his father's strength and agility, was already able at archery, far more than I, and excelled at any skill that required a keen eye and a steady hand. I would carry him around on my shoulders playing at cavalry; he wielded a wooden sword. I was better at knucklebones than he, but he did not like me to lose deliberately out of deference to his age. The first time he caught me doing this he sulked; I treated him as an equal afterwards and he quickly came to beat me. We played other games too. His favorite was morra. You make a fist behind your back and then "shoot" a number of fingers. The idea is to guess the number of fingers before they are displayed, and the first to guess correctly wins the round. We played for sweets or pebbles. He liked to cheat, pretending his fingers had slipped, or that he had miscounted and really meant four, the right number, when he said three, or delaying his guess so his quick gaze could count mine. I would stay and dine, and read Homer and the epics to him before he went to sleep. Morra is still very popular in Sicily, where they say it originated, and here in North Africa.

I had come early that morning to her house. I was to go rabbit hunting with young Pericles. As I was being admitted I found Aristophanes sitting in the entrance hall waiting for his slave to return from an errand before he went home.

"You are out and about early, Aristophanes," I said, greeting him.

He had a reputation for sleeping in late after a night of drinking, but he grumbled, "In fact, I was up all night writing."

He had come to give Aspasia a draft of his new play. Nicias was to produce it, but Aspasia sometimes gave him money privately. I had not seen him for some time and noticed that he had let his beard grow untrimmed and unkempt. It suited him, giving him a rather wild, unpredictable look. In other words, his appearance and his personality were more in balance and closer to the spirit of his writing. His sharp clear eyes filled with paternal warmth when we met. I was fifteen at the time, and he was twenty-eight or nine, so he just might have sired me. He saw a son in me.

I asked, "Were you working on a new play or still on the revision of *Clouds*? Aspasia told me you were redoing

428

it. I liked it the way it was and hope you haven't changed much."

"I am glad you liked it. I myself was displeased. Apparently, so was the public, if disdaining me for any prize is an indication. In any case, I finished the revision long ago. Rather I abandoned it. I never think anything is finished and could tinker with a play for years if I did not have to get them staged to make a living. It was time to abandon *Clouds* and move on to another. I have written a first and second draft of the new one. No telling if there will be a third. It seemed to flow easier than *Clouds* but not even the gods know what my public will say about it. The public is worse than tyrants, you know. You are lucky to be a goldsmith. There are buyers, but rarely critics."

I hardly dared ask, but he knew I was a fan, and so I said, "Is your new play a secret?"

"A secret? Well, I suppose it would be damaging were a play to become familiar before the competitions. Someone else can copy your plot after all. It may have contributed to my defeat last time around. The other comedies featured Socrates, and as mine was the last to be staged it looked as if I had copied everyone else rather than the other way around; the jackals. But if you give your word not to spread my plot line to your classmates and keep it between us, well I could tell you a little about it."

I had lost none of my enthusiasm for theater and said, "You have my word!"

"Well, in fact, I had ideas for two plays. The one I've dropped off for Aspasia to read is called *Wasps*. It lampoons Cleon again, or a least a character I've named Philocleon, Friend-of-Cleon."

429

"Cleon again! Oh I look forward to that. He and Alcibiades can be whipped any day as far I am concerned, at least verbally, on or off stage."

"Alcibiades too? Hmm. There is an idea for a play all right. Yes, there's a lot to lampoon there. But are you still smarting from that Mania business? I heard you suspect he played a role in that. Aphrodite is quite capable of putting him up to it, not to mention Mania herself. She was quite a little vixen. I thought the whole thing quite funny, but don't worry, I won't put it in a play. At least, not in the next one."

I groaned. "Oh please, not in any! Does all of Athens know about Mania and me? No one wants their follies paraded before the public!"

"Follies? I heard you were capable of five times some nights. I would call that an accomplishment and hardly a folly."

"Five times! Where on earth did you hear that? From Leagros?"

"Is it not true then?"

"Certainly not. Three was the most, at the very beginning when I was totally besotted. And then I could not manage it for a week afterwards."

"Before you're off with someone else again let me know. I have this wonderful doctor who supplies the most amazing aphrodisiacs, guaranteed to give you three elysions per night, night after night."

"From the sounds of it, it would only give Athens that much more to talk about."

"Now don't pride yourself, I don't think that everyone knows about your little affair. Let me see. My barber does, and my doctor, and oh yes the local sausage seller too."

"What!"

"I am teasing you, Amyntas, teasing you. I would never write about your affair, not when I have Cleon to trash; none better than he."

I wanted to say sarcastically, 'except Socrates', but Aristophanes was my friend and I did not want to offend him. I said, "I know you are teasing. Now what about telling me more about the new play?"

"Well, the plot revolves around a law suit brought against a dog for stealing some Sicilian cheese. There is a mock trial, and the dog is acquitted, but only after children dressed up like puppies parade around gaining everyone's sympathy. Oh yes, the chorus are all wasps, with quite a sting, if you catch my drift."

The mock trial, I vaguely recalled, probably referred to a lawsuit Cleon had brought against General Laches for accepting bribes from the Sicilians. I said, "I have heard something about Cleon's lawsuit. No one likes litigation more than he. And Wasps is a wonderful title! That is just what he deserves, to be stung by wasps."

"You and I see eye to eye about that oligarch Cleon. After his speech at the last Assembly I had half a mind to title it *Viper's Tangle*. I take it that you were not there, not after your little incident at the Pynx?"

"You heard of that too! That Leagros. Or Chaerephon!" I sighed and said, "I did not dare go; Athenades would have had me whipped. Socrates told me some. What was your impression?"

"The old fool wants to be general, all right. There is no doubt about it. He loves his glory that one as much as he

431

does his courtesans and wine. And they'll make him a general too. They cannot afford not to, unless Alcibiades beats him to the sword. But Cleon did mention something that may be of interest to you. Were you told about his Lemnian and Imbrian remarks? He made them at the very end of the day when a lot of people had already drifted off, and perhaps Socrates did not stay to the end."

"No, Socrates said nothing about this. Lemnos is not that far from our ancestral lands, you know. But those islands have always been loyal to Athens. There is no news there. Father has secret allies on them too."

"I know. That is why I mention it. Granted, you can't always trust what Cleon says. A good deal of his rhetoric is self-serving, or serves his war faction more than the truth. But for what it is worth, he said that his intelligence agents report that Brasidas is conspiring to take over these and the other islands around. It is part of a grand plan to check Athenian sea power, which would suit Macedonian interests I suppose. Of course, who knows if what Cleon says is true. At the time he was arguing for money to build more triremes, so he could have made it all up, for 'the glory and honor of Greater Hellas', as he likes to say."

A chill went through me, hearing that phrase, much as it had when Prince Argaeus talked about Greater Macedon. I said, "I also wonder if Cleon tells the truth. Father writes to me most every week, at least when he can get letters through, and he would have mentioned this. Cleon will do anything for war, won't he?" I hastily added, "And Perdiccas!"

"Yes, well, Perdiccas. But he's mad, isn't he? Cleon is not mad. He has unrequited rage, and that makes him more dangerous. Is your father as sure as the rumormongers here that Perdiccas will choose Sparta this time?"

"He writes that he already has. But can't we talk about something else. Talking about politics and war makes me a little sick these days. Let's talk about your plays instead. *Wasps* is such a splendid title, the best of all your titles, I think. Perhaps I can get Socrates to take me to the preview, with your permission of course."

"Of course you can come."

"But you said there was an idea for another?"

"Well, yes, but I really shouldn't talk about it. It is only a vague idea, about peace of course, like some mole rummaging around a seeded field, and it rather depends on history, as all my plays do, although no one ever seems to notice."

It sounded intriguing but our conversation went no further. It was ended by the eruption of young Pericles into the anti-chamber. He had heard that I had arrived and had raced to find me. We were going up-country to hunt. He was eager to start and wanted to show me his new gear.

"Amyntas! There you are. I was wondering when you would arrive. Come on. I have a new bow and a new sling, and I want to show them to you." He tugged at my hand.

I said to Aristophanes, "I am afraid I shall have to go, but I wish you success with Wasps."

"Thank you, Amyntas. And don't forget that offer I made. You know, my doctor's special brew and all."

I laughed and said, "I won't forget."

Pericles wanted to know what brew he meant, but I did not tell him. He was pulling me to one of the living quarters of the house, not the back where we could depart

433

for the stables.

"Where are you taking me?" I asked. "I thought you were in a rush?"

"I want to show you something first, but you have to be quiet."

We sneaked up to the open doorway of one of the studies giving off the central courtyard. Socrates was sitting cross-legged in the middle of the floor, his hands on his knees, palms upward.

Pericles whispered, "He has been sitting there like that since last evening. Do you think he is all right?"

"I'm sure he is. He sits and thinks like this sometimes. But we should not disturb him. Come, let's go hunting."

Before I could pull him away, Socrates opened his eyes and stared straight at us fixing us in our place. A full minute passed, as if he were traveling back in mind from a far place to intercept outer recognition.

He smiled and said, "You two are going hunting today, I hear?" He rose and brushed himself off.

I said, "Yes. That is the plan. Will you join us?"

"Riding? I am not much of a rider. And I have to get to my morning routine in the Agora."

He went there most every morning for questions and answers, and I asked, "Are you all right then?"

"Yes." He came over and took each of us by the hand. "Come. I'll walk you to the back entrance. The slaves will be waiting already. You are to spend the whole day away I hear, and they have packed a lunch for you. It is warm today, but with a light wind, a fine day for chasing rabbit, stag, or whatever you are after."

Pericles said, "We are after rabbit, up at the villa. They

434

are eating the garden and mother's manager said he would pay us for everyone we shoot. Mother gave me a new bow, just for today." He danced about and tugged at Socrates' hand. "What were you doing Socrates? Were you sleeping sitting up? Is this something you learn for the hoplites? I would like to learn that. Will you teach me to sleep sitting up? I am sure it will be very useful when I am a soldier."

"I was not sleeping."

"You weren't sleeping? Then what were you doing? Amyntas says you do this all the time. Is it a secret? If it is I can't see why. All you were doing was sitting. Does it have something to do with that voice of yours? Mother told me about your voice. She said it was a god. What does he look like? Is he handsome, like Polydamus? Polydamus is mother's favorite, you know. I like him too. His shoulders are so broad he can carry me around on just one and calls me his pet parrot."

I said, "Hush now, Pericles. You must not bother Socrates with so many questions."

"But I wasn't bothering him. I was just asking. Mother says that Socrates asks questions better than anyone. You do not mind my asking questions, do you, Socrates?"

"No I do not mind. But I do not have answers for all of them."

"Mother says your voice gives you directions. Is that what it was doing last night? Is it speaking to you right now? Please tell me what he said. I would very much like to know."

I thought I should reprimand Pericles again, but did not want to seem too paternal. My older brother had often guided me, but as often had left me to make my own

435

mistakes so long as they did not endanger me. Socrates could very well answer for himself, which he did.

Socrates looked directly at me, and he said quietly, "My voice did not say I should not go to battle."

His answer chilled me and I could not respond. Pericles babbled on but we had come to the rear door and he ran off to find the slaves and guards that would accompany us on our ride. I thought our retinue all a bit exaggerated. My Nubian slave was very tall, half again as tall as the rest; he would have scared off any thief with or without our breast-plated convoy. Aspasia came out to greet us, while Pericles ran off to fetch his new bow and arrows.

She kissed me on the cheeks. "Amyntas. Are you sure you can put up with that son of mine today? He gets over excited when he goes hunting you know. "

"He really does not bother me. Actually, I am looking forward to it myself, as a break in routine." I knew she read signs every morning, and asked, "Did the signs show that we would be successful today? If he doesn't get at least two rabbits he will be disappointed, no less if he came home with nothing."

"The signs were oddly neutral today. There was an owl on a branch. And in one of the charts I found the sign of the owl."

I said, "The owl is skillful at hunting its prey. Athena hunts."

Just then Pericles came running back followed fast at his heals by his favorite hunting hound, a fine red Laconian with the cunning of a fox. Pericles looked like a proper hunter, with a bow strung over his shoulder and an arrow-filled quiver to hang on the side of his horse; there was a new sling tucked in his belt. He gave his mother a quick peck, his eyes darting excitedly with the imaginings of the chase, his horse rushing break-neck at some terrified hare fleeing for its life across a field.

The stables were not more than five minutes from Aspasia's door. It was a district for the wealthy and the aristocracy and they liked to keep horses for their sons, and teach them to ride, nearly from birth it seemed. The street was deserted as we exited; our retinue made a clamor. The road faced the sun and was warmer than the courtyard. It had rained the night before and there was a fresh smell in the air, but the day would be warm. Pericles slipped from my hand and rushed ahead. I called him back and his guard rebuked him. We reached the corner of Aspasia's street. A long, busy road intersected it and we were just weaving our way across it, for the last steps to the stable entrance, when I heard my name called. I saw a youth I recognized waving to me from the crowded thoroughfare. His name was Callimachus. He had been at the Lyceum in my first month there, but had been expelled for theft, at least that is what the rumors said.

He waved his arm and shouted over the head of the guard, "Amyntas! Hello there! Where are you off to?"

The guards stopped him from approaching. He argued that we were old school chums, that he was just saying hello. I told the head of the guard that we had been at school together, and they let him through.

I said, "Well, well, Callimachus! I heard you had gone to sea. Are you still in Athens or only back for a visit? Was it you I caught a glimpse of the other day when I was out and about with Lady Aspasia?" Pericles tugged my hand

and I added, "Let me introduce you to Pericles son of Pericles. This is Callimachus, an old school chum. I am sorry, Callimachus I do not know your father's name."

Callimachus said, "Well, well, imagine that, Pericles son of Pericles, and a hunter no doubt. Why that looks like a fine bow, a fine bow indeed. I say, Amyntas, you are running with the rich and powerful these days. I thought it was you with that grand Lady the other day, and yes it was me. You must be going to the stables down there I suppose? May I walk with you a bit?"

Our party had threaded across the busy way into a short, quiet byway, filled with plane trees, as were many of the other streets in this elegant district.

I said, "So tell me, what have you been doing with yourself since leaving the gymnasium?"

"Leaving? All right leaving, if that's what you want to call it."

He was handsome in a rather rough way, perhaps a year older than I. His arms were thick, and strong. His beard had already begun; chest hair poked out over the fringe of his tunic. He was smiling and letting his hand graze mine, and I wondered if he were flirting.

I said, "I heard there was some incident or other. But you know I had just started there and never heard the whole story. We're on our way to the country for the day, but perhaps you would like to come by the shop some other time. There is a small circus in town right now and we could do that some afternoon. If you are free. Are you working? What brings you to this part of the city."

"A circus? Well that does sound fun." He glanced around; his hand brushed mine again as if to take it. He leaned closer, I though for some suggestion, and he whispered, "Actually, I do have work and it's why I am here. I have a message for you. You are to tell your father this."

At that very moment a very odd thing happened. Time slowed to a crawl. This is hard to explain, and when I told Socrates about it he thought it told us something about the nature of time; that it was might be relative to something else, and less fixed than we thought. Time slowed to a hundredth its rate. My Nubian was just behind me and I heard him gasp, or give a small cry, something that made me turn. I saw a look of alarm cross his face, then rage. I glanced at Callimachus. He was trying to slip away through the entourage and run. Each of his steps was immensely slow; I could see each gesture, his arm push a guard to the side, his knee raise, then both arms ascending above his head, his neck bent backwards and his back arched. The spear was entering at mid-point just beneath his shoulder blades; large drops of blood floated out infinitely slow. "Praise be Apollo," I heard myself say as if it were someone else's voice. I looked down and saw a red stain spreading slowly over my white tunic. And then there was blackness.

When I regained consciousness I was in Aspasia's house. She sat beside me, and Socrates was sitting on the floor, asleep, his arm extended over me. She leaned forward, held my head, and encouraged me to drink.

"Praise the gods," she said.

My mouth was parched; my throat and all my muscles ached. I managed to say, "Where am I?"

Aspasia said, "In my house."

I felt pain and looking down saw there was a large poultice dressing attached to my side.

She took my hand. "You must rest. You will be all right now that you have awakened. We were worried."

"How long?"

"This is the third day."

"The third day," I said as if in a dream. "Callimachus?"

Aspasia said, "Yes, Callimachus."

"I saw a spear. I am sure I saw a spear. Is he alive?"

"No."

"He did this."

"Yes. The wound was shallow but his knife was poisoned."

"Poisoned. Why?" I closed my eyes but hearing Socrates rouse, opened them again. He bent and kissed me, his face filled with joy, yet as if he might cry. I fell again into an unknowing, dreamless sleep.

I was a long time recovering and remained the whole time at Aspasia's. Socrates came every day to read to me, Pericles to play games, and entertain me by mimicking people we knew. He was very good at getting Chaerephon's voice. The laughter hurt, but helped me to heal more quickly, that and Aspasia's skills. I owe her my life.

The poison made me nauseous, and took away all appetite. It gave me sweats that further weakened me. I could hardly move from bed and when I did I had to return quickly to rest. Some two weeks later, waking in the middle of the afternoon from troubled sleep, I found father sitting next to me.

"Oh, father. My father!" I began to cry.

"You must not be upset, my son. Everything will be all right."

"But father, I must tell you. There are things I must tell you."

"There will be time."

He put his arms around me and we wept together. But I was not only crying out of joy at seeing him, but also because his being there meant the end of my being in Athens.

VI: Epilogue: The Poison Cup.

1. 399 B.C. Hestia.

We were still three days march from Paraitonion. I roused the encampment at dawn so that there would be no more delay than necessary in reaching the coast. Our Baktrian camels were stubborn animals that would not be urged faster, their tempo fitted to the day's great heat by habit. I longed for the hearth of Hestia; for the comfort of routine my wife and daughter provided, and for the cool sea breezes prevailing in spring. But I feared bad news from Athens, as my dream of Socrates foretold. Approaching from the arid south, what a welcome sight the green tips of palms blown by sea winds, the first sight of my villa glistening on its high knoll. There was still much work to be done, but I returned with more plans than I had set out with, inspired by Philiscus and Alexis, now keen on the new medicine. Fresh spring flowers lined the pilgrim route that last morning. I looked for darker signs, vultures after carrion, or patches of parsley sown by Thanatos, but there was only deep peace.

When at last I entered our house, eager to bathe away the desert dust, my wife greeted me soberly. She often told me important or difficult things first, instead of Djadao, my overseer: the birth of a niece, the marriage of her youngest brother, or the death of my friend Chaerephon. I knew from her face that this news would be hard. I had brought her expensive creams and oils from Ammon, not as fine as Aspasia's but fine. They must wait.

Eshe said, "A messenger has arrived from Athens."

"From your face, I see that is not good news. Is it

Socrates? There was a dream."

She looked surprised, nodded and said, "I do not know how to soften the blow for you. I am sorry."

"It is all right. My dreams told of dark things. What has happened?"

"He was arrested on charges so serious as to warrant death. You will have to make all haste to Athens."

I was stunned and sank into a chair. Arrested? Socrates? And death? Was this the same Socrates I knew and loved? I said, "I heard rumors in Ammon of a plot against him, but there is always talk of plots there and I did not take them seriously."

"You dreamt?"

"The gods showed me Socrates in a cage with his hands shackled, but I thought it must be a sign of something else, of illness perhaps. I never knew him to commit a minor infraction. A serious crime is impossible for someone so virtuous and wise."

She was silent, her head bowed. "There is more." She took my hand. "I am sorry to be the one to tell you. The trial was the day before the messenger left. He waited for the results before coming here. It is hard to say these things."

"I would rather hear them from you than Djadao." Had he been ostracized? For an Athenian, this was worse than death.

Eshe said, "The sentence was death by hemlock. I am sorry, Amyntas. I know how you love your friend. There are messages from Crito and Chaerephon's brother giving the details." I began to tremble like a frightened child. She put her arms around me and said, "You have just returned

443

but you should leave for Athens as soon as possible. The news is nearly a week old. Djadao has information about ships."

I cried out, "But Athenian law is clear! Upon sentencing, the sentence is carried out. There is no appeal in Athenian law. You Egyptians you can at least throw yourself on the mercy of the Pharaoh. What use is there? He is already dead!"

"The messages say that he is not dead because of some law or other that I do not understand. There is a thirty days respite. Djadao knows all about it."

"Thirty days? I do not understand. I must go to Djadao at once. No, I must collect my thoughts first. Where is our dear Azeneth? I have not seen her yet and would bring my presents to her, perhaps take her for a walk down to the sea. I must calm myself down if I am to think clearly. I'll see Djadao in my study afterwards."

I went to the open windows. From our knoll the colors of the sea were dazzling. It was calm that day as if the gods were drawing me across it. I did not hear our daughter playing and said, "Is Azeneth well?"

"She is with her nurse. I told her you might be arriving this morning and she is very excited."

"I have brought her toys from Ammon, and you gifts as well. The new physician is also with us. I told you about Philiscus in my last message. Did you receive it?"

"It was splendid news. I look forward to meeting him. I had the guest wing prepared and arranged he should join you for dinner. I asked some of the town midwives about the new methods. They seem threatened, which can only be a good thing."

"I am eager for him to examine Azeneth. I'll go find her now. She is well enough today for a walk?"

"Yes, I think she would like that. And Alexis? I would not forget to ask about him. He fared well on the desert crossing?"

"Yes. He is quite taken with the new medicine and has been asking poor Philiscus a thousand questions. I am encouraging him. He would make an excellent physician, don't you think?"

"But of course he would. Perhaps he should also join you for dinner?"

"If he would not be taken from his wife and baby tonight, after being away."

Shock and rage were confusing my grief. I wanted to be by the sea, vast beyond feelings, into which feelings could sink into calm. My daughter came running to greet me as soon as she saw me and threw herself into my arms, clinging fast to my neck. She held my hand, as we took our private path down to the water's edge, and told me in a long babble all she had done since I had left for Ammon some weeks before: her pet lizard had died but she had found another, she had not had any faints; a wizard had come to the town who could make things disappear in smoke. Eshe had hired him to come to the house to perform for the children. If it had not been for Azeneth I might not have survived the day, but her small hand in mine, her innocent enthusiasm over my return, restored me through affection.

She ran down to the sea to look for shells. I awarded her whenever she found a conch whole. She turned and waved at me and I saw in her face her mother's intelligence and kindness. Eshe. Eshe had said hemlock. How could a sentence of death be passed against the wisest man alive? It could not be. But Eshe had said that Socrates lived. How could that he? There must be some mistake, some error on the messenger's part, or on the part of that great city. I found a stick and traced Greek words in the sand, pondering my life in Athens. But what could justify hemlock? I could see nothing. I called Azeneth to me.

"But father, I have not found any shells yet."

"We can come again tomorrow, and I shall award you double for what you find. Besides, you have not seen all the gifts I brought you! Do you not want the rest?"

She came over meekly. "Of course I do, but I want to be with you. Can we look at them together?"

"Yes, we can do that. But then father has work to do. I promise I shall come to your playroom as soon as I have seen Djadao."

She was a little frightened of Djadao, because of his hooked nose and the scar on his cheek. She and her small friends called him 'hawk-man', but he was the soul of kindness.

We turned to walk back, the villa gleaming white against the cloudless azure sky. I was very angry but resolved. If Socrates were still alive, then it was imperative that I leave for Athens as soon as possible. The merchant fleet stayed in sheltered harbors until the storm season was over, but the still sea that day was full of sail. Until summer they might still hug the coast for safety against a sudden gale. Finding a captain to risk open water before the calm would be possible for a price. How I

446

wished at that moment that I were Zeus and could change into an eagle not for abduction but for rescue. By bird flight the time to Athens was half a day and timing could be of the essence. I was no eagle.

Azeneth was whining and I took her in my arms to carry her across the inclines. I had brought her a straw toy camel nearly as large as she, a string of colorful beads, and a new dress of Egyptian cotton. I said, "You will like the other gifts, I think. And I have also brought someone I want you to meet. His name is Philiscus of Kos. He is a very clever man who thinks he can help you with your fevers and fits."

"More gifts? What are they, father? You must not tease me. But do I have to see another healer? You know how they hurt me." She would have cried had I not said, "He is quite different from the others and will not bleed or hurt you. I promise this."

She had experienced too many cures to be entirely convinced, but thinking of her welfare, and giving her comfort, further helped me that black day.

An irony awaited me, as in the dramas of Euripides I so admired. When I returned to the villa with Azeneth I went to my study and found Djadao waiting. His name meant "the fat one" but he was thin and clever. He was both our overseer and my personal secretary, a shrewd man sent to us from Memphis by Eshe's family, and respected for his competence and unflinching loyalty. When I saw the scrolls laid out I felt dread again.

I said, "So Djadao, the word is not good from Athens. Azeneth has already told me some. But a respite for Socrates?"

447

"The sentencing was on the eve of the feast of Apollo, and the yearly offering at Delos, or he would have been executed."

The Apollonian feast of Delos! Apollo was the irony. Every year Athens decorated and sent a ship to Delos to celebrate the defeat of the Persians. No executions could take place within the thirty days it took for the ship to go and return, the thirty days of the festival. Socrates had been tried and condemned on that eve, and so he was still alive. Still alive!

I said, "Thirty days then, praise the fair God! When was the sentencing? Do you know the exact date?"

"It was precisely ten days ago today."

Twenty days left. There was no time to lose. I went to the open window of my study as if to check the prospects of the sea again. Would I be aided or prevented?

Djadao was explaining, "I heard of a Corinthian trireme outfitting in the sheds at Crete. She is transporting pottery but I think can be convinced to transport you in all haste. I sent word to the captain of our emergency, and a generous down payment, were he to accept our commission. There have been reports of pirates in those waters, too great a risk for a merchant ship or penteconter. But I hear he is competent and brave, or reckless enough to risk the wrath of Poseidon for a special mission. His ship is fast, the Arete. I have ordered special offerings to all the sea gods. With Godspeed you could be in Athens within the week."

I said, "It will not leave much time in Athens, but time enough to rescue him. And if the Arete does not arrive?"

"I am looking into other options. There are a handful of merchant round ships and fishing boats down in the

448

harbor, but they are not ideal. There was a bad storm here not a week ago, and it would be hard to convince them to risk Piraeus. I am still asking around, but the Arete has a full rowing complement of 170 and the captain is in heavy debt and we, well, agreed to pay it off if he took you with all haste."

"And sponge boats? Are any of Alexis' relatives here?"

"There were none as of yesterday. It is not their season. But I shall check again. I did find a small fishing boat willing to take letters to Oloros; and to Crito telling him you may be coming. The boat set off the day after I received your instructions from the desert, again for an extravagant sum. The sea has been calm since his departure, so I think he must have gotten through. There is another standing by to take more messages. Both boats have had not much of a catch so far this season and are desperate for money. As you can see I took several liberties with your purse, but under the circumstances . . . "

"Say no more. You acted correctly. I am especially eager to see Oloros. He will know more about what is really happening from his riff-raff connections in the Piraeus underworld than Crito or Chaerephon's brother could know."

"If word reaches Oloros he should have bearers waiting when you dock. I already asked him to look out for a house for you to rent for as long as you need to stay. And shall we tell him to find a buyer for the dates? Did you bring them back with you?"

"Yes, the dates. We shall need the profit for bribes in Athens not just for the jailers and prison guards, but also to hire mercenaries to break him free if all else fails. Have them stored securely until we embark. They are worth more than gold and Socrates' life may depend on them."

"I shall post a twenty four hour watch, double guard in three shifts."

"There is so much to do. Please ask Alexis to come when he can break away from his wife and son. Go to him yourself Djadao and if he does not know about Socrates, well, it is better he hears it from you before he comes here. He'll want to go to Athens, and we need to make plans for our departure. And send word to Philiscus that the three of us will dine here together tonight."

"A plan is forming Master? I can see it in your eyes. I have put all things aside for you today."

"You are worth your weight in, well dates, Djadao, dates."

"A fortune you can eat!" he said, joking about his fondness for delicacies. "I would be sorely tempted, and grow fat rather than rich. Do you require anything else?"

I replied, "Refreshments. I am still dehydrated from the desert. I see there is enough writing material. And Alexis. There is a great deal to do before we embark. There is a Macedonian saying. In matters of the gods it is good to have a sense of urgency. A plan? Yes, a plan is forming. Now which of the scrolls are messages and which have to do with the charges?"

"I have laid them out in order. These three are from Oloros, Crito, and Chaerephon's brother; and these are the charges and a list of the accusers. There is not much detail, but as you say, Oloros will know more."

"And charge a steeper price than usual, you can be sure.

450

He knows how fond I am of Socrates. And will see it as a rare opportunity for profiteering."

As he was leaving I said, "And oh yes, there is something else. When you have returned from seeing Alexis', please take Azeneth and her nurse to Philiscus. Invite him to dinner. And tell Azeneth that I shall give her a large reward for being brave, although she will see that Philiscus' method are quite different from the others."

"So I have heard. May Asclepius bless her!"

When he left the room I did not settle down immediately to read the charges, but paced in confusion. It seemed to me that the gods were asking something of me, clear from my dreams and the timing of the sentencing. I prayed first for understanding, and with a heavy heart unfurled the first scroll.

I, Meletus, son of Meletus of Pitthos, most solemnly make this affidavit and swear the following charges against Socrates, the son of Sophroniscus of Alopece. That Socrates is guilty of refusing to recognize the state gods; that he is guilty of introducing new gods, and that he is further guilty of corrupting youth. The penalty we demand for any and all these charges is death.

Who was this Meletus that he had the arrogance to charge someone like Socrates with such ignoble crimes? The charges were three, but in fact they were really one, all religious.

I was sitting at my desk reading and writing when

Alexis rushed in to find me. He said, "I heard, and came as quickly as I could."

I gave him the charges to read and asked, "Do you see anything odd in them?"

"What do you mean?"

"The three charges are really one. It was very clever of the accusers to make them into three, but in fact they are all the same; Socrates' voice, are they not? Denying the state gods, introducing new gods, and so corrupting the young, they are all this voice of his, this god with no name that no one else can worship or hear."

"Yes, I see that. But what does it mean?"

"It might mean, that only the God who is his voice can save him by revealing who he is."

"But he has not so far."

"No, he has not. But then there is the feast of Apollo, and the ship to Delos. It is very strange that the sentencing and feast should coincide."

"How so?"

"Perhaps it means that the God of his voice intends to reveal Himself in some dramatic way, so as to make the people fearful of executing Socrates."

"You think then that his voice is Apollo?"

"I asked Socrates this once long ago and he said he did not know because it had never told him so."

"Then what are you saying?"

"Only that perhaps, we might be about to find out, and, of course, it would change everything."

"And if not?"

"Then we must have a backup plan, to entice Socrates here. Rescue or kidnap him by force if need be."

I could see the gleam of adventure in Alexis' youthful eyes. He exclaimed, "My sword and shield are yours. When do we leave?"

"As soon as the gods will it. I feel it in my bones, Alexis. The gods want us in Athens."

2. Piraeus.

And so we set sail that fateful spring, Alexis and I, with heavy hearts gazing out over the endless sea from the prow of our trireme, dreading what we might find in Athens upon our return. The sea was calm but we used full oar to dash northwards for Crete, rather than proceeding more cautiously westward to Kurene, hugging the coast before venturing across open waters. We sighted mythical Ogypia on the second day, a propitious marker for a journey in the hands of the sea gods. The oars bit deeply, the island of Antikythera soon promised Piraeus.

If we had time before Socrates execution, there was no time to spare. The Feast of Delos was two thirds over before we could embark, our trireme unadorned, not as the stern of the consecrated ship sent to Delos to commemorate Theseus' voyage to Crete when he saved the fourteen youths. Theseus made a vow to Apollo that, were they saved, there would be an annual pilgrimage. Athenians were if nothing fearful of their gods; there was never any doubt about Socrates' life during that month. The sacred ship was crowned on the day of Socrates' trial, after which he was confined in prison, giving time for his friends to visit and conceive plans for his rescue and escape from Hellas. This month was a sacred time; Socrates life was in the hands of his inner god.

I had hit upon a simple plan to entice Socrates away form Athens, but one I felt would succeed, and had laid it out for Alexis and Philiscus the night of our arrival from Ammon. The fortune I had built from gold was considerable, if not quite the equivalent of what Nicias had amassed from silver, or Cleon from tanning, more than sufficient for our plan. We would start our own Lyceum in Paraitonion, which Socrates would head. Alongside it we would build for Philiscus a clinic and school to train physicians in the new methods, with the ambition of being the largest and best outside Kos. There would be a temple to Asclepius, and the finest library for the new medical treatises, philosophy, and history. The best and brightest from everywhere would come to study. Our palaistra would be second to none. There was no reason why our complex could not outstrip the reputation of the Lyceum or Taureas, the fulfillment of my wealth, but more importantly the fulfillment of Socrates' talent as a teacher, if not his life.

Alexis and Philiscus were enthusiastic about my plan, but Alexis had raised doubts. He said, "It will not be easy to convince Socrates. He has always been a good citizen and will obey the sentence. You also know how he hates to put one foot outside the city, no less abandon Hellas for Africa."

"But his life has never been on the line as it is now."

"Yes, but I remember you telling me how he could not be cajoled into going on a picnic with you to the countryside. Both of you were stung then. There was the promise of tender friendship in open air. How do you expect to convince him now, when he is old and more set

454

in his ways, not less."

"He was never under a sentence of death."

Philiscus interrupted, "I agree with you Amyntas. A school where he will be appreciated and of great value to all around him, should make a forceful argument for Socrates, should it not? I do not know him but he will surely be attracted by the idea of doing good for the many."

I said, "And he need not leave his wife and children either. We can bring them all here. And Aeschines, Crito, Plato, and anyone else he wants."

Alexis did not like Socrates' wife, and in fact hardly anyone did. He said, "I would not exactly look forward to having Xanthippe as my neighbor, but if it saves Socrates, well I suppose we should all be ready to make some sacrifices."

I did not share the general distaste for her and said, "We shall see her in Athens too and tell her of our plan. No matter what calumny is spoken against her I am convinced that she loves Socrates and will help us convince him."

Alexis said, "If she thinks she will have a grand home, and Socrates a sizeable income, she will be on our side. She complains constantly about never having enough for herself and her sons. It is an endless bone of contention in their marriage, you know that Amyntas."

Philiscus was very taken with the idea of a library. He had brought from Kos several rare volumes by his teacher, Hippocrates, and these could become the cornerstone of the collection. Paraitonion, unlike Athens, did not have a civic archive and this I had already started, as well as collecting the burgeoning field of histories. But medicine

455

would be the largest part of the collection. A home would be built for Socrates among books and scholars, Asclepian priests, and doctors of the new order. We would hire scribes to take down his wisdom so that it might be taught and disseminated. That was our master plan.

During the voyage Alexis and I also began to work out the means of his escape. In Piraeus anyone could be hired for anything, as was true of almost any port city. We would hire a band of mercenaries to remove him forcibly from prison, if bribes were to fail. Our contact, Oloros, would hopefully be waiting for us at the dock and would make all the arrangements. We stood often at the prow to discuss our plans, as if we might pull the ship forward by impatience. Alexis missed the sea and diving, and I felt guilty sometimes for taking him away from it. He did not complain, and liked his life in Africa, but then word would come from home, or one of his brothers would visit, and melancholy would overtake him.

Such a mood had come on him now, and I asked, "Are you thinking of the sea again? They say that those who dive into its depths are possessed by it forever."

He turned and smiled, "No, this time I am thinking of Athens. We have not been back since the walls fell. I am afraid of what we shall find."

"At the hands of that Spartan, General Lysander! I am glad I was not there to see them fall. There has been so much madness in Athens in recent years. There was the edict against resident aliens. Aspasia had to flee back to Miletus. Imagine, the mistress of Pericles having to flee the city she loved most."

Alexis said, "Perhaps it was willed by the gods? She

456

was tried for impiety herself back in the time of Pericles, was she not? And Socrates was charged with impiety, so her old charges might have corroborated his guilt by association."

I said, "She was charged by the comic poet Hermippus who wished to promote himself and his bad poetry in the public eye. He also charged her with procuring freeborn women for Pericles' bed. She was acquitted of both charges. But Socrates has not been acquitted. It shows how things have changed, no doubt because of that endless war." I added, "You know, I heard that she gave her house to her old lover, Polydamus. He was freeborn and could move into her villa with his wife and children. If there is time, we should visit him."

Alexis was fond of Aspasia. "Athens will seem empty and forlorn without Aspasia to visit."

"Or the courtesans who were so crazed about you?"

"I am not seventeen any longer."

"Past your prime and hardly past twenty? I think not. You are able to satisfy a wife and a mistress in Paraitonion. And not a few in Ammon you left with smiles."

He said, "The secret is those precious white dates of yours. Two or three make you ready."

"Broadcast that about in Athens! It will raise their value still higher if they are thought to be aphrodisiacs. Have they been stored under guard?"

"Yes, of course."

We made light, but each hour we drew closer I dreaded more and more the first sighting of Piraeus, beautiful as it was. Glints of the marble Temple of Artemis on the fortified hill of Munychia would be our fateful beacon. She was the sister of Apollo; the Guide of our voyage. On the last two or three days we made slow speed against head winds despite full oar.

***

Aboard ship we had discussed the other messages that had come from Athens before we sailed. We knew the names of the conspirators, but not many details about each of them.

Meletus was their spokesperson; he had delivered the charges to the High Judge who heard religious cases, confirming my theory that they were all religious. An upstart poet of very low talent, Meletus seemed to have been delegated because of his golden voice. Our report said, "It is generally agreed that Meletus is too stupid to have concocted the plot himself."

The second accuser was the orator Lycon, "a populist famous for stirring up sentiment in the Agora by making outlandish proposals that have an air of reason. He was very vocal a year or two ago over the banning of resident aliens, and it is partly due to his lobbying the Assembly that the ban was enacted. He has been grumbling about Socrates' voice, and weeks ago declaimed it in the Assembly. His shock of wild white hair gives him instant recognition." I thought how he must resemble Cleon, in more ways than one.

"General Anytas is, perhaps, the most interesting. Our sources say he is the real instigator of the indictment against Socrates. He had vehemently opposed the Thirty

458

Tyrants, and especially scorned the role that Critias played in overthrowing the democracy. For this he blames Socrates, as Critias' teacher, some say lover. In the Assembly we heard him shout, 'What kind of wisdom spawns tyranny?' By seeming to question the words of the Delphic Oracle many thought he had gone too far. There are also rumors that Socrates had an affair with Anytas' son, and that the son owes the brothels large debts. We think that this is the real source of the charges. Anytas sees Socrates as the corrupting influence on his son and will not own up to his own responsibility for not controlling him. This is Crito's view. Anytas is, perhaps, the most formidable of the three, but others lurk behind them and they seem to act for many."

Surely madness was afoot again in Athens, as it often was. The city suffered plagues of false leaders as periodically as it did other pestilences. Thirty years since the plague, I reflected, and more than twenty since I had lived there as a boy, before my fortune was made in Egypt and Scythia, before I took ill, before I met my wife on Crete, saw my daughter born, met Alexis, standing close in comfort now, sensing my unease, my apprehension of arrival.

He said, "The headwind has become a calm. We will have to use the oars again, and should dock in Piraeus at dawn."

I looked out over the placid sea. "The signs from the gods have been mixed."

"Yes, they urge us to hasten, and yet delay us."

"It reflects my own state. I want to be there, but dread arriving."

Alexis said, "Something heavy lingers over us. In part Socrates, but not only."

I trusted his instincts and asked, "Do you sense danger?"

"Athens sounds crazed again. We must be careful."

I did not like this talk and to lighten matters said, "It is certainly different this visit. When we were in sight of land the last time you were trembling in anticipation of the brothels. You disappeared for days. What was her name again? The one who commanded all your time?"

He said, "I can't remember now, but it certainly was not Mania."

"Oh heavens. Mania! I wonder what became of her? She was clever and ambitious, and I suspect that she has fared pretty well. But don't you want a little of the same this time? With your natural Persian curls you would be swarmed. "

His black beard and hair curled naturally, in a style the Persians affected. He said, "Did not one of your messages say something about Anytas' son frequenting brothels? If we found out which, it would give us a way of meeting him and getting to the truth."

"A good thought. Oloros will know."

"Yes, Oloros."

A fish broke surface, but not a dolphin. Alexis said, "I did not tell you of the dream I had last night. I stopped by a door, and peering through the keyhole saw three dolphins leaping, like those painted on Aspasia's walls."

"Three? I shall have to think about it." We had our soothsayers with us and I would ask him later. I said again, "Let us call it a good sign."

The captain came on deck, perhaps to summon more speed from the oarsmen in a becalmed sea, but the wind had changed abruptly and we were being blown forward again. He would make sail.

3. Oloros the Informant.

We waited out at sea that night, the Captain sending word ahead by fishing skiff; our trireme docked in Piraeus at dawn under a red sky, not a good omen. As we slipped closer to shore, the morning cries of the city drifted out to us: dogs barking; the news hawkers; the bleating of sheep held for slaughter. The square main sail and the smaller foremast sails were furled. Two rows of oars were raised; only a few of the third were needed to guide us into dock. My heart quickened to see Attica again. Fortified with our plan, my dread had given way to determination. We would throw ourselves into the rescue.

Returning to Athens had always meant more of a homecoming than my few visits to Macedon. Upon the death of the mad Perdiccas some twelve or so years before, the ruthless Archelaus had acceded to the throne. He was Perdiccas' son through a slave woman. The new king had immediately set out to consolidate his power by assassinating his chief rivals, including his brothers, uncles, and my cousin Prince Argaeus about whom I have spoken earlier. Archelaus was a lover of all things Hellenic. Intending to build a new Athens in the manner of Pericles, he had moved the capital from Aigai to Pella and undertaken an ambitious building plan. He was a supporter of the arts, to encourage Macedonian pride and ambitions.

There is reason to mention this here. In this same year,

461

not weeks after the death of Socrates, while on the hunt Archelaus was assassinated by his young lover Craterus. There followed a period of great confusion in Macedon until my cousin's son, Amyntas III, took power. He finally brought stability to the country. In the year I write he reigns still and I have returned many times to visit him and am close to his son Philip II. My father died of a broken heart to see Macedon ruled by Archelaus. If he had lived long enough he might have seen that the sweep of history cannot be predicted by events of the moment. Passing final judgment on Macedon because of Perdiccas or his successor would have missed the rise of Amyntas III. Macedon grows daily in influence now. Was Perdiccas so wrong in his ambitions, or was Prince Argaeus so wrong about his scheme for a Greater Macedon that he laid out all those years ago?

As we crept into shore we had a view of the harbor, usually crowded with the bulk of the Athenian trireme fleet, most now still in their sheds upshore. Themistocles had fortified the rocky island on which the city was built. Pericles had finished it. But fallen walls and rubble were clearly visible from the water. Piraeus was to some a shining light, its glistening temple dominating the town. To me it was a place of blacks and grays haunted by ambiguous souls with shadow identities, especially in the districts adjoining the docks and shipbuilding yards, the center of the Athenian underworld among whom I had contacts. Long ago I had made it clear to a group of reliable informants that I would pay handsomely so long as the information proved true; correct information was essential were you to trade in gold. Lies and liars were weeded out over time, perhaps some would say at needless expense, but by this visit I knew I could obtain reliable information about Socrates' plight and secure help with his escape. We would be greedily awaited. The smell of money energizes.

We were close enough to the dock now to identify the usual assortment of prostitutes, vendors, workers ready to do the unloading, and the destitute children begging. Alexis interrupted my brooding to reassure me that the crates with the precious dates were safe and sound. Our own baggage and slaves were already on the dock.

He asked, "Will Oloros' men greet us? I see no one yet."

"There, the tall man at the back there, that is his head slave. Those others must be his men. But I do not see Aeschines or Crito's slaves. It does not bode well."

"A rough looking crew. One has only one eye."

"We may need them if we meet resistance securing Socrates' release. If Oloros followed the instructions Djadao sent him he will have rented a house for us on one of the hillsides. He may want us to see him first. He will be eager to tell us how much he knows about the case, and I am eager to hear."

"Sell us you mean. It is a strange return, stranger than all the others."

"Yes. The sky portends storm, but we must not let Oloros know of our distress. He will take advantage of it. And we shall consult our diviners first thing we are settled."

Oloros' man pushed through the dockside crowd to greet us.

Alexis squeezed my arm and said, "I am with you."
In spite of our apprehensions I could sense his resolve, and was grateful that he was at my side.

Of all my paid informants Oloros had proven to be the best. He claimed to be an Athenian citizen, and his name could be accepted as such in the city, but I knew he was Thracian. Daryush had provided the introduction several years before. He had been Dareios' spy in Thrace, and thereafter Daryush's liaison in Athens. If Daryush had cultivated the art of seducing other men's wives and fleeing the consequences, Oloros was more likely to dispose of the husband and on occasion the wife. He owned a tannery in the old quarter of Piraeus, but information was his trade and craft. He might have amassed a fortune from tanning as had Cleon, but he had other ambitions. If he had done his work, he would have consolidated the documents and statements necessary for us to form a clear picture of Socrates' situation.

The slave said, "Your Excellency! You were much delayed reaching Piraeus. We heard at the last minute that you would be docking this morning."

"Yes, first a storm blew us off course, and then we met a headwind. "

"Ah! The connivances of the gods."

"Indeed."

"Do you wish to go directly to your villa to settle and refresh yourselves, or see my Master first?"

"He found us a house on the hillside?"

"Yes, my Lord, a fine new house with cool breezes. The spring has been warm here. Master is sure you will be pleased. It is yours for as long as you wish to stay."

The ride to Athens was half an hour or less at a trot, and there was no need to rent a house there. We could use Piraeus as our base and stay better informed. I said, "We were refreshed enough in the long voyage, don't you think Alexis? Take us first to Oloros, and then bring our cases and slaves to the house for us."

"Yes, your Excellency. Master Oloros has put me at your disposal for your stay. If there is anything you want, you need only ask me."

Oloros greeted us warmly. He had an innocent air belying his slyness. He was small, with a fringe of white hair circumscribing baldness red with skin lesions. His eyes were narrow and black; he squinted, narrowing them further, when taking your measure or deciding whether trickery or honesty were the best course. His full mouth suggested a sensual temperament and his ears protruded as if the gods had granted him a physical tool for trading in information. He spoke flawless Attic, but, when nervous, threatened, or tired, Thracian sounds would infiltrate. I had known him some ten years, but always found him challenging. His true loyalty was what he called "the business", of course not tanning but his shadow trade, or trades. Perhaps he was loyal to his son, who was as sly as he, and to his current mistress. His hands were nervous, not expressive as were most, but restless, aggressively tapping, his nails bitten. His hands alone might have made me mistrust him. I had begun to use him as one of my principal Athenian informants while I still lived in Crete, and he had thus far not let me down. It was in his best interest to have regular wealthy customers who might

465

provide basic income for years on end. So long as I made regular demands, and payments, he had remained reliable and loyal. Ares protect me, were I to use someone else!

We were at the door of his shop. I did not like going in there because of the foul smells from the compounds used in the tanning process. Philiscus the Physician had already started me on a purification regimen, to rid me of the effects of gold smelting. Since then I had less tolerance for foreign substances such as those used to cure the leather worked into sandals, sword straps, cuirasses, and the hundred other objects necessary for war or personal adornment. Tanning is a large part of the industry of war, more so than gold, which is closer to ritual and religion. Profiteering in war, or the industry of war, was a natural undertaking for Oloros.

As I walked through the beaded fly curtain my eyes smarted and I felt at a disadvantage. You needed your wits about you when dealing with Oloros; tearing eyes and pulsing headache did not make me self-confident. I knew as soon as I saw him that the news was not good. Although he greeted us warmly enough he was on edge. Instead of lingering at the front to share a welcome drink, he took us immediately to the back of the house to a room with thick walls where we could talk unobserved and unheard. He summoned a slave to fetch "that wooden box next to my bed". I had a special gift for him, six of the rare white dates each carefully preserved and wrapped, "worth thrice their weight in gold" as he exclaimed, popping one immediately in his mouth. His eyes gleamed at the news that there were several boxes to sell.

He said, "We shall make a handsome profit. Djadao's

previous messages said you might be bringing them, but I had no idea how fine they would be. You will be in sore need of extra funds."

I said, "Is there bad news?"

He gave typical, guarded response. "What was the last you heard?"

"That Socrates was in jail, condemned to death, an outline but not the details. Is he well? Has something happened?"

"I saw Aeschines a few days ago thinking you would dock at any moment. Socrates is well. He receives many visitors and Aeschines said he was putting Aesop's fables to verse. His jailers like him and he is well attended. Except perhaps by Xanthippe. She is in hysterics. But there are many difficulties. You will need mercenaries? I take it for an escape plan?"

"Yes. And the difficulties?"

"The jail has put on extra guards, perhaps because Socrates' friends and supporters are angry. There is also unrest and tension in the city and extra police patrolling the streets. If you are thinking of forcibly rescuing him it is going to take twice as many men as we thought. I delicately put the plan to Aeschines, 'What if, just what if, someone wanted to break Socrates free?' I asked. He called it a 'foolhardy idea hardly worth considering'."

"Foolhardy? Hardly worth considering? Those were his words?"

"Yes. He had a good reason. He had already proposed to Socrates that he go into exile. He and Crito had made arrangements for him to flee to Thessaly. But Socrates flatly refused."

"I am not surprised by that. In fact, we expected it, did we not, Alexis?" Alexis nodded. "Did Aeschines tell you Socrates' reason for not wanting to go? My guess is that Aeschines was not offering to provide Socrates with any plan or opportunity at the other end, anything that would give meaning to his life and justify the flight. Aeschines has been impractical about money his whole life. Everyone knows that."

Oloros said, "I did ask him with what means he tried to entice Socrates."

"And what did he say?"

"Only that the matter was simple. That Socrates' voice told him not to flee."

"And face hemlock? This is hard to believe."

"This is what Aeschines said. And others tell me the same."

I was upset by this but would not show it to Oloros. I said, "Socrates has always obeyed his voice, but we must know the nature of the question Socrates put to his inner god before we judge the answer. Other questions might elicit other answers."

Oloros said, "In any case there is still time to rescue him. I have mercenaries standing by if you need them. A word from me and thirty will be at my door."

We did not know what rescue plan Socrates' friends might have concocted, or the nature of Aeschines' question to Socrates about leaving, or precisely the circumstances of the answer. Just as Socrates had felt free to explore the Delphic Oracle's statement of his wisdom, I felt it imperative to question this. His daimon might have only meant that Socrates should not leave for Aeschines' reasons, but his god might approve my plan, and have anticipated it. One thing seemed impossible, that his god would want him to die when his life could find fulfillment through meaningful work. What divine purpose could his death possibly serve, when his teaching could inspire so many? Our plan had every chance of working.

I said, "We must go to Athens at once to see for ourselves. Can you arrange for us to see Socrates this afternoon?"

Oloros said, "When I heard yesterday that you would dock today I applied for permission for you and Alexis, but the first visit that you could be granted is early tomorrow morning."

"And how many days before the … the cup."

"Six days would make the month."

"Six. Then there is no time to lose, is there? We must see Aeschines as soon as possible. Have you sent word to him of our arrival this morning?"

"Oh yes, and I heard back already. He has left the whole day open for you, and knows that you want to free Socrates. There are fast horses at the house I have rented for you. You should go to the house first. There are some men there you should take with you to the city. It is not entirely safe. I have been careful to conceal your visit, but if Socrates' enemies know of your arrival and purpose, well there is no telling what may occur. The mood is dark in Athens. There are also some documents that I have gathered for you: profiles of the accusers, the list of jailers. You should familiarize yourself with these before going into the city.

"It is always wise to arrive in Athens informed. I have a

469

quick question. There were rumors that General Lycon's son was Socrates' lover. I thought, if we could discretely talk with the boy, without his knowing who we are, we might gain some insights into the case that could prove useful to the rescue."

"I have heard the same. The boy gambles of the cockfights and has run up quite a debt, and at the bar attached to the ring. It should not be a problem to meet him there. He has an eye for the dark types, such as you, Alexis. I know someone who could make sure he was there tonight without suspecting it is a setup. With a little wine and certain glances I think you might learn what you want."

Alexis laughed. "I am not sure how good I am at the flirting-for-information game, but I am willing to give it a go."

I said, "We had better get to the house. There is much work to be done. But we should work out a signal, in case we need to reach you immediately, Oloros, or vice versa, of course."

"I shall assign a slave to you at all times just for emergency messages. He is a fast runner and one of my most trusted. He also has been trained in memory, so you need put nothing in writing. Tell him clearly what you need to relay to me and he shall arrive at my door before you can take two breaths."

"Good. And a password, if you send someone to me?"

"What would you suggest?"

I had no trouble suggesting one. "That is easy; Apollo's Bow. We need His war skills now and are in his hands."

4. Fallen walls.

We rode out that afternoon from Piraeus never having seen the fallen Long Walls. I remembered that road to and from Athens to be like a low river between high banks; the boulevard as wide as the arm-span of a hundred men standing side by side and the walls towered the height of twelve men standing on each other's shoulders, the watchtowers twice as high. Walking, or on horseback, or riding on a cart, once between the gigantic walls nothing could be seen of the surrounding farmland, and little heard. In summer refreshing breezes were blocked, and if you had to travel to Piraeus you did so in the early morning or at evening; in winter the reflecting sun could still raise sweat. The walls were security. They had made the city impregnable to siege. The walls were power. By protecting the fleet and Athens from land invasion they fulfilled Pericles' strategy of naval might, conceived by Themistocles just before the great victory against the Persians at Salamis. I had first seen them with Simonides. He had taken me one day, early in our friendship, to see the temples in Piraeus. The west gate of the city gave directly onto the road with no break, and suddenly there were the walls towering over us. The road was as busy a market as the Agora. Stalls were set up all the way to Piraeus. It was a better place to buy fish and other food stuffs brought in through the port, and many of the foreign traders, of silk, flax, cheap jewelry, and trinkets regularly sold along there. A journey that could be done on foot comfortably in an hour took much longer because we stopped to browse. To me the walls were great architecture, as was the Parthenon, or the Temple of

Hephaistos. In their eerie splendor, the archers staring down on us from their lofty height, they inspired awe, as did the sacred. But there had always been a dark side to that road. Here the city executions were held, and I refused to go to see any of them. The walls were very much an Athenian construction.

That late afternoon, when the road should have been teeming, there was an eerie stillness. We came on the destruction at once; we reined in abruptly. Before us lay a long, desolate, windswept track. Hardly a stone on stone had been left standing. On all sides there was rubble, worse than we could possibly have imagined. Great clumps of jagged wall as far ahead as we could see made me think of temples felled by those barbarians disrespectful of Attic gods. The sun behind us was already slanting across the ravaged fields lengthening the shadows, the burnt and ravaged houses. Trees stood as charred sticks; the land left fallow for lack of workers. I prodded my horse forward, half hoping that as we proceeded the walls would miraculously rise again as we neared the city. Everywhere the huge limestone foundation blocks, and the smaller sun-dried bricks were scattered, or smashed. Here and there were meager signs of rebuilding, some of the old wall being used for new farm houses. Crows rose from among the rubble, providing more chances for food than the fallow fields. We saw no one plowing. An air of futility hung over everything. Attica was a land enervated and ravished by war; it had the air of the primeval emptiness we call chaos; that too was war,

In the distance we could see the rose tinted city shimmering as the sun lowered. The Parthenon looked intact. Why had the Spartans spared the Acropolis, I wondered, when around us all else was in ruin?

Alexis said, "It does not look as if Lysander burnt any of the city."

We had heard false rumors of this. I said, "No, but the countryside is worse than I thought. Desolate, really."

"Yes. I was not prepared."

"Nor I."

We rode on. Men were scratching half-heartedly at the ground with makeshift tools. They paused to stare at us vacantly as we rode by. We must have seemed wealthy foreign merchants to them, and the looks we received were envious and hostile.

I said, "We had better adopt simpler dress in the city."

It was not necessary to explain. Alexis saw what I saw. He said, "Flax but not cotton, and certainly not expensive wool. We don't have any flax with us but we can find some in the Agora. Farmer but not philosopher?"

I knew he was trying to lighten the moment and said, "Not the most popular sort in Athens just now?"

"Or ever, to hear Aristophanes go on about them."

"Yes, the sophists! He hated the sophists. It will be good to see him again."

"He must be old by now."

"If fifty is old. He is not quite that."

The dust of the road had parched us. It was a relief to leave behind the fallen walls. We stopped at a corner to discuss our plan.

Alexis said, "Do you want me to come to Aeschines' house with you? It is already getting late. Perhaps I should go around to the bathhouse which Anytus' son haunts and meet up with you later. Oloros said he was likely to be there in the evening or at that seedy tavern he mentioned, with the cockfights.."

"Yes, perhaps you should try to find him. We can meet up at Aeschines' later in the evening before we return to Piraeus."

Alexis said, "Oloros said the tavern was at the other end of the Panathenaic, up by the Ceramica, so I can come part way with you. It does not seem safe and I would have worried about you anyway. Now I know why Oloros insisted on these chaperone thugs. It sounded like greed to me, but now that I've seen the road and the looks we had along the way, I have to admit he was right."

"Yes. There was never too much danger of bandits between the Long Walls because of the frequent police patrols, but now it should be renamed Brigands Way. They can lurk behind any clump of rubble. We'll divide the men, three with you, three with me. That way if we need to get messages to each other we shall have runners."

"Good idea. We must be prepared for eventualities. What was Anytus' son's name again? Wasn't it Krios?"

I said, "Yes, it was Krios."

"One of the Titans! It figures that Anytus would name his son so vaingloriously."

I said, "Or foolishly. Zeus defeated them."

"It will be interesting to see what I can wheedle out of him."

"One of Oloros' documents said there was some sort of proof of Krios' claim that he and Socrates were lovers. He sounds a bit of a liar, so be careful." I added, "Here, let us get off the main road and take to the side streets. I know a

474

short cut to where we are going and we are getting hostile looks again."

"Our dress is definitely too foreign. The mood in Athens has definitely changed hasn't it? Let us hope it is not permanent. We are looked on as strangers now; made less welcome."

"We have another look about us. Cleansing the city of the resident aliens brought to the surface an old debate about Attic purity, and suspicion of outsiders. The real Athenian. I hate the 'us or them' mentality. The law overturned the ban but the intolerance lingers because economic uncertainty lingers."

Alexis said, "Athenians are always looking after their purses."

We had passed through the city gate and were now in a byway shaded with laurel. The city at least seemed intact, spared pillage and burning. Lysander had shown some wisdom. Leveling Athens would have bred generations of angry soldiers seeking revenge. It was enough what he had done to the walls to humiliate. Children played around us. There was a smell of cooking. Doors were open. We were watched from the shadows. I remembered a way that blinded and deafened you to the Agora until you rounded a corner and came upon it suddenly in all its color and bustle. I never ceased to take delight in the childish surprise, today more reassuring than ever. We lingered to hear the gossip, but there was nothing much about Socrates, and none about war. There was a shortage of lamp oil because some carts had overturned coming into the city; some said deliberately to raise prices, some blamed the gods. There was a heated argument in a group

475

of some ten or fifteen gathered by one of the herms about who would excel at the next games. Wagers were already being placed although they were months away.

"Has anything changed?" I said to Alexis. But we knew it had.

We paused again at the intersection of the Panathenaic Way.

I said, "Our tasks are clear then?"

Alexis said, "Yes, wheedling as much as possible out of Krios, and all that his father would rather keep hidden. To tell you the truth that seems easier than arguing with the likes of Aeschines."

"Yes, but if Anytus is really the one behind things, as Oloros thinks, we might use his influence to secure Socrates, well, flight, if not release, in exchange for protecting his son's reputation. But you shall do your best. Of that I have no doubt. We must try every possibility to free Socrates."

"Then we will meet later, at Aeschines?"

"Yes, unless there is cause for either of us to send word."

Alexis said, half in jest, "If the password for Oloros is 'Apollo's Bow', then perhaps ours should be 'Clash of the Titans'?"

I had to laugh. "Well chosen. Why not simply Titans? That is an obscure private joke and no one will catch on.'

"Titans it is then."

***

Leaving Alexis at the edge of the Agora I started in the

direction of Aeschines' house. Aristophanes had introduced me to him on my last visit to Athens; he lived in the same district of the city as Aristophanes, or "downwind of the sausage-sellers", as we use to joke, and as Aristophanes would retort, "better than downwind of the sausage-eaters." Aeschines father was a sausage-maker. He had pretensions to be a philosopher. At the time of Socrates' trial he was still young, perhaps in his mid-twenties or so, and afterwards tried to reconstruct Socrates' dialogues by comparing his memories with others of Socrates' friends, including myself. His versions are reliable, if our memories do not betray us by projecting the ideal onto mortal talk. To make a living, he had recently opened a perfume shop with Aspasia's assistance, and inventions. He made a modest living from this, enough to support his "Socratic project" as he called his dialogues. As a philosopher he was not original, and I always thought his gift for oratory was greater than his ability to reason. He was hot headed, but I never questioned his loyalty and devotion to Socrates.

I had hardly gone ten steps when I met him. "Aeschines!" I cried. We rushed together to embrace. He was carrying a scroll and I said, "Are you going to read poems this late in the Agora?" He had already published the first of his Socratic tracts, some in verse.

"My friend! I was wondering if we would meet. I was just rushing out to the stationers before they closed to complain about the quality of this papyrus. Look at the flaws in it. I couldn't write a word on it without the nib catching on fiber! Honestly, what is Athens coming to when you cannot buy a sheet of decent paper? Why not go

477

along? If there are two of us that stationer crook will feel overwhelmed and give me another without argument. Otherwise I will have to be there an hour arguing."

He was not a great beauty either then or as a boy, but he was warm and emotional, short of stature, thin but not emaciated as Chaerephon had been. On seeing him I felt my fondness, and how much I missed by living on an isolated coast. I said, "Of course I will. But what are you writing now? I loved your book on Alcibiades. But you were not half harsh enough."

"Haven't you got over your ambivalence towards him now that he had died? Our view of someone often changes when life divides us from them."

I laughed. "Ambivalence, to say the least! I hope you are not writing a sequel?"

"Well, of sorts. In fact, the idea came to me quite suddenly when I had the letter from you saying you were coming."

"From me? What is it then? It is good to hear that I can still inspire at my advanced age."

"Your advanced age? You can't be more than forty."

"Not quite yet. But your new work?"

"I know you will approve. It is called Aspasia. I feel I owe her so much, and hope to hear as much as possible about her from you. I never knew her well, not as you did. We had a professional connection. Will you have time for an interview or two so I can make some notes?"

"For a tract about Aspasia I shall make time and give you any help I can. It is a splendid idea. Is it a dialogue?"

"It is; at least at the moment. I am still working on the outline, so it might change. I've wanted to write something arguing that women were as fit for politics as men. So I have Socrates and someone else, possibly Callias, argue about the civic virtues of women, using Aspasia as the main model. After all she was one of the leaders of the peace party, was she not? That is certainly one thing I want to hear from you."

"I suppose now that she is safely in Miletus her support for the peace faction can be told. It was controversial."

"Indeed it was. You know, I have a theory. It is that Aspasia was the model for Aristophanes' Lysistrata. But when I put my suggestion to him all he would say was that it was interesting. What do you think?"

"Perhaps. She certainly supported peace and the peace factions, in Persia as well as Athens. I always considered her to favor those sympathies, but without Aristophanes or Aspasia saying she was I am not sure you could prove it."

Aeschines said, "I shall have to badger Aristophanes again. The evidence is strong, but you are right, it is circumstantial. Socrates often told me that, in his opinion, the real political genius was Aspasia and not Pericles. As a matter of fact you told me the same thing, didn't you?"

"Well, yes, I did. But have you news of her?"

We had come back out into the Agora. The stationers were along the Panathenaic colonnade. He turned a somber face to me and said, "She has not taken the news of Socrates very well. I had a message from her this week. She is a little older than he is, and perhaps age has made her more vulnerable to bad news, but they say it has plunged her into anger and grief beyond reckoning. She tears her hair and throws herself about, has let herself go and looks a fright. That is what my reports say."

"It was hard for her to lose her son General Pericles in such an unjust way. And now there is this injustice against Socrates, whom she loves as much as she has loved her son, or anyone. It will be a double grief for her."

"I heard from her overseer that she has taken to her bed and will not eat."

"Perhaps I should plan to go to Miletus from Athens and not return to Africa. I will send her words of support as soon as possible. It makes me all the more determined to do something to save him."

"Save him? The messages from Djadao hinted at things but did not say much."

"None have been to me as Socrates has been. I could not stay home in Paraitonion and think I was doing nothing. We have come up with an exciting plan. I am eager to tell you."

Aeschines asked, I thought a non sequitur, "Aspasia has a great gift for divination, would you not agree?"

"Yes, I would agree."

"And if she had cast the signs about Socrates, would you believe these?"

"Did she cast the signs?"

"Yes."

"Did you hear what they said?"

"Yes. All the signs said that he was fated to die by the cup."

It was hard to believe that before hearing the full story from Aspasia, but I was not there to make accusations against Aeschines. I said, "And Socrates? I would have news. Arrangements were made for Alexis and I to visit him first thing tomorrow."

"Then you will see for yourself. He is in marvelous spirits, peaceful, at one with himself. It is quite extraordinary really."

"I heard from Oloros that you tried to convince him to flee."

"Oh yes, certainly we did. Antiphon and Crito have friends in Thessaly who extended an invitation. But we failed miserably. He could go there straightaway. Two towns have formally invited him. No, you can't accuse us of not trying. At the sentencing hearing he himself raised the question you know, and answered it. 'Should I suggest banishment?' That is precisely what he asked. And he answered that if Athenians could not put up with him, his constant questions, and his philosophizing, then no one could, so there was no sense in the city banishing him. On top of that he claimed he was too old for exile. His life was near its end and he would rather die in Athens."

I exclaimed, "But that is an opening then! I am here to tell him just how much we want to put up with him in Africa! As for his being too old, well, the older the wine the better, as far as I am concerned! We can ferry him to Africa in such style that he will hardly feel the strain."

I outlined our plan for Aeschines, but when I was done he shook his head doubtfully, "Crito and I appealed to him to flee, in the name of all his other friends. No matter where he went, he said, he would be a gadfly, and only get into trouble, so he might as well stay in Athens, which he loved and which was his home. He gave many other reasons like this too but I am sure you will hear them from him yourself when you see him in the morning. If you do not believe me you can also ask Crito."

I said I believed him, and added, "But don't you see? Everything you said gives me hope, not despair, that we can convince him to head our new Lyceum in Paraitonion." I told him of our plan, going so far as to invite him to join us as well.

He looked skeptical, and said, "Perhaps."

This was beginning to anger me. I said coldly, "Only perhaps?"

He replied, "We have tried. All of us have tried: Crito, Plato, Antiphon; all the others. And I myself have tried several times so that I can try no more. We all want him alive and if I thought there was any chance of your convincing him to go to Africa I would back the effort completely. And so would the others I am sure. But the simple truth is, Socrates is ready to die and does not wish to escape death, nor does his voice tell him otherwise. And that voice of his usually has the final word."

I agreed that it had, but said, "His voice speaks to circumstances, so if we can create new circumstances then we cannot predict what his voice will advise. It seems to me worth trying."

Aeschines said angrily, "New circumstances! But it is fated! Death is his sentence. The gods inspired the people to go mad. There is no appeal and the time for exile is past! What possible circumstance could you be talking about? My view is simpler. Out of respect to his inner god, and the direction it signals all of us, I bow before its wisdom. Like the oracle it is difficult to understand, but there is a divine purpose about his death, and if his voice and Socrates are trying to tell us this then we should listen. I do not know, Amyntas. You have been too long from

Athens."

I lowered my voice, "I agree with what you say, but still, I have men waiting if need be."

He looked incredulous, "To free him by force?"

"Yes."

"But Socrates would never agree to that, no less his voice! Never! No, I could not support that either."

"Calm down, my friend. Calm down. Let me talk to Crito and Socrates tomorrow. And let us also see what Alexis finds out tonight."

"Alexis? Find out? Where is he anyway?"

"Meeting Anytus son, perhaps Anytus too."

"For what purpose? I do not at all see what you are trying to do."

"If we are to spirit him out of the city we shall need many people to turn the other way."

"Then you have no idea how deep Anytus' hatred of Socrates goes. He will never 'look the other way' as you say."

"I have heard he has debts. He may be open to persuasion."

"Hardly! He thinks that Socrates corrupted his son. It is a falsehood, of course, but he believes it passionately and to be convinced otherwise would be to admit that he was himself at fault with his son, and this he will never admit."

"Money turns hearts and minds."

Aeschines suddenly stopped in the middle of the Way, threw up his hands and said, "I have heard enough Amyntas. I think you have gone stark raving mad and I want nothing further to do with this whole business. If you come to your senses come and see me again, but otherwise good luck to your efforts with Socrates. Or should I say, your failure?"

With that he walked angrily away.

5. General Anytus, the boxer.

Alexis had planned to meet me at Aeschines' house, or send a messenger there, but Aeschines' sudden departure meant a change of plan. Just as well, I thought, if he will not hear me out, then I am better off without him. Better regroup with Alexis and get on with our own rescue plan. I blamed Aeschines and Crito for not spiriting Socrates away already, blinded as I was by anger and grief.

It was early in the evening. A tavern was nearby. I was parched and upset by the argument. I sent messengers to both the bathhouse up by the Ceramica and decided to wait where I was until I heard back from Alexis. As we had been passing through the Agora we had thought of stopping by a cheap clothing shop to buy simpler tunics, and while I waited I wondered whether I should not take the opportunity to do this. But defiance and determination surged through me. I would not change my appearance for Athens' madness. In fact, I called my slave, and threw my silk trimmed cloak over my shoulders, much as I had disdained such with Simonides. How foolish I felt that I had nearly led Alexis into such stupidity.

A slave brought a pitcher of expensive chilled wine. I might have used my good Attic Greek, and the district slang words I knew, to make him and myself think that I belonged. I shrugged that off too. As I settled again at the same table I noticed that malevolent glances were still being cast my way from the street. If I had not made the ride from Piraeus that same day I would still have known that the defeat had happened. The destruction of the walls lurked beneath the city skin as some hidden disease sullenly infecting. The comings and goings, the buying and selling, the prostituting and begging, those were the same. As in my youth boys were beginning to scurry home after a day confined at school, their pent energy erupting in pranks and raucous jokes. The news criers were shouting the latest prices, promising the "real truth" about the latest scandals. There too mingling among the throngs were the war wounded I had seen in my boyhood, neither more nor less. If anything, what seemed most changed was that there was no war news or discussion, whereas it had dominated the Agora of my youth. But the city had changed.

In my youth the war and plague had been to blame for a certain sense of purging despair that would periodically wash over Athens like a torrential spring rain. Was the long war and defeat, the stark losses that war brought upon us, or the imposition of symbols by the Spartan conquerors, to blame not just for the hostility we encountered, but also for the trial and sentencing of Socrates? Athenians honored their gods, Athena and Apollo above all, but these two powerful deities frightened Athenians too and they often tried to appease them and win back their affections. Were they offering Apollo the life of Socrates as expiation, as sacrifice, to earn back good fortune? The charges of impiety and corruption against him seemed so absurd and patently stupid that I could not believe that any Athenian could truly believe them. Were Athenians trying to negate the past and move

485

on with their lives, and did Socrates symbolize the old order they wished to deny? There were hidden things in this trial not being spoken about, things of men and things of the gods.

More than an hour passed before the messenger returned with a message from Alexis. I was to come at once and followed through the now emptying and darkening streets. The Ceramica had not changed much. It was still as seedy as ever. I had to be protected from the whores trying to grab my hand, drag me inside some hovel. We went down a narrow alley and through a dark entranceway into a private drinking club attached to a cockfight arena. I told my three guards to wait outside, but there was still a moment's lull as I walked in. Alexis was across the room, saw me and waved me over. I thought again how glad I was he still wore his Egyptian clothes, and that the gods would have it that we stood apart. He was reclining near a youth whom I took to be Krios, too drunk to do more than raise his head.

Krios attempted to say through blurred speech, "So, you are the friend Alexis has been speaking about, Lord . . . Lord." His head fell back onto the couch.

Alexis took me off to the side, and said, "I was about to send word to you just as your message arrive. There's a lot to tell you."

"I as well. I did not go to Aeschines as planned. I shall tell you later. Perhaps we should go elsewhere?"

"Not just yet. When I saw the state he was in I suggested to his slaves that they take him home but he has ordered them not to touch him no matter what his condition. He also has a sizable debt to settle from gambling on the cockfights. The innkeeper is saying he won't allow him to leave until General Anytus himself pays it and gives guarantees for future debts. He sent a slave to the General telling him such. It is worth waiting to see how it plays itself out, don't you think? That is why I was about to send for you."

I said, "An opportunity then. Of course we should wait."

"Should we have a story ready if the General arrives, or should we use our right names? Would General Anytus recognize you as a friend of Socrates? We might think of a disguise."

It had been more than twenty years since my bond with Socrates; it never had the cuurency in Athenian gossip that Alcibiades' love for him had, no doubt because I was foreign and Alcibiades a high born citizen relative and ward of Pericles himself. I said, "It would be great fun to invent a disguise but I do not think we will need it. If the General asks I'll simply say that I am a Macedonian trader and leave it at that. What have you learned so far?"

"Krios hates his father, but he also brags about him. Do you know how the General made his fortune? Through tanning."

"Tanning!"

"Yes. The same as Oloros, whatever it says about his loyalties."

"And Cleon," I added. "What else?"

"Krios claims to be Socrates' friend, but the innkeeper says his drunkenness is nothing new and it is hard to believe that Socrates would be friends with such a drunk. When I finally found him, I ordered drinks all around, which immediately ingratiated me. He was not at all loath to talk about Socrates, although I should say in the crudest of ways."

"How so?"

"Well, he said that not only did Socrates look like a satyr but that he conducted himself like one in bed and would fling himself on his back and ride him all night until the birds sang at dawn. He made the room believe that he could provoke Socrates into a lustful frenzy, although I would not describe it in the same words he used."

"I understand, but it is not Socrates at all. No matter how smitten he always had virtue."

Alexis said, "Of course. You need not have said that to me."

"No, I suppose not. I was reflecting out loud."

"Krios said that his father was jealous of Socrates' influence over him right from the start, and vowed to take revenge."

We were interrupted. Several men entered and I heard General Anytus' name mentioned, although he was too surrounded to get a good look. The men went over to Krios to lift and carry him out and as they passed close I saw that he was just a beardless boy. Had he done his military service yet? How could his father allow such a youth, perhaps seventeen or so, to fall apart so? As it happened Krios was twenty-one, of the fair type who grew facial hair late.

Alexis pointed and whispered to me, "There, that is Anytus. He was a boxer in his youth, Krios told me, and has written a book of rules for boxing."

488

"Anytas the Olympian? I had not made the connection. And he has written a book? Perhaps I can use it as an introduction."

Anytus was speaking with the proprietor, an obsequious man who bowed and scraped. I saw a string bag change hands, no doubt minas not drachmas. The proprietor gestured in our direction and Anytus turned to look. He was strongly built; his mouth was thin and cruel. He had never been too successful as a general, having lost his main campaign in the war with Sparta. They say he publicly exaggerated his opposition to the Thirty Tyrants in order to prove his loyalty to the democracy. His shoulders were broad, his arms thick and bullish. He wore his beard trimmed closely.

I was about to approach him, when he approached us, introduced himself, and said, "The innkeeper says that the two of you have been kind to my son. Let me thank you; perhaps invite you for a drink. He says you are Macedonians? I have some fine wines at home, though none from Macedon I fear. Will you at least walk with us? I want to get my son away from this place. Let me apologize for his disgrace."

We rose to leave together and I said, "Thank you for the invitation, General Anytus, but you need not apologize for your son. We were all a little wild in our youth, were we not?"

"Perhaps, although I dare say most of us could count on good influences to set us right again. Not so poor Krios."

"We are just visitors but we have heard rumors. We were told something about a lawsuit, and you as one of the litigants. A nasty business from what we heard."

489

"You heard correctly. A very nasty business! If I had had my way I would not have brought the matter to the courts at all but settled it all with a sound thrashing."

I glanced at him and saw cold cruelty. Perhaps we might find out how he had treated the men under his command, and whether beatings had lost him morale and was a reason for his lack of military success. I said, "Sometimes a firm hand is needed."

As we walked through the now quiet streets, Anytus asked, "Have you been long in Athens? May I ask how matters are in Macedon now? We are pleased with the changes there since the court moved to Pella. The new regime promises well for our future alliance. Your new king is somewhat more enlightened than the last. Are you involved in court life?"

"You are well informed, General Anytus. But we came directly from Africa. I have been living there on the coast for many years because of my health. We are simply here on business, a few days or a week at most. I trade in gold, and we also have a shipment of precious white dates to sell, and pay honor to the Athenian gods. Then we shall have to return to Africa I am afraid."

"You have not been to Macedon recently?"

"No, not for two or three years, although we keep in touch regularly. My cousin is an adviser to the new King. But let me ask you something. You were a boxer I am told? And have written a book? I am asking for a reason. You see, I collect books, and hope to build a library in Paraitonion, where I have a villa."

Vanity washed over his face. He said, "You also are well informed. It is true, and I would be honored to present you with a copy."

I said, "I shall, of course, pay the copier's cost. They tell me there are fine copyists in Athens."

"I will not hear of it. It will be a gift."

"You are too kind."

Anytus said, "Your son, here, has seen that my Krios came to no harm tonight. It is I who am in your debt."

I did not stop to correct the impression. I wanted him to talk about Socrates and said, "The outside influence on your son must have been strong, to countermand that of such a strong and devoted father."

"I used on my son all the means of persuasion that I know, but you see he came under the influence of this Socrates. He is crafty and manipulative and calls himself a philosopher. You know, years ago I interrupted his ranting in the Agora where he held forth every day, and castigated him for his preaching that politicians were not good examples for youths, which was close to treason. Worse, he did not dissociate himself enough from the action of those friends of his among the Thirty Tyrants, as if friendship should come before the common good. He calls himself apolitical, but I call him, at the least, irresponsible. He knows the black arts of seduction too, having learned them from that witch Aspasia. Good riddance to the resident aliens I say, and would not have them back if it were my wish. Who knows what gods they really worship in Miletus. Perhaps those dark, destructive gods they are fond of in the east, and the real god behind Socrates' voice no doubt. Let the fruit of his teaching be proof!"

I said, "He sounds like a terrible villain. "

"You do not know half the story. This Socrates spread it

491

about that all I had to teach my son was the tannery business. And what would be wrong with that if it were true, which it was not? His exact words were, "He should not confine Krios' education to hides!" Imagine saying that about a devoted father. Poor Krios. He wanted to organize a band of youths to rescue Socrates, you know, but I put a stop to that. The sooner the hemlock takes him the better it will be not just for my son but for Athens. Too bad the festival intervened or we would be rid of him already. Jail is too good for such a corrupter of souls. Soul murderer he is, plain and simple."

We had left the inn and were walking through the deserted night streets, towards the same district where Aspasia had lived I noted. It was difficult to restrain my rage, but I managed to ask in a calm voice. "Was your son involved with this Socrates long?"

"I made the foolish mistake of sending him to the Taureas, the haunt where that old monster preyed like Kronos devouring his children. Dear Krios was only fifteen when he began to come under his influence but he hid it well from me. He bribed his slaves not to tell me either, but one of the teachers reported that Krios was sneaking off after classes to Socrates' house. When Krios came of age I made sure he was sent to a far camp for his military service. But no sooner was he back than he took up with that scoundrel again. It did not take me long to find others who would join me in making official charges. Some groundwork also had to be laid to make sure the city was against him. Praise the gods we succeeded. Or rather Socrates condemned himself by and having ignoble friends such as Critias and by never revealing the name of his god. If he had done this he would have reassured the city and the god would have gained new worshippers. What god would not want that? No, his god was a black god, a foreign god, not one that we wanted in Athens. Aristophanes was right all those years ago."

"And you say this Socrates has been condemned to death?"

"Yes, by hemlock. No less than for crimes against religion. There was a plea for banishment by his duped friends, but I would never have accepted anything less than death to protect Krios, and Athens for that matter. The world should know that we do not trifle with justice, or the gods."

I cautiously said, "Yes, the world will know that."

Anytus said, "After our defeat and disgrace at the hands of Lysander, Athens needs to make new beginnings, regroup, rid itself of blasphemies."

I was about to respond. But suddenly, there in the street, Alexis was sick. I put my arm around his shoulder. "Alexis. My dear. What is it?"

"It is nothing. Something I drank, or ate."

I said, "I hope that you will not be offended, but I fear that we must come visit you another evening General Anytus. It would be wiser to take Alexis back to the house we have let."

"Of course, of course. Let me send a slave with you. Please feel free to ask anything you want. I know excellent physicians."

"You are too kind, but we have physicians with us."

"Let me send a messenger to you tomorrow then?"

"For sure."

Alexis loved Socrates and was overcome by the strain of Anytus' talk. He told me this as soon as we were out of his sight.

I said, "I am sorry, Alexis. I did not know you would become so upset. But I had to see if Anytus could be brought into a plot to rescue Socrates, and of course he cannot."

"I knew you were doing this, but holding back my rage was too much. Will you really have his book in your library?"

"If there were the slightest chance that he could be of assistance in Socrates' escape, then I would. But there isn't and I shall not. Nor shall I see him again. Come. Let us get back to Piraeus."

***

When we returned to our rented villa there was word from Oloros. He had arranged that same night that I meet a man who would have important information about the jailers, the hiring of mercenaries, and the means of rescue. Alexis was feeling upset and ill and so I went alone, if having strapping guards along can be said to be alone. The night streets of the port were sinister and I did not like hastening through them. My guards only signaled a man of means, fair game to those drawing back into the shadows. Word is spread swiftly among bands of thieves.

The bar I entered was none too consoling, dimly lit by a few sputtering oil lamps to keep faces hidden already darkened by hooded cloaks. I was to meet a man called Drakon, a name meant to inspire fear I suppose. He was waiting at a corner table. Knife cuts had scarred his face and neck; his right arm was tattooed with a fighting cock; it fought to the death. At his shoulder the tattoo was a scorpion, its tail curled to sting itself; they killed themselves when trapped. Would he do either? Thracians did this, they said, and I wondered if he were some relative of Oloros. I placed the bag weighed with silver in his hand as Oloros had instructed. He hefted it to test its weight, looked within, and poured some out on the dirty table, bidding me to sit and waving to the innkeeper to bring more of the cheap brew that was worse than swill.

"When will you need our services?" he said, drawing the bag closed.

"I hope never. It depends on the return of the ship from Delos and it is due in three or four days. I am to see Socrates tomorrow morning and that will give me a better idea. If I can convince him perhaps we could break him free tomorrow night? But I would have to make sure the guards are bribed to stand aside. I don't want lives lost. Can you be ready as early as this time tomorrow night?"

"It will be difficult, costly, but I might be able to arrange it. And if the guards will not be bribed, or someone else interferes, well, there is always the knife and sword."

How far would I go for Socrates? I said, "I doubt there will be need of that. The guards will cooperate. They will have been well paid. That will be seen to by tomorrow. A show of strength is merely a precaution."

"It is better to prepare for the worse and not tie our hands. Otherwise, I cannot guarantee success. But whatever you wish."

"I do not want to risk Socrates' safety by chancing a mishap. And he would not want anyone harmed to save himself. It must be this way or we do not have an agreement."

"We have an agreement."

"Are the other terms clear too? Have you, for example, thought of the city police patrols near the prison?"

"Yes. They will be taken care of. We're to meet you at midnight behind the Stoa with twenty men, and a chariot. I would recommend a two horse. There is too much rubble along the Piraeus Road, and four will make the chariot unwieldy. After we meet up we go directly to the jail. If things go the way you say, they should let us in with no fuss. The rest is straightforward. We whisk him out as fast as we can straight to dockside here."

"Yes. The Captain of the Arete will know we are coming."

He said, "A suggestion. We might time the escape to the sailing tides instead of midnight, to narrow the danger of being pursued."

I said, "It is a good idea so long as the augurs agree. And you and your men are to stay with Socrates on board, to the very last second before sailing. Is that clear?"

"Perfectly clear."

"You've been paid half now, and I shall pay you the remainder just before you leave the ship."

"Agreed. I can also have some men stay on board for the voyage to make sure he is protected for the journey." He pointed out two or three types as rough as he. They raised their chins to acknowledge.

"That will not be necessary. The Arete is well armed."

496

Drakon said, "She is a good ship, one of the fastest and costliest." He added, "Now, if our business is over, there is a girl here I can get for you for a good price. She is clean and artful, or a boy if you want, fresh out of the army and needing some means right now, a Cretan skilled in Cretan ways."

I thought of my youthful encounter with the soldier in the Ceramica. I declined, and said, "Perhaps another time. I have more work to do tonight."

"An hour for the boy? You will not regret it. He is there, standing over against that pillar." He made a signal and the boy moved into the light. He was pretty, small of stature, nervous, and sympathetic; I waved him over. He looked surprised and approached. "Here" I said, pressing pure silver into his hand, and closing his fingers before he could see how many there were. "I have no time tonight, but this will keep you."

The boy said, "Will you return tomorrow?"

"I am not sure."

Drakon dismissed him with a wave. But as he was walking off he opened his palm, turned and smiled, weighing the tetradrachmas in his hand. If he were wise they would feed and shelter him a month, but I had no delusions.

6. Led by God.

When I returned later that night from my meeting with Drakon I found a messenger waiting by the door of our rented villa. The guards rushed forward and seized him, but Crito had sent him. He bowed and handed me the scroll.

Crito wrote, "I propose that we meet at dawn outside the jail, before you go in to see Socrates. Aeschines came to me angry after your meeting, but I, and the rest, do not share his sentiments. We would give you all our support and our very lives to help you save Socrates, and have one condition and one condition only, Socrates must agree." He would meet me in front of the courthouse next to the jail an hour before sunrise.

It barely gave me two or three hours to sleep before having to return to the city. "Time is pressing", he had also written, of which I hardly needed reminding. Two other remarks upset me. He thought we should see Socrates together because two of us together might better sway him than one. But I wanted to see Socrates alone, and did not relish an argument over this. What he further wrote chilled me. "We have sent our runners to Sunium, to keep watch on the sea. When they have caught sight of the ship returning from the festival at Delos we will know that only one day remains before the hemlock. They will race back to warn us, in fact letting us know that it will be our last hours to rescue him." A fast runner might make it back from Sunium with word in under an hour.

Alexis arose, planning to accompany me to the jail, but as we prepared to ride to the city, still in the black of night, another of Oloros' slave accosted us. Oloros had found buyers for our dates at the premium price we had set, which probably meant, as Alexis suggested, that Oloros would sell them for much more and keep the difference, besides his commission. Alexis would have to stay behind in order to oversee the transaction, while I went up alone to Athens to meet Crito and see Socrates. We had the impression that there was time enough to see Socrates on another day and if he were staying behind in Piraeus he could visit the Arete and make sure it was being outfitted to sail as quickly as possible. I knew nothing about ships, and relied on Alexis for this.

The sky was starlit, the predawn air was still cool enough to be bracing as I mounted the fast Thessalian and prepared to head east to the city again. Alexis pulled my hand down to his and did not seem to want to let me go. Leaning down I whispered affection before goading the horse forward. I felt it shiver, eager as I for a run. I muttered a prayer, "Poseidon, father of Pegasus, bring me swiftly to Socrates' side."

How eerie the desolate countryside again seemed, moon shadows like bogeymen lurking to snatch children, stories of which my nursemaid told to frighten me into obedience. The rubble reminded me of Homeric cities in ruins, of Troy perhaps, whose massive walls were also felled. How could the work of so many men be so easily undone, as if permanence itself had been undone and everything was now impermanent? War was all I could think of as I rode towards the dark outline of the city, war that took all that you loved from you. I tried to shake the feeling and renew my determination to save Socrates, from himself if need be. I wished to be free from war and loss as if held in servitude to a god I did not wish to serve. The city loomed intact before me. The sky began to glow a soft white behind the great temples and I felt a surge of hope. As I entered the first streets I slowed my horse among the houses to dampen the echoing hoof beats. In a few minutes I would be sitting with Socrates. My efforts to rescue him would truly begin.

***

The courthouse and prison where I was to meet Crito were at the top end of the Agora and I had to traverse the entire length of the city to reach it. Nothing stirred. If anything I had come early, only the barest glint of dawn lighted the sky. As a boy, I had never been out and about in the city so early because of Athenades' strictures, or scuttling through before dawn from Mania's side. I felt an intruder, as if the noise my small party made might disturb the sick and children.

Having been tried in the court of the Heliasts, the jurors' court, he had been remanded to the prison next door. The Athenians with their black humor called it "The House", though not one in which anyone would have lived willingly. Prisoners were generally well treated, allowed visitors, and given good food.

Crito was waiting outside the plain façade of the courthouse, and we greeted each other emotionally. I had not seen him for several years and he looked haggard and aged. He was the same age as Socrates, seventy. Having been born in roughly the same year and in the same district of the city, the Alopece, they had, in fact, been friends from boyhood, although no other of Socrates' friends was as dissimilar. Crito had no pretensions to philosophy. He owned farms to the north of the city, and larger holdings in Euboea, a gentleman farmer very much involved in farming, as his ruddy complexion and solid frame suggested. He had two sons, his oldest, Critobulus

500

being a favorite of Socrates. Critobulus also became infatuated with Alcibiades youngest son, who rivaled his father in beauty, and the passion was much discussed in Athens. Crito was a quiet, solid sort, always ready with practical suggestions. I liked him a great deal, but had never been able to coax him to a visit me in Africa. Like Socrates, he was very much an Athenian stay-at-home. If born into the Athenian aristocracy, he nonetheless lived unpretentiously under the influence of Socrates. If he had a fault it was that he was too modest, and I wondered whether or not his modesty might impede our efforts. But if he was modest, he was not meek.

He said, "I am so glad to see you. There was great excitement among all of us when we received word that you would sail as soon as possible, but I had feared you would not reach Athens in time."

"But I have. And I am eager to hear what you have to say."

"It was why I asked you to come so early. We have an hour or so before they will let us in to see our dear Socrates and I thought we should discuss the situation."

"Aeschines told you?"

"Yes. As I wrote in my message, he came to me very angry last night, and it took a great deal to calm him down. I hope you will not hold it against him?"

"By no means. We are all under duress."

"Indeed, Aeschines and the rest, I do not exclude myself, are a little crazed from the thought of Socrates' death. I can hardly utter the dreadful word."

"I as well. It is good to talk of it with you, my friend. I have missed you."

"And I you. You cannot know how angry we all are with the city. Except Socrates. You will see for yourself this morning but he is entirely at peace with Athens and himself and sets a great example for us all, which I for one am not up to at all. No, I have to say, grief and impending loss have driven us all a little mad."

"I know. Despite his anger did Aeschines at least present my plan fairly?"

"I think so. We discussed it at great length. After he calmed down a bit we also made the rounds of some of our other friends, so I think it was discussed very thoroughly. None of the rest of us agrees with Aeschines. Your plan for the new Lyceum has more virtues than anything we proposed and the, well, consensus, if not unanimous, was overwhelmingly positive. Most of us thought it just might sway Socrates' voice."

"Despite the fact, as Aeschines said, that Socrates has already refused your proposal to go straightaway to Thessaly? It was your proposal I think, with Antiphon's support."

"Yes, it was indeed. We had gone so far as to secure formal invitations from two towns."

"And he still refused?"

"Yes. He said that if he were a gadfly getting into trouble in Athens then he would be a gadfly getting into trouble in Thessaly and, therefore, it did not matter if he fled."

"Yes, he would say that."

"I think he was trying to shield us. His refusal to flee could be because of Athenian law. Any Athenian who helps another Athenian flee justice can be made to pay a heavy fine or forfeit all his property. I don't think Socrates wants to see that befall any of his friends for the sake of his life when he sees it as nearing its natural end anyway. But, what we realized in our discussions last night, was that, well as you are no longer a boy and ward of Athenades, and do not live here, the law is moot."

"Exactly! Socrates might agree. I have mercenaries standing by. It must appear as if none of you are involved so as to protect your property and families. Besides, I shall be fleeing with him, and on a Corinthian trireme. I am sure this is all the plan of the gods."

"Yes, it has the earmarks. There was another reason he would not flee. At his trial I myself gave assurance to the Assembly that I would be responsible for his not escaping. It was a point of law, to insure that he is well cared for in prison and have some freedoms, but it has rather tied my hands too. When I personally proposed to Socrates that he flee and was more than ready to bribe the guards and get him out of the city, he would not hear of it because of the consequences he foresaw to me and my family. But, you see, for these very reasons, we are ready to support you. We can argue with Socrates that there would be no consequences to any of us were he to accept your offer." There was no one about but he lowered his voice. "And is your plan to free him by force ready. At this late date it may be the only option."

I too lowered my voice. "I completely agree. Everything is ready."

"And if you need extra money I am ready to give that too. None of us would be shamed by putting money over friendship."

"There is more than enough for the rescue, but perhaps extra offerings to the gods might sway them?"

"A good idea. I shall see to sacrifices at once. Praise Athena you have come, my friend. Praise her."

I said, "But tell me. How is Socrates? I hear he is well?"

Crito replied, "Remarkably well. So much so that you would think he had just seen a comedy. He spends his days translating Aesop's fables, and marveling over them as if he were a child again. 'Dieing is a return' he said to me just yesterday, when I teased him about Aesop."

"Oh, it is just like him! Then he has not found the confinement too terrible?"

"Not at all. He has had so many visitors that he hardly has a moment to himself. Xanthippe and his sons are here for most of the day, Aeschines, Critobulus, and all the rest of his inner circle as well. I told him myself yesterday of your arrival and that you would visit this morning. Do you know what the first thing he said was when I told him you were coming? You will like this. He said, 'Perhaps Amyntas will think my Aesop worthy to be put to song. I always liked his voice. It had such purity.' Can you imagine? In his situation he is thinking of song."

"Did he really say that? Purity?"

"Yes. He is so excited that you are coming. When he utters your name his face lights up with that old love."

"It is good of you to say that Crito. You cannot know how much this has made me suffer. Are the jailers treating him well?"

"Very. The guards seem embarrassed that he is here and do everything they can to make him comfortable, at least

504

everything that Socrates will permit. He does not want to put anyone out, he says. They bring him rich foods but he saves it for his boys so that when they come to see him there are always treats as if they were on a picnic. It softens the situation for them."

"And Xanthippe? Is she holding up?"

"It is a good thing you are asking me that and not Aeschines, who dislikes her. She has a very expressive personality, which does not put me off as it does the others. I hide my sorrow, but she weeps and tears her garments and I find it rather satisfying. She can hardly bear it and just yesterday she had to be taken out. The boys are holding up well. Oh, you should see them. Both Menexenus and Lamprocles are stoics. Sophroniscus is suffering the most. He is seventeen now and understands the most. You will spend the whole day today with Socrates, I hope? All the boys will be coming later. By the way, I saw Xanthippe and Sophroniscus last night and told them of your plan. Sophroniscus especially is excited about living in Africa. Do you know what he said? He said, 'Perhaps we can turn death into an adventure yet.'"

I was overjoyed to hear this and said, "True son of Socrates. They will have a grand house and anything they want. The plan is to build a whole complex overlooking the sea for the new school. The house of the Master will have to be imposing."

"You have done well in your trade, Amyntas. Praise Athena, goddess of trade, that it is so useful now."

"Yes, whatever it takes I am ready to give. There is no question of sparing one owl, one mina, or a thousand. But let's not talk about money at such a time. You were telling me about Socrates? How is his health? That might have a bearing on his escape and I have heard that the House is damp and has rats."

"He has not been bothered by either, although his ankles are chafed from the irons. Xanthippe puts salve on them every day."

"Irons! They have not!"

"The law insists."

"We shall have them off him soon enough."

Crito moved closer. Again he looked around anxiously, and kept his voice low. "We have spoken with the jailers."

I took his arm and pulled him further into the shadows. Already, below us, there were signs of the city's first stirrings. "And?"

"They will more than gladly cooperate. They are fond of Socrates. One of them told me that a month from now, when, well the event is over, the whole city to a man would regret the poison cup and he for one will make sure the path is clear and that the others turn a blind eye. We will have to move quickly once the ship is sighted returning from Delos."

I said, "I can have enough men here for the job in a thrice. And the Arete is standing by waiting word to sail at a moment's notice. Tonight, in fact, if the gods wills it."

Crito said, "And Socrates cooperates. He would obey the decision of the people's court, and the law. The law and the people are not the same to him, and he feels he must respect the Law as if it were a person. I would agree if the Assembly had acted justly. But they have acted unjustly. There seems to me no need to honor the vote of a jury that is so clearly wrong, or the Law that caused it to be so. But Socrates does not see it that way and says that he always did his duty as a citizen and would not violate that now. Besides, he does not see death the way the rest of us do. Death is freedom. To disobey the law because he would die, after all his years upholding it, does not make sense to him. Or rather, it would only make sense if death were not a continuation and culmination. His death will leave us all bereft. But if he goes to Africa with you we shall be relieved to see him leave and be somewhere where he can do great good. It was always one of his goals in life." He suddenly seized my hand. "We are grateful to you Amyntas, that you have come at the eleventh hour. Now it is up to his voice."

I said, "I am ready to drink the hemlock myself if need be, and beseech him with my final breath."

Suddenly Crito threw his arms around me. He was trembling with grief, as was I. "Oh Amyntas. If anyone can save him you can!"

And as suddenly I felt the burden of my rescue plan weigh upon me, a plan that had taken me from the middle of the desert across the Great Sea to this prison. I gently pushed Crito away and said, "There, there. I shall succeed, if the gods have not gone mad, as have the Athenians."

＊

I had only to ask Crito to allow me to see Socrates alone for an hour or two before the others arrived for him to agree. It was the hour of sunrise when I was conducted to the door of the prison, a modest building; ill adorned and foreboding. My heart raced with anxiety as the aged jailer

507

led me to the room where Socrates was being held. He told me that Socrates was already awake. "When I told him last night you were visiting this morning his face lit up as fresh as the dawn sun." The sputtering lamps in the narrow hall through which he led me, the sounds of coughs and restless breathing from other cells, made me think chillingly of the underworld. He unlocked a heavy wooden door and stepped aside to let me pass.

Socrates was sitting at a low table next to a pallet bed, writing. He looked up and raised his arms to embrace me, but my first thought was that he was in shackles exactly as I had seen in my dream. I knelt beside him, and lay my head on his knee.

He said gently, "Now, now, my friend. You're not going to weep I hope? You always were a sensitive sort."

"Oh Socrates! Chains!" I wanted to tear them off or have them magically transferred to me.

"Come now, tell me your news. You can't imagine how joyful I was when I heard from Crito that you were on your way here from Africa, and ecstatic when I knew you were visiting this morning."

But I was still overcome. "But Socrates! My dear Socrates! Look what they have done to you! I shall never forgive Athens! Never!"

He was looking at me with great kindness and affection. He said, "It is not all that dreadful. I am sure you will see that as soon as you are calm and reason returns."

I shook my head. "I was told that it was the full citizen's jury that condemned you. When I think of it I can hardly breathe from anger."

"But why should you feel that way when I do not? We

508

Athenians are the way we are: passionate, irrational, idealistic, brave, foolish, heroic. I do not agree with their judgment against me, just as I have not agreed with many things they decided and carried out, but I am no less Athenian."

"But how could they have done this to you? It is stupid, unjust and cruel, nor is it the least bit grateful for all you have done for the city."

"It is the law, and you know I would obey the law."

"If it is the law then the law is a fool. We shall have these shackles off you soon enough."

"Why? Has the ship from Delos been sighted then? How much time is there? What does the water clock say?"

He made mention of this dire sign with such equanimity that I was taken aback.

I said, "No, that is not what I meant." I leaned closer and lowered my voice, less than a whisper. "We have plans, to take you out of here. There is so much to go over before the regular visiting hours begin. I know that Xanthippe is coming, and your sons. I shall be glad to see them. I have heard that Sophroniscus is a handsome youth, and Menexenus and Lamprocles too. This must be hard on all of them. But I have a plan. Do you think they are listening at the door?"

"I doubt it. The jailers have shown me every respect. They leave the door open sometimes and let me walk in the courtyard. But what is this talk about a plan?"

"It is to found a school in Africa with you as its head, a school greater than the Lyceum, a palaistra greater than the Taureas. I have already set things in motion back in Paraitonion. A brilliant physician, Philiscus... But where

509

do I begin? Seeing you like this confuses me. I am so sorry, so sorry. I should have come sooner, when you were accused, but I did not know. I was down in the desert at Ammon making sacrifices to Zeus when a dream! A dream! Yes, I must tell you. You in a cage is you here, not the play of Aristophanes ... " I went on in this jumbled fashion for a time, filling him in on the entire plan for the African Lyceum, if not too coherently. I concluded, "It will be a glorious school such as has never been seen before. It will fulfill your life. We shall hire the finest scribes to take down your philosophy. Your books will reach to the farthest shores. What a glorious life we shall make there. Students will flock from everywhere to study at your feet. There is already great excitement there over the possibility. Come away today. You are sure we are not overheard?"

He had been listening attentively, nodding now and then, a very bemused expression on his face. "Go to the door if you are concerned, but I assure you they do not treat me like that."

"It is only that I would tell you of the rescue. We can do it this very night. I have men standing by, a Corinthian ship, the Arete, to take us to Africa. We can sail on the night tide. Oh Socrates. There is so much life yet for you to lead."

He said gently, "I could have chosen exile at the sentencing hearing but I did not. Crito or Aeschines should have told you this."

"But they did! Their plans were nothing. And even if you refused exile then, things are different now. Aeschines' plan for Thessaly was at best bleak." Before he

510

could say anything I added quickly, "Let me ask you, if you knew of my plan at the sentencing hearing would you have asked for exile? What does your voice say?"

I was sure he would say that he would have chosen my plan, but he did not. He said, "This is my home. I would not dishonor the law then or now, not when I myself refused the plea of exile." He pressed my hand again. "I see that you are grieving, but that is because you think you are losing me, which is not true. Try to calm yourself. When I heard you were coming I was glad because I knew that you had the capacity to understand."

"But I am losing you."

"No. That is not true. I wanted you of anyone to come. You need only look into yourself now. It will be clear."

We sat in silence for a time in that plain room. The walls were streaked with moisture. There was a simple chair, a table at which he had been writing his versions of Aesop by a simple oil lamp, a straw bed, the coverlet threadbare, and the door with a little window for air. I did not know what he meant, or what I was supposed to think. Calmed by his warm dry hands, I began to feel my whole plan fade away.

I said, "I am sorry."

"Sorry?"

"I have been only thinking of myself."

"It is normal at such times. Death makes people a little crazy. I understand. Let me ask you something. It is an important question, and at the heart of why I eagerly awaited you."

"I shall try to answer truthfully."

"I know that."

"Then?"

"What has always guided me?"

"Oh that is easy Socrates. Your voice. Your inner voice."

"And?"

I said hesitantly, because I had always known the truth. "Your voice has not told you to choose exile or to flee. I heard this from Aeschines and Crito. It has in fact never told you not to do anything that you have not done and so you find yourself here today."

"Yes. That is all true."

"And you are only obeying your inner god?"

"Yes."

I said, "But would your inner god want you to die?"

"Why would it not?"

"I don't know. I know that the gods sometimes have taken the lives of other gods and mortals. Zeus struck Asclepius with lightning because he resurrected the dead and commanded what only Zeus can command and so by this Zeus would let us know who in heaven presides over life and death. If your inner voice has told you not to avoid death, or not to do anything to avoid it, then might it be this god's wish for you to die? Does it fulfill some divine purpose?"

"How can I know that?"

"But it is your voice you wish me to understand."

"Yes. It is why I waited for you. I knew in dreams that you would come. God has led you here, and led me here too."

"But I do not understand."

"You remember when the Oracle spoke about me, that I

512

was wise, and how I came to understand wisdom as knowing what I do not know?"

"Of course I remember. You went around Athens trying to find others wiser than you, or whether people thought you were indeed wise. Let's travel the world and ask why Athens has done this."

He said, "My life has been simple. For all of it, since the time I was a small child, I have obeyed my inner voice, and somehow it has led me here, but I do not know why. In other words, I know what I do not know, and I know that I need not grieve, and can be joyful. I am not going to be able to travel around and ask questions so that I can understand His will. He is not giving me time for that, but this I accept."

"And should I? Is it why the dreams have summoned me here? To see you die and accept it? No! I cannot, I will not accept this. I would have you come away to Africa. Let me argue with your inner god if need be. Please, Socrates, come away. You, God of Socrates' voice, let me rescue him."

He said, "Rise from the floor now, and come, let us sit near each other, here on the bed. Straw is all I have to offer you, I am afraid. Come sit closer." I did as he wished, my hands folded in my lap, my head bowed in sadness. He said, "Now, ask yourself if it is the right thing to free me from prison and take me to Africa. Close your eyes. Concentrate on this."

I did as he instructed. Suddenly he put his warm hands on either side of my head and said firmly, "Concentrate."

I did, and suddenly as clear as a bell I heard a young strong voice say within me, "No." And that was all.

513

He took his hands away and I looked at him, startled.
He said, not a question, "You heard."
"Yes, I heard."
"You must be faithful to this."
"Yes, I shall be faithful to this."
But that was not all. He took my face in his hands again, and looked hard into my eyes. And then he said quietly, but I am sure I heard correctly, "God guides us."
We sat for a long time not speaking, until Crito interrupted us.

7. Peace.

The following day I was to go back with Crito to see Socrates again, this time with Alexis, but when Alexis and I arrived an hour or so past dawn, we found Crito and Xanthippe huddled together on the courthouse steps weeping. The runner had arrived from Sunium. Crito had already been in to tell Socrates. The ship from Delos had been sighted. Socrates would have only one day to live. Tomorrow, it meant, he must die.

Crito said, "His face filled with bliss when I told him. I could not understand it."

My purpose that day was different than I had planned, not the rescue of Socrates from sanctioned murder, but the rescue of Xanthippe and the children from want. I felt I should comfort her. There was a large profit from the sale of the dates that Alexis had transacted the day before, money I had not spent on the mercenaries, or needed to spend on the Arete, or for bribes for Anytus, the jailers, or anything else that I had planned. It would serve a better purpose. Crito would manage the large amount, and give some every month to Xanthippe so that neither she nor Socrates' sons would lack anything. There was also enough for a proper funeral rite. Socrates would be cremated and his remains lain in his family tomb outside the city walls. His father, Sophroniscus, was there. Was this another reason for Socrates not to flee? He loved his father, and he loved Athens, and would not be buried away from either. Lavish sacrifices would also be made to Persephone and the other gods to guide him on his passage.

There were twelve of us in the room by his side when he took the fatal cup from the executioner's hand and drank the hemlock with dignity. I think of myself as the twelfth friend, that is the last among his friends, because I was the last to arrive on the scene, all the others having gathered around him when the accusations first surfaced and before the trials ever began. The god did not summon the others in dream or otherwise, and this also set me apart. I do not know why I was visited in dream, only that it was so.

Crito and I sat on either side of him on the bed and held him in our arms during his last moments, and it was to Crito and me that he said, "Don't forget to make a sacrifice of one cock to Asclepius on my behalf." These were his last words. Some have found this a strange thing for someone to say who is condemned to death for denying the gods. To me it was logical. A cock was also the traditional offering to Apollo, and so Apollo must have been much on his mind. And Asclepius? That also seems clear to me. For Socrates, death was the final healing. He wished to thank the healer god for his fulfillment. He also knew that I was building a temple to Asclepius in Africa, and perhaps he wished to reassure me of his support or was merely being practical? But I do not hold that his last words held a special meaning just for me. That was not his way. Death was very matter of fact, not an end, but a beginning. His final words would have been meant practically.

For reasons I cannot fathom no one has told the tale of the moments after his death, to me as important as his last. Some were sobbing, but as he breathed his last, a tangible peace filled the room. We all stopped weeping, and a profound stillness settled over us so thick as to be palpable. As I looked around the room I could see that everyone there, Crito, Aeschines, Alexis and the others were all sharing the same profound peace; their faces were tranquil.

As Alexis and I left the cell, nearly an hour later, one of the guards said, "It is a very peaceful day today, is it not Master?" He looked startled and added, "Oh, then Socrates is dead?"

I was struck by the fact that the peace of Socrates' death had been cast over the wider world around. One last thing too, and perhaps this was meant especially for me. I sat on the step of the courthouse for a moment, sad but peaceful, thinking of Alexis there beside me and my wife and daughter waiting back in Paraitonion, grateful for their love. I sat in the same place where I had sat with Crito, when my head was so full of foolishness. A raven, bird of Apollo, alighted on the step next to me, raised its head, and cawed, sending a shiver through me. It hopped closer, cocked its head staring at me before flying up; it turned

516

southward, towards Africa.

Many years were to pass before I began to write this history. I do not know why it was so long before Socrates came to me in a dream, dressed in white and resplendent. He laid a plume upon my breast and I cried out, "Socrates! Should I write?" He said, "Listen." And my voice did not tell me not to write.

THE END

Breinigsville, PA USA
04 January 2010
230188BV00003B/1/P